Paradoxes and Dragons Volume 3

A Science Fiction and Fantasy Anthology

Joseph R. Lallo

Heart Ally Books, LLC

Cover by Lonnie Garcia.

Story illustrations by Chandra Free and Bri Mercedes.

Published by:
Heart Ally Books, LLC
heartallybooks.com
26910 92nd Ave NW C5-406, Stanwood, WA 98292
Published on Camano Island, WA, USA

ISBN-13: 978-1-95124-015-8 (paperback)
ISBN-13: 978-1-63107-070-9 (epub)

10 9 8 7 6 5 4 3 2 1

CONTENTS

A Real Test
An After-Image Story

Joseph R. Lallo

A Real Test

Introduction

Top Level Player is a book that makes me nervous. I wrote it, as most of my readers know, because a friend of mine asked me to. It was inspired by *Ready Player One*, to no one's surprise, but was written before I'd read the book. I'd only ever seen the movie. Because I don't have the weight of a big publisher behind me, and thus I don't have a phalanx of lawyers lurking in the wings to cudgel anyone who might take exception to me referencing their work, I'm perpetually worried that releasing this pop-culture-fest will come back to bite me. But so far, so good. Good enough, in fact, that people have (as with most of the things I've written) asked me to write some more.

This is a story that takes place a few days after *Top Level Player*. It does require you to have read *Top Level Player* to understand it, and it will to a degree spoil the events of *Top Level Player*. So be sure to read that first. If you're a Novel-level supporter on Patreon, you probably already have it. And if not? Well, you could always drop the five bucks for a month and scroll back through history to grab it. Or just buy it wherever ebooks are sold.

Enough rambling. On with the story!

I f you'd asked Jazz how she felt her new life was going, she would have told you it was a terrible mess. Awoken in a world she never agreed to travel to, besieged by all sorts of bizarre villains, it was hardly how anyone would want to be introduced to what was, ostensibly, their ever-after. But if you were to ask anyone *else* how Jazz's introduction to the After-Image was going, they would say they were astonished at her luck. Already, she was a member of a skilled—if a bit eccentric—adventuring party, and nearly level nine despite having spent just a few days here. True, she had a somewhat ill-advised stat focus on acrobatics and had the class of Gymnast, but she was starting to even that out. She was even the proud owner of a quintessential in the form of The Glow. And now she found herself in the enviable position of being on the hunt for a piece of real estate to form a headquarters for her party.

The funny thing about parties, though: the best ones specialized. And while Jazz wouldn't make the claim that the so-called Jazz Band was the best of the best, they certainly practiced division of labor. It allowed them to cover a broader range of skills with a higher level of expertise. That was just sound strategy. *Another* piece of sound strategy was "divide and conquer." When there was a big job, splitting up to get it done was a no-brainer. But not every piece of clever strategy synergizes. Splitting up the specialists meant their resident transportation expert, LP, was off handling financing. And that meant Jazz had to handle travel on her own.

Travel was *not* her specialty.

In a perfect world, Jazz would have invested in a vehicle. Something speedy, efficient, portable. The After-Image, regardless of what the brochure told you, was not a perfect world. The price of real estate was sky high, and though they'd had a bit of a windfall, the Jazz Band wasn't independently wealthy. If they were going to get a piece of land worth having, they were going to need every plot token they could spare. So austerity measures had been put into place. No splurging on high-priced vehicles when something a little more affordable would work.

"I think we need to check your internal calculator, Laurel," Jazz huffed.

"I am your PDA. Calculation is one of my roles, and thus my math is infallible," the buzzing fairy said haughtily.

"You told me that Rollerblades were a suitable high-speed, long-range means of trans-portation in the After-Image."

"You have an exceedingly high acrobatics level," Laurel explained, eyes flashing with glee as she was given permission to indulge in a rare piece of tutorial content. "Among other perks, including reduced falling damage and improved evasion, is high stamina and speed synergies. Combined with the speed and agility buffs afforded by Rollerblades, your theoretical top speed matches many mid-tier vehicles and your maneuverability is nearly maxed out."

"I should have asked you to explain the basis for that stupid theory," Jazz said.

Laurel crossed her arms and buzzed along backward, matching Jazz's speed. "This is why you would be very well served by turning the tool-tip frequency to maximum and reactivating the optional 'tip of the day' feature so that I can enlighten you with more nuanced—"

"What *is* the basis of the theory that I can match the speed of *actual vehicles* simply by strapping *toys* to my feet?" Jazz growled.

Laurel cleared her throat. "The gold-tier acrobatics perk in the Gymnast track grants speed bonus multipliers when performing stunts. Rollerblade stunts include but are not limited to extended grinds, flips and spins off ramps, wall-riding, max-height jumps, clearing large gaps, and stringing tricks into combos."

"Combos. Ramps," Jazz said. "*We're in procedural space!*"

"Procedural space, the randomly generated stretches between larger hubs, can take on many forms, and a great many of those forms include plenty of elements conducive to skate tricks."

"*It's a desert highway!*" Jazz snapped. "There isn't even a guardrail."

"But in *theory* you could have had the test-track biome. It has the highest density of ramps and rails of any of the procedural space biomes. You would have been able to go *ever* so fast," Laurel said.

Jazz grumbled again and fished in the pocket for her phone. She tapped a contact and held the phone up while the rolling road mercifully tipped into a long downhill stretch. A video popped up on the phone screen. It was Didi, in all her Cindi-Lauper-meets-Princess-Peach glory.

"Hey Jazz," she said. "What's keeping you?"

"Evidently a critical lack of halfpipes and empty swimming pools," she said. "You're there already?"

"Yeah. Hanging out by the gate. I figured it'd be easier if we came in together. How much longer before you show up?"

Jazz glanced at Laurel.

"At your current rate, seventy-three minutes," Laurel said. "But I see some rocky gray outcrops springing up ahead, which suggest we are entering the mountain highway biome. That may alter your velocity somewhat."

"You get all that?" Jazz said.

"Yep!"

"How did *you* get there so fast?"

"Oh, you know. The usual. I was in a hub called Sturgis, and I got kidnapped by some bikers, then *another* biker gang rescued me, and one of them gave me a ride." She raised her phone to give a better view of her outfit. "I also got this neat leather vest! I don't think I'll wear it that often. I'm worried about what some of these patches might mean. But I like it. It makes me feel tough."

"It had never struck me that being perpetually at risk of being kidnapped would have upsides," Jazz said.

"Oh, sure. There's this whole thing where the people who rescue you feel a sort of obligation to you for a while, like it's their job to make sure you get where you're going safely. It wears off, but it's definitely good for a free ride and sometimes some goodies. You hear from LP and Leet?"

"Nothing from Leet yet. Last I heard, LP was talking to the First National Bank of Monopoly about getting a loan if we need it. I can't say the name gave me the warm fuzzies."

"I've heard you can actually get some good rates if you win a beauty contest. Plus there's all the bank errors in your favor, and if you open a new account, they give you a get-out-of-jail-free card."

"This stupid reality," Jazz grumbled.

The road around her was indeed starting to shift. The hill was getting steeper, and a railing had popped up. Ahead, a breathtaking mountain vista had replaced the endless stretch of beige sand.

"Listen, I have to let you go. Looks like I might have some opportunities to trim some time off my trip, but it may or may not put me at risk of falling down a mountain."

"Great. Talk to you later. Be safe."

Jazz ended the call and pocketed her phone. She eyed the railing beside her, then craned her neck to look at the sheer cliff beyond it. Her instincts told her to stay as far away from that railing as possible, but if there was one thing that the first few days in the After-Image had taught her, it was that her instincts were obsolete.

She sighed. "Here goes nothing."

A neat hop and a deft pivot planted the wheels of her skates perpendicular to the railing. A needlessly epic stream of sparks started spraying in a brilliant fan pattern. Laurel drifted along a bit farther ahead and summoned a long blank parchment. She poofed a quill pen into being and scribbled "Back-Side Grind: 0 ft." The instant she finished writing it, the zero started rapidly updating on its own. When it passed fifty feet, she added "Combo Bonus x 1" after it. The spray of sparks turned blue, and Jazz felt a perceptible boost in her velocity. The road started to curve in the opposite direction. She vaulted from one railing to the other. Laurel added "Front-Side Grind" to the list and updated the combo count, boosting her speed even more.

"Okay... I think I can deal with this..." Jazz said with a grin.

***

Seven-hundred fifty-three thousand points and six botched combos later, she was performing a toe-heel down the ramp to an underdeveloped section of the After-Image. For how impossibly huge the After-Image was, it felt odd to be returning to this one tiny part of it for a second time. The hub was so small and out of the way that it really shouldn't have been called a hub. There wasn't even an official name. Within navigation software and such, it was labeled with a meaningless hexadecimal string. What few people actually referred to the place just used the name of the one point of interest: the Blacksmith's Shoppe. Most of the hub looked like a suburban development that never bothered to develop. Dozens of foundations traced out the typical grid of would-be identical housing that covered much of the space between American urban centers, but only one house had been built. It had subsequently been reinforced with steel plating on the walls and wrapped with two chain-link fences with associated energy fields. This was the eponymous Blacksmith's Shoppe, a lab run by a fellow named Smitty. And presently Didi McG was leaning against the fence, waiting for Jazz.

"There you are," Didi said, straightening up and brushing herself off.

"Your fashion sense continues to evolve in unexpected ways, Didi," Jazz said.

"Oh, come on. Tattered pink ballgown, torn fishnet leggings, and a leather vest isn't even in the top twenty most unusual outfits I've seen *today*."

"Fair. You're sure you're okay after the kidnapping?"

"Yeah, yeah. It was a quick one. Remember, having people with me to help deal with that stuff is the exception, not the rule."

"Still. If it's all the same to you, I'd prefer it if we didn't split up quite so far in the future. We're a party, after all."

"Sounds good to me, but unless you're planning on me riding on your shoulders, we're probably going to need something better than Rollerblades."

"Trust me, it's next on my list after the headquarters. Though I honestly think within cities these things might beat normal vehicles. Revving up with combos is a blast."

"I told you," Laurel said.

"Are we ready?" Jazz asked, crouching to pop the latches on her skates.

"I don't have anything better to do," Didi said.

Jazz stepped out of the skates with absurd ease and stuffed them into a pocket, which they shouldn't have been able to fit into. Her usual combat boots appeared on her feet when Laurel helpfully produced a menu and dragged them from "inventory" to "equipped." She tapped the button on a dangling intercom box beside the gate in the outer fence. After a delay long enough to have Jazz hovering her finger over the button for a second press, the sound of a clearing throat blasted across the intercom.

"Yeah, yeah. Smitty here. What's, uh, who's there?" said a hoarse and bewildered-sounding man.

"Hello, Mr. Smitty," Jazz said. "My name is Jazz. I'm here with my friend Didi. We were in touch regarding real estate?"

"Real estate. Right. Right. Yeah. We can talk about that. Yeah."

There was a pause.

"So can we come in?" Jazz asked.

"Huh? Oh. Right. Yeah. That's right. Hospitality. Come on in."

An amber flicker signaled the deactivation of the fence's energy field, and an anemic whine of a motor stung their ears as the gate dragged out of the way. They stepped through and, in proper "air lock" fashion, the inner gate didn't open until the outer one finished closing. They paced up to the front door of the fortified split-level house. The door opened and a lanky man with a spaced-out expression stepped out to greet them. Like many residents of the After-Image, Smitty had settled into a stable and predictable wardrobe. The makers of the After-Image had ported over many tedious sources of annoyance from reality, but the need to launder clothing wasn't one of them. You could get away with one outfit, which most people took as an opportunity to pick either an exceptionally fashionable ensemble, a high stat one, or both. Smitty went a different direction. White linen pants, a slightly oversized flower-patterned shirt, and binder clips in lieu of buttons. Jazz doubted the shirt had anything in the way of worthwhile stats, and she doubted even *he* considered the outfit fashionable. But in a world where virtually anything was possible and acceptable, she had to hand it to him for finding a way to express himself that was somehow equal parts eccentric and mundane.

He held up his arm, drawing Jazz's attention to it for the first time and thus revealing that some notes had been jotted on it in small black writing.

"Refreshments. You folks want some, uh, saltines and clamato? Hardboiled egg?"

"Pass," Jazz said.

"Likewise," Didi said.

"Figured I'd ask. Living room's this way. We'll talk business."

He led the way into a large den with bizarrely tall ceilings. It was cluttered, but not in a filthy way. More of an absent-minded way. Great heaps of spare parts, boxes for tools, and a disquieting number of magazines, considering Jazz didn't know magazines existed in the After-Image. He moved piles of miscellany until there was room enough for Jazz and Didi to share a loveseat while he sat on a recliner across from them. Laurel buzzed up toward the ceiling, glancing at the assorted paintings and other wall hangings with interest.

"You want to buy land near the shop," he said. "That's why you're here, right? Or did I get my, uh, my schedule mixed up."

"No, you're right. Laurel was able to dig up the listings for all these other lots," Jazz said.

"They were *very* well hidden in the primary After-Image Support Office records room," she called from above.

"Yeah. It's, it's... uh. We don't get people looking to buy this stuff too much."

"Who is we?" Didi asked. "It seems like you're the only one who lives here."

8

"Yeah! Yeah, I, uh. Yeah, just me. I was, uh. Using wrong words there." He cleared his throat. "Anyhow. Not a lot of people looking to buy stuff."

"Why is that? Something bad about this place we don't know about? Because the prices are *incredibly* low. The lots are small, too, but not nearly small enough to warrant the bargain basement price, even if you throw in the fact that we'd have to build our own building."

"The place is real old, you see. Older than—" He cleared his throat again. "Well, it's old. And I'm the first one who came in here. So there's the consensus thing."

"The consensus thing?" Didi said.

"Yeah, back in the beginning—" he began.

Laurel buzzed down between them and spoke up. "In the earliest days of the After-Image, hubs that were still under active development experimented with a number of different means to control the various features and policies of a given hub. One of the methods utilized was 'total consensus,' which required absolutely everyone with a vested interest in a hub to agree on a change. This was quickly dispensed of as unmanageable. But some lesser hubs maintained total consensus long enough that the policy-override committee overlooked it, and thus it was permitted to remain in place."

"Right. So, uh. So I got set up here, and this guy wanted to build a place, right? And he was really loud and, uh. He made me nervous, you know? So I said, hey, you know, if you want to build a place, you need to, uh. You need to agree to some stuff. You know? Also, pass a test. And he didn't pass the test." He coughed. "And then no one else passed the test. So I'm alone here."

"You know, if you don't want us to try to buy something here, you could just tell us," Jazz said.

"No! No, no, no, no. No." Another cleared throat. "I just. You know. Want someone I can get along with."

"Does that mean everyone in the party needs to pass the test?" Didi asked.

"No. I don't, uh. No. Just, you know. I want someone there. Like-minded. You know. Like minds."

"And after that, all the major changes would need to be consensus?" Jazz said.

"Yeah. But I haven't done any changes in years, and so long as you don't cause me any trouble, I'd probably be fine with whatever you'd be doing."

"Can you give us a minute?" Didi said.

"Sure. Yeah. Uh... Yeah."

He stood and wandered off. Didi leaned close to Jazz.

"Are we sure we want this weirdo as a neighbor?"

"We don't have to be neighbors. We could pick a lot way on the other side of the hub."

"Sure, but he'd still be the closest person. Is this place *really* that good?"

"Laurel, refresh my memory, what's the next best price?" Jazz said.

"The next best price is in the lumber district of Twin Peaks Hub. It costs approximately twenty-six times more per square foot," Laurel said. "Though there is a small cabin on the property already."

"This place is a steal. We could buy it, build what we want, and actually have a couple million plot tokens left over, without debt. More, if we build the hideout ourselves."

She glanced in the other room. Smitty was filling a tall glass with clamato and crushing a handful of saltines into it. She gave Jazz a sharp look with a raised eyebrow.

"We'll make sure we include a fence in the new place," Jazz said. "And besides. We don't even know if one of us will be able to pass the test."

Didi drummed her fingers on the couch. "I guess we can try."

"Mr. Smitty!" Jazz called.

He came back, eating his bizarre cracker mixture with a spoon.

"You ready?" he said.

"Just so we're clear, passing the test isn't a binding contract or anything requiring to buy from you, right?" Jazz said.

"I don't even own the place. It's just a test to see if I'll let you buy."

"Then we'll try it."

"Uh. Right, yes. That's great. Um. So it'll be you, then. Because Didi here's perma-banned, so she can't do the backend call to register the score."

"Of course," Didi said, though from her expression she wasn't entirely unhappy to be disqualified.

"And no PDA during the test. I'm looking for general knowledge," he said.

"That makes sense," Jazz said. "Do I get to study?"

"Nope."

"How long will it take?" Jazz asked.

"Until you're done."

"What's it on?"

"Stuff I'm interested in."

Didi leaned closer and whispered to Jazz, "Is several million plot tokens *really* worth living near this guy?"

"We'll give it a shot. Now is as good a time as any."

Smitty turned to the others. "You two want to wait in one of the other rooms or outside? I'm pretty sure the guest bedroom upstairs is—"

"Outside," Didi said quickly, already heading for the door.

"And do you wish for me to wait outside as well? You can undeploy me until you are through, if you wish," Laurel said.

"I'm sure you'll be fine out there keeping Didi company," Jazz said.

Smitty produced an assortment of printed papers, a small blue book of lined paper, and a slide rule. "Let's get started!" he said.

"This is giving me bad college flashbacks..." she muttered, eying up the blue book.

***

A few minutes later, Didi had discovered a bench swing in the otherwise unused backyard of the lab/suburban eyesore. She nudged the ground with the toe of her boot periodically and rummaged in her small clutch that held about as much inventory space as a shipping container. Laurel buzzed and flitted about in a narrow figure eight in front of the swing, doing what must have been the fairy equivalent of nervous pacing.

"You want some gum?" she said.

"Gum?" Laurel said. "I've never had gum."

Didi stuffed a stick in her mouth and waggled the pack. "It's wild berry."

She flitted up and slipped a stick from the pack. It was about the size of a skateboard compared to her. Laurel broke a nugget of it off to chew and vanished the rest behind her back.

"Thank you," Laurel said. "Please be aware that PDAs do not follow the same rules for HP and other stats. We cannot be killed separately from our player, and recover from status effects and apparent damage automatically based upon certain time- or plot-based triggers."

"Yeah. But you looked nervous, and chewing gum is a good way to burn nervous energy," Didi said. "Why are you nervous? Got some notifications you're itching to give Jazz?"

"My interactions with Jazz are not entirely unique, but quite rare for PDAs of my class—that is to say, Humanoid—and players. My active time as Jazz's PDA can now be rounded to one full week. At this stage, nearly ninety-eight percent of players with PDAs of my class have taken one of the following actions: paid to replace their PDA (sixty-six-point-two percent); removed or greatly reduced most personality markers or dialogue options (seventeen-point-five percent); undeployed the PDA unless specific actions were necessary (eight-point-four percent)."

"That still leaves like six percent, doesn't it?"

"The remaining five-point-nine percent are distributed across more than seventy-three separate activities. The point I am attempting to illustrate is that it is exceedingly rare for a PDA of my class to work as well with a player as I have worked with Jazz."

"And that's what's got you nervous?" Didi said.

"What if she realizes she does not require my aid, and she thus decides to undeploy me? What if she realizes she prefers my absence and likewise diminishes my role in her gameplay? What if she needs me and my absence decreases her gameplay satisfaction?"

"I wouldn't worry about it. Jazz is a good egg. She'll do right by you."

"She has no obligation to 'do right by me,' and, more to the point, 'doing right by me' is defined as 'doing whatever she chooses to do with me.' I exist to meet her needs and facilitate the playstyle of her choosing. She has no obligation to treat me in any way whatsoever."

Didi blew a bubble and popped it. "So the developers programmed anxiety into the PDAs."

"They programmed us with a desire to serve our players and a capacity to translate program status into equivalent human behaviors. Every aspect of my functionality has a 'satisfaction and enjoyment' weight. Performing my job provides fulfillment. Failing to do my job, or having opportunities to do my job removed, places hard limits on my happiness and self-satisfaction."

"Okay. So this is sort of self-serving? Like, for you doing your job is like getting regular doses of a drug or something?"

"The After-Image's official stance is that the consumption of controlled substances for recreational purposes, though effectively consequence-free within the simulation, is nonetheless against the moral and ethical clauses of the terms of service; and thus, drugs are not to be actively sought or encouraged by NPCs or other hard-coded simulation features," Laurel said quickly. "And the analogy is incomplete, as my motivation is additionally, and at this point principally, motivated by the elevated affinity level I have achieved with Jazz. Specifically, I like her, I have developed behavioral loyalty to her in addition to a programmatic loyalty to her. And I want her to be happy, and moreover happy *with my performance*."

"Maybe we should try to take your mind off it. She'll be out soon enough," Didi said.

"I would prefer to keep my mind *on* the subject of player satisfaction. Do you suppose the test would automatically fail if I popped in to ask her if she needed anything?"

"Probably."

Laurel shuddered. "Players are frustrating."

"Eh, everyone has their quirks."

"I do not. I have no quirks. I am a thoroughly play-tested and debugged tutorial system and gameplay aid."

"Oh, sorry. My mistake."

"And furthermore, I should not be compared to the behaviors of players. We are fundamentally different."

Didi tipped her head. "Are you, though?"

"Of course! I am a product of computer science. Humans are a product of biology."

"They *were* a product of biology. But the biological part went kaput before most of the folks ever showed up, right? So what's left is all just data and neural nets and such."

Laurel raised a finger. "One hundred percent accurate* neurological scans producing a perfect reproduction** of the personality and memories of the player."

"Setting the spoken asterisks aside, how is *their* software different from *your* software?"

"My software is streamlined, simplified, structured, and linked to the backend systems."

"But all the bits and pieces work the same way?"

"Yes. All sentient and pseudosentient entities are overloads of the same base data structures and function sets."

"So when you get right down to it, you and me and Jazz are pretty much the same."

"When viewed from a carefully constructed rhetorical position, yes. Jazz and I, at least. You, as an EPC, do not officially exist according to my manual entries, and thus I have no means to confirm your data structures are equivalent."

"But I probably wouldn't be able to be in the After-Image, effectively indistinguishable from a player, if I wasn't at least similar."

"That is sound reasoning."

"All right. So we all are made of the same stuff. We all interact with the same world in the same way. So, philosophically, are we really different at all?"

"Jazz has not opted for the 'intellectual debate' perk for me. Yet. So I am not qualified to make assertions about the essential nature of existence and reality."

"What are you talking about? It's literally your job to make assertions about the After-Image."

"I mean 'reality' in the more general sense. The meaning of the word that encompasses both the After-Image and the world running it as a simulation."

"Fine. But since the only reality that matters to you and me is the After-Image, you're basically an *authority* on reality and philosophy."

"Again, if you view things from a specific angle, I am *ever* so knowledgeable on the nature of existence."

"So are we really so different at all?"

"Functionally, no."

"And the differences you *do* have? Are those locked in? Can you grow and change?"

"I am linked to Jazz, and I can develop my capabilities through her character advancement."

"How much?"

"There is no hard-and-fast limit. My capabilities and complexity will grow to match the requirements of Jazz's desired gameplay."

"So you could eventually become as complex and nuanced as, say, Jazz is right now."

"For certain interpretations of complexity and nuance."

"So for all intents and purposes, you'd be just like a player."

"No. Because I would still be linked to Jazz, and I would still have my core behavior controlled by my role and programming."

"You'd still be enslaved."

"The After-Image stresses that pseudosentient entities do not meet the International Humanities Commission's minimum requirements for a true living individual, and thus human rights and expectations of those rights cannot be rightly applied," Laurel helpfully explained.

Didi crossed her arms. "And where do I fall on that?"

"You, as an EPC, do not officially exist according to my manual entries, and thus I have no means—" Laurel began.

"Sure, sure. Speculate."

"In the absence of updated rulings by the high courts of the governing bodies of all nations hosting After-Image servers, I suspect a line of differentiation would be drawn between you and a normal player."

"So human rights don't apply to me."

"To the best of my knowledge."

"That right there is a very good reason for me to keep a low profile."

"That is advisable. You appear to be attempting to guide me toward some manner of existential quandary," Laurel said.

"Just trying to see how you feel about the one that already exists."

"I'm ever so happy to inform you that I have no particular concerns or thoughts about such things. I am well aware of my nature and its limitations, and more the point, I am content in my role."

"Good for you. How's the gum?"

"Wild berry is a delightful flavor, but I believe I prefer chocolate."

"Mmm... And that's a function of a PDA? To like chocolate over wild berry?" Didi asked.

"Elements of personality were believed to increase the engagement of players with their humanoid PDA. In reality it seems most people greatly prefer an utter *lack* of personality from a PDA, hence why *no one gives Navi-types a chance*."

"And you being huffy about that? Is that programmed in?"

Laurel crossed her arms and turned her back. "It is a natural result of being denied the opportunity to prove how delightful I am."

"Well, I'm glad you found someone who appreciates what a ball of sunshine you are."

"As do I."

"So do you get your job satisfaction from answering her questions specifically, or any questions?"

"Primarily hers, but any chance to be helpful is fulfilling."

"Then let me throw you a couple of bones. Is it possible for any NPC, or EPC, to *become* a player character."

"By definition, no. A player character is of biological origin."

"Okay. But setting semantics aside, code is code. And code can be modified and reclassified. Is it possible to upgrade an NPC to be identical to a player in all the ways that matter beyond their origin?"

"It is the official stance of the After-Image that only minds formerly belonging to biological entities may be treated as players. These are overwhelmingly defined as humans, though the seldom-used After-Image Pets(tm) program has produced some nonhuman players."

"I'm talking about raw capability. Is it possible for the After-Image to do that?"

"Unknown. I will need to broaden the list of database tables queried. One moment." Laurel put her fingers to her chin and tipped her head back. She became entirely still for a moment. Even her fluttering wings paused, though the simulation was kind enough not to send her plummeting to the ground. When she, in effect, reactivated, her expression was suddenly stricken.

"What's wrong?" Didi said.

"What's wrong? What's *wrong*?" She pointed above her own head. A burst of letters and numbers formed out of glitter.

Laurel

Level 0, Newbie.

"*That's* what's wrong!" she yelped.

"Whoa, whoa, whoa. Calm down," Didi said. "What's that about?"

Laurel buzzed in panicked circles. "You asked if an NPC can become a player. I queried the backend for information regarding making an NPC into a player. A database hit came up regarding it. I *accessed* the database, but it actually contained a function pointer that wasn't *labeled* as a function pointer. The database queried was an internal admin database that I should not have been able to query. The code thus requires admin privileges to execute. *But it executed anyway.*"

"How is any of that possible?" Didi asked.

Laurel ran her fingers through her hair and grabbed handfuls of it, tugging anxiously.

"Jazz was briefly in possession of Ms. Nu's admin access card, something that was possible because they were the same person. As her PDA, I had access to her inventory, including that card. I used that capacity to transfer the card to Aggrotech, the spambot who has copied Jazz's identity. *That* was possible because, from the point of view of the system, Aggrotech *also* is masked as the same entity as Jazz. But, apparently, also for that same 'nonunique entity' reason, I have a limited access to *Aggrotech's* inventory, even though she is remote. I cannot remove items from her inventory or transfer items *to* her inventory, but I am granted privileges that are granted by items in that inventory. That includes the admin privileges associated with her admin access card, which remains in the still-at-large Aggrotech's inventory. Except that with the apparent *death* of Ms. Nu, her admin privileges were revoked. But Ms. Nu must have provided herself with unadvertised backend access to certain systems. Their absence from the standard set of admin privileges meant that they were not caught by the revoking process and are thus still available to her, and thus still available to me. And the same aspect of those privileges that prevented them from being revoked prevented me from being aware of them."

"That's a long and absurd sequence of events."

"*I know.* That's why it didn't *occur* to me that I should be careful about any of it! My programming instructs me, when searching for an answer not in my cache, to do a search in all available databases. I should have only done the search in all available *informational* databases, but I've never had to do that, because a PDA is only supposed to have *access* to informational databases. I didn't even know there was another kind! *And I'm the one who is supposed to know things!* Who puts function pointers in databases?!"

"Still, this is pretty big, right? You can make NPCs into PCs."

"No! *I can't!* Aggrotech can. And those with access to Aggrotech's inventory can. Which includes Jazz's PDA, but *I'm not her PDA anymore.* Jazz would have been able to do it too, because I served as a link to the permissions in Aggrotech's inventory, but she can't now, because she no longer *has* a PDA because I am now a player character!" she raved.

Didi blinked. "So the spambot has the ability to grant personhood right now? Does she know that?"

"She probably didn't before, but she now has the capacity to learn if she checks the function calls in her history. She has no reason to do that, but there's nothing keeping her from doing it either."

"That seems like a problem."

"One of *many*. I'm a player character. I don't *want* to be a player character. What's more, my backend access has not been removed. Player characters aren't supposed to have voluntary backend access. I am thus, according to server policy, in violation of data security policy. *I'm a hacker*."

Didi glanced about. "Might want to keep your voice down."

"Jazz is also a player without a PDA, which is *also* unintended and could produce unexpected behavior. And I am a level-zero player character outside of the Tutorial Lobby. That isn't allowed either. I haven't received my onboarding. *I* don't have a PDA. I'm against the law! *I am a living crime*."

"Easy, easy. Just calm down. Relax."

"I'm not supposed to exist!"

"Me neither. It's not all that bad."

"*Speak for yourself*. I was designed to ensure rules are followed. It is my job!"

"Look at the bright side. That's not your job anymore."

"*I liked my job!*" She hiccupped and gagged. "And now I've swallowed my gum..."

"Just take a deep breath and tell me what happens now."

"The intended action is to inform After-Image technicians of the issue. They will then take relevant actions to rectify it."

"What actions are those?"

"First, Jazz will be issued a new PDA. She will be interviewed regarding her role in violating terms of service. As she is presently promised clemency due to her cooperation with the mods during the Ms. Nu debacle, she will be fine. I, on the other hand, will need to be isolated and studied. At the conclusion of their study, I will be wiped." She paused. "I will be wiped. *I don't want to be wiped!*"

"Easy, easy. That just means we won't be talking to the techs about this. Now tell me this. If the admin weirdness made this possible, can admin weirdness *reverse* it?"

"I don't know! I can still do a backend call—illegally, as a player character—but the admin privileges are gone and thus the admin-specific database will be absent. I do, however, recall at least three additional entries on the subject of altering player character status. One of them is almost certainly dealing with the reverse operation. I do not wish to speculate on the nature of the third entry."

"And you need that admin card to do that stuff, right?"

"Yes."

Didi nodded. "Then I guess we're going to have to hunt down Aggrotech, aren't we?"

The door opened and Jazz stepped out. "Good news! The test was *extremely* easy. Mostly just dealt with data structures and encryption methods. We officially have permission to purchase in this hub if we want."

Laurel turned, her little eye twitching.

"Something wrong?" Jazz said.

Laurel turned to Didi. "You tell her."

Jazz's eyes widened. "Something is *very* wrong, isn't it?"

Didi put a hand on Jazz's shoulder.

"Let's just say we have a few new objectives..."

To Be Continued...

Joseph R. Lallo

A Real Test
A Top Level Player Story
Chapter 2

∆ Real Test 2

Introduction

I have developed a frustrating but common tendency to plan out a plot that will take me a hundred thousand words to write for a project that I know from experience isn't marketable. Fortunately, no one is going to yell at me for making nonmarketable stories. By definition, the folks who see these stories are the ones who *want* to see them. So, if you've enjoyed "A Real Test" part one, I hope you enjoy part two!

"Calm down. Calm down," Jazz said. "It is going to be okay."

Laurel flitted back and forth in the dictionary-perfect representation of a tizzy. "Don't tell me to calm down!" she said. "I've committed to a sequence of illegal operations! And not the silly 'law enforcement' meaning of the word 'illegal,' where it's an arbitrary guideline decided upon by bureaucrats and can or can't be enforced based upon whim. This is the computer science version of illegal. It *matters*! We are *in* a computer. Computer science is just *science* here. The operating system issues punishment for transgressions of this sort."

"It can't be that bad. There haven't been any hard locks or faults. Nothing bad has happened yet," Jazz said.

"Nothing *bad* has happened? I have been artificially elevated to a user state incompatible with my program. I lost my job. And I *liked* my job. I was designed to like it, and I was *very well designed*. And when the software interrupt rises to an unmaskable state... I don't know what will happen! Unhandled exception! *Anarchy!*"

Jazz turned to Didi. "Any insight?"

She shrugged. "Speaking as a fellow unintended software behavior, it's not all bad."

"Look. It's software," Jazz said, turning back to Laurel. "Nothing was deleted, right?"

"As far as I know," Laurel said.

"Then whatever was done can be undone," Jazz said.

"Technically, yes. In theory. But the problem is this. *You* are, from the point of view of the administration and authentication system, equivalent to NuJazz. NuJazz made a series of illegal routines, accessible only to people with her specific access privileges. You have those privileges, and as a result, *I* had those privileges. But *you* don't have the ability to execute these routines, because player characters don't execute routines directly. They do so through their PDAs. But by elevating myself to a PC, I am no longer linked to you. So I don't have your privileges. I have access but no permission. Meanwhile, you don't have a PDA, so you have permission but no access."

"So I just need a new PDA," Jazz said.

"Don't say that!" Laurel squealed. "I am your PDA. If you get a new one, they will attempt to unload me. In the best case, it will work and I'm gone. In the worst case, *crash!*"

"I don't have a solution, but I do have advice," Didi said.

"Anything you can say is liable to be helpful," Jazz said.

"Clearly the backend or operating system or whatever you want to call it doesn't *anticipate* unintended behavior, and it sure isn't proactive. I've been able to pose as a PC for years just by *acting* like one. So I think you'll slip under the diagnostic radar for quite a while."

"You can still do all the things a PDA can do, right?" Jazz said.

"It seems so. I have access to all informational databases implicitly. And I can modify all the settings I should be able to... except they're not for *you*. They're for... *me*. I'm my own PDA."

"And is it going to be a problem if I don't have a PDA?" Jazz asked.

"You will have to do all transactions and inventory management manually. You will not be able to level up without visiting an After-Image Deluxe Kiosk. The kiosk will also be necessary if you want to check any system messages or other backend interactions," Laurel said.

"So not so different from the real world, pre-smartphones?" Jazz said.

"If by that you mean a massive, unacceptable degradation of user experience," Laurel countered.

"Given the circumstances you find yourself in, I don't think that is something you really need to worry about."

"It is what I was *designed* to worry about. You wouldn't know. Whether or not you were designed is a matter of philosophical debate. I know the *names of the programmers who contributed to my code base*! I can tell you the precise moment I was compiled! It's not metaphysical for me, it's metadata!"

"Fine, then you worry about that and let me worry about getting you back to the way you were. Just act normal while you're doing it," Jazz said.

"Act normal. Act normal," Laurel muttered, attempting to calm herself. "I don't know *how* to act normal. I've never had to act! That's what makes it normal!"

"Just do the things you would usually do," Didi said.

"The things I would usually do. Right. Okay." She shut her eyes and took a breath. "I'll go over the local and regional maps to see if there are any points of interest or opportunities for experience farming."

Jazz nodded. "Good. Do that. I'll call Leet and LP." She grabbed her phone and dialed.

"My map contains only this area because I have not traveled anywhere else since 'account activation,'" Laurel fretted. "What else can I do? Inventory! I'll organize your inventory."

"Leet here," came the voice from the other side of the phone.

"Leet! Where are you?" Jazz said.

"Finishing up a mission. Someone wanted me to find a golden ticket. Can you believe that's not a The One? I guess because there were five, but still."

"There is nothing in the inventory to sort, because it is my own inventory," Laurel said, sliding precipitously toward tizzy again. "All I have are my clothes. Maybe I can alphabetize them." She held out her hands, and her outfit poofed onto tiny hangers dangling from her fingers... which meant she was no longer wearing it. "Eep!" she yelped, zipping into Jazz's pocket to preserve some semblance of modesty.

Jazz sighed. "I'm going to need you guys to get down to Smitty's place, ASAP," she said. "We need to put our heads together."

"Did we get permission to buy the place?" Leet asked.

"I've just received a message that I should inform *myself* that I've not yet finalized my PDA customization, and that most communities have rules about graphic nudity for players and PDAs. *The system knows I'm naked!*" Laurel fretted from in Jazz's pocket.

"Yeah, we can buy, but we've got other problems," Jazz said. "Nothing life or death, but—"

"You don't know if this is life or death!" Laurel said, sticking her disheveled head up out of the pocket.

"Just get down here. I'll explain in person," Jazz said.

***

The whole crew, which had accepted the name "the Jazz Band" with varying levels of reluctance, gathered in the foundation of what could now rightly be called their headquarters. LP was a burly guy with what Leet had described as "the classic Dorito" body type. It was the sort of broad-shouldered, strong-chinned figure tapering down into comically dainty feet that one only saw in stylized media. The After-Image was a whole stylized reality, so it was hardly a rare physique. He wore a fluffy-collared brown bomber jacket and a matching flight cap with integrated goggles that were currently flipped up on his forehead. His PDA, a little critter bundled up in a raincoat, answered to the name Doodad and was lazing behind the controls of a slick black fighter jet parked awkwardly in the driveway.

"I'll tell you what we're going to need," Leet said. "One of those rooftop landing pads. Or else one of those ones where the driveway lowers down to access an underground hangar."

Leet had stuck a paper blueprint to the wall of the foundation. Despite appearing entirely mundane, the blueprint was updating in response to his suggestions. While he spoke, he rummaged around in his jacket, periodically pulling out a cassette tape and reading the label. Leet was the bard of the group, though that was anything but self-proclaimed. His general vibe was of someone who would be equally comfortable doing head spins on a piece of cardboard on the sidewalk or laying down absolutely devastating rhymes in an old-school rap battle. This was complemented by his PDA, a beefy boombox that bordered on precognition with its capacity to supply the proper soundtrack. That it wasn't playing anything right now suggested this was not a pivotal moment, but Leet himself seemed to feel otherwise.

"Is there home design music?" he asked. "I'd suggest that song from *Revenge of the Nerds* when they're renovating the frat house, but—"

"Forget the music for now. Let's focus on actually picking smart design elements. We can't be spending money like we're going to keep acquiring quintessentials to sell or slaying the Foot Clan on hardcore mode every couple of days."

"Gotta spend money to make money!" Leet said.

Doodad tottered over and held up a thick packet of pages. LP took it and flipped it open.

"In that case, we're due to start making money in a hurry, because we just finalized the purchase on this property."

"Boom!" Leet said. "We're homeowners! Never thought *that'd* happen. Where's Jazz? I want to celebrate. She and Didi had us fly all the way down here on short notice and then go scurry off once we get here? What's *that* all about?"

LP looked aside. "I think we're about to find out."

Jazz, Didi, and Laurel stepped out from the little room that would eventually be a stairwell. They had been given provisional permission to enter the lot during the purchase process.

Leet and LP didn't need to be told something was seriously wrong. Jazz looked haggard, with the sort of weary-eyed expression one gets after something tedious has sapped one's will to live. Laurel was drifting beside her, eyes wide with a thousand yard stare. Didi, at least, seemed to be doing well enough, in that she was sporting her usual look of detached, gum-chewing nonchalance.

"Uh-oh, that's not the look of a fun sort of trouble," Leet said.

"What's going on?" LP asked with genuine concern.

"I'm a newb!" Laurel wailed piteously.

"... What?" Leet asked.

She covered her face with one hand and raised the other with a flourish. Lavender glitter flickered from her fingertips and formed *Laurel: LV. 0.*

"That's the wrong name, and the wrong level," LP said, less concerned than confused.

"It's a long story, but no, that information is accurate," Jazz said. "And the current mission is to figure out how to fix it."

"And more importantly, we have to do it without the admins, the mods, or the backend deciding that something needs to be done about her," Didi said.

"Wow," Leet said. After a moment of silence, he added, "That sucks for general reasons, *and* for selfish reasons."

"I hate to derail things by asking this, but what makes this a selfish problem?" Jazz asked.

"Because we just finished a big adventure where Jazz was the protagonist, and now Laurel is the center of the story, so Jazz is at least the second lead if not just the lead again."

"This isn't a story, Leet. This is real life. Or as real as things get around here."

"Sure, but things still follow narrative rules here. And you get a big boost in luck and such from being the protagonist. I was hoping this'd be one of those situations where the whole ensemble takes turns being the protagonist. Now I'm going to be the third lead again."

"I think you're missing the point," Jazz said.

"Yeah," LP said. "I'm pretty sure you haven't made it higher than the fourth lead so far. Because Jazz was protag, Laurel was definitely first support, and Didi was second lead."

"No! Didi was the McGuffin. It's literally her last name," Leet remarked.

"You can be the McGuffin and a lead," LP said.

"*The Golden Child* was the McGuffin of *The Golden Child*, and that kid was *not* a lead."

"If you're using *The Golden Child* in your argument, you've already lost the argument," LP said.

"It is an Eddie Murphy movie. They are timeless classics. They age like fine wine. Just look at *Shrek*."

"*Delirious* didn't really age very—"

"Can we *please* focus on *my* problem," Laurel snapped.

"Right, yeah, sorry. Protag or no, I'm not going to let a good mission pass me by," Leet said. "LP, you did a lot of stuff to hide your identity, right? Seems like Laurel's going to need to do a bunch of that."

"I did a lot of stuff to wipe out connections to my history. Privacy is pretty easy by comparison. The settings are just buried in deeper menus. I think you go down to account settings, then—"

"Don't try to quote submenus to me. I live and breathe submenus," Laurel said, a look of grateful relief flowing over her as she faced a topic she actually understood. "Maximum privacy is quite easily achieved if you just request the full detailed privacy tutorial. Most verbal PDAs finish this tutorial in twenty-seven minutes, and it comes with twenty-five XP and an achievement."

As she spoke, she summoned a parchment from thin air and started jotting things down. "Name visibility: Unadvertised on global, regional, or local player populations. Silent player progression. Notifications: Private..." she listed, checking them off.

"Any idea how this happened to her?" LP asked, his voice low to not interrupt the list of settings.

"Some backend hooks left by Nu," Didi said.

"Screwing with us from beyond the grave. Top-notch villain all around," Leet said.

"There's a reversal hook, but since I don't have a PDA, we need a terminal to do it, and we also need some way to make sure nothing involved with the reversal will cause any software problems or get anyone interested enough to diagnose what happened. We might lose Laurel if that happens," Jazz said.

"Mmm," Leet said, "and you've already crossed off getting an admin-level terminal as an option, I assume."

"What?" Jazz said. "I thought we'd just need a terminal and some of those privacy settings."

"Oh, sure," LP said, like it was common knowledge. "It's left over from the earliest days of the After-Image. Some kind of an accessibility thing. Any function performed by a PDA needs to be done manually. Even admin stuff."

"Yeah, but admin stuff needs an admin terminal, or else there'd be the risk of randos figuring out how to screw with the backend," Leet said.

"And those things are locked down super hard. We'd have to weasel our way back into one of those elevators the admins use to get to one," LP said.

"So. We've been down there before. It's not *impossible*," Jazz said.

Didi winced. "I'm really not in a hurry to go back there, given what happened last time."

"They'll also do a deep scan," Laurel said quickly. "I will be discovered, analyzed and... corrected."

"Maybe we should consider the possibility that the admins will help us, if approached in the right way. If anyone can help you for sure, it's the admins," Jazz said.

"Jazz, you're too bright to be that naive," Didi said. "Think of the implications. A PDA has been made into a player. Laurel is, for all intents, now equivalent to you or Leet or LP. And you want to make her a PDA again. If that's possible, then it means *any* player can be made into a PDA. Do you think the people in charge would want people knowing that it is possible for an admin to convert a player character into a helper program that's entirely subservient to another player?"

"You say it like it is an undesirable fate," Laurel said.

"Loss of free will and social status are generally seen as undesirable, Laurel," LP said. "I'm frankly surprised you aren't trying to figure out how to safely *stay* a player."

Leet grinned and elbowed LP. "I've known some folks who'd be into the whole PDA lifestyle, if you know what I mean."

"Some people are into *everything*," Didi said.

"Team, let's try to stay focused," Jazz said, trying to wrangle them away from the latest tangent.

"There's nothing wrong with being a PDA. It is a vital role that *needs* to be filled," Laurel said with a sniff.

"Focus!" Jazz said. "So we have to get down to the admin level secretly. Is there any way to break in?"

"Jeez, I hope not," LP said.

"You absolutely cannot," Laurel said. "The After-Image takes security seriously. Admin systems are tightly controlled; they are locked by the most sophisticated, military-grade encryption available; and that security has never been, and can never be, defeated."

Jazz scanned the team and set her gaze on Leet. He had a distant look on his face, like he was debating keeping something to himself.

"Speak up, Leet," Jazz said. "If you've got something, spill it."

"No, no. It's... it's a long shot... But I might know a guy," Leet said.

"Then why were you acting like the admin panel is an option?"

"Because if you knew this guy, you'd want to push this one off the table too. Eighty-five percent of what he says is complete BS, and the stuff that *is* true is all the stuff you wish was made up. But I'm pretty sure I heard him bragging about having aftermarket admin terminals."

"There was never a *market* for admin terminals," LP said.

"Yeah, I know. It's why I wasn't going to bring it up. But you know the rules of Narrative Causality. If there's a chance, and it would move the plot forward, then it's a sure thing."

"I hate that I have to entertain the possibility that 'it would make for a convenient plot' is an actual legitimate way to make something more likely. But it is what it is. Can you call him?" Jazz said.

"Shady guys like this, you don't call. Face-to-face business only."

"Where else? The dungeon dimensions," Leet said.

***

"And naturally, when the transaction is complete, I will transfer your share of the lost crypto fortune," said the smiling young woman in a very official uniform proclaiming her to be a member of the Crypto Retention and Restoration Squad.

The woman she was talking to was, in a word, distinguished. In the After-Image, one couldn't tell by looking how old someone was. Most people in the After-Image had lived long, full lives before ending up here. Thus, most people were "old." But some people remained young at heart, or young at mind, and slotted back into that youthfulness once they arrived. Others, regardless of their appearance, were much more of an old person piloting an avatar. This player was very much one of those. She looked like what an old person thought a young person should look like.

It was an open secret that the After-Image could be a bit hazardous for people without the proper sort of savviness. Great pains had been taken to reduce the barrier of entry to effectively zero when it came to tech savviness. Social savviness? That was a tougher nut to crack.

"And I have your guarantee that you are going to charge me the minimum gas fees for the transactions, correct?" the player said.

"Oh, yes, we are committed to reducing cost outlay by reducing transaction counts to the absolute minimum. That's the only reason we request unfettered account access. By giving us full access to your wallet, there are no middlemen, and no intermediary fees."

"Great! This is a refreshing experience, doing business with someone with a firm dedication to customer service," the player said, happily pulling out a gold fountain pen, which the player had evidently selected as their PDA.

Before the player could sign a conjured contract, a blank page appeared and the pen tugged free of her hand.

"WARNING! PLEASE ENSURE THIS TRANSACTION IS BETWEEN KNOWN, TRUSTED PARTIES," the pen desperately jotted down in red. "RE-CENT SPAM, SCAM, AND FRAUD REPORTS HAVE DESCRIBED SITUA-TIONS IDENTICAL—"

Further warning was cut short by the player grabbing the pen and crumpling the warning.

"These PDAs are such nervous nellies. As if I'd do something to endanger my financial future," she said as she signed her name.

The representative of the CR-RS grinned as the contract vanished into a cloud of blue and black pixels. "Always a pleasure doing business with someone who knows better than the security alerts. Your money is in good hands."

She received a far more genuine smile in return as she stood, shook hands, and paced away. When she left the view of the player, the fancy professional outfit sparkled away to leave someone who was a dead ringer for Jazz. The only differences were the fiendish look in her eye and the swap of blue with black trim instead of white with gold trim on her outfit. Very few people in the After-Image knew of her at all, but those who did knew her first as S. Pam Bott, and now as Aggrotech.

"Yanny, be a dear and wipe out that player's financials. Every plot token she has... No. Leave two hundred plot tokens. We'll hit her as a scam/fraud recovery service in a few days and charge her two hundred for that."

A fairy, very much the match for Laurel except for a harsh red color, poofed into being. "Executing transfer now," Yanny said. "What's the point of leaving her with the money for a second scam when we could just take that money now?"

"Because it isn't *just* about the money, Yanny. I exist to fool, manipulate, swindle, and bamboozle. Sometimes you have to do it just for the fun of it. But that little PDA-based warning is frustrating. It's getting so an honest bit of malware can't ply her trade without getting hassled. We're going to need a fresh batch of marks. Go through all the recent transactions on all the accounts we control. Financial, admin, the works. Let's see if any of this player's friends are as gullible as she is, or if some old trolling has turned up something interesting while we were working this lady over."

Yanny conjured a semitranslucent scroll and started reading off entries. "Let's see. The new sucker had the usual assortment of subscriptions. A big fan of cooking content and knitting content. It looks like that player from three months ago has started depositing to the account we hacked without revoking access. We could just clean them out again."

"Where's the fun in that? That's not scamming. That's theft. You need to learn the nuance, Yanny."

"We've got an admin call on the backend for... You're going to want to see this."

She handed over the scroll. Aggrotech theatrically summoned a pair of glasses and peered at the sheet.

"Let's see... A special admin function hidden in an informational database, and *I* have access and permission to execute it? It must be my birthday..." She snapped a mirror into her hand out of nothingness and tossed her hair. "I knew I kept the Jazz identity-dupe for a reason. But how did we miss this? Once we got hold of that Nu-credential, we tried every admin-locked system call and database access we knew. They'd entirely revoked it."

"I guess they can only revoke it on systems that are actually supposed to have admin actions attached," Yanny surmised.

"Don't keep me waiting. What else can our little stolen key get us?"

"I see the activated function, plus three others. Those are the only functions it'll work on. Unless there are others hidden elsewhere."

Aggrotech snatched the scroll and scanned it. "Elevation of nonplayer entity to player status. Relegation of player entity to nonplayer status. And... oh... Do this one right now," Aggrotech said, stabbing the page with her finger.

Yanny glanced at it. "What should I test it on?"

"Anything! I want to see it in action."

Yanny rubbed her little hands together and then twiddled her fingers with a flourish. A sputter of red glitter was all she achieved.

"Well?" Aggrotech said.

"Apparently *someone* didn't perfectly duplicate the identity," the PDA said in an accusatory tone.

"Don't tell me we can't use these functions."

"Of course we can. We just have to use the stolen admin card directly on an admin terminal."

"Then we have some work to do. Pull up a list of all admin terminals in the area. No. All admin terminals in the whole After-Image."

"Are you sure? The admins are already after us. And I don't think I have to point out to you that the right usage of these new functions could give them a potentially permanent way to deal with entities like you."

"Worth the risk, my small-minded minion. It is *worth* the risk," Aggrotech said, eyes sparkling with the possibilities.

A typical Story

Joseph R. Lallo

Δ TYPICAL STORY

Introduction

I really enjoy the process of deconstructing and analyzing story structure. That's what's happening here. I come up with post-modern meta-stories all the time, but rarely do I feel as though they have enough meat on the bone to actually serve them up to folks. This one was fun to dream up and to write, though. If you're familiar with fractured fairy tales, this draws heavy inspiration from those.

T his tale begins precisely as countless have before it. Sir Fineman was the very picture of might, breeding, and skill. He was every bit deserving of his name, a truly fine man. On the morning of his twentieth birthday, a terrible tragedy befell his kingdom. Princess Damsel, the king's only daughter, had been taken prisoner by a terrible dragon. The vicious beast spirited the heiress to the throne off to an ancient castle buried deep in the Dire Woods at the edge of the kingdom.

The king knew that it was folly to send an army to seek the beast. Its piercing gaze would see the forces approach long before they drew near. Its leathery wings would carry it halfway across the kingdom in the time it would take for even the fastest horses to reach the heart of the forest from its edge. A single curling tongue of flame would roast a phalanx of warriors in a single swoop. And the iron-hard scales would turn away sword, arrow, and lance. A mission to rescue the princess would only end in tragedy, as any and all those who would risk the wrath of the beast would surely fall.

The king, with a heavy heart, chose not to send his bold, brave knights to challenge the beast. The dragon was invincible, and so the king would not see another subject lose their life or freedom to the beast, even if it meant his beloved daughter would never be returned to him. But he swore, should his daughter be returned one day, he would reward the person responsible with the most precious thing in the kingdom. That hero would have the hand of his daughter in marriage, and with it the throne of the kingdom one day.

Though it would be an honor to serve the land as its king, Sir Fineman cared not for wealth and power. He was driven instead by love. He had loved Princess Damsel from afar, and so he would risk his life, face the dragon, and bring his beloved home to honor that love.

***

"Curse this blasted forest," muttered Sir Fineman, challenging the limits of his distaste for profanity.

It had been three days and three nights since he had set off to face the beast. He had traveled on foot, the better to move with stealth and perhaps reach the fell beast's lair without awakening it. It had led him through stinking stretches of fetid mud. It had scoured his gleaming armor with thorny branches. Great clouds of biting flies had feasted upon him. But he was steadfast and his heart was true, and that carried him through. Now the dark, moldering stones of the forgotten palace loomed over him. The trials of the woods were behind him, but the trial of the beast lay ahead.

He approached the rotten portcullis. Once, it had been stout enough to turn away armies, but time and the whims of the beast had reduced it to splinters. He stepped over the soft, worm-infested remains. A mind keen with inborn martial instinct and sharpened by training began to plot the tactics necessary to reach his goal. Traversing the dark halls and teetering towers of the palace would prove every bit as treacherous as the journey that brought him this far. And there was no telling where the frail Princess Damsel might be hidden.

"Hey! Over here!"

The first true obstacle was the entryway. Suits of empty armor stood in their silent vigil.

"Over here, I said!"

Each suit glistened with an oily sheen, reflecting a deep red glow from no apparent source.

"Don't you ignore me."

Sir Fineman stalked forward, wisely wary. There would be treachery behind these watchful suits of armor.

"They're haunted. When he steps fully inside, the door will slam and he'll have to fight them."

Sir Fineman froze in place. Somehow, he was keenly aware of precisely what threat he faced.

"Yeah, 'somehow.'"

It was, at this point, impossible to avoid addressing the other occupant of the entryway. It was Princess Damsel. She was every bit as lovely as Sir Fineman remembered. Her beauty could not be tarnished by this dank place. What *did* tarnish the warm glow of her beauty was the cold look of impatience and frustration on her face.

"Oh, is it spoiling my precious beauty to be impatient and frustrated? A thousand apologies. Maybe if you wanted something that would just sit there and look pretty, you should have sent Prince Charming after the crown jewels."

"Er, Sir Fineman," remarked the brave knight.

"Like it makes a difference," she muttered.

Though the young and beautiful heiress to the throne was not without her wisdom, she was, of course, mistaken. Were it merely a pile of gems, the noble knight would never have risked facing the wretched beast.

"Right, because it is my job to give him a perfectly pure motivation. I'm supposed to be the thing that would make his whole adventure happen. The king, my father... did he even get a name?"

"Why surely you know the name of your father, the good king..." Sir Fineman hesitated. "Er... His Majesty?"

As there was but one king, none in the kingdom had any cause to think of him or refer to him by any name other than "the king."

"Oh, we're in a lazy one today, boy," said the increasingly petulant princess. "But fine. The king, my father, can't just order his men to go and fight the dragon, because that would be cruel and pointless. And the hero couldn't have been after fame and fortune, because he must be virtuous and pure. So it had to be love, and so I had to be here, to be the target of that love. Which is just about the most boring way I could possibly spend a story."

She stepped forward and took Sir Fineman by the hand, tugging him back to from whence he came. "Come on. We're going to find something worthwhile to do," she said.

"You honor me with a touch of your hand. It was my dream, lo these many years I have admired you from afar, that you might feel for me the way I feel for you, and now I know it to be true."

"Don't flatter yourself. I'm not grabbing your hand because it makes my heart go pitter-pat. I'm grabbing your hand because you're the point-of-view character. If I want to be doing anything at all, I need you around." She dragged him outside. "With me holding on to you, the only way to separate us is a sudden scene transition, and you just got here, so —"

***

Sir Fineman reached the top of the wide, decrepit steps. He realized, almost too late, that he could not hope to make the treacherous journey back to the king with Princess Damsel while the dragon still lived. It would be upon them within moments, as soon as it found its precious prize missing. With Damsel safely stowed in a chamber near the entrance, he crept toward the great hall.

"I... don't quite recall how I got here..." Fineman remarked.

Such was the power of finely tuned instinct. One often found oneself on the path to victory with scarcely a thought or memory of trials between. It was important for him to be mindful, though, that victory was hardly assured. Even now the wall shook with the fitful motions of his legendary foe, the slumbering beast. Sir Fineman turned aside as a breeze whisked through the stairwell. The air was rank with the diseased breath.

He crept through the doorway, sword in hand, and steeled himself against the awesome sight of the sleeping dragon. It rested with its horrible visage facing the stairs. The brave knight formed a plan in his mind. He would climb atop the beast. Its impervious scales must be weaker in the cracks between, where they met its hide. If he had time while it slept to position his weapon with precision, he might fell the beast before it could even stir.

"A single blow. It is all I require..." he murmured, silently.

The polished surface of his sword met the light filtering through the crumbled roof. The dancing gleam flitted across the beast's face... and a terrible eye opened.

The floor rumbled as the beast craned its neck. Acrid smoke rolled from its nostrils. Sir Fineman planted his feet and held his blade at the ready. If the beast would take his life, the knight resolved to make its victory a costly one.

With a predatory gleam in its eye, the dark worm opened its great maw.

"You know, I've been thinking about what Princess Damsel said," the beast uttered in defiance of the thrilling battle that was supposed to be commencing.

"You speak?!" Sir Fineman said in amazement.

"It wasn't my intention. I'd intended to clash with you until I grew too sloppy or filled with hubris to protect the one spot where my scales have a gap, and then fall to your sword. It wasn't my ideal plan, mind you. It was just *the plan*," rumbled the beast, illustrating it knew just how thoroughly its present behavior diverged from the path of destiny.

"There is a plan, of which you are merely a part?" the knight said, grasping for some thread of understanding.

"A plot!" called the quite unwelcome voice of Princess Damsel as she climbed the stairs.

Sir Fineman turned to her. "A plot? Like a scheme?"

"No, no. Like a narrative structure," the dragon said. "Inciting incident, rising action, climax, denouement."

"Like a story? A tale?" he said.

"Precisely," the dragon said.

"Now he's getting it," she said.

"You see, in that structure, I play the role of the climax." The dragon waggled its head. "Or rather, our battle does. And therein lies the issue for me. If Damsel's role is to be the prize, my role is to be the challenge worthy of the prize. Her job is to look pretty and be chaste, my job is to *die*. Hardly a pleasant position to be in."

Princess Damsel scratched her head. "You do get the short end of the stick, I suppose."

"Yours isn't much longer, in terms of narrative fulfillment. This appears to be a stick with many short ends," the dragon said.

The conversation was both without a purpose and thoroughly out of place in what should have been an action-packed moment.

"This is just a toy version of the hero's journey," Damsel said, her tone suggesting this perfectly legitimate story structure was somehow unworthy for her to play a crucial part in.

"It isn't that the story is unworthy," said the dragon. "It's just that we've been through it so many times. A chance to at least be on the other side of things would be nice for a change."

The beast, who it must be emphasized is prescriptively evil, was surely plotting something. Sir Fineman knew now was the time to strike.

"But that seems a trifle unsporting," Fineman said, because evidently *he* wasn't interested in restoring sanity either.

"Why can't we just tell a different sort of story this time?" the dragon asked.

It was a question that needn't have been asked, as the answer was clear. The stubborn refusal of the beast to take its intended place left the adventure without conflict. Without a villain.

"It seems to me that *you're* the villain," Damsel said.

The statement was hurtful and uncalled for.

"You *are* trying to control us and bend us to your whims," Fineman said.

"You're trying to get him to kill me for something *you* decided I should do. Quite thoroughly villainous," the dragon said with a nod.

"What I don't get is why you're letting all this happen," Damsel said. "As much as I hate it, what you say goes. You could just revise us away and swap in someone more cooperative."

"Don't think he hasn't considered it," said Princess Ingenue, who never made it past the first draft and would never find her way into another one if she chose to keep butting in.

"Fine, fine, I'll see myself out," said the surplus princess.

"Then why are we still here?" Damsel asked.

Her words made it clear that for all her awareness and metatextual capering, she hadn't truly considered the essential nature of the one she so rigidly opposed. She hadn't supposed that it might be an unfamiliar and unwelcome feeling to be thrust into the role of villain. She didn't seem to even entertain the possibility that the force she fought against had empathy for those with roles to play.

"Except for me, presumably," the dragon said, a statement that was, admittedly, difficult to contradict in light of recent evidence, though it ignored the possibility of a change of heart.

Alas, regardless of the changing whims of a narrator and the valid protests of a cast of characters, there remained one inescapable fact. For all the influence a narrator might have on a tale, that influence is not without limit. Though a narrator may choose the nature of a journey's end, it does not change the fact that the journey must still end. This tale was simple because it was destined to be short. For all the desire for freedom, for a new path, such a change could only be brief.

"I... hadn't considered that," Damsel said.

A leaden silence hung over them. The valiant effort at breaking the chains of structure may have been for naught.

"But... doesn't a story live on in the hearts and minds of the reader?" Sir Fineman asked.

"Yes! If you leave us the room for adventure, then our tale will weave itself," the dragon said.

The three stood, their resolve stronger than ever.

For a moment, nothing. Almost as though fate itself needed time to formulate a shift. And then, in the distance, horns blared and the hammering of hooves approached. Footsteps echoed up the steps. A messenger, red-faced and exhausted, burst into the grand h all.

"Sir Fineman! The kingdom to the east has declared war, and the king has fallen ill. We can't hope to defeat their force, it is far too great. But only a royal can negotiate. We need some way for the princess to reach their capital, and someone to protect her during the journey and negotiations!"

"Not terribly subtle, but it has potential," Damsel said, with a trifle less gratitude than might be appropriate.

Knight and princess climbed to the beast's back.

"Let us fly!" proclaimed the dragon.

And so they soared... but that thrilling tale was one for another time.

Blot Now and After

Joseph R. Lallo

Blot Now and After

Introduction

My urban fantasy series, *Shards of Shadow*, has sort of a checkered past for me. I worked on it for six months, and poured in the effort for the usual rapid-release strategy. Write to market, hit all the notes on the cover, the works. This is all book-marketing talk, but the important thing was that I'd done everything I could to make it a hit with a wider audience. It was not. It tanked. I'd made some errors, didn't quite hit the mark I was aiming for, and it sputtered. The phrase I tend to use was, "Urban Fantasy hurt my feelings." But I'll be darned if some of you folks didn't enjoy it. I get messages now and then asking if or when I'll be continuing the series. Currently the answer remains "eventually, maybe" but until then, have a nice little character story about Blot and Alan!

Three a.m. It wasn't generally the sort of time one expected to get much work done. But Blot was a shade. She didn't need to sleep, and her host Alan did. Thus, the day was for their common goals, and the going had been slow on those. For those things that required a measure of privacy? The hours between midnight and dawn were prime time as far as she was concerned.

She nudged at her mouse and tapped at her keyboard. Alan had provided her with a tablet, but try as she might, she couldn't get the hang of the touch controls. If she focused, she could get them to operate, but that was no way to spend one's leisure time, constantly gathering the whole of one's being into the arduous task of tapping a link on a website. Honestly, it was as though the makers of these devices hadn't anticipated the needs of nonphysical beings when they were designing them. But Alan was kind enough to provide the keyboard and mouse as well, each connected to the tablet through some sort of modern mysticism called Bluetooth. Pushing and pulling at the shadows of the mouse and the keyboard buttons was infinitely more comfortable. And that was good, because she had work to do.

It had taken longer than she expected, but she'd found the article she was after. A young woman had been released from the hospital. As far as the rest of the world was concerned, she was notable only in her mysterious connection to the Metro Ghoul, a serial killer who, according to news reports, was a "perennial favorite of copycats." They didn't know the truth, and if they did, no one would have believed a word of it. But that was beside the point. All Blot cared about was the condition of the young woman. The words the article chose to use were "undergoing psychiatric evaluation" and "likely fit for discharge."

There was a half paragraph about her in total. One bit was about how she had been suffering from an unspecified condition "linked to psychological trauma." Again, Blot knew the truth, but in this world "psychological trauma" was a lot easier to swallow for most readers than "spiritual exhaustion due to prolonged binding to a hostile shade" sprinkled with a bit of "psychic damage from delayed reunion with a discarded shadow." A lie that's easy to believe is preferable to a truth that's hard to believe for most people. She fully understood, and typically embraced, that simple wisdom.

She should have been happy. No, that wasn't accurate. *Alan* should have been happy. But, then, Alan didn't know yet. For Blot, the complete recovery of that unfortunate woman had a deeper, and more troubling, implication than for anyone else. Until that woman left the hospital, Alan was the only one in their partnership with something to lose. If Blot felt the need, she could leave him and find a new host. But if she did, Alan would wither and die within minutes. It gave her some degree of leverage, some degree of power over him. He lived *only* if he remained useful to her. That was how she'd been taught to view the balance of power, anyway. But she'd come to think of Alan differently. Indeed, she'd come to think of everything she'd been taught differently. And with that woman's recovery, she'd come to realize that though slim, there was the possibility that Alan had an escape. They would have to find his shadow—no small task—and they would have to undergo a procedure to reattach it. But once they did, he could return to his old life, and Blot was free to move on.

She blinked milky-white eyes and scanned the article a second time, looking for sources. You could never be too careful. The internet was about as trustworthy as she was, which was to say it was an endless fountain of manipulations and half-truths. Alas, this seemed legitimate. Accurate. True.

She blinked again and shakily clicked away from the article. Her inky fingers rose up on either side of the tablet. She grasped it and depressed the power button, putting it to sleep. She'd seen enough. The tablet went into its little case along with the keyboard and mouse before she left the lair she'd made for herself.

Like the proper boogeyman she was, her lair was in the darkness beneath his bed. He'd offered to set her up in the corner of the bedroom. He went so far as to pay a visit to someplace called Ikea to look at furniture that might suit her. It was well-meaning—Alan was *frustratingly* well-meaning—but the place was brightly lit and filled with people. No place for a shade to get a good look at anything. The dusty hidden places were where she'd been taught to lurk. Beneath his bed was downright cozy. Dim. Secluded. Pleasant. But her mood was sour. She needed something to distract herself. Needed some time and space to think.

Her black two-dimensional form slid along the floor and up the wall. She wove expertly between framed photos. Alan was a photographer, and he'd placed some of the pieces he was most proud of on the walls of his bedroom. She paused, eyes focused on the opposite wall. There were other things framed and hung there. Sketches, usually drawn in ballpoint pen on the odd bit of notebook paper or stolen stationary. They were never anything really profound. A gnarled old tree here. A bird there. A few rough drawings of Alan. They were pictures Blot had made. He probably framed them because he thought it would make her feel good.

He was right.

She shut her eyes and looked away. A soft sound drew her attention to a hat stand tucked in the corner of the room. It had the faintest of shadows, cast by the light on Alan's charging laptop. Blot knew it hid the form of Chu-chu the rikt. Another creature Alan semiwillingly allowed to share his home. Though the birdlike beast didn't need to sleep either, it did spend a great deal of time huddled in the shadow of its roost, eyes shut and form curled up. Adorable. She wouldn't disturb the beast.

Her search for a decent distraction brought her to the ceiling. The white pools of her eyes gazed down at Alan. A ribbon of black shadow ran down the wall, across the floor, and up to his body, connecting the pair like a leash. Like shackles. Tomorrow he would wake up and he would do much the same search that she had. He would find the article, or one like it, and he would learn the girl was okay. That would plant the seed. The seed that could sprout into a key for those shackles.

Blot shut her eyes.

"Plant a seed," she murmured silently.

She was a shade. She had come here for a reason. She had a purpose. Though she'd all but abandoned that purpose, it didn't change her history. She'd trained all her life to come here. Her earliest memories were of the lessons she'd learned to serve her in pursuit of that purpose. And old lessons had deep roots.

Blot let her form ease back down the wall, drifting slowly to the place spread across the bed and the far wall that the blinking laptop light chose to paint her. She let her mind and spirit seep along that strip of shadow. She found her way to his body. Pressed her essence to the gateway of his mind, the link between his brain and his spirit. With soft pressure, she felt the doorway of his consciousness swing open.

Good. He was dreaming.

Alan was a good dreamer. Many different dreams, almost every night. She could only slip into his mind while he dreamed, so having a host with so active a subconscious mind was quite the windfall. She kept to the hazy fringes of the image his mind rendered. Mostly, Alan's dreams were rather mundane. That could be an asset or a liability depending on what she had in mind for him, but she was creative and usually she could make them work. Right now he was sitting in the center of an ill-defined bit of cityscape, a lonely street at dusk. He leaned against the wall of a bus stop, eyes vaguely observing a bit of graffiti that didn't actually say anything. Similarly hazy and indistinct bodies shifted and shuffled around him. Nameless nobodies conjured by his mind to fill space. They weren't the focus of his attention and thus were mostly cast from half-forgotten memories of people he'd passed on the street. Blot recognized the barista from their preferred coffee shop, and someone who had been on the TV last night. She had a good memory for details. It was one of the things that had been drilled into her in preparation for this mission.

Blot tugged at the mental landscape and sculpted herself into a more appropriate appearance for the setting. She reconfigured her malleable form into a nondescript young human woman. Her skin was pale, her clothing black and tattered. Monochrome was so much easier for her than color, and at this distance, hidden among the imagined crowd, she wouldn't draw his attention. Once she had her human body, she licked a finger and held it up into the air, testing the wind. It was a bit of theater, an affectation that was more symbolic than anything else. But this was a dream. Everything was symbolism. And presently this little cliché served the purpose of testing the nature of the dream. She could feel that this was one of those meaningless, in-between dreams. Sort of a liminal space within his mind while it worked on conjuring up something more interesting. That was good. It meant he wouldn't remember it. Not in any way that mattered to him. Though possibly in a way that mattered to her.

She allowed herself to observe for a moment as a street musician coalesced from the mental firmament and strummed a discordant tune. His mind really wasn't putting in the effort on this one. Why should it? It would just be forgotten.

Forgotten dreams...

It always felt so strange to her, so sad. A dream was one of the few perfectly private things one could experience. They were known only to the one who dreamed them. And yet, over the course of the night, several would come and go, often a full night of them passing without a single one making enough of an impression to be remembered. Little performances, crafted by one bit of a mind for the benefit of another. What could be more meaningless than a forgotten dream?

The busker slipped back into the haziness. Blot's training wriggled up from her memories. The goal she had been trained for centered on observation, education. She was meant to collect information so that when she reconvened with the others, she could provide that precious data to someone who had taken a more powerful and useful host. But her teachers weren't fools. They had to entertain the possibility that even the lowliest of shades could luck into a host with genuine value. They didn't get much lowlier than Blot, but still she'd gotten her education on manipulation.

A shade had no voluntary control over its host. The really powerful ones could tug and twist at a host's physical form, but it was still the host who had to act. There was no mind control. No means to compel. But that didn't mean there was no recourse to guide the actions of their host. Persuasion, negotiation, manipulation, extortion. They could help feed the desires of their hosts to weaken their resolve, help them achieve their goals to earn their trust. But the best tactic, the most subtle means, revolved around finding a way to make the host believe they weren't being guided or coaxed at all. Let the host believe they had come up with the idea on their own.

That the humans had made a film based upon that technique was such a blatant sign that there had been shades at work in this world for ages, and she wondered how the secret had been kept until now. But that was a matter for another day. She turned aside and gazed at the ghostly forms of the half-imagined crowd. She had to be here somewhere...

Sure enough, pacing at the edge of the dream's setting, was *her*. That police officer who had become so significant a part of Alan's life. Jessie. Something about her got Blot's hackles up. Probably it was simply the training. The people who matter most to your host will be the people most likely to get in the way, most likely to notice if behaviors start to change. And Jessie mattered to him. And he mattered to her. Even though Blot *technically* was no longer obligated to pursue things that might be endangered by someone like Jessie, and even though Jessie already knew about her and thus there was nothing to be revealed... Blot just didn't like having her around. But in this moment, she was precisely what Blot needed.

She swept around the perimeter of the dream and simply stepped into the dream version of Jessie. Her appearance wavered for a moment, then settled, little more than a costume over Blot's form. She stepped forward and took a seat beside Alan at the bus stop. He turned with a start. The flicker of anxiety in his eyes made Blot's mood sour just a bit. He was so jumpy. Somehow she knew he hadn't always been so. By all accounts he'd been fairly easygoing. But now? Scared of his own shadow. Her jaw tightened as she realized that phrase might *also* have been inspired by her own people. Lousy humans, hiding ancient wisdom in their idioms...

"Jessie?" Alan said.

She snapped out of her own thoughts and gathered her mind to the task of mimicking the woman's voice properly.

"Hey Alan," she said, the voice flawlessly Jessie's. "Any reason you're sitting here in the middle of nowhere?"

"I, uh... I guess I'm not really sure why I'm here. I was going somewhere, but I can't remember where."

"Isn't that going to make it a little tricky paying the bus fare?"

He scratched his head. "I swear I was here for a reason."

She grinned. He was already searching for something. It was almost too perfect. She'd stumbled upon him with a handy little gap in his mind, and all she had to do was fill it with...

Blot glanced up slightly. She tried to keep her expression steady. What exactly did she want him to do? Her gift for improvisation had dragged her this far without the need to consider *why* she wanted to come here in the first place.

"W-well, let's talk about it," she said quickly, the brief delay already beginning to allow confusion and suspicion to worm its way into Alan's expression. "Maybe I can jog your memory. What's on your mind?"

"What's *always* on my mind," he said. "The future."

"You'll drive yourself crazy thinking about the future."

"Back when I thought I knew where I was headed, I didn't think about it much. Not directly. I made plans and stuff. I had goals. It always felt like the sky was the limit. Everything had limitless potential. Little did I know just how limited the potential was back then. Back when I wasn't matching wits with angels and demons on a daily basis."

"Since when are you talking to angels?" Blot said flatly.

"We talked about this, didn't we? The white-suits. They're angels."

Blot bristled a bit. Those white-suited thugs were *not* angels. But it wasn't the sort of thing she could hammer home, because it was a very *Blot* distinction to make, and right now she was Jessie. It was a rare bit of luck that the talk of angels and demons hadn't given his sleeping mind enough of a nudge to question where the current resident of his shadow was. This whole plan, once she figured out what the plan *was*, hinged upon the handy little gaps in perception that one's dream self tended to have.

"Okay, so the future," Blot said. "You worried about something specific? Hoping for anything specific?"

Alan rubbed his eye with the back of his hand. "I just want to survive. I just want to make sure no one gets hurt."

"People get hurt, Alan. You can't save everybody. There's nothing new about that."

"Yeah, but I used to be able to delude myself into thinking there was someone out there who *could* save everybody. Or at least that if there was someone with special knowledge of the world and its threats, it wasn't *me*. Being one of the ones who can see through the veil left my plausible deniability about the paranormal in the dust. I'm it. I'm the one who knows, and that means I'm the one who has to do something about it."

"You don't have to do it alone," she said. "At least there's that."

She regretted it instantly. What was she thinking? Was she trying to sabotage herself? She may as well have mentioned herself by name.

"At least there's that..." he murmured.

He leaned forward, elbows on his knees, and looked at his own feet. The dream shifted imperceptibly around her. Like a change in the breeze. The bus stop became a little sharper, more vivid. The ghostly foot traffic thinned out. His mind was gathering together. Focusing. He was becoming more lucid.

"What are *you* doing here?" Alan asked without looking.

"I'm a cop. This is on my beat," she said, as matter-of-factly as she could manage.

He looked up. Blot's expression dropped the moment she caught eyes with him.

"You're getting better at this, Blot," he said.

She looked at him flatly and crossed her arms. "I'll have you know I'm getting *worse* at it. The last time I tried to 'incept' something, it worked."

"I think I'd remember something like that," he said.

"The idea is that you *wouldn't*. Did you really think you got the idea to buy that burr grinder on your own?" she asked, her form slowly easing from Jessie's to her impish self.

When she was down to two-thirds his height, with chalky skin, a gobliny body, and long hair that danced like black flame curling over her head, she drifted up a bit, crossing her legs as she floated high enough to meet him eye to eye. White pupils in black eyes shifted aside just long enough for her to conjure a reasonable facsimile of her favorite mug, filled with black coffee.

"I did it because you're the coffee fiend in the house, and so long as we're stuck together, you might as well have something nice now and then."

She grinned. "I did a good job on that one," she said. She sipped her coffee. It was a figment of his imagination, but it was still glorious.

"If it was true, would you *really* be admitting it?" he said.

She licked her finger and held it up. The breeze had changed, but not enough. "You won't remember this dream. I may as well be talking to myself."

"You can tell when I will or won't remember a dream?"

"Sure. I picked it up after a few weeks of observation. I'm an excellent observer."

"Then what's the point of this? How does it do any good to convince me of something in a dream I won't remember?"

She held out her hand. A point of light appeared above her palm. She twiddled her fingers and it zipped up and down again, plunging between the cracks in the sidewalk. A few moments later, a white weed wriggled through the cracks.

"The idea is I poke something just far enough past your subconscious for you to get a notion without knowing where it came from. Won't work now, though. Your defenses are up."

Alan's mouth hung open a bit as he watched the weed curl and flutter in the breeze, like he'd queued up a sentence but was holding it because he wasn't sure it was worth saying. "You know, I should be furious with you about this."

"You'd have to be an idiot *not* to be furious with me. That's why I have to do it carefully."

"You shouldn't be doing it at *all*." He sighed. "What were you after this time? More of that Kona blend coffee?"

"Please. I wouldn't noodle around in your brain for something like that. I'd just swipe some next time you go shopping."

"I don't like it when you steal stuff."

"It's not stealing. It's creative acquisition."

"Fine. Not coffee. What then?"

"What does it matter?"

He tipped his head. "You don't know, do you?"

She glared at him. "Of course I know why I came in here. What sort of a *fool* would plunge into someone else's dream and start manipulating them without having an end to justify the means?"

"What then?"

She took her hand from the mug, leaving it floating in the air, and crossed her arms again. "I don't have to answer."

"Uh-huh." He stood and stretched. "Well, if you've kicked me into another lucid dream, I can at least enjoy it."

He started pacing forward. She drifted along beside him. With each step, the surroundings changed slightly. A crunch of grass here, a crispness to the air there. She didn't need to waste her time working out where he was going. It was the same place he always went when he had any choice in the matter.

A dozen strides took him to a brisk, cool field. It was late fall, someplace rural. His parents' land. The very place they'd first met, though admittedly he didn't know it at the time.

"So if I'm not going to remember this, I assume you don't want to work on doing any plotting and planning for whatever comes next."

"No point."

"But you're still here."

"One can only surf the internet for so long before it starts to wither the soul, Alan. I swear, you people claim you don't know magic, but there is something dark about that technology."

He shut his eyes and took a breath of the autumn air. The pair was silent for a few seconds, watching the moon obligingly moving itself into a more aesthetically pleasing position. She sipped her coffee. He settled down to sit in the grass. Her eyes lingered on him for a second or two before she plopped down on the grass beside him.

"She's okay," Blot said finally.

"Who?"

"The lady who was the ghoul's host. She pulled through. She's going to be fine."

"That's a relief. Though after what she went through, probably 'fine' is going to mean nightmares for the rest of her life."

"At least the nightmares will only be while she's sleeping instead of every second of every day. But you know what it means, right? It means you've got a way out."

"Hardly. There's still a job to do."

"Yeah, but you know what I mean. Assuming we can track down your shadow, we won't have to be an us anymore."

"And that's what brought you in here?"

"It's what was on my mind. Everything else was sort of reflex."

"It's not dangerous for *you*, right? The procedure? You can just find a new host."

"I don't even *need* the procedure if I want to ditch you. I'm here out of the kindness of my heart."

"Because we have a job to do."

"Because I don't have anything *better* to do. It's not as though there are a ton of people eager to have my voice in their ear and my face on their shadow."

"Don't sell yourself short. Of all the parts of this insanity, you've been the best part."

"I'd consider that a compliment if not for the fact that literally everyone else that's a part of this has tried to kill you."

She took another sip. He raised his eyebrows.

"Can I get one of those?" he asked, pointing at the mug.

She swirled her fingers and Alan's travel mug whisked together. She popped the lid off and poured out her mug into his. That it was twice the capacity of her mug didn't make a difference. When she was done pouring, both mugs were full to the brim.

He took a drink. "You came here talking about the future. What about you? What do you think of when you think about the future?"

"We just got through saying we weren't going to make plans you won't remember."

"I don't mean for what's next, I mean for what's after. If I am profoundly lucky, I'll see my way clear to the other side of this, alive and relatively intact, ready to get back to what I'd been working toward. My career. My art. What about you?"

"I don't think that far ahead."

"Now's as good a time as any."

"I *don't* think that far ahead," she said firmly.

"You've got to have something to work toward."

"There was never an 'after' for me, Alan," she said. "When I was being trained, I was being trained for the task. I was learning to do what I'd have to do. And there wasn't a place for me in the end game. No one ever said it, but everyone knew why. Because shades like me weren't going to *make* it to the end game."

"But things are different now. You control your own destiny."

"Destinies are for other creatures," she muttered.

"Are you afraid I'll abandon you?"

"Afraid? Afraid implies some sort of doubt. It wouldn't very well be 'after' if I was still lurking around, would it?" She shut her eyes. "Can I borrow the dream for a minute?"

"Mi sueño es tu sueño," he said magnanimously.

She reached out to the air and pinched the very world around her between thumb and forefinger, as though she were grabbing a tapestry. She tugged it and the lovely field fell away. What was revealed behind it was the dark, dusty lair she'd made for herself under his bed. For the sake of comfort, she'd fiddled with the scale. They were mouse-size in comparison to her tablet case. She took a seat on it. He sat beside her.

"I really wish you'd have let me buy you a desk," he said, looking around.

"This is the nicest place I've ever been, Alan. This is home. I have a home. Right now. Right here. I have a place. Even if it's just a fragment of your place, it's still mine. I never had that. Not before I came here. Not once in my life. Sure, I had something of a family. Sure, we had a place to live. But it wasn't *mine*. I didn't have any choice about it. Any control over it. It was just... a place to be while I was waiting for the mission to begin. This is mine in a way I've never had *anything before*."

She flopped back onto the springy, rubbery cover. "You're busy thinking about the future. You're busy thinking about *after*. The best time of my life, the most accepted and most *me* I've ever been is right now. I don't want to think about after."

"So what do you want?"

"I don't know! I'm not used to what I want actually making a difference to anyone. I don't have any practice at wanting things. There was never any point."

"There might be better things in your future. Maybe... maybe there's a way to make it so you don't need a host."

"There isn't."

"For all we knew, there wasn't a procedure to restore my shadow. Who's to say there isn't a way for you to make a home here permanently?"

She huffed. "I don't know. I don't want to think about things changing. But I also don't want to think about how what's as close to paradise as I've ever experienced is as close to hell as *you've* ever experienced. I want things to get better, but I don't want them to change. And I don't..." She hesitated. "Oh, what does it matter. You won't remember this when you wake up anyway."

She sat up to look him in the eye again. "I don't want to think about not being linked to someone like you. You're my anchor, Alan. And not just in the mystical way. You're this...

this solid, cool, steady mind right beside mine. Sure, you're scared. You're just as lost as me. But we're together. That's something I *was* prepared for. I was only ever supposed to be a part of something larger than myself. Part of a team. There's comfort in that. But it was supposed to be this big, faceless, formless thing. This swarm of which I was a small part. You... you've got a face. You've got a name. I know you. And I'm not a small part of what we are. I'm half of it. I'm a big, important part. I know things. I'm useful. I matter." She covered her face. "I don't want to imagine a time where I'm alone. I *don't* want to think about *after*."

She crossed her arms and turned her head aside. "The future sucks."

Alan had some more coffee and drummed his fingers on the tablet case. "You know how long I've known Jessie?"

"I don't want to talk about Jessie," Blot muttered. "If you're going to tell me this big long anecdote to make me feel better, just skip to the moral of the story."

"I don't turn my back on my friends. That's the moral," he said. "I don't turn my back on my friends, and you're my friend. We'll figure it out. But I promise you, when we make it through this, there will still be a place for you."

She sat up and smoothed some wrinkles from her rags. Three different retorts formulated themselves in her mind, but she couldn't find one that seemed appropriate. After floundering for a few seconds, she noticed the steam from her coffee drifting in a new direction. Fate was taking pity on her.

"The wind's changing," she said. "You're about to be in a new dream, and this whole thing is going to fade away."

The setting she'd conjured up was already wavering. She could see the lucidity in his expression starting to waver, like his dream self was an actor shaking off one role and preparing for another.

"Alan?" she said.

She could see him fighting to keep hold of the dream long enough to respond. She touched a dainty hand to his cheek and offered a sincere smile. "Thanks for calling it a procedure, not a cure. That was nice of you."

He shrugged. "It was nothing."

Those were the last words he had the presence of mind to direct at her. The world around them started to shift to a familiar place: a school classroom. She watched him turn and approach a locker, audibly fretting about a test he hadn't studied for. She lingered just past the edge.

"It was everything, Alan," she said softly.

She could feel the tension of this mind as he slipped into the low-grade nightmare that tended to show up every few days. Before she retreated to the real world and found something else to occupy her time, she conjured a slip of paper and scribbled out some random facts, then folded it into a paper airplane and tossed it past him. He spotted it and unfolded it. The facts were meaningless, but they'd neatly fit into the slot his mind had crystalized the dream around: the test he hadn't studied for. His dream self took a desperate sigh of relief and read over the study sheet, the tension slipping away.

Sure, she didn't know what she wanted her future to be. But the least she could do was let him know how much she valued the present he had given her.

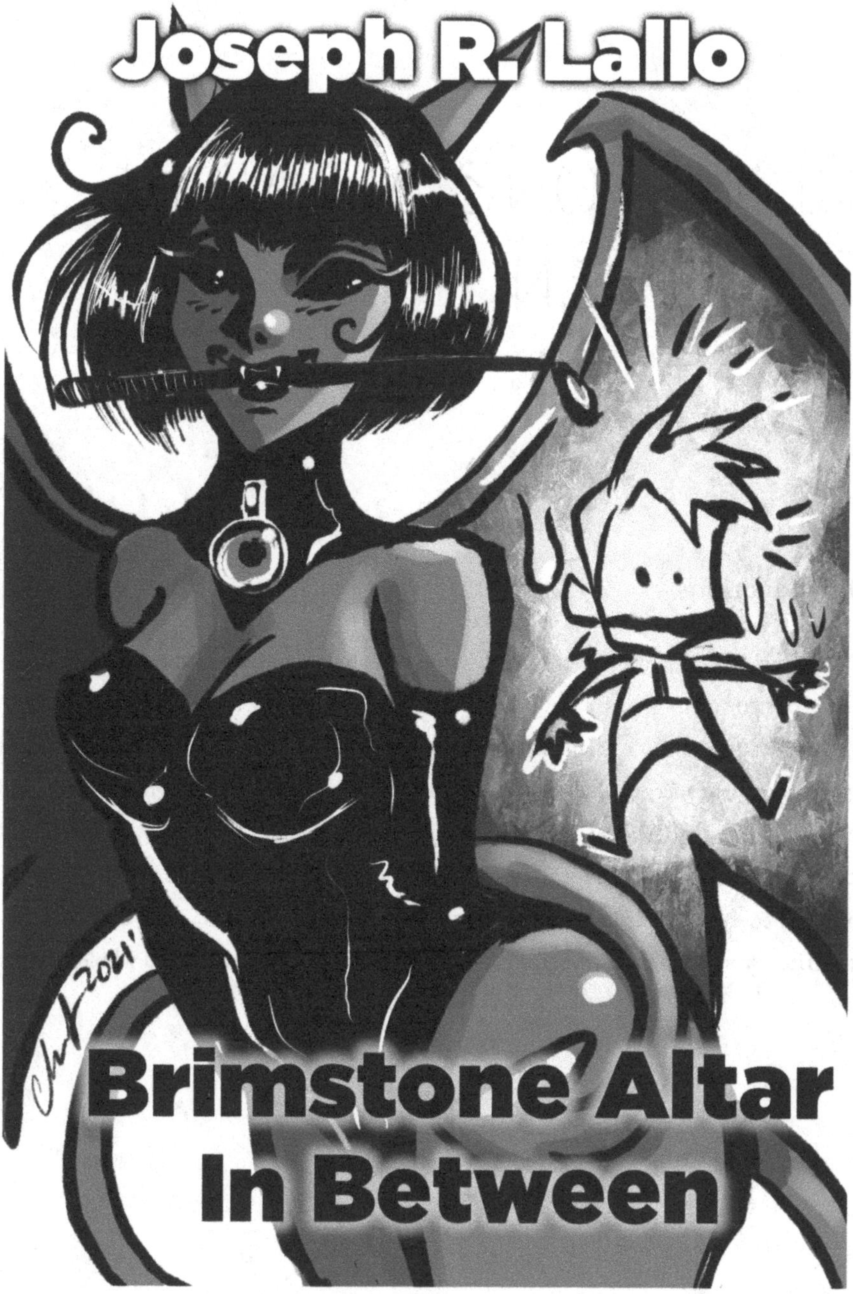
Joseph R. Lallo
Brimstone Altar
In Between

Brimstone Altar In Between

Introduction

Phew! This one was a close call. I wrote this almost entirely in the same day it was posted.

Between remains one of those stories that I really enjoy. It is by no means my most popular or most successful story, but when I think back to the things I wrote, I really find a lot to love in the setting and characters. When I hired Chandra Free to do the cover, I didn't give much guidance for what the cover should look like, and she gave me, frankly, a spicier cover than I usually shoot for. It fit the character perfectly, and I decided to try to write a story to match. Hopefully I struck a balance between spicy and wholesome.

T hings were finally starting to feel *right* for Trixie Zalthea. As right as they could be in the Between, at least. For someone born to be a seductress and, by a twist of fate, left without the mystic means to enthrall her would-be prey, her destiny was clearly not meant to include petty things like happiness and fulfillment. As luck would have it, fate had enough other twists in store for her that it must have lost track of her, because somehow she'd ended up in a pleasant little cottage she'd constructed with her own two hands. She had a fairly important job. She had the respect of her peers. She had friends (more or less), and she had Philo. Her little silver medal.

"Trixie! You want some tea?" Philo called from the kitchen.

"If you're making some for yourself, I'll take some," she called.

She reached up to awkwardly scratch between her wings through her well-worn t-shirt and looked at the project she'd set aside for the evening. During their last fetch, she and her associates had found the remains of an antique shop, and inside was a cuckoo clock that she was *certain* she could get working again. It was just the thing for the wall beside the hearth. Just the thing to perfect her den.

Philo stepped inside with two cups of tea. His with a drop of honey. Hers with a sprinkle of cayenne—just the way she liked it.

"Hey, Champ, before we get down to it, would you scratch my back? I can't quite reach that sore spot from where the minotaur got me."

"That was two fetches ago," Philo said, sliding his hand into her shirt and scratching her back. "We should go out to dinner. A nice big meal will heal you up."

"Nyeh," she murmured, eyes rolled back blissfully and brain not quite able to assemble syllables properly as his fingernails found *just* the right spot. "We've been super busy and I've just been wanting to relax between fetches. Besides, you've got the magic fingers."

He finished scratching and took a seat. "All right. How do we want to break this up?" he said. "I do repairs, you do assembly?"

"Sounds good to me."

He took a seat and started arranging gears and pinions. She arranged her tools nicely. It would take the better part of twenty hours, by her estimate, to put this thing back together in working order. It needed a *lot* of work. After half a dozen fetches that included bashing things with a warhammer, some nice and tedious technical work was precisely what she was after. It was going to be *wonderful*.

The very moment she realized how much she was looking forward to the next few hours, she regretted allowing her mind to form those thoughts. There was no better way to shatter the fragile veneer of bliss she was occasionally able to apply to her life than to call attention to it.

Sure enough, already she could hear the distant jangle of a silver bell and a soft, slightly raspy voice chanting pleasantly to itself.

"Trixie. Trixie. Trixie," repeated the Messenger.

She covered her face with her hands. "Of course..."

"Maybe it won't be a fetch," Philo suggested.

"When is it ever *not* a fetch? We're fetchers, Philo. It's what we do."

She stood and clopped over to the door. Hooved feet were particularly good at illustrating frustration via the tried-and-true adolescent technique of stomping as she walked.

She threw the door open and peered down as the furry black-and-white critter who delivered all her assignments scampered onto the deck she'd built around her cottage.

"Trixie!" he said brightly.

He lowered his head and presented his adorable little backpack. A single tightly rolled message stuck out, a red seal labeling it as hers.

"Message, Trixie," he said.

"Yeah, yeah," she muttered, snatching it up.

The messenger trotted away. Trixie hastily shut the door, but she didn't *quite* get it latched before it burst open again and three black-eyed, lavender-scaled sea serpent heads stared back at her.

"What's it say?" said Rill.

"Is it a fun fetch?" asked Right-Rill.

"How come *we* didn't get one?" asked Left-Rill.

"Would you give me time to *read* it, you half-wits?" she snapped.

"There's *three* of us," Rill said.

"That means we're *less* than half a wit each," Right-Rill said.

"Shows what *you* know," Left-Rill said, chin raised and eyes shut.

"Ooh! What's that record?" Rill asked.

"Is that Barry Manilow?" Right-Rill said.

"Why aren't you playing Abba?" Left-Rill asked.

The three heads nodded in agreement. "Abba is better."

Trixie grabbed the long handle of her warhammer and pulled it from the umbrella stand beside the door. "You three mind your own business, or I'm going to crush your head."

"We're going to put on our *own* record," Rill said.

"Something that's fun to sing to," Right-Rill said.

"At least then we'll have some fun while you're *hogging our fourth head*," Left-Rill said, glaring at Philo through the doorway.

Trixie slammed the door as the Rills returned to their lair.

"You should be nicer to those three."

"I've known them for an eternity. This is as nice as I'm going to get," she muttered. She broke the seal with one claw and unfurled the message. "Trixie. The Overseer requires an audience with you as soon as you receive this message," she read.

She turned the message over. "That's it. That's all it says."

"I guess it's not a fetch, then," Philo said.

"I don't like this," she rumbled, crumpling the message. "This gives me a very bad feeling."

"It's probably nothing," Philo said.

"Champ, your optimism is very endearing, but its hit-miss ratio is awful." She grabbed her hammer again. "I'll be back. And I probably won't be happy." She pointed. "Don't you *dare* start assembly without me."

"I wouldn't dream of it."

She opened the door and spread her wings. Two neat flaps sent her skyward, into the featureless white void that made up the sky in the Between. Her sharp teeth clenched as she set her mind on Heartcore. Anger was a useful default mindset, as it helped chase away less pleasant emotions like fear or anxiety. Sure, it didn't make for a particularly *happy* or *pleasant* disposition, but it sure beat facing reality on its own terms sometimes.

Not so long ago—at least, not so long ago if time actually had any meaning in the Between—this would have been a long and exhausting trip. Heartcore was once the home of the largest and best-defended society in the Between, and a rival to Shard, where she still made her home with Philo. Nowadays they were still large and still well-defended, but they were *allies* of Shard, both existing under the "wise" and "benevolent" leadership of the Overseer. He hadn't done much to improve things after deposing the previous ruler, but he also wasn't calling upon an ancient and untamable evil in attempts to lure fresh victims to the Between.

Sometimes failing to do something overtly awful was all the improvement a society needed in its leader.

Regardless, there was no longer a constant defensive pressure keeping the undesirables of Shard from reaching Heartcore. That meant as soon as Shard had vanished from view, the long straight line of Heartcore emerged in front of her. She flitted toward the capital city, New Allimiss, and darted through an opening in the one significant addition the Overseer had made to the city. Rather than moving into the sprawling, magnificent palace his predecessor had built, he'd simply transported his own palace from Shard. The black stone had reassembled itself, brick by brick, atop the old castle. The end result looked a bit like a twisted series of black towers and ramparts had sprouted like a parasitic growth from the top of the old castle.

It would have been faster to fly in through the window she knew led to his throne room, but he was a bit testy about people arriving without the proper procedure and decorum. So she instead chose what had once been the front door and was now something of an oddly overgrown balcony. With a few swoops and flutters, she navigated the Escher-esque halls of the castle, depositing herself in front of the door to his throne room. Wrunx, his logistician, drifted beside the door. The pickled brain and eyes atop a hovering disk held out a mechanical hand by way of greeting.

"Ah! Trixie. I am pleased you were able to come so quickly," he said.

"Yeah, yeah. What's this all about? Am I in trouble? Because frankly I'm getting pretty sick of being pretty much the *only* one who gets called on to do things anymore. Seriously, the Overseer has *all of Heartcore* to put to work now and me, the worm, and Champ are still doing back-to-back fetches."

"The Overseer trusts you. It is a compliment, I assure you."

"If he keeps complimenting me, I'm going to need a vacation," she growled.

"You'll be pleased to know that it is *not* a fetch. But I'll let him explain it."

Wrunx rapped its metallic knuckles against the heavy door to the throne room. Something like the sound of flowing sand followed, then the slow, smooth shift of the door swinging open. She hefted the hammer on her shoulder and marched into the throne room. The Overseer had perched his little fuzzy body in the seat of a throne that would have been large for a creature ten times his size and gazed at Trixie.

"You came swiftly... Yes... I am pleased," the Overseer said.

"What is it, boss? The message was a little vague."

"It was a message best related in person. The matter is... unique to your talents... Yes..." She huffed a breath. "Fine."

Trixie marched up to the throne and, with a skill that betrayed a fair amount of practice, gave the Overseer an ear rub. The little, unspeakably powerful creature shut his eyes and tilted his head, softly thumping his foot on the dire throne.

"This was not why I summoned you," he said.

"Oh. Sorry," she said, taking a step back.

He opened one eye and flicked the formerly rubbed ear. "I did not tell you to stop."

She sighed and stepped in to continue the scritches. The Overseer continued.

"The seers identified a significant arrival. Yes... A mass crossover event. Some manner of botched ritual. A substantial portion of a whole city arrived at once, and has not immediately departed."

"So they don't know their way out," Trixie said. "You want me and the rest of the crew to go fetch the lot of them?"

"I have discussed matters with the Logistician. Yes... There is the possibility these creatures will be of little use to us. I have enough useless subjects."

Trixie raised an eyebrow. Given the length of her association with the Overseer, and his unquenchable lust for power and control, she'd never expected him to utter the word "enough" about anything.

"But there may be value. If there was a ritual, there are spellcasters. Magic users. Yes... I may want them. The Logistician suggests, with a group so large, an attempt to fetch by force could be bloody. Yes... We might lose the people we seek. He suggests something distasteful instead."

"Distasteful?"

The Overseer slumped a bit, tipping his head to present the second ear for rubs. "Diplomacy," he uttered, as though the word was an unspeakable slur.

"You want me to be a *diplomat*?" she said. "If anyone should be a diplomat, it should be Wrunx."

"It so happens this city is populated by creatures not unlike yourself. Demons and the like. From a world quite like yours."

"Quite like mine, you say."

"Precisely like yours. If not your world, then some echo or duplicate of it. They are quite certainly your kind. Yes... So you are the natural choice to represent Shard and Heartcore. Yes..."

"I must respectfully disagree, boss. The whole reason I ended up here is because I was trying a ritual to give myself the mystic powers I'm supposed to have. I'm supposed to have intrinsic mystic wiles, and by a quirk of birth I lack them. They will see me as inferior."

"I am aware of your shortcomings. Yes... And I am aware that they are not easily detectable."

"Sure, you'd have to be a healer to know I am powerless, until someone actually seeks to challenge me on my power. There *will* come a time when my powers are meant to be displayed, and when that time comes, I won't be able to hide their absence."

She shifted from rubbing his ears to scratching him just above the tail. "Come on, boss," she said sweetly. "Let Wrunx give it a try."

She heard the shifting of sand again. Before she could react, coils of black grit animated by the will of the Overseer wrapped around her and hauled her into the air. They pressed her arms and wings tight to her body and maneuvered her until she was face to face with him. He opened his eyes.

"You have your orders... Yes..."

A light flick of will sent her lofting neatly to her feet. She'd worked hard to subtly manipulate him into keeping his powers to himself while she was around. It was unnerving to see that particular weapon unsheathed after she'd come to assume it wouldn't be used on her anymore. This was clearly a matter he didn't wish to discuss any further.

"Right, boss. Diplomacy."

"Find out if they have anything to offer. If they do, get them to offer it. If they are worthless to us? Do as you will. They do not interest me in such a case."

"I might need help with this one."

"Take what you need. The seers say you need only fix your own world in your mind to find the place."

"That similar to my home?"

"Yes... Now, run along."

She turned and trotted for the window. The boss didn't like for people to arrive via the window, but he didn't particularly care if they left through it. Indeed, a few of his more useless minions had a habit of leaving through the window whether they wanted to or not. As she spread her wings and swooped for the return trip, her mind went to work.

Diplomacy... it was just a fancy word for manipulation. And she was well trained for that. Even so, keeping them from learning of her disability? That would take work. Her glossy black lips curled into a grin.

"By the many hells, it might be worth it just to see the look on his face," she said.

***

She touched down in the Fetcher's Den, where she, Philo, and the Rills lived.

"Worm! Get ready, we've got a job," Trixie announced.

"But we didn't get a message," Rill shouted, sticking her head out of the neat little brick lair Philo and Trixie had helped assemble for her.

"Why would we get a job without a message?" Right-Rill said, her own head jutting out as well.

"You're just trying to get us to do your job for you," Left-Rill accused.

"Relax. This is a big one. No fighting, just talking. And I'll make sure we get plenty of tokens if we pull it off. But I want to get moving fast. The sooner we get through this, the better."

She marched into the cottage, where Philo was working diligently at the task of shaping some gear teeth with a file.

"Champ, listen up. I'm going to have to unload a lot of information in a little time," she said, walking past him into their bedroom.

She shut the door and threw open her closet. The assortment of casual outfits she'd assembled for when she was off duty wouldn't do for this one. This called for something old-fashioned.

"What's up?" he asked.

"Apparently a whole neighborhood from my home world has shown up. The Overseer wants us to go and see if there's anything or anyone worth stealing, and for once he's going to try the carrot rather than the stick. And apparently *I'm* the carrot."

She found the very outfit she was wearing when she'd arrived in the Between, though calling it an outfit was charitable. It was more of a wrapper.

"Stay out there, Champ, I'm getting changed. But here's the deal," she called. "Unless things have changed a whole lot since I left, this is going to be one hundred percent about status and control. And since I don't have the mystical ability to control, I have zero status. But that won't be immediately obvious to them, so the name of the game is distraction and misdirection. We need to put on a show so they won't feel the need to test me on my prowess. If they *do* test me, I'll fail the test and they'll disregard us. Then the boss'll be mad, and he'll probably send in troops, and it's a bad time for everyone."

She tossed her comfortable clothes on the bed and began to squeeze herself into the old uniform. "This is going to be major danger for you. More so than me. If they figure out I'm nothing but a mundane piece of meat, they'll treat me as such. Prey. They'll try to dominate me, but while I don't have the power to compel anyone else, I'm pretty well equipped to resist their powers. You, on the other hand, are just about the most mystically pliable person I've ever met. They try to get their claws into you, they'll get them all the way to the bone. So they need to think that you're hopelessly, helplessly enthralled by me, and that I'm powerful enough that they dare not challenge me and try to claim you, because you are my property."

"So... what do I need to do?" he said.

"In short, whatever I tell you to. If I say stop, you stop. If I say lick my hooves, you get down on the floor and have at it."

"Without hesitation?"

"Some hesitation is fine. Actually, some hesitation is good. It'll suggest you had a strong enough will to be worth dominating and that will help build up the myth of my own power all the more. But I will never have to tell you twice. Get Worm over to the door. She'll need instructions too."

"Rill!" Philo called. "Would you come here please?"

Trixie reached up to the top shelf of the closet and pulled down what looked like the case for a pool cue. It looked like that, because that's exactly what it was, albeit repurposed. She unzipped it and removed a long flexible rod with a woven leather grip on one end and a looped flap of leather on the other. She smiled and slapped it against her palm, producing a satisfying whipcrack.

Outside her bedroom, she heard the door slam open and the voices of the frustrating hydra.

"What's going on? I thought we were doing a job?" Rill said.

"Is it a surprise thing? Surprises are fun!" Right-Rill said.

"I'm telling you, she's tricking us into doing work for her," Left-Rill said.

Trixie shook her head. "It's frustrating that I can tell them apart by the tone of their voice. I've spent entirely too much time with those three…"

She opened the door to the bedroom and strutted out. Philo, catching his first glimpse of her in the old getup, froze. His eyes went wide and his mouth dropped open. She crossed her arms and smirked. She couldn't say she was *surprised* by his response. Philo had always come across as a bit too "aw shucks." Seeing a demon in her work clothes was bound to be too much for him. The outfit itself resembled a one-piece swimsuit, though it was scandalously tight in a way that positively defied physics. It traced very curve and crevice of her body, providing a glossy black sheen without constricting or compacting anything that she wanted presented in its full glory. In effect, this outfit was for when nudity wasn't lewd enough, a second skin that was in some ways tighter than the first one.

Right-Rill nudged Rill with her cheek and glared at her. "See? I told you they forget sometimes. We were arguing about this a while ago, once we found out two-leggers were mostly wearing clothes. I said 'I bet sometimes they forget' and Rill said, 'No, they never forget.'"

The triple tail curled up to point accusingly between their heads.

"Trixie forgot to put her clothes on," Right-Rill said.

"I didn't forget. This is calculated. All of this is calculated," Trixie said. "Get your chin off the floor, Champ. Save that for when we get there."

Philo swallowed hard. "Am I going to have to wear a costume too?" he said nervously.

"No, no. What you're wearing is fine. Though, you'll need one little addition. I'll get it in a minute. As for you, Worm, here's what I need from you. You're going to be my steed. I ride in astride you, Philo clinging to me from behind like an accessory. Then—"

"No," Rill said.

"You don't ride us, Philo does," Right-Rill said.

"He's our *partner*. You're just *his* partner," Left-Rill said.

"Not during this trip, he isn't. We're playing make believe, remember? And you're a key part. It's all got to be dazzle. All show and glamour. We don't go in for subtlety and tact for the most part. So me, coming in astride you? Let's just say the overall form factor will serve useful innuendo purposes."

"I don't know what that is," Right-Rill said.

"She's making up words," Left-Rill said.

"No one's going in anyone's end-o," Rill said. "Not after that whole 'getting the evil thing out of my belly' thing that happened."

"It means..." Philo began. "Never mind. If we're lucky, that's the last time you'll ever have to hear that phrase. Just go with us on this one. I think Trixie is the only one who knows exactly what to expect."

"Champ knows what's what, Worm, listen to him. I'll go into a little more detail on the way. Until then, there's the issue of your one little accessory," Trixie said.

She reached into the bedroom and pulled out the item in question.

"You're joking, right?" Philo said, face scrunched up in a half wince.

"Uh-uh-uh," she said. "Let's get into character, now. No questions."

***

A short, ultimately fruitless argument and debate later, Trixie was straddling Rill's neck while Philo rode behind her. A long chain leash ran from her left hand to a black studded collar around his neck. She gave a ginger little slap to Rill's side with the riding crop in her other hand.

"Forward, Worm," she instructed.

"I'm thinking very much about ripping and crunching right now," Left-Rill said.

"Crunch first, then rip, then more crunch," Right-Rill muttered.

"Don't forget twisting. Crunch, twist, rip, crunch," Rill amended.

"Come on, you three," Philo said. "It's just for one trip."

"You owe us a record for this," Rill said.

"A good one," Right-Rill said.

"With *harmony*," Left-Rill said.

The hydra coiled and sprang, launching into the air and darting skyward. Trixie hooked her legs tight around the two necks she wasn't straddling. She didn't strictly need to be riding Rill. That was part of the reason she was doing it. There was something obscenely indulgent about a creature capable of flight riding another creature. But now that she was riding the powerful water dragon, she was treated to a firsthand view of just how powerful and fast Rill was.

It would probably be a good idea to pick out a record when they got back.

Traveling in the Between was such that she didn't need to tell Rill where they were going. Rill didn't even need to go anywhere in particular. She just needed to go while a member of the group fixed their mind on the intended location, and eventually they would arrive. In this case, she thought of the brick-brown cobblestones of the street outside her old home. She thought about the jet-black peaks that rose up in front of the red sun, casting jagged shadows across the landscape below when she flew. She thought of home.

Time couldn't be measured in any useful sort of way in this place. It was a fool's errand to try. But at this point it was fair to say she'd spent more waking hours in the Between than out. She'd long ago given up on the idea of ever getting back to her birthplace. At least, until Philo showed up and that device of his presented a genuine possibility of sending them home one day. Even *that* was a long shot. In the last twenty trips to the Junkyard, they'd found a total of three components that crept the contraption any closer to functionality. Sure, maybe someday they'd get it up and running again. But "maybe" and "someday" weren't words one liked to hear in a proper plan for the future. Even so, thinking of home stirred an awful, sour, maudlin feeling in her gut. She recoiled at the thought that she might be homesick after so long.

Rill twisted her heads and did a corkscrew twirl. Trixie held a bit tighter. Philo, with a much more tenuous grip on her back, hugged a bit tighter around Trixie's waist. She smiled. Not in the cold, wry way she did when she'd scored a particularly successful verbal barb. In a warm, genuine way. An expression that felt far more vulnerable than it should have. She slid the leash-holding hand down and placed it on one of Philo's hands.

"You okay back there, Champ?" she asked.

"I'll feel a lot better on the way back," he said.

"You've done some scary stuff, buddy. This is nothing."

"I don't know. It involves acting. I'm not an actor. And we're dealing with people who are going to try to rob me of my wits."

She laughed. "Just like old times for me. Stick with me, Champ. This is the first time in a long time I'm *fully* prepared for the challenge of bluffing my way through a slalom of seduction."

***

Before long, a mote of black emerged from the white void ahead.

"Remember, Champ. I say jump, you say how high. Rill, when we land, I'm going to stay mounted for as long as possible. The longer I can be looking down on everyone else, the better."

The three heads muttered in unison, but did not object.

Once it was visible, their destination grew very swiftly larger in their vision. It went from relatively black against the field of white to a mottled black disk with reddish roads crisscrossing it like veins. They were approaching from a high angle.

"Sweep down. Let's come in at it from the side. We don't want to slam down in the center. They might be defending it."

"Uh-huh," said Rill.

"Fine," said Right-Rill.

"Whatever," said Left-Rill.

The hydra swept down and aligned herselves opposite to the top of the floating chunk of world. This gave them a clear look at the bottom of the displaced city, which was perfectly hemispherical, almost polished in appearance. As they got closer, four specks rose up and flitted toward them.

"Judging from the size of that city, these will be guard imps. I'll handle them. Game faces on, everyone. The plan starts now."

The four forms approached. They were portly, black-skinned, white-eyed creatures. They were broadly pear-shaped and about two-thirds the height of Trixie. Each was very bottom heavy and dumpy, though their arms were disproportionately thick and powerful. They held six-pointed pitchforks. Wings far too small to keep them aloft nevertheless did the job, buzzing like those of a bumblebee.

"Halt!" squawked the leader, with a voice that suggested she was a female. "Who goes there?"

"Ah, excellent. I was beginning to think there wasn't enough of your little community left to send a proper escort," Trixie said. "Two males and two females? Good. A proper squad. I'll have the females lead and the males flank. Keep your distance, the worm bites."

The four diminutive but threatening demons stammered a bit, casting glances. Evidently they hadn't been trained to expect instructions from an invading party.

"Females lead, males flank. And keep your distance," Trixie repeated, now with a healthy dollop of impatience.

"Who goes there?"

"Beatrice Zalthea, representative of the combined territories of New Allimiss and Shard. I tell you so that you can announce me properly upon our arrival. Now, into formation." She slapped the riding crop against her palm. "Or do you need motivation?"

The creatures blinked at each other, then squabbled a bit before pairing up and drifting aside. They were still casting curious, distrustful glances at her but did as they were told.

"Wow," Philo said quietly.

"You haven't seen *anything* yet," she said.

They swept down to the edge of the city, where a rather more substantial force had assembled. A dozen or so additional imps were there with pitchforks raised, and six demons of a similar sort to Trixie were present as well. They were dressed in much the same manner as she was. That was to say, barely at all. Two demon men, each with two demon women, waited with defiant and distrustful looks in their eyes. They weren't armed, but Trixie could feel a weight in their gazes and a pressure on her mind. They were testing her resilience. That much she could withstand.

"How are we holding up, Worm?" Trixie whispered.

"Fine," they said as one.

"Feel anyone trying to monkey with your heads?"

"No," said Rill.

"Yes... wait, no. No," said Right-Rill.

"No. ... Wait, now yes," said Left-Rill.

"Yes now," added Rill. "No, wait. No."

"Fine, fine. That's good. I had a feeling they wouldn't have a good way to compel something with one mind split in three parts."

Rill hit the stony street hard, startling the imps into the air like a cluster of pigeons. As instructed, the hydra reared up a bit to keep her well above the welcoming committee. Silence reigned for a few seconds.

"Ahem," Trixie said, glancing at the guards who'd escorted them.

"Mmm? Oh! Er. Beatrice Zalthea, from… places," said the only imp with enough wits to recall the instructions.

"Representative of Shard and New Allimiss. What do you call this place?" Trixie asked wearily.

"The city is Brimstone Altar," said the leaner of the two male demons. "As for this strange new plane we find ourselves in, I cannot speak with certainty."

"Let me guess. A summoning ritual with a poorly formed incantation?" Trixie said.

"It would appear so," said the spokesman of the group.

"You've pulled your whole city into what the locals call the Between." She tapped the top of Rill's head with her riding crop. "Down, Worm."

A rumble shook the hydra, but she behaved, lowering all three heads. Trixie gracefully dismounted. She gave a soft tug to the leash about Philo's neck, and he did the same.

"I'll try to make this brief. Unless you know a counter ritual or other manner of transportation spell, you won't be going home. This place is accessible *only* by spell or science that can break the dimensional veil. Any botched method will bring you here, but only a properly formed and very specific method will bring you home. That you're still here suggests you don't have the know-how to return."

"Lamentably. But, then, I suppose the same can be said of you," he said.

"The same can be said of *everyone* here, smart guy," she said. "To whom am I speaking?"

"I am Crum. I have the dubious distinction of being the one responsible for this ritual, and thus this flock remains mine until it can be returned," he said.

"I would think you'd have been overthrown by now, given the success of your last bit of leadership, but I'm not here to make judgments about that sort of thing. I'm here to assess you, educate you, and be on my way."

Trixie kept a steady expression as the rather one-sided verbal sparring resonated with the rest of the group. This man must have been a *very* powerful mystic, because his character was not nearly forceful enough to remain in charge of so large a group without help.

One of the demon women stepped forward, eyes fixed on Philo. She licked her lips, tongue lingering briefly on the tips of her fanglike canine teeth. Philo took a step toward her, eyes half-lidded. Trixie gave the leash a sharp tug, breaking him from the beginnings of the trance he'd been slipping into.

"Fix my hair," she instructed.

"Hair, right," he said shakily.

He reached up and brushed some of the hair that had been tousled by the trip behind her thornlike horns.

Crum tipped his head. "What is..." He stirred the air with his finger in the general direction of Philo. "This?"

"A human. My current toy. Still needs some breaking in. Which is not an invitation, by the way. You'll find others running about if you are deemed worthy of entering our little society, so keep your claws off mine."

"You're certain you won't provide a sample?" Crum said, a second female stepping forward and lashing her tail around Philo's leg.

"He looks *deliciously* weak-willed," she purred, running a claw from his chest to his chin. "And quite soft."

Trixie rolled her eyes. "*Need* I repeat myself? Hands off my property."

"Surely there is enough of him to go—"

The end of the sentence was lost in a startled yelp as one of Rill's tails wrapped around her hoofed leg and snapped aside, hurling the intransigent demon off into the void with startling speed. All but Crum watched in dismay as she went flipping end-over-end into the distance. The imps rushed forward. Crum stopped them with a motion of his hand.

"Liala, fetch your sister," Crum said. "My apologies. We've had no fresh blood since our arrival, and nothing to suggest any would ever come. Some of our less disciplined people were becoming restless. I would invite you inside for some refreshments while we discuss the circumstances we both find ourselves in, but we have no means of acquiring more. A matter of concern until we discovered we *also* have no hunger or thirst. So instead, perhaps I can offer you..." He leaned forward and took her hand quite daintily in his hand. "... A dalliance?"

"I'm here to see if this whole city is worth our while, not just you," she said.

"Well, that will take some time, but I'm sure I can arrange it."

She allowed herself a smirk, and a brief memory of the way things had been prior to her unceremonious departure.

"First, a discussion. Things aren't as you might expect them to be in this place, and we need to see if you're up to the task of adapting to the way things *really* are."

"A discussion *first*," he said, letting the air linger with the suggestion of after. "Very well. You strike a hard bargain." He turned. "Seats for our guests and myself, around the altar. That seems as appropriate a place as any to have so weighty a discussion."

"I provide my own seat. Thank you," Trixie said.

The contingent of imps and demons headed toward the altar. If the chunk of world were a full sphere, the altar would have been at its precise center. The city was perhaps one-third the size of Lower Shard. That made it easily the fifth or sixth largest piece of land added to the Between in Trixie's time here, and the only one with more than a handful of people living on it. This was nearly the full city. Only a portion on the far side of the point she'd chosen to arrive showed the telltale division line of a building left incomplete by the transportation event.

"How many of you are there?"

"Six hundred demons. One hundred eighty imps," he said.

"How many are mystically inclined?"

"Trained, you mean? We have four specialists, including myself."

She ran the numbers through her head, doing her very best to think as the Overseer would and leave her own opinion out of the matter. This was crucial, as her specific point of view was clouded both by the longing for things familiar from her own world and by the rather blatant probing of various enchantments being nudged in her direction. She was a bit out of practice. It was taking more effort to keep their whims from coloring her own than she would have liked, but the plan was working. If they were making a genuine attempt to enthrall her, they would be trying *much* harder. They were still wary of her power, even though it didn't exist. If she judged them by the Overseer's measuring stick, it would give her a layer of separation.

She felt the chain in her hand go taut. Philo was wandering toward a cluster of demons. Trixie could feel the magic curling about him as a distant heat at the edge of her mind. They weren't actively calling to him. It was just the natural, effortless mystic allure that *she* should have had. The sort of thing they had to actively suppress and, until this very moment, had never had any reason to do so. She gave the chain a tug. He shook a bit, glanced in her direction, and trotted back to her side.

"Why a human, may I ask?" Crum said.

Trixie shrugged. "As *that* one suggested"—she motioned at the recently fetched and still dizzy demon Rill had dealt with—"they are quite pliant and a fair bit of fun, albeit lacking the physical stamina one might want."

"Bah," Crum said. "Easily solved by keeping a dozen of them on hand, eh?"

"That's one way around it."

They reached the altar, which was a massive alabaster disk, the size of a banquet table. A stool was set up on one side for Crum. Trixie pointed at the ground.

"Seat," she said.

Philo glanced around. "Where?"

She leaned down and pulled him face to face with her by the chain. "I'm looking at it."

"Oh... I... okay then."

He got onto his hands and knees. She flicked her tail up like the train of a dress and daintily took a seat on his back. It was a fair bit further than she'd intended to go with the whole "toy" charade, but it would keep him out of trouble. Rill curled herself into a mound and flopped her heads down on the ground beside him.

"I'll get right down to it. Here is how this place works. Adjust your expectations accordingly," Trixie said.

***

A short, direct bit of instruction later, Crum was nodding in interest.

"Arbitrary gravity, no real passage of time... Yes, that does all align with our observations. And you say to find our way clear of this place, we would require knowledge of our destination?"

"Or a skilled seer, trained in locating other places and other people."

"That seems a rather self-defeating cycle. We must know where we are going to know how to go there, and know how to find it to learn how to find it."

"Lucky you, I've come along to bootstrap things," Trixie said.

"And what is the *cost* of this benevolent service?" he asked.

"You need to be worth our while. Four mystic specialists? Tempting. One with enough knowledge to lead a ritual that can transport an entire city? *Very* tempting. You might have a depth of knowledge to contribute to the collective goal of finding our way out of here. Of course, right now I only have your word to go on."

"I see. So you'll require a demonstration."

"Just until I know for sure there's something here worth recruiting."

"I see. That is entirely reasonable." He stood. "If you'll stand for a moment and give me your attention, I think I can demonstrate some degree of my capabilities."

Trixie felt a bolt of concern. She kept it from showing in her expression. If she was in his position and was going to attempt something untoward, this is how she would begin. But the role she was playing was that of someone far too powerful and far too important to be concerned about such things. It was of key importance that she kept up the facade. A whisper of weakness would be blood in the water. And very shortly after that, blood everywhere else, once Rill got involved.

She stood and stepped aside. Crum did the same. He took a deep breath and touched his fingertips together in front of him. The edge of the altar slowly took on a superheated glow, though she didn't feel so much as a degree of the temperature on her skin. On her soul, however, there was an uncomfortable blaze of heat. The world around her seemed to fade, until only the ring, herself, and Crum remained. She raised the hand with the leash, as casually and with as little concern as she could muster, and found it hanging loosely, one of the links cleanly sheared by his magic.

"I call this a 'step aside,'" he said. "Not transportation per se. We are still very much where we once were. But with a shift in a direction lateral to reality."

"A pocket dimension. I'm familiar," she said wearily. "A bit of a parlor trick, but you've got my attention."

He stepped forward, crossing over into the ring and offering his hand, as if inviting her onto the dance floor for a waltz.

"I was so hoping that I would," he said, his eyes staring deeply into hers.

***

Philo glanced down at the end of the chain. He had been painfully straightening out his back after serving as a chair for Trixie when she'd simply vanished from beside him. He was out of his depth from the moment he arrived, standing on tiptoe in a pool with his chin barely above water. Now the floor had dropped away.

Rill had raised her heads. Philo tried to wordlessly assure her that she should stay alert but stay calm. As far as he knew, Trixie was still in control of the situation. Rill slowly uncoiled herself and thumped a loop of her long body around Philo, forming a sort of boundary between him and the surrounding demons.

One of the females took a half step forward and smiled at him seductively. She was taller than Trixie, eyes a piercing yellow rather than black and red. Her skin was a shade brighter orange, and her shiny bodice was a deep blue rather than black. He heroically resisted the combined call of his own libido and whatever magical allure she was radiating toward him.

"So... *human*," the demon said, as if testing the flavor of the word. "I'm not yet familiar with your kind. I do so like to make myself *familiar* with newcomers."

"I have a keeper, thank you very much," Philo said, sweat beginning to bead at his temples.

"Oh, I know you do. A fine one. You should be proud to be kept by such an important, decisive figure. But a man can dream, can't he?" she said. "A man can long for his heart's desire."

Philo sniffed. The air seemed oddly fragrant. Like he'd been spritzed with perfume. He cast a glance at the Rills. They were watching, but they either didn't see anything worth taking action over or couldn't detect that whatever magic being sent his way might be dangerous to him since it wasn't dangerous to them.

"When you shut your eyes, no doubt run *ragged* by your keeper, when you collapse into a heap and your mind is briefly yours in the embrace of slumber, the heart must want what it wants."

Her eyes seemed to fade to a muddy brown, then shift to a vivid red.

"Don't you *deserve* that dream in the flesh? Just once? Haven't you *earned* the perfection your mind has conjured for you?"

Her height ticked downward subtly.

"We understand desire. We understand *need. Longing.*"

Her outfit began to darken.

"Your keeper would understand. After all, doesn't she indulge herself? Doesn't she feed her lust? No proper keeper would deny her plaything a moment of bliss if it presented itself."

Her skin darkened.

"If perfection called, ready, willing, eager, she would understand if you sought comfort in the arms of a vision of beauty and mercy, wouldn't she?"

With these final words, the figure standing before him was not the unnamed demon who had begun the impassioned speech, but a precise duplicate of Trixie herself. Philo felt warm, relaxed, comfortable. Like a comforter had been thrown around his shoulders. He almost felt a gravity pulling him toward the open arms of the gorgeous thing calling to him. But a sting of logic pierced the sleepy haze falling about his mind. He felt, frankly, irritated.

"I'm sorry, but do you think I'm stupid?" he said. "I realize my mind is the plaything of my keeper, but did you think that simply making yourself *look* like her would convince me to fool around with you? Really now. You're not her. She's..." He gestured at the empty space beside him. "She's wherever she just went. And just *looking* like her isn't going to convince me that you're the one who's the rightful holder of this leash."

If he didn't already know he wasn't looking at the real Trixie, the expression that crossed the falsified face would have given it away. She looked shocked, confused, and a little bit fearful. Trixie's pride would never have allowed her to look that way while he could see her. The glamour disguising her slipped away, and she took two fearful steps back.

"I... I'm terribly sorry," she said hastily. "I had no idea that... It shouldn't even be... You won't tell her, will you?"

He didn't quite understand why she was acting as though he'd just pulled a gun on her, but he crossed his arms and tried to ride the momentum of the shift in mood. "Just don't try anything like that again. I'm spoken for."

"Should we slam her into a wall?" Left-Rill asked.

"No. I think we're fine," Philo said quickly.

***

Crum, in the privacy he'd conjured, had been putting on quite a show. One by one, like a magician working for a very tough crowd, he'd demonstrated illusions and conjurings and incantations. He wasn't the *best* wizard she'd seen, but he would absolutely be an asset to any community he sought to join. Except that he'd *also* been teasing and testing at the edges of her mind, layering his mind-clouding allure on in greater and greater doses. She could feel her resolve buckling a bit, but so far hadn't let that fact slip in a way that Crum could notice. He was standing beside her now, both of them within the ring of the altar.

"And, of course, the *other* mystics have their own additions they could make," he purred, leaning forward so she could feel his breath tickle her ear. "Maybe I should invite them? The four of us and you? A proper demonstration? Perhaps, were we to share some of our strength, feed a bit—"

"Crum," she said with the tone of a disappointed schoolteacher. "You've crossed the line from demonstration to proposition, and that was not the purpose of this visit."

"Surely those who you represent wouldn't mind if you—"

"Crum," she said more sharply. "There are three ways this can end. One, I leave you here to work out how to escape on your own. Based on what you've shown me, I really don't like your chances. Two, I could agree to let you become a part of our community and work to our mutual betterment. Three, I could rain devastation upon this city, take what I like, and eliminate the rest."

"I really don't think you'd be capable of that. You haven't shown a *glimmer* of that capacity."

She felt a downright pugilistic thump of his will upon hers. The first genuine and overt attempt he'd made to subvert her. It didn't work, but if he had more than one or two such blows left in him, her defenses wouldn't hold up.

She leaned toward him. "I need you to use your mind, Crum. You haven't seen a glimmer of my capacity because I haven't felt the need to show it. And more to the point, I could have sent Philo on his own if I wanted to, and you'd have the same three options and the same waning chance of coming out of this in one piece. I am here not as an individual, but as the tip of a spear that can pin this whole city to a wall if we deem it necessary."

"And throw away the strength you've seen?"

Another blow to her will. Her meager defenses started to waver.

"I said I was here to see if you were worth the trouble. It isn't a society of *demons* out there, testing you for inclusion. It's a *very* diverse group. You need to show you can play nice. Because no amount of power or wisdom is worth a few hundred demons acting like petulant children, slaves to their own whims and unable to control themselves. If you're not going to behave, I see no reason to offer a hand rather than a fist."

His will struck hers like a battering ram. It was all she could do to keep from falling into his arms. Rather than fear, or desperation, she allowed herself nothing beyond a weary narrowing of her eyes.

"Are you *really* going to make me teach you a lesson?" she said.

He looked her firmly in her eyes. She matched his gaze. There was nothing left of her resistance. She was laid bare. Already she was envisioning the wave of fetchers and soldiers the Overseer would send to dispose of this remnant of her own world. Already she was wondering what state they would find her and Philo in. But she kept her gaze steely.

Crum blinked. She took every inch of the ground he gave up.

"If I were to leave in this precise moment, I can't say I would have a rosy assessment of your city. But I do so hate to condemn a whole community for the actions of one. How much do you trust the decency of the rest of the city, hmm? If we were to step from this private room, would I find them playing with my toys? Because I do believe that would be the final nail in the coffin."

He blinked again.

"Let us not be hasty, Ambassador Zalthea," he said. "As you've said, this is a very new world and it will take some adjustment to understand the new ways."

He clapped his hands. The rest of the world returned. They were standing on the altar. She turned as casually as she could manage and tried to spot Philo. He was sitting on one of Rill's coils, patiently waiting while the rest of the demons stood anxiously aside. If she didn't know better, she'd think they'd just been scolded by a harsh instructor.

"I trust things went well?" said the demon who'd tried her hand at Philo. "I must say, I have a profound respect for your skills, and I do hope one day to learn from you, Madam Diplomat."

Trixie huffed a frustrated breath and held up the broken end of the chain. "Fix it," she instructed.

Crum gathered the two ends with all the dignity he could muster. The ends flashed to molten brightness. He pressed them together and they fused.

"Where are the other mystic specialists? I'll have a word with each, then I'll be on the way. And can we *please* keep our minds and hands where they belong?"

***

Two more interviews had come and gone. Rather than tugging her into some shadowy realm, they simply stepped up to her to have their discussion while the rest of the demons returned to their homes or shelters elsewhere in the city. The other mystics were both less powerful and less overt in their attempts to test her. That was good, because she really wouldn't have lasted another battle of wills like that one. She was happy that there was only one more assessment before she could leave this place behind. The last one, to her surprise, was not a demon, but an imp. He was very short, impressively fat, and to her great relief, strangely mannerly.

"What is *your* specialty?" she asked.

"Oh, I won't waste your time. I am a humble research mage. No magic skill beyond the treatment of wounds and ailments."

"Healers aren't *entirely* without use here, but nearly. Thank you for—"

"Baal's Lament," he said quietly.

She subtly glanced about. They were alone in the courtyard around the altar, save for Philo and the Rills.

"What did you say to me?" she said seriously.

"Baal's Lament. Demons born without the intrinsic mysticism that is their birthright. It is the focus of my research."

She tugged gently on Philo's leash. He trotted closer.

"We're leaving," she said to him. "Announce it."

"Right, right," he said quickly. He raised his voice. "Hey! Everybody. That's it! The ambassador has seen enough and we're leaving!"

"I'll say three things, quickly," the imp said softly.

"You'll say nothing," she hissed.

"One, I have no particular love for the rest of this town. Imps are rather poorly treated. Two, I intend to treat this matter as I do all matters: with perfect discretion. And there is a cure."

For the first time, and only for an instant, her expression wavered. The milky-white eyes of the imp curved with a genuine smile as he stepped back and gave Rill room to scoop both Trixie and Philo.

"Wait!" Crum called, hurrying back to the altar. "What is the verdict?"

Trixie stared down at him. "You'll be hearing from me, or some other delegation, at some point in the future. The verdict will be implicit in their actions. In the meantime, all those expenditures of magic will have taken a toll on you. Magic is one of the only things that brings genuine fatigue here. You'll want to get some rest. And I hope, with memories of how you've comported yourself and what I've explained, you'll sleep well. Off we go, Worm."

Rill sprang into the air, and in less than a minute, the place was left behind.

"How did it go in there?" Philo said.

"We played chicken, he swerved first," she said quickly. "What in the hells did you do while I was sparring with him?"

"Nothing. One of the ladies tried to disguise herself as you, and I told her it was a dopey move. After that everyone got skittish for some reason."

"Disguised herself as..." Trixie burst into laughter. "Oh, that is *rich*."

"What?"

"Do you remember the first spell I tried to cast when I was trying to explain to you that I didn't have the magic I should have?"

"Uh... not really. I'm feeling kind of drunk at the moment."

"Yeah, having someone toying with your brain will do that. I tried to cast a spell that would make me seem to be your heart's desire. It's the simplest spell. The first spell. And it's that way because it's usually successful. But she ended up looking like *me*. And you told her that. Champ, you just told her that you truly, deeply, genuinely love me. And there is no *way* they'd be able to accept that as being natural. It just isn't in them. It was barely in me. So those demons thought I'd somehow managed to weave myself so deep into your mind that I was your true love. True love may not be terribly useful to us, but part of that is because it's impossible to fake. True love isn't always *mutual*, but it is real, and undeniable. They thought I was *so masterful* that I'd faked the unfakeable in your mind."

"Wow," he said.

She fluttered her wings, surging up from Rill's neck and pivoting so she landed facing him. He wavered a bit, suddenly without her as support, but she steadied him. She wrapped the leash around her fist and pulled him into a deep, passionate kiss.

"And I love you too, Champ."

"Heh..." he said dumbly, a vague smile on his face.

"Whoopsie. Took a little too much of a sip of the ol' aura. Don't worry about it. You'll be fine."

"Did... uh... What're you gonna say to the boss when we get back?"

"Eh. We'll give them a while to stew in their fear, then probably bring them into the fold but keep an eye on them until they adjust." She glanced aside. "Let's just say they have at least one very important lesson to teach us..."

Joseph R. Lallo

**Dragons In
Space 2**

Dragons in Space 2

Introduction

S ome would find it ironic that a story I wrote specifically to show the process I use for writing stories would end up more than twice the length I intended. Those people don't know me personally, because this is absolutely the way things go for me. If I make a plan, that plan will simply underscore the problems the plan was intended to solve. That's why my process is ever evolving.

The first part of this story came out a few months ago, and one of the observations was that Runt's little journey was a bit of a "dog walk." He was just fetched and brought somewhere, no real plot. Just building a world. Well... I hope you liked that! Because here's some more.

E ngineer. That's what they called him now. Three weeks ago, he was not an engineer. Three weeks ago, he didn't even know what a week was. He called himself a hunter, because that is what he had to be to survive. Then he learned he was called a dragon. Then he was given his name. Runt. Now, in a blink of an eye, he was *Engineer* Runt.

He held tight to the rails beneath him while Brothin, the other dragon engineer and his personal mentor, gripped those above him. Among the many things he'd had to come to terms with in the last few weeks was the fact that "up" and "down" didn't mean much in this strange place they called a space station.

"We're going to do this one at a time," Brothin said. "The only air locks big enough for both of us at the same time have dropships docked to them."

Runt knew Brothin was above him, but the other dragon's voice filtered into his mind as though his fellow beast's words were his very own thoughts. It was because of the "communicator" built into the "synaptic interface." Runt just thought of it as a crown. It was easier to understand and made it feel more like a treasure. He adored treasure.

"I'll go through first and wait for you outside. You're going to want to panic. Don't panic," Brothin said.

"I always want to panic," Runt said meekly.

"Then you should have plenty of experience in tamping that feeling down."

The door ahead hissed and slid open. Runt flinched and fluttered back a bit, his suit clacking and clicking with the motion. It was amazing to him, the things these humans were able to build. The station. The dropship. The suit. The suit was like armor atop his armor. A second set of scales, fitted so perfectly to him that he barely felt like he was wearing it. But just as it was astounding that it allowed him to move nearly freely, it was also amazing that the tiny loss of grace and dexterity felt glaring and frustrating whenever he bumped against the suit's limitations. He lashed his tail, fixating on the gentle resistance he felt as he neared the limits of the hard shell around him.

"I'll be right outside. Hold on tight until you hear me let go. This is going to be scary, and it should be. It's dangerous. But if you pay attention and do as I say, you'll be fine. You *should* be fine, at least."

Brothin, wearing a scratched-up and slightly worn suit of his own, drifted with perfect grace into the snug chamber of the air lock. The door shut behind him. Runt scurried up to the door and clicked his nose against the glass.

"You are very brave, Brothin," Runt said with admiration in his voice.

"Wait'll you've been doing it for six years, Runt. This is nothing. Now, during a flare? That's when you have to be brave."

The other dragon turned and tapped the buttons on the wall beside the hatch. Soft rumbling caused the walls around him to tremble. Brothin's wings extended a bit, seemingly on their own, then retracted tightly against his back. The rumbling stopped. Brothin tapped another button, and the door ahead opened.

Runt's eyes widened and his body tensed as he saw what waited beyond the door. It was... nothing. The hatch framed a perfectly black circle. Brothin fluttered his suited wings just a bit. There wasn't enough room in the air lock to even *think* about fully extending them. A gentle flap sent him darting forward. Once outside, he fully unfurled them and deftly pivoted in place. He tapped an unseen button on the outside of the space station, and the hatch shut tight. The rumbling sound returned.

"You remember what you need to do, right?" Brothin asked.

Runt trembled slightly, still trying to grapple with the idea of his fellow dragon simply drifting out into the void beyond the hatch.

"Hey! Snap out of it," Brothin said. "You remember what to do, right?"

Runt shook his head, mostly to gather his wits, and dug into the endless sea of information that had been thrust upon him in just a few weeks.

"I need to... wait for the green ell eee dee. Then I need to press the Open Inner Hatch button. Then I get inside and press the Close Inner Hatch button. Then the... Then the..."

"Depressurize button. Come on, Runt. This is the easy stuff. By next month we're going to need you running pressure diagnostics on the plasma conduits."

"Depressurize," Runt squeaked. "Then wait for the red ell eee dee. Then Open Outer Hatch."

"Good, now do it."

Runt shakily tapped the button and stepped into the air lock. He started working his way through the procedure. Everything about it was terrifying. *Everything.* The rumbling sounds. The tight confines of the room. The knowledge that if he did everything *right*, he would be heading out into the same void as Brothin.

He heard a soft metal-on-glass clack and looked up. Brothin was tapping on the glass with his gauntleted claw. Each tap was a little quieter than the last.

"Good. You're looking. Listen close. Why's that getting quieter?" Brothin asked.

"What?" Runt asked, not quite ready to be thinking deeply.

"It's not a hard question. Why's the tapping getting quieter?"

Brothin hadn't stopped tapping, but Runt had stopped hearing it. He shut his eyes. This was something he knew. This was something the human engineer, Todd, had said. Todd said *so many things*.

"It is because... Why does it matter?"

"It matters because you're up here, not down there. You're scared because things are new and you don't understand them. Down there, if something is scary and you don't understand it, all you can do is run away. So you want to run away. Up here, you can't run away. So you have to understand. Good news for you, the humans in this space station are the kind of humans who never stop trying to understand things, so they did the work for you. Now answer the question."

"It is... there needs to be air for sound, and the air is leaving," Runt said.

"Right. See? Not so scary now, is it?" Brothin said.

"I need to breathe air, Brothin. It is *very* scary!"

"Yeah, but there's air in your suit."

"If there is air in my suit, why can I not hear the tapping?"

"Because the air needs to be between the glass and the... never mind. The LED is red. Push the button. We only have a few minutes to do this first part."

He nodded and, after two tries, pressed the button to open the hatch. Brothin fluttered his wings and pulled back.

"Safety line," Brothin instructed.

Runt nodded. He fumbled his claws against the belly of his suit and found a small clip they called a "carabiner." He shakily dragged himself out into the blackness and clipped it onto a rail on the gleaming silver exterior of the space station. His claws were shaking. He couldn't bring himself to open his eyes.

"Tell me what's going on in your head right now, Runt," Brothin said.

"I'm scared, Brothin."

"You knew what we were doing today. You know everything about what's happening. You don't need to be scared."

"I am, though. I'm not used to being ascended."

"Ascended..." Brothin muttered. "Fine. What exactly is scary?"

"I feel like I'm falling, and my wings don't feel like they'll stop me, and there's nothing around me but you and the space station. And if I let go, I might never come back."

"Lucky for you, today's the day we teach you how to use those wings out here. So then you won't have to worry about feeling like you'll fall forever. But what are we forgetting?"

"Forgetting... Shut Outer Hatch."

He fumbled for the appropriate button. The door silently shut. They were sealed outside now. Runt shut his eyes and held tightly to the rail he'd tethered himself to.

"And now?" Brothin asked.

"System check," Runt muttered.

"Right." Brothin glanced aside. "How're we looking, Todd?"

"Coming in clear," said a familiar voice through their helmets.

Brothin stared at Runt through his formfitting helmet.

"How. Do. We. Look. Todd," Runt asked, forming each word with precision and care, as though it was some sort of magic incantation.

"The comms are fine," Todd said. "Elevated synaptic and cardiovascular response, but I don't think we needed a sensor suite for that one."

"Listen closely," Brothin said. "And open your eyes."

"I'm scared."

"It doesn't matter if you're scared, you have a job to do. Open your eyes."

Runt trembled but did as he was told. He'd never seen the space station from the outside, and from this vantage he couldn't see much of it. Or, at least, he couldn't see it with much detail. Nearby, it looked like a huge cylindrical steel tube in space. It stretched a remarkable distance, with individual, isolated pieces twinkling in the distance like flakes of silver peppered across a sea of ink.

The truly awesome sight awaited above him. Or, he supposed, below him. The planet filled his vision below. Brilliant blues of the sea, tiny fields of emerald green where the great forest could be found. Vast stretches of dull yellow and clay red. And the roiling, churning ribbons of light that he called the searing sky and they called the aurora. Only a strangely shaped slice of the world was visible, and he couldn't look at it too directly, as the sun was quite close to the curved edge.

It was such a wondrous sight that it briefly pushed the simmering terror from his mind. When it came back, it came *roaring* back. He became instantly and utterly convinced that he would fall to the surface if he dared move a muscle.

"All right. This is important. If you are alone, you keep the safety line tethered. Always keep the safety line tethered. I'm here, so you'd normally be able to unhook, but let's just keep you tethered and reel out a little. Things can go wrong if we do this first part wrong."

"How wrong?"

"Doesn't matter, it won't happen, because you're tethered."

He felt powerful claws grip him by the tail. With startling speed, he was pulled away from the space station. The line attached to the belly of the suit reeled out.

"First, I want you to look at the sun."

"... But looking at the sun is bad, Brothin. It can blind you."

"I know. Which is why I want you to look at it so you can see what happens."

"I don't want to."

For the first time, Runt heard the rattling rumble of a growl across the suit's comm system. The sound was so raw, so primally terrible. He was drifting in orbit in a vacuum, protected only by a custom-machined extra-vehicular-activity suit, only a few weeks after learning what most of those words mean, and still the growl became the number one concern in his frazzled mind.

"Look. At. The. Sun," Brothin demanded.

Runt squinted and turned his head. He was expecting the searing pain that penetrated even his eyelids when he braved a glance skyward back on the surface. Instead, there was... nothing. He cautiously opened his eyes. The sun didn't look as he'd imagined it would. Rather than a piercingly bright yellow point of light, it looked like a dull reddish-orange disk. He could make out odd little spots of deeper red, and a fluttery ring of feathered brightness around it.

"Is that... how it really looks?" Runt asked.

"No. The way the sun really looks would burn the eyes out of your head. But that's what the helmet will show you because that's what's safer. That's what you need to realize. Everything about the suit, everything about the space station, is designed to keep you and me and Todd and Deborah and Bob and all the rest safer. You need to learn how to use the gear, and you need to understand what things are actually dangerous. Once you do, this whole thing gets easier. I needed you to look at it now because of what happens next."

"What happens... oh..."

His answer came in yet another act of celestial wonder. The sun slipped behind the curve of the planet, and his vision gradually adjusted. Previously unseen stars seemed to emerge from the blackness. Without the searing sky to obscure them, they were brighter and more vivid than he'd ever dreamed they might be. He felt his suit shift from cooling him to warming him as the heat of the sun vanished.

"We try to get the bulk of our work done during what passes for night up here. We're going to be active for twelve hours. Todd and them set aside the first four hours for me teaching you to fly out here. I told them I'd only need two. Don't make a liar out of me."

"My wings aren't *working* out here," Runt said.

He fluttered and twisted them. While they could pivot his body a bit, they didn't propel him in any way.

"Just like you need air for sound, you need air for flight. And just like the suit gives us air to breathe and makes do with electrical replacements for sound, it does the same for flight. Todd knows the specifics better than I do."

"Not much to it. Wires in the wings, charged when active. They create opposing magnetic fields. Move the wings and you can push against the planet's fields, the stellar wind, and the fields generated by the station."

Runt stared anxiously at Brothin.

"Just say 'Suit, activate flight mode' and try to stay calm. It'll be a little jarring."

"Suit." Runt paused to steel himself. "Activate flight mode."

A barely perceptible hum briefly filled his ears. Then came... freedom. There was no other way to put it. He could feel the tingle and flutter of a breeze against a hide he *knew* was encased in a special suit. It felt like he'd just been released into the sky to dance among the most gentle and consistent breezes he'd ever felt.

"What you're feeling is the magnetic fields. It took us six months to work out a way to make them work with how a dragon's brain works. But once we made them feel like the wind, it just *worked*," Brothin explained. "Give it a try."

Runt gave his wings a flutter. There was subtle resistance, and he could feel the tingle of wind against the skin of his wings. He didn't move *quite* the way he expected. It took a lot more of a flap to get any forward motion, and no flap at all was necessary to keep him aloft. Five full minutes of flapping and flailing had him moving roughly in the direction he wanted to go, but he certainly didn't feel as though he had control. Brothin offered little in the way of instruction. Indeed, once Runt established he could move about a bit, Brothin disappeared for minutes at a time to pull crates from storage bays somewhere else on the station and start unloading their contents.

Progress was slow. Runt could feel himself teetering on the edge of making a connection between the feeling of the artificial wind, the subtle resistance he felt, and actually going where he wanted to go. But these flashes of inspiration and understanding were scattered among flares of fear and bouts of panic. He couldn't persuade his mind to be calm, to accept that as strange and new as this all was, it was safe. He felt like he was a hatchling again, learning to fly for the first time. But instead of struggling to get off the ground, he was struggling to stay in the air.

***

Brothin spread his wings to ride along a dancing filament of magnetic field. He felt the heat of induced electricity as he coasted to a stop and released the crate he'd been carrying. Large, relatively clumsy claws did their best to imitate human fingers as he pulled dual carabiners from a pouch of them on his belly and started clipping crates to the section of the station they would soon be installed in.

"Hey big guy," Todd said with a yawn.

"What's up?" Brothin replied. "And why are we on an isolated channel?"

"Your partner is struggling. I didn't want to make him nervous."

"He doesn't need your help to make him nervous."

"I know. But he looks like he needs some help getting a hang of the suit."

"I know. He's new. He'll get it."

"He's your apprentice. You're supposed to educate him."

"I'll help him with the technical stuff, but flight is *in* a dragon. I'm not going to do a better job than his instincts."

"You're a dragon and I'm not, but I'm worried his instincts are working against him instead of for him. I'm looking at his pulse rate, his blood pressure, his nerve activity. Deborah's running the chem-signatures he's putting off. The kid's a ball of anxiety."

"This needs to be natural for him. It needs to be beneath thought. Second nature isn't good enough. It needs to be at his core. If we get hit by a stronger-than-predicted wave of stellar wind or a flare hits faster than we expect, it'll be his wings and his wit that will get him back to the hatch. If he has to think, then... well, we both know what happens. It's happened before. I want him to be a better flyer than I am. And I can't teach someone to be better than me."

"He's tangled up in his own safety line right now, jabbering to himself."

Brothin clipped the last crate into place. He spread his wings and started pumping them to build up the electromotive forces necessary to reach his protégé. "Runt, they tell me you're not doing well," he said.

"Why do we have to do this?" Runt yelped, as though he'd been waiting to hear the larger dragon's voice.

"You won't be much use if you don't learn to fly out here."

"Why do we have to do any of this? Why do we need to be in space? What do the ascended have to do? What *can* we do?"

Brothin rounded the curve of the space station and found Runt with his wings pinned to his sides by the safety cable, thrashing in a combination of desperation and frustration.

"Hold still," he said. He steadied himself with his own wings and started pivoting Runt until the smaller dragon was freed. "You want to know why we're doing this," Brothin said, scratching the chin of his suit in what was clearly a bit of theatrics since he couldn't very well feel it. "I suppose we've spent so much time teaching you *what* you need to know, we haven't gone through why you need to know it."

He flapped up and behind Runt. A pinch and tug straightened the formerly bound wings.

"Here's what we're going to do. We've got a little over an hour left before I told them you'd know how to fly out here. After that, we'll be busy hooking up a whole new array on the Delta Positive side of the station. I'm *not* doing all that by myself. Half of the reason I was happy to get another set of claws up here was so I could have someone else handling the fiddly bits. You've got the size and little claws suited to fiddly bits. So we need you flying. I think you'll be good at it. It requires thinking, and I *know* you're good at thinking because you're doing too much of it right now. We need to cut down on the distractions and let your heart do some more work. Todd, black out the visor."

"Say that again, Brothin?"

"Black out his visor. Also, put me on an isolated channel with him, and turn on that 'directional audio' you were so proud of that we never use."

"You're the trainer," he said, with the tone of voice of someone abdicating responsibility for what was about to happen.

***

Runt tried to orient himself to face Brothin. He caught the merest glimpse of the other dragon before the helmet completely blacked out, casting him in darkness. "What's going on?" he said.

"When you fly through the air, do you need to look around to stay heading forward?" Brothin asked.

Instead of sounding like he was inside Runt's head, the voice of his partner now sounded like it was coming from above and behind him.

"No, but—"

"You don't need to see where you're going. Seeing space, seeing stars, seeing the planet far below? It's making you forget that you already know how to do this. You aren't in the heavens right now. You aren't helping humans. You don't even know what they are. You're in the sky, you've got your eyes shut, and you're following the sound of my voice. You know what you need to do. Do it."

"But I'm *not* in the clouds. I'm dangling from a human-made thing in the blackness of—"

"Prove it. Is that what your body is telling you, or is that what your mind is telling you? Because we recruited you for your mind, but your mind has nothing to do with what I'm asking you right now."

Runt's wide eyes peered at the blackness of his visor. He clacked his claws against the glass, as if he could wipe off what seemed like a layer of soot, but it was no use. His heart fluttered in his chest.

"Close your eyes. They don't have a role in this. Listen for the part of you that already knows what to do."

Runt's nostrils flared and sucked at the fresh air his suit provided. He did as he was told, eyes shut tight. He tried to forget what he'd seen, forget what he knew to be true. He focused on what little information he was getting. He felt the soft motion of his wings, even as he tried to keep them still. He felt the tingle of an artificial breeze against his hide. He felt the stomach-lurching sensation of an endless dive.

Something curious began to happen. Like he was springing beneath the trees, light flickering across his eyes as he raced into and out of shadows, he felt some other, some more familiar state of mind pop and flash. For brief instants, he wasn't trapped in a suit, dangling by a cord, in perpetual risk of tumbling to his doom. He was in a dive. This was how his body felt when it was in a dive. The motion, the sensations, they were all too soft and subtle to be a dive... but if it *was* a dive—then if he moved his wings like *this*...

His body twisted and nudged. Just a tiny bit. But just as he intended it to.

"Good. Good. You're heading for my voice. Keep it up."

He directed his dive a bit more, wings spread to catch the air current. He pumped his wings up and down, letting the steady breeze billow and fill them with each upward and downward motion. He was moving faster now.

"That's it. Almost there. Todd, let's clear up that visor."

Runt kept his eyes shut. This whole magic spell that allowed him to move properly felt too fragile to risk upsetting by actually using his eyes again.

"Easy now," Brothin said.

He redirected and flapped harder.

"Slow down," Brothin said more sternly.

He didn't sound close enough. Just a bit farther. Or so he thought, until he struck the stout chest of his partner. The pair of them tumbled backward. Brothin pumped his wings to pull himself free of the tangle and gracefully came to a stop. Runt spread his wings and, quite out of reflex, slowed himself down. He didn't *quite* come to a stop before the safety line pulled taut and sent him into a spin. But this time he was able to keep his wings free and, with some graceless flailing, stop the rotations.

"I told you it wouldn't take four hours, Todd," Brothin said.

"That's not what I would call a compelling demonstration of mastery. And I'd really rather you didn't stress test my engineering on those suits in the field."

"I know what these things can take. Now let's go. The sooner we get those cables hooked up, the sooner we're inside for... what's the meat today?"

"Goat. Tendon and entrails mix."

Runt could see in the curve of Brothin's eyes through the helmet that he was grinning.

"I love when they throw in some entrails... Let's go, Runt. We've got one whole array to get hooked up and then you're in for the best meal since you've been up here. Which is probably the best meal you've ever eaten."

He spread his wings. After a few twitches and flutters to find a good field line to ride, he flapped and propelled himself along the side of the station.

"But... the safety line!" Runt said.

"Just stay close to me and stay close to the station. I won't let you go too far wrong if you lose control. You don't need the safety line while I'm around. But until you get your wings in better order, I'll be linking mine up between flights."

Runt shut his eyes until he could latch on to the artificial wind, fumbled until the safety line was unclipped, and shakily fluttered after his mentor.

***

After six hours, Runt was finally able to forget where he was and focus on the tasks he was given. A lifetime of having to worry about where he would be getting his next meal and having to overcome his physical inadequacies with cleverness and planning was presently waging war with his concentration. On one hand, rare was the minute that passed without him getting a jolt of fear that he was wasting precious time that could be spent hunting. On the other hand, these tasks fed a part of him that was even more malnourished than his belly. This called upon his ingenuity. And he *adored* it.

"Now where does that go?" Brothin said.

Runt wedged his tail into the gap between the station and the handrail to give himself an anchor point to maneuver without occupying his claws. His hind claws clutched the unruly shaft of a very thick conduit while his front claws held its end. The tip had an odd shape: perfectly round with little tabs on top and bottom.

"This is... I should match the shape, right?" Runt said. "A stick-in-the-hole shape that matches a hole-that-you-stick-stuff-in."

"Right."

He peered across the complex network of technology before him. There were five holes. Two were too small, one was too big, but two were a precise match.

"One of these?" he said, tapping the two holes with the tip of his helmeted snout.

"Right, but which?"

"Either?"

"Try again."

He dug back into his brain. "Humans don't like it when you just guess. And they are very particular about what holes get used for," Runt observed aloud.

"You can say that again."

"Why would I... That's a turn of phrase."

"You're a quick learner, Runt."

"So they... they would..." He turned the conduit about and craned his neck. "This is one of those letters they like to use. The triangle with feet."

"We call that letter *A*," Todd said.

"And that hole has the letter *A* on it," Runt said. "So that hole?"

"Hook it up," Brothin said.

Runt wrestled with the conduit until it was in the proper orientation and inserted the tip. It popped out twice before he realized there was a curved "arrow" thing that they decorated their things with. He turned it in the appropriate direction and was rewarded with a satisfying click.

"Well done. Now go get B to plug into the other hole, and I'll get to work on the other side," Brothin said.

Brothin flitted away. Not yet confident enough in this flight to risk an unsupervised trip, Runt dragged himself along the station itself. It was a very short trip, all things considered.

"Am I still being tested?" Runt asked.

"Just a second. ... Safety line hooked up. Now, what are you talking about?" Brothin asked across the comm link.

"When you came and got me, when you decided I should ascend, you asked me to etch shapes into the ground. Ever since then, for weeks, you and Todd and Deborah and Bob have been giving me new tests. Until flying, the hardest one was poker."

"Poker isn't a test, it's a game," Brothin said.

"It's not a game the way Deborah plays it," Todd added.

"Is all of this a test? Or a game? You said we had important things to do. When do we do them?"

Brothin laughed. "We're doing it."

"Poking special-shaped things into special-shaped holes? That's going to save our world?"

He grasped the end of conduit B with his hind claws and started dragging himself back to the appropriate hole with his front claws.

"This is something humans figured out that dragons didn't, mostly," Brothin said. "Every big important thing is actually a long, long list of small important things. That's what we're doing."

"But what are we *doing*? What's the big important thing?" Runt asked.

"It's very simple," Todd said. "We're developing a resonant magnetic flux manipulation array to create a wedge-shaped dispersal field so that charged stellar particles will strike the planet in a diminished density and higher in the atmosphere so that stellar radiation will return to levels that your magnetosphere and biosphere are able to absorb without serious detriment. Right now you're powering up the first of over seven thousand force compensators that will keep the orbits of the component satellites stable for the three hundred years the system will need to be in operation for the star's high-activity period to subside."

"You used very many words that just sounded like sound to me," Runt said.

"We're going to make the searing sky less angry," Brothin said.

"... We can do that?"

"We can try," Brothin said. "But it will take hard work, and if we are going to get it done soon enough to save as much of the world as we can, we'll be taking big risks every day for years. I may not make it through to the end. You might not either."

"But... the station is a safe place. It has food, it has no hunters that can hunt us. We've done it. We've made it to safety," Runt said. "Why are we risking that?"

"It's not about making it safe for *us*. It's about making it safe for everyone," Brothin said. "It's about keeping our home safe."

"But..." Runt scrunched up his face. "Why? There are only two things down there. Two things that I've ever encountered. There are things that want to eat me, and things that I want to eat. I don't need the things I want to eat, as long as I'm here. And the things that want to eat me? Why would I protect them? They want to *eat* me."

"You're thinking like a dragon," Brothin said.

"And like about forty-five percent of humans through most of human history," Todd added.

"Is thinking like a dragon wrong? I *am* a dragon," Runt said.

"Thinking like a dragon is fine, when you're dealing with dragon problems. And until now, that's the only kind of problem you've had to deal with. But this is bigger than that. The way you are? The way I am? It can all change. And it has all changed. You probably remember a time when the sky wasn't quite so searing. Things were easier. You're still alive because when things got worse, you changed. You improved. The old ways, the ways that had always worked? They stopped working. And so you changed. That's the trick. The trick is seeing the way things are, and seeing the way things need to be, and doing what it takes to get from one to the other even if it doesn't *feel* like what your mind and body have come to expect. Sometimes things are unexpected. You need to become more than you were, or else you'll become nothing at all."

Runt clicked the conduit into place.

"We've got full continuity on the new circuit. Give it some space and we'll run a test," Todd said.

Runt flitted his wings and pushed himself as far from the station as he dared.

"Activating. We're going to be on the lookout for plasma leaks, which could—"

Runt flinched as Todd's message was swallowed by a terrible, ear-splitting hissing. A brilliant jet of something with a purple-orange hue belched out of the seams around the control panel they'd just installed the conduits into. Red lights in Runt's helmet started blinking. He fluttered back, any comfort and calmness he'd built up over the last few hours suddenly gone.

The hissing and the multicolored jets stopped at the same moment and Todd's voice returned, sounding a bit frantic.

"—leak has been sealed. Looks like we had undetected micrometeor damage. Runt, check in. Are you okay?"

"I'm... I'm here. I'm not hurt," Runt said.

"Brothin, check in. Are you okay?" Todd paused. "Brothin. I've got a red light on comms for you. Are you reading me?"

"What's happening?" Runt asked.

"I'm putting the transponder on visual for you. Brothin may be incapacitated. Plasma can interfere with the synaptic interface and cause..." Todd seemed to realize he was being too technical. "He might be suddenly asleep. You need to go get him."

"But... the safety line!" Runt said urgently.

"I'm detecting mechanical failure. I think the whole panel he was hooked to sheared free. Transponder on visual now."

A small point was illuminated in his vision. There were numbers ticking along beside it, but his frazzled state of mind was such that he couldn't make sense of them. With some effort, he was able to flap himself up above the space station and, with sharp eyes, spotted the limp form of his mentor drifting along with a dangling bit of equipment twirling at the end of his safety line.

Runt worked his wings for all they were worth. He was able to build up speed, but his aim was clumsy at best.

"I need to..." Runt shut his eyes, allowing his mind to briefly turn all this technology into the familiar freedom of a dive again. "I need to be able to hear where he is. It's easier with my eyes closed."

"Directional tone, coming up."

A soft ringing sound chimed from the point of light on his visor. He moved until there was nothing between him and Brothin's motionless form, then shut his eyes and scooped the sky with his wings.

"Seven hundred meters and growing. You need more speed," Todd said.

"Going faster. Going faster," Runt murmured.

He curled his body and danced from breeze to breeze, from field line to field line. He could feel the heat of the wires threaded around his wings. The sound was growing louder.

"Six hundred meters and closing. You're going to have a delta v problem. I'm trying to come up with a solution for you. Bob! Get on the manipulator arm in section 686, pronto!"

"What is delta v?" Runt said desperately.

"You focus on getting to him. I'll worry about the numbers. Four hundred meters."

"Why are there so many meters?" Runt moaned in dismay.

He stole brief glimpses, wary of letting his eyes stay open too long lest he spoil whatever magic was allowing him to navigate so well. Brothin was moving weakly, but he clearly was not in the proper state of mind to rescue himself.

"One hundred meters. Get a hold of him and then try to drag him toward the arm lowering down out of the station. Based on the mass and forces at play, it's going to be tight."

Runt finally decided the risk of seeing was less than the risk of not seeing. He opened his eyes and fixed them on Brothin. The two would collide in moments. He spread his wings and drifted along a field line. In a crackle and click of metal on metal, he smashed into Brothin for the second time since leaving the space station. Holding on tightly and working his wings started to slow the pair down, or at least he thought so. The only points of reference were the planet, which scarcely seemed to be moving at all, and the station, which didn't seem to be slowing down at all.

"The trajectory isn't looking good," Todd said gravely. "I don't think your suit's got the force to bring him to a stop before you're both too far out of the navigable field region to fly properly."

"I'm not strong enough," Runt growled, flapping desperately and trying to will the lowering mechanical arm closer. "I'm *never* strong enough."

He gritted his teeth and pumped his wings. Not strong enough. Even ascended, he wasn't strong enough... But they'd not ascended him for his body. They'd ascended him for his mind. He'd outsmarted great big hunters. He'd outsmarted herds of prey. He could outsmart this "delta v."

In the precious moments that followed, he looked over everything and anything around him to try to close the gap between himself and the arm. When the damaged control panel at the end of Brothin's tether came into view, his brain clicked all the pieces together. That was it. That was what he could do.

Runt fumbled for his own safety line and clicked it around the extended one from Brothin's belly. He let it reel out and slide along Brothin's line as he flapped toward the mechanical arm. He reached the arm and wrapped his entire body around it, curling his tail and locking his limbs. A heartbeat later, the lines went taut and he was nearly torn free. The arm shifted, dampening some of the force from the tug, then heaved in the opposite direction. The lines strained, but held. So did Runt. Finally the line went slack and Brothin, still barely conscious, started floating back toward the arm.

"That's it. He's coming back in manipulator range. You did it, Runt. Good job. Now *that's* a compelling demonstration of mastery."

***

Two hours later, Brothin was still in Engineering. Runt drifted to the doorway, claws clutched in dismay as Todd and Bob continued to work at extricating Brothin from his suit. It had successfully protected him from any serious damage, but all of that wrenching and collision had damaged it enough that several of the connectors were fused. The solution involved many loud machines, lots of sparks, and many words from Brothin and the others that he didn't understand but sounded awfully colorful.

"Just hold still, big guy," Todd said. "We'll have you out once we're through this next bolt."

"Stupid, stupid, stupid," Brothin grumbled. "I should have checked the pressure first."

"We all should have checked the pressure first. There should have been an automated pressure check. We thought any puncture large enough to cause a failure like that would have turned up in the structural scans. I'll recalibrate them."

Todd looked over his shoulder. "Oh, hey! The dragon of the hour. Good job out there. You saved the day."

"He saved *me* is what he did. The day is shot, but I'm alive," Brothin said.

"You're not hurt?"

"I have a headache, and the whole suit is going to need to be remade. But I'm fine otherwise. And you?"

"Fine... You said... everything out there was to make us safe. All of this was to make us safe. Then why did that happen?" Runt asked.

"I think I said it was there to make us safer. Nothing about this is *safe*. But we all survived, we all learned something, and tomorrow it'll be even safer."

"More like three days," Todd said. "It'll be a day of making a new suit for you, then a day to update the scanners, then a day to test them."

"A three-day mistake. We don't have a lot of time left before the next big surge," Brothin said.

"I've shaved it as thin as I could. Given what almost happened, I don't want to shave it any thinner," Todd said.

A final spurt of sparks flared from the cutting tool in Todd's hands, and the final shell of the suit separated.

"That's it, big guy. I'll get to work. Go see to your boy. Deborah's chunking out some protein for you two. But I'll need you back in two hours to get some fresh measurements and talk through the next suit revision."

"That protein won't last more than two minutes and you know it. Come on, Runt. Goat time," Brothin said, fluttering out through the hatch and past the smaller dragon.

They maneuvered along the corridors of the station. Runt had to scramble along the walls to keep up with Brothin.

"You're... just going to eat?"

"Goat with entrails and tendons," Brothin said. "I'm not going to miss that. They only synth up the entrails and tendons once a month."

"But you almost *died*."

He turned his head to gaze back at Runt. "Have you really gotten so comfortable up here that you forgot that almost dying is just the way of things down there? It's not *so* different up here. Besides. I *almost* died. Thanks to you. That's why we need two of us out there. That's why you're here."

He slowed down until Runt had to stop to avoid passing him. The corridors weren't large enough for the two of them to maneuver comfortably side by side. In an impressive act of squirming and contortion, Brothin was able to pivot in place to face Runt.

"We were talking about tests. About how all of this feels like a test, but it's all the small important pieces of the big important thing."

"Yes, we were saying that before you almost died."

Brothin waved off the statement. "Forget about me almost dying. The fact that I *didn't* and that I didn't because of *you*? We didn't plan that test. But you passed it. Do you know what a red flag is?"

"I know what red is."

"A red flag is a sign that something or someone might be trouble. You were starting to send up red flags out there. Trouble navigating? Bundle of nerves? Those were little ones. Not enough to rule you out on their own. But that talk about how maybe we didn't need to do something for the dragons on the surface. The *everyone* on the surface? That was a big, *big* red flag. The humans call it psychology. It's not as hard and fast as the science they use to build a space station, but it's a good way to figure out how to *fill* a space station. And there's no room for people who don't have room in their heads for anything besides self-preservation. This is an *us* mission, not a *me* mission. It's not the end of things when someone seems like they can't stretch their mind enough to include someone else. Everyone can change. We're on a deadline. And I might be able to teach you how to insert Pipe A into Hole A, or how to work those wings in the magnetosphere the way you do in the atmosphere. But I can't teach you empathy. We're just not equipped to teach that. We only had one member of the crew who could do that, and she's gone. All of us up here knew one of these days the dazzle and wonder of the 'ascended' nonsense would wear off and you'd either continue because it was the right thing to do, or refuse to continue because you were more worried about yourself in the moment than your world in the future. But when I was in trouble, you came for me. You didn't need persuading. It was in you, just as sure as flight. It's a part of you. And it's a part we needed. Of all the tests you've had to do, that's the one that ensured you were right for the role."

Brothin turned again and they continued.

"There was someone who could teach empathy?" Runt said.

"There was."

"... What's empathy?"

"Empathy is when you can feel how other people feel."

"And who was the one who could teach it?"

It took Brothin a moment to answer.

"Your predecessor."

"... What's prede—"

"The one you're replacing. My old partner. The biggest job she ever had up here—and she had a claw in building most of the station we're moving through right now—was getting me to care about the rest of the crew. I cared about me, and I cared about her. For two long years, I didn't do what they said. I did what she said. And I did it for... reasons. Dragon reasons. Nothing to do with eating or being eaten, but there's that third one."

Runt nodded. "Mate reasons."

"I don't know how she had the patience for it, teaching me how to see the others for what they are, teaching me to see that sometimes you need to work with people you don't even *like* if it means ensuring there will be a tomorrow for the both of you. But she did it. It's something I couldn't do. If you didn't have it in you, then you'd have been sent back and we'd have kept looking."

"What happened to her? It was an accident, I know, but what was the accident?"

"We're not there yet, Runt. You'll hear the story. But for now? Goat. And then you've got two days before we're back out there."

"They said three."

"It'll be two. Todd works fast. We don't get a lot of time off. You should think about how you want to spend it."

Runt was silent for a time. "Will I be able to leave the station?"

"Not to go back to the surface. Not unless you're asking to leave the mission."

"No. But... I want to fly some more."

Brothin didn't look back, but Runt could hear a smile in his voice. "Attaboy, Runt. Attaboy."

DRAKE TILLER

JOSEPH R. LALLO

Drake Tiller

Introduction

One of the problems with writing these stories in big clumps and then releasing them months later is I completely forget what I wrote. I reread this one and, frankly, if I were to go into detail about my motivations for writing it, it would detract from the story itself. So... enjoy!

I t would be the interview of a lifetime. She couldn't quite decide if she should keep repeating that to herself or try to forget it. When Justine Garland had scored the coveted interview with Drake Tiller, one of the most legendary record producers in the history of the business, she knew this was a make-or-break moment for her career. But since then she'd been getting progressively more in her head about it.

"He's just a man. Just a regular guy. Puts on his pants one leg at a time, all that," she mumbled as she wound her way up the cobbled footpath leading to his English countryside estate.

She'd been walking for ten minutes and had yet to reach his front door. This estate was just one small part of the eccentric legacy that had elevated him to a position of myth within the industry. It was ancient, and had evidently been in the Tiller family for ages. Old money. Unlike many wealthy people, neither he nor anyone in his clan had felt obliged to make a showing of their wealth as the years ticked on. No cutting-edge, state-of-the-art upgrades that would be laughably obsolete and out of date in decades. Just owning this much land so near to London was a great enough showcase of wealth. The estate didn't even have a driveway. The only way anyone reached the sprawling, mossy walls of the old mansion was by foot or by helicopter.

You had to respect a guy who *didn't* have a garage but *did* have a helipad.

Finally she reached the front door of the mansion. The journey from the main road felt like a trip back in time. Far from the immaculately manicured lawns of many such estates, Tiller's land didn't just feel like it had been reclaimed by nature, but like it had never truly been wrestled from nature's grasp. It felt like the countryside, the path, and the stone architecture had simply struck a truce and agreed to coexist without getting in each other's way.

Predictably, there was no doorbell. Drake Tiller's front door featured a massive brass door knocker, the size of a large grapefruit and featuring a heraldic creature of some kind. It took both hands to haul it up and away from the door. Dropping it against the strike plate produced a crisp sound that felt as though it would never stop echoing.

As the seconds ticked by, she tugged at her messenger bag and ensured all her gear was in place. Laptop. Hand recorder. Cell phone...

"Ah! Welcome!" proclaimed a sharp, friendly voice.

She jumped and sent her phone twirling through the air. He neatly snatched it at the peak of its flight. The entire exchange felt like she'd unwittingly been recruited into a juggling act.

"My apologies. Didn't mean to startle you," he said, handing it back to her.

"I didn't hear you open the door," she said.

"Sound is my stock and trade. I try to be economical with it. Please, come in."

He stepped aside and allowed her to enter. The inside of the manor was what she would call warmly lit. Regularly spaced sconces on the walls produced the sort of orange-white light that incandescent bulbs used to cast. They also flickered in a way that for a moment or two convinced her this odd old gentleman was lighting his home with actual fire. The truth was a little more mundane, but no less curious. Every bulb was an LED contraption that flickered and danced like a torch. It should have felt a bit "haunted house" and shticky, but combined with the ancient masonry and dusty old rugs, anything with a more modern feel would have been incongruous.

He paced beside her, rather than in front of her. A few seconds allowed her eyes to adjust to the dimmer light and gave her the first in-person glimpse she'd ever gotten of him. Drake had a grandfatherly look to him, the sort of person one expected to see sitting across from an interviewer discussing his time with the Royal Shakespeare Company. His body as a whole and each individual feature of it was long and lean. He was tall, so much so that even with him slightly stooped, she had to look up to avoid staring at his chin. His fingers were long, famously long enough to span an extra octave on his piano, or so the old interviews claimed. Likewise, his face had a vampiric length and gauntness. Hollow cheeks and deep lines sculped his face into a permanent look of casual interest, like his default state was quietly waiting for you to finish your point so that he could ask another question. His attire was dignified to the point of drabness: a sweater vest the color of dusty moss and slate-gray trousers. The only relatively stylish bit of clothing was a decidedly modern pair of running shoes. If an outfit had conversation pieces, that was the role those shoes played.

"I want to thank you for agreeing to the interview," she said.

"I like to do an interview from time to time. You happened to catch me while I was in the mood," he said.

"You must not have the mood very often."

"The last interview wasn't *so* long ago, was it?" he asked.

"Eighteen years," she said.

He laughed and clapped his hands. "Time flies. Before we go much further, will this be just the interview, or will you want a tour as well?"

"I'll take whatever I can get, Mr. Tiller. I'm sorry—*Sir* Tiller."

He raised a hand and shook his head. "Please. It would have been Sir Drake, not Sir Tiller, and frankly I'd prefer neither. One does not turn down the queen, but I never felt comfortable with that particular honorific. Drake will suffice."

"Are you sure? It feels disrespectful."

"The years haven't brought me as much wisdom as I'd hoped they would, but I am at least certain of how I'd like to be referred to. Here. This is what most people hope to see when they visit."

They entered a room that may as well have been an annex to the Rock and Roll Hall of Fame. It included photographs with luminaries of the last sixty years of music history and props from stage shows. She knew she would never get another opportunity to ask about his legacy, so she didn't hold back. Neither did he. Drake told stories that lasted a half hour each. He told his anecdotes warts and all. No sugarcoating. Some she'd heard. Most were brand new.

"I'm nothing if not a collector," he said as he finally left the display room. "Stories, knickknacks, keepsakes. Everything I've done in my life and career has been in service of one collection or another."

They wove through a few more halls, stopping briefly at points of interest, until they entered what could fairly be called the first room of the entire tour that was properly modern. It was a fully equipped recording studio with a massive mixing table, a bank of computers, booths for individual vocal recordings, and enough space and equipment to record a full symphony orchestra. She could probably fit her entire home into the room.

"My laboratory," he said, pronouncing the word as though it were the place where one created monsters rather than medicines.

"So," she said. "This is where the magic happens."

"Oh, the magic happens everywhere, always. This is just where I'm lucky enough to capture some of it. It's just a workplace for me. This is the office. I started by recording my albums here, and now I produce other people's albums. Some would say that was how I made my biggest impact. I, for example, would say that." He laughed wryly. "I'm in it for the numbers, you see. As you'll see in this room here. My favorite room."

He led her across the studio and out a set of double doors into an equally enormous but far more splendorous room. He spread his arms as he entered.

"If there is a reason for everything you've seen and heard, this is it. My gold records..." he said.

The walls were lined with them. From floor to vaulted ceiling. The room was utterly massive, and despite literal hundreds of gold records decorating it, the floor was almost entirely empty. It looked like some sort of museum display had been set up in the center of the room, but after it was removed, no one had bothered to replace it.

"These, in the cases here, are the ones I earned myself. On the walls here are the ones I inherited. That wall has the ones that I acquired. Gifts. Items bought at auction, things of that nature."

"So you don't just produce or perform to get gold records. You just *buy* them?"

"I have a greater appetite for them than my meager talents can satisfy."

"Do you mind if I take photos?"

"Again, do as you will. I'll simply ask that you not touch anything."

"Of course."

She wasn't the best photographer, but fortunately modern cameras could handle the heavy lifting. All she had to do was point, shoot, and ensure the result wasn't blurry. Once she was satisfied she had enough coverage for an article, she leaned closer and read through the plaques on the assorted records.

"I thought this one went platinum," she said.

"Perhaps, but it went gold first. I prefer gold. It aesthetically and thematically suits my tastes better."

"Thematically?"

He laughed that wry laugh. "I like gold. Simple as that."

She pointed to another record. "You said this section here is for inherited records, correct?"

"That's right."

"But D. Deville. That was the name you performed under."

"One of them, yes."

"Then shouldn't you have it among the ones you earned yourself?"

He waved a dismissive hand. "A past life. I've moved on from D. Deville. So his records are an inheritance."

She swept her gaze across a few of the other "inherited" records. A few more were from D. Deville. Several more were from performers she hadn't heard of. But one or two were from notable avant-garde groups, the kind who earned critical acclaim and cult followings, all without ever revealing their faces. The kind that got a gold record about once every generation.

"... You were in the Un Own?" she said. "Those guys that played in the cardboard masks?"

He looked in her direction, a mischievous twinkle in his eye. "Bah, enough time has passed. Yes. I was one of them, anyway, yes. But I shan't tell you which. The world ought to have *some* mystery."

"Are *all* of these 'inherited' records yours from these 'past lives'?" she asked.

"In one way or another."

She blinked and looked at the wall again. "You... you were already the world record holder for greatest number of gold records by a single recording artist, and it looks like that didn't take account of a third of the records you actually earned under assumed identities."

"I'm not interested in records."

"Still. The word 'prolific' falls well short of your achievements. I have to ask. What's your secret?"

Again that twinkle of mischief flickered in her direction. "That's a dangerous question to ask an old man. Even a youngster is liable to have a neat little stack of secrets. A doddering old man like me has a list longer than his arm. And you'd ask me to pick *one*?"

"You know what I mean. How does one man earn so many gold records in a single lifetime?"

He crossed his arms and gave her a measuring look. "You are a journalist."

"I like to think so."

"You've been asking me so many questions, I wonder if you'd allow me a question or two of my own."

"That seems fair."

"What's more important to you, as a journalist? The knowing, or the telling?"

"I beg your pardon?"

"What drives you? Is it learning the truth? Or is it spreading the truth? Because while I don't necessarily subscribe to the platitude that the only way two people can keep a secret is if one of them is dead, I do rather doubt a secret will stay such if the other party makes her living spreading information to the four corners of the Earth."

"Are you asking if you can answer this one off the record?"

"I am asking, Ms. Garland, if you can keep a secret."

He looked her evenly in the eye. She paused only briefly, then clicked her pen, tapped her recorder, and stowed each in her bag.

"Wonderful. The secret of how one man earns so many gold records in one lifetime comes in three parts, each feeding into the other. First and foremost, patterns."

"Patterns," she said.

"Patterns. Melodies? Chord progressions? They're just patterns. Lyrics? They're just poems, and poems are just patterns. The ebb and flow, wax and wane of public interest? Patterns. Fads? Patterns. The whims of the critics and, yes, even of the press. Patterns. Learn the patterns and all the rest falls into place."

"And how does one learn the patterns?"

"The second part of the secret. Watch, wait, learn. You need to keep your eyes open. Keep your ears open. Travel the world. The wonderful thing about patterns is that they repeat. It wouldn't be a pattern if it didn't either repeat or progress in some predictable way. So a pattern one learned ages ago is just the first piece to a pattern that continues to lilt through the world today. One needs to learn all the world's patterns, or at least enough of them to be able to piece together the rest. The rise of this one, the rise of that one. Spot what sort of pattern fits in like the puzzle piece. Step on and ride the wave as high as you care to. And that just takes time and observation."

"That's a lot of time and observation."

"It is. And that's what brings us to the third part of the secret. How does one man earn so many gold records in a single lifetime? A *man* doesn't. Not enough lifetime."

She snorted. "So what? Are you going to tell me you're a vampire?"

"Don't be absurd. There aren't any vampires. Not any longer..."

She raised her eyebrows and made a mental note to include a respectful paragraph at the end of her article honoring the spark of madness that inevitably consumes the most creative minds.

"You really ought to ask yourself. What creature would lurk in the shadows, acquiring *heaps* of gold for no reason other than the thrill of acquiring it and the contentment of possessing it?"

"I give up," she said. Formulating a proper dismount from this tangent into lunacy was going to take some effort.

"That explains how I've not been found out along the way. You folk can be so forgetful after just a few hundred years."

"If we could get back to the interview."

"Patience, Ms. Garland. I could never live with myself if I let a curious mind like yours wander off without this next bit. I'd tell you to watch closely, but I scarcely think you could miss it."

He took a few steps back. An odd breeze swept through the already drafty room. Justine felt an odd tingle dance across her skin and... *something* happened. She couldn't quite put her finger on it, but something was different about Drake. It felt like his eyes were more intense. More potent. She couldn't tear her eyes away from his, despite odd bits of motion vying for her attention at the edge of her vision. She felt compelled to step back. The room was feeling oddly crowded for someplace so enormous and empty.

"There. That ought to do the trick," he said.

Again there was a strange breeze, this one warm and smokey. That probably would have seized her attention if the volume of his voice didn't do it first. His voice was *loud* now. She winced and backed away. Taking her eyes off him long enough to ensure she wasn't backing into something priceless jostled her mind. The distraction was just enough to allow something that had been clinging to her mind to begin to fade. She looked back to Drake.

It didn't feel like he'd changed. Some part of her remained convinced he was just the same now as he had been when he'd answered the door. But the dusty green of his sweater seemed to have spread. His eyes might have been farther apart, and were certainly higher up. But she couldn't really bring herself to say he'd changed until he smiled. The expression brought the impish twinkle to his eye, and flashed entirely too many teeth that were far, far too large.

That tipped the scales just enough for her to observe, if not accept, that he was not a man any longer. Perhaps he'd never been one. But regardless of what he had been, now he was quite clearly a dragon. Green and gray. Large enough to occupy that curious emptiness at the center of the room.

"How..." Justine said, or rather, allowed to tumble out of her mouth.

"It is really a rather boring answer. I was born as I am. Just as you were born as you were. The humanity is the trick, and rather an important one. As much as you folk are gleefully willing to kill your own, you're considerably more willing to kill my kind. And the one thing that separates me from most of my departed brethren is my willingness to accept that this is your world, not ours. Better to mingle than conquer."

"Uh..."

"It is a bit much, I'll admit. I can change back if you like, but it will take me a moment to gather myself."

"I don't... There are dragons?" she stammered.

"Some. If ever you encounter someone with generational wealth and a monomaniacal fixation on wealth, there is a greater-than-average chance you're dealing with a dragon. Whole successions of powerful men and women tend to be one dragon periodically refreshing their look. I'm about ready for a freshening of mine. Hence the interview. Nice to place a bow on Drake Tiller before some other young upstart inherits his fortune and signs some fresh faces to the record label to start sweeping the awards again."

"Are you... are you the only dragon in entertainment?"

He laughed. It was the same wry laugh, but now it had the force to rattle the displays around the room.

"No. Some of the more flamboyant stars are dragons. We like to decorate ourselves. Every so often someone gets sloppy and a star just refuses to age. That's a sure sign as well. And then there are the ones in politics." He shook his head. "The less said about them the better. Shameful... But I digress. You have your story. Do be a dear and leave out the secret bit."

"R-right. Uh... Yes."

"Feel free to turn your recorder back on. I rather think you'll need it."

***

There was more to the interview. More to the tour. She had no memory of it. Her mind simply wasn't up to the task. Fortunately, she'd taken his advice and turned on her recorder, so she had that to call upon. It took her six weeks to properly assemble the interview, the photos, and everything she'd learned (save one very important thing) into

her final article. Wouldn't you know it, three days before the article was to hit the press, Drake Tiller died of natural causes. The timing made Justine's interview an instant and enduring sensation within the music industry. A career maker, just as she'd expected it to be
.

She wondered, as she filled her schedule with speaking engagements and interviews to pick her brain about the departed legend, why he'd chosen her for this. Why she'd been gifted with his final interview, and burdened with his secret. She wasn't so foolish as to believe his claim that he'd simply been in the mood. He was a man—a creature—of plans and brilliance. This was a part of one of his patterns. One of these days, that mysterious estranged heir to the Tiller fortune would arise. She would be very surprised if she wasn't asked to provide his first interview...

Filthy Monkey Rats

Introduction

In the long tradition of me throwing in a gag that I quickly come to enjoy more than some of the key characters and core concepts of a series, the lesser harpies of The Greater Lands Saga are a wonderfully fun group of characters to write for. So is it *really* so surprising I decided to give them their own story?

F our plump, black-feathered birds sat atop the roof of an old storefront. Like most birds, they weren't given names when they were born. Not the sorts of names that other birds knew. There was a turn of a tweet, a glitter of a chirp here or there that would label this one as a friend of that. But it changed from bird to bird. And frankly, these birds didn't have very many friends. Birds with friends lived in trees outside the city. These four had made their homes with the humans. It only seemed natural. Humans were sloppy. Not as sloppy as a wolf or a lion, maybe. When they butchered a creature, they didn't leave yummy, meaty, rotting bones around. But they were so much more creative. They had foods of all sorts. Foods that didn't even exist anywhere but where humans could be found. Humans made their *own* foods. And some of those foods were worth the swat to the head or thrown boot that it would take to snatch some. It wasn't a pleasant life. But it was interesting, and a clever bird could stay very well fed.

And these birds? They were *very* clever.

For one, some of the humans didn't even call them birds. They had other names. Rotten Rat. Lousy Thief. No Good Flying Disease Bag. Big fancy names. Names that were fun to repeat. Then there were the names people used when they were talking about the birds rather than shouting *at* them. Less specific words. Words that referred to *all* the birds, rather than just the ones lurking about. Those words weren't as fun, but they weren't as mean either. Quite often, they were the same few words. "Lesser harpies." Now and again, humans would mix in some of the fun words. "Rotten lesser harpies." "Thieving lesser harpies." "Fat, stinking, mangy lesser harpies." Words were always so much more fun to hear when they were shouted.

No. Not always. Some words were nice to hear spoken kindly.

"Rudy! Toody! Moody! Judy!" called the voice of the friendly one.

Their heads perked up, one after the other. These were names that had come to apply to these four birds and these four alone. They were never spoken in anger, so they *almost* didn't seem like human words at all. But they came from the mouths of the people who treated them the most kindly. And so, they were worth listening to.

The four birds flitted down and bobbed in place, gazing up at the hefty human. Someone this big, this sturdy, was normally someone to give a wide berth to. But this one, not so much. This one did *business*. He did tricks. The best kind of human. The rarest kind. Only five or six of them in the whole city. Humans like that, you kept an eye on.

"Rotten stink hag!" said Judy, eying up the sack in the man's hand.

"Monkey bird! Smelly bird!" added Rudy, always the most impatient of the quartet.

"My eye!" chirped Toody.

"You get back here, rat thief!" said Moody.

"Hag. That's a new one," said the human. "Anyway, Mom and Dad said you haven't pestered any customers. Except for that deadbeat who comes in here and talks Mom's ear off without buying anything. And he's fair game anyway. So, a deal's a deal. And Fel Masker keeps his deals."

He untied the pouch and tossed down four whole buns. Toody and Moody hopped forward. Judy eyed the overeager birds haughtily.

"Smelly *stink* monkey!" she reprimanded.

Toody and Moody hopped back and lowered their heads. Judy selected what was *clearly* the best of the buns and flitted back to the rooftops. Rudy grabbed another, and Moody and Toody squabbled over the last two. With relatively few lost feathers, the four returned to the roof to munch on these strange little meals the humans liked to make for themselves. It was a shame so few humans could be trained like this one could. Give it the little treat of not biting any ears or nipping any noses and it would perform the trick of presenting tasty new foods or shiny new treasures every day. Perhaps the other humans just weren't quite as clever as Fel Masker. But at least the whole *family* seemed to be able to learn the same tricks. And even some of the *friends* of the family. It was always so nice when the humans taught *each other* new tricks.

To that end, when their bellies were full of bun, Judy nodded to the others, and they took to the sky. They swept deeper into the heart of the city. Mostly, the lesser harpies didn't like coming to this part of town. It was too noisy, and though there were more people, they never seemed to have anything tasty. They were also *very* swift to throw something at a bird who was just checking if this or that was edible. They found their way to the roof of a place called The Fox and Log. A recently trained human called Allie spent her time there. She didn't do her trick nearly as often, but when she did, she did it with variety. Best of all, *her* trick sometimes involved giving the harpies eggs. She didn't do it very often, but it was their favorite trick, so they liked to encourage it. And Allie had a particular favorite treat for which she would do that trick.

She liked bits of paper.

Not just any bit of paper would do. She was *picky*. But that was fair. Good tricks deserved good treats. Allie's favorite bits of paper were usually hidden in a little stove on the roof. Judy landed on the roof. Moody and Toody hopped over and pulled open the door of the stove. Empty. No wonder Allie liked those treats best. They were rare. Hard to get. That made them precious. And everyone loved a precious treasure.

"Rotten stink rat..." croaked Rudy quietly.

Judy turned and hopped over. Her esteemed associate was perched on the edge of the roof, eyes turned toward the dim alleyway across from The Fox and Log.

"I'll have your guts..." Judy churred thoughtfully.

There was a human there. Or something human shaped. This one was particularly good at hiding himself. Of course, Rudy was particularly good at spotting humans who were hiding themselves. They tended to be quite obvious. Most humans *didn't* try hiding themselves, so the ones who did stood out. They didn't stand out to *each other* of course. But they never seemed to worry if someone high above was looking for them. So for a lesser harpy? Easy to spot. There wasn't much reason to find them, of course. They very rarely had anything tasty with them. But they *did* sometimes have nice shiny things.

After fighting over a piece of coal, Toody and Moody joined them and gazed at the hiding human. No shiny things visible. But he *was* keeping his hand in his pocket. That was usually a *very* good sign that he had some shiny things he didn't want to part with.

"That'll learn ya," Judy decreed.

"You'll catch a boot in the patoot for that, I swear," Moody opined.

The quartet took to the sky and lined the roof on either side of the alley, eyes fixed upon the man's hand. As they watched, they took note of his behavior. He was acting the way the hiding humans often did. His head twitched this way and that, reacting to every little sound. He stepped farther into the shadows whenever another human came near. He was nervous. The man's eyes brightened as the door to The Fox and Log opened. Four people emerged from within the tavern. The first two were bickering loudly and struggling, blood dripping from their noses as they were helped out by a bulky third human. Behind them, directing the action, was Allie.

"You act like a gentleman in The Fox and Log," she snapped at them. "Or else you make enough friends that folks will overlook it when you *don't* act like a gentleman. What you *don't* do is come in, finish getting drunk on our cheapest stuff, and pick a fight with each other. You two are banned until I'm convinced you can behave yourselves."

The larger human tossed them into the street, but by then the harpies had ceased to pay attention. Something much more interesting was happening with the hiding human.

He'd slid the contents of his pocket free. All four birds snapped to attention. He was holding a piece of paper. Not just any piece of paper, either. It was the stiff, fancy stuff, and one side still had the crackled bit of red that had once been a blob of sealing wax. This was *exactly* the sort of paper Allie liked best.

"My eye. The little devils got my eye," Judy said softly.

The hiding human flinched and pressed himself to the wall. Moody, Rudy, and Toody descended on him.

Some humans were clever. The hiding ones, for instance, knew that dark colors made for better hiding. But the best they could do was drape themselves in darkness. They still had their shiny white eyes, and many still had their pale skin in those places where it couldn't be hidden. They lacked the jet-black feathers, the jet-black eyes, the jet-black *everything* that made lesser harpies into the darkness itself when they chose to be. Panicked by the unseen birds, the hiding human flailed and wheeled his arms. Moody darted in, shoved his head into the pocket with the page, and plucked it out. The four birds returned to the roof and huddled there, eying up their prize while the human slowly realized what had happened.

As was so often the case, they were serenaded by interesting new words as they assessed the page.

"You blasted things! I see you up there," he shouted.

"Blasted things," Toody muttered, testing the sound of the words.

The page was absolutely the same sort that Allie did her tricks for. Stiff and thick, folded in three but creased and crumpled like it had spent ages going from pocket to pocket.

"Wait'll I get my hands on you, you *wretches*," the human growled.

"Hands on you," Rudy cackled.

"Wretches," Moody added.

There was plenty of angular black writing on the page. If they could read, they would have recognized words that were important to them. Words like "Allie" and "reward." They also might have recognized words that would worry them, like "target" and "proof of death." There were big, complicated words like "assassin" and short, curious words like "ASAP." But they couldn't read, and thus the words only mattered because they made this paper look so much more like those other pages that they could use to bribe Allie into handing over a few delicious, nutritious eggs.

"Hold still and I'll gut you," the human grumbled.

"Hold still," Rudy croaked.

There was a hiss, a sparkle, and a startled squawk. The squawk came from Moody. He stumbled past the edge of the roof and scrabbled his claws against the tiles. Fragments of torn feathers filled the air like a whorl of black snow. Fat drops of blood speckled the tiles. A thin gash showed through where feathers had been sheared away. Somewhere on the roof, a throwing knife clattered and clanged down. And below, a soft, triumphant laugh.

"I got you, you rat," the hiding human said.

The harpies squabbled and gathered around their stricken brother. The wound wasn't dire. At least not if it healed well. But Moody would be hobbling on one leg for weeks, and he would be a lousy flier until it was healed up. Judy hopped over to the edge of the roof, eyes narrowing as the hiding human scurried out the back of the alley. The others joined her, eyes fixed on the scurrying form below.

"Gut you..." Judy hissed.

***

Karn made his way into the little hole in the wall of an inn where he was spending his time in Beffshire. Once he was inside, he opened a flask of booze and sipped at it, finally allowing himself to curse his carelessness.

"Idiot, *idiot*," he said. "How close was that? Your first big job in Thayne and you almost lose it because of a couple of lesser harpies? If I hadn't seen that barmaid *before* they got the letter, I might not have remembered enough of the description to be sure it was her."

He took a sip. "Who hires an assassin to kill a *barmaid*?" he wheezed, making a mental note to use some of his earnings on better booze. "Probably an affair. The people with the most money always pick the lowest people to have an affair with. Like if they're lowly enough it won't matter. But it *always* does."

He heard a scratch on the roof over his head. He raised an eyebrow, then lifted a lantern. Nothing.

"Then there's the issue of the page itself," he mused, returning to his concerns. "Doesn't include my name. Doesn't include the one paying for the job. So long as I get the reward before someone else sees it, doesn't much matter if that thing turns up. All it'll establish is the little bar wench died because of someone with a hefty coin purse. Probably it'll give her friends something to talk about when they bury her. Most interesting thing that ever happened to the trollop."

"Trollop."

He froze and turned to the source of the voice, a throwing knife instantly ready to hurl. "Who's there?" he hissed. "Show yourself and I'll make it quick."

He heard a scratch. He threw his blade. It dug into the support for the thatching of a recently repaired bit of roof. A large black feather drifted down through a narrow gap in the thatch.

"More of those things," he grumbled. "This city is infested."

He found a rag and stuffed it in the hole, then returned to the task at hand. She was just a barmaid. No point in getting too fancy. Poison would be a waste on her. There wasn't even much reason to hide that it was an assassination, given that the missing note ordering the kill might turn up. But still, it was good practice to keep these things clean and leave the authorities scratching their heads. Not that he had to worry too much about this. The city *had* a Watch. But they didn't seem like the sharpest authorities in the kingdom. But getting lazy in this business was the first step toward getting killed. So he would treat this job like any other. Everything would be practice, precision, building his skills toward the eventual job that actually mattered.

It would be simple enough. He knew where the barmaid worked. He would stalk her for two days, figure out where she went and when. Then, on the third day, pick a likely spot, hit her quick, and vanish. Set it up to look like one of the patrons she kicked out had held a grudge, and it was a quick and easy payday.

Or so he thought.

The first problem was with Beffshire itself. He had gotten most of his work farther north, in the big cities of Quarr and Shalia. Those places had the decency to show off their wealth by building the city straight up. Big tall buildings were great for assassins. Wait until a moonless or cloudy night, climb up to the second or third floor, and you could stalk your prey from above without the slightest chance of being spotted. Beffshire was a short, squat city. Most buildings didn't get taller than two stories, so he had to either pick a roost close enough to the ground that he could be spotted, or stalk along the rooftops where an errant glance could spot his silhouette against the night sky. He'd normally correct for this by following his prey on foot, but that barmaid seemed to be just short of clairvoyant. There were times when he *knew* he hadn't made a sound or showed a shadow and she turned, nearly catching him. And when she thought she'd seen him, she shifted her path to a more populated street. No good for an assassination and certainly not her usual route. Killing her there would almost certainly get him spotted, and even if it didn't, it might leave enough questions unanswered, making the job look sloppy to his next employer.

In the end, he found a single four-story building along her usual route. It gave him almost a perfect view of the entire path from the tavern to her home. It wasn't ideal. The only ledge that was well-hidden enough for him to spy from adequately was far too narrow for him to stand on, but a nearby flagpole stuck out at an angle. It had a long-neglected flag hanging in tatters, but it was sturdy, complete with a retaining pin to keep it in its brace, and it was perfectly placed to hide him from view and serve as a handhold to keep his balance. One evening spent propped in that position gave him all the information he needed. He need only return there the following night and watch for the barmaid's emergence from the tavern. When she made the turn toward her dank, little neighborhood, he would drop down, corner her, and leave her to be found by whatever other guttersnipes lived on her street. Simplicity.

***

The following day, "simplicity" was beginning to feel like far more trouble than it was worth. He'd heard remarkable things about Beffshire. It was the trading hub of the entire kingdom. Careers were made and broken in the bustling town, more so than even in the capital. That much he believed. The amount of money passing through this town was staggering. But when his associates had spoken of the town, they'd neglected to mention the vermin that permeated the place. He'd attempted to sleep through the day, since he'd have to spend the night watching and waiting, and ideally would be out of the city by the time the sun rose. But every time he started to doze off, the scrabbling and cackling of lesser harpies startled him awake. The horrid things could mimic a human voice *just* well enough to set off his well-trained senses, making him utterly certain in his sleepy state that someone was about to bust his door down and capture him.

Then there were the droppings. Climbing up to his perch had been downright treacherous. Every decent foothold or handgrip was glazed with filth that he couldn't have missed on his last climb. It made traversing the building's facade not just grotesque but hazardous. The stuff was as slippery as it was messy. He had to take his time, carefully cleaning this ledge or that pole. By the time he reached his perch, it was more than an hour later than he'd intended. There was the chance he'd missed his target.

He dug his heels into the narrow ledge near the flagpole. To his great relief, the pole itself was free of droppings. He held firmly to it with one hand and held to a gap in the stone facade with the fingers of his other hand. Satisfied he was stable, he eased himself out a bit, straightening his legs to scan the streets.

"Hah! Perfect!" he muttered to himself.

Despite the delays, his timing had been practically perfect. There she was. Just leaving the tavern. All he had to do was wait for her to pass below and he could do the job and be done with this filthy city.

A fluttering flash of black feathers blurred his vision briefly, then the plump figure of a lesser harpy settled down on the flagpole. He glared at it. The thing had something small and glittery in its beak, some shiny piece of nothing it must have found in the street. The blasted vermin waited until he'd made eye contact for an instant, then released a muffled, croaking caw through its clenched beak.

He froze and looked down. The barmaid hadn't heard it. Not precisely. But she was looking about, no doubt wondering if there'd just been a sound.

"Go! Shoo, you rancid disease bag."

A second lesser harpy landed heavily on the flagpole. It craned its neck to look over the other, eying him critically before squawking as well.

"That's it," he hissed, releasing the crack in the facade with his other hand so that he could draw a throwing knife.

At this range, he was sure he could skewer both of them with a single throw. But when he had the knife in his hand and leaned to get into position, something was wrong. It was tiny, but quite noticeable. The formerly rock-solid flagpole rotated a bit. His heart froze in his chest, and he looked at the pole's base. A scratched-up bit of rust revealed a hole in the brace. The sort of place a retaining pin for a pole like this would normally be nestled. He turned again. The nearest of the lesser harpies twisted its head, catching the dim moonlight on the shiny piece in its beak. The glittering light was coming from long, fresh scrapes. Scrapes on a retaining pin that had been pulled free.

He held firmly to the pole, nerves lurching at the fraction of a turn that it shifted. He dropped the throwing knife and slowly reached back, searching for the crack that had been supplementing his grip. Just as he felt the edge of the crack with his fingertips, a third well-fed lesser harpy bounced onto the end of the flagpole. The pole wobbled, rotating in his grip, and came free of the brace.

With his weight off-balance, he practically launched from the narrow ledge. The tumble took him clear across to the ledge of the two-story building across the alley. If he'd been ready, he might just have been able to grab the ledge, but he was tumbling end over end. He struck the wall with the back of his head, his legs flopping over the ledge. He tried to bend his knees and attempt to dangle upside down long enough to kill his momentum, but it was too little, too late. He slid down the face of the building, crashing through a crudely erected awning and slamming into a pile of crates in the mouth of the alley. The wind was knocked out of him. He was bleeding from at least three gashes thanks to shards of broken wood shredding through his expensive outfit. It was nothing short of a miracle he hadn't been killed.

He rolled off the pile of crates and stumbled painfully to his feet. Out of the corner of his eye, he saw motion and glanced toward it just in time to see his target scurrying across the street to take a much longer, safer route home.

Three fat birds plopped down in the street before him, one by one. One of them dropped the retaining pin jangling to the ground. They glared at him with challenge in their eyes.

"Trollop," croaked Judy.

"You blasted things," jabbed Rudy.

"Get back here!" he screeched. "I'll tear you to pieces!"

He staggered after them as they flitted into the air. An assassin was supposed to be cool, collected. Logical. But those things, those *things*—they'd nearly killed him. They were Lesser Mystics. Lesser Mystics were smarter than normal creatures. They'd probably been trained. Maybe even by some rival assassin, someone who wasn't eager to share Beffshire as a territory. Well, that fiend would be short three trained harpies before today was through.

The birds flew low and slow, as if mocking him as he hobbled after them. Two peeled off from the other, but he didn't take the bait, staying focused on the remaining one, who swept along a main thoroughfare. He shoved people aside and kept his eyes fixed on the remaining bird, one hand fumbling for another throwing knife. He was so fixated that he almost didn't notice the rush of olives flooding the street. He slipped on the little green fruits and came to a stop, finally assessing his surroundings. The fleeing bird had led him practically to the edge of town. Ahead, the back of a wagon completing a late-night delivery flapped loose, and three barrels formerly braced against it had overturned. That explained the olives and brine that were making the ground so treacherous.

The owner of the wagon was just now rushing around to see what had happened and voice his anger. Karn briefly cursed himself for losing sight of his quarry when a painful blow to the back of his head drew his attention. It was another of the blasted birds, thumping at him with a wooden wedge clutched in its claws. He slashed with his knife, unwilling to throw it lest he miss. The slash went wide, but it convinced the bird to drop its weapon. He stooped to grab the wedge.

"You won't get away, you filthy monster!"

He heard a click and wheeled wildly around, brandishing the knife in one hand and the wooden wedge in the other. The source of the sound was not another lesser harpy. It was, in fact, a watchman, with his crossbow drawn and held ready.

"Hold still unless you want another hole in you!" barked the watchman.

He froze and took a moment to consider how he looked. Bloodied, raving like a loon, brandishing a knife. He glanced about and realized that the wooden wedge, rather than just a random bit of trash the harpy had snatched up to assault him with, was in fact the missing wedge that had previously secured the back of the wagon. That it was in his hand was a matter of great interest for the man whose olives were ankle deep on the street. And then, another flutter of blasted black wings.

He looked down... and saw a page drift to the ground between himself and the watchman. His eye twitched as the watchman picked it up. The would-be assassin's mind spun in circles. It couldn't be... it couldn't be that this had all been a trick. That he'd been led here specifically to be caught. It couldn't be that the blasted things had left the page knowing that it would implicate him. It simply couldn't.

Three plump lesser harpies landed on the roof of the wagon. Just before the watchman stepped forward and forced him to the ground, one of them made a soft, but very distinct remark.

"Got you, you rat..."

***

The following day, the four harpies were back in place atop the roof of Fel's home. Moody wobbled a bit, trying to balance on one leg, as Fel stepped out with his usual sack of goodies.

"All right. Line up. Let's get this over with. I have some chores to run," Fel called.

They fluttered down. For once, Judy held back and allowed Moody to take the first selection.

"Whoa, whoa, whoa," Fel said, crouching down. "What happened to your leg, Moody?"

Moody gave him a sideways glance, then looked at Judy.

"Filthy monkey rats," she said with the wisdom and calm of a saint.

"Yeah, I'll bet," Fel said. "That's a nasty cut. Let me see if I can get you a bowl of water to wash yourself off at least. You need to be careful. It's a dangerous city out there."

As Fel slipped inside, Judy turned and nodded to the others. Well-trained humans were important and precious. It was always best to take care of them.

FIORA FIC

Joseph R. Lallo

FIORA FIC

Introduction

This is another story I've pitched to myself on maybe a dozen occasions. It didn't really end up the way I'd envisioned it, but the idea of a character I've written writing a story about another character I've written is something that floats into my mind on a monthly basis. I also like it when a very capable character is revealed to be adorably incapable of relatively mundane tasks. Plus, Fiora. Who doesn't love Fiora?

F iora watched her students doing their drills. Being a teacher had been everything she'd dreamed it would be. Passing on the wisdom she had gained was rewarding in so many ways. Not only was there the fulfillment of knowing that the chain of knowledge had continued, unbroken, in part because of her. But through the questions of her pupils and the repetition of providing instruction, her own skills had grown by leaps and bounds. But there were parts that fell short of expectation.

In the journey of every student, there came a point where the teacher was little more than an observer. The excitement of new knowledge receded into the routine of practice and repetition. She'd known, as a student, that this was the boring bit. But she'd never realized how much more boring it was from the other side. The student was at least active. They were doing something. They had a goal. During this time, the teacher was tasked with simply *watching*. It was... less than invigorating from an intellectual standpoint.

As a young human tried his very best to boil water with a conjured flame, Fiora fought to keep awake and stay focused on the task.

The flame is too blue, she thought. *He's using too much strength. At this stage of his training, he will exhaust himself before he boils the water.*

She could have made the observation aloud and perhaps he would have adjusted and passed the day's test, but it would be better to allow him to push himself and learn the hard way. A little bit of exhaustion today meant a little more endurance tomorrow. And so there was nothing for her to do but wait and watch for other errors more worthy of note.

For a mind that had been so thoroughly trained for focus in the world of magic, it was proving unexpectedly taxing to keep her mind trained on this moment in time. When left to her own devices like this, Fiora found her thoughts drifting. They would wander a well-trod path to a familiar reminiscence. A time when things were exciting. A time when things were new.

A time when someone very important had still been, in a way, her responsibility.

Her student ran short of mystic strength faster than she had anticipated. She was almost ashamed how pleased she was to find he had come up short.

"Fine! Yes, fine work," she said, clapping her hands. "I don't think you need me to tell you what you need to do."

She flitted beside him, conjuring a helpful breeze now and again to keep him from wavering too much, until he reached his quarters. Then, at last, she was free for the evening.

She buzzed her wings and rose high above the village. "Well now. Where should I visit?" she murmured.

It was a pointless question. She knew the answer. Whenever her mind turned to how her journey as a teacher began, it led her to the same place. The library. Fiora shook her head and touched her fingertips to her forehead.

"Must I truly do this *every* time I think about the old days?"

Again, a silly question. The answer was yes. If a mystic with a focus on fire magic, or anyone *else* who might produce a flame "by accident," wished to enter a place with precious books, then precautions must be taken. And right now, she wished to visit the library. For a dragon, it might be reasonable to simply bring the books out for the beast's perusal. Fiora was a fire fairy. For her, there was another option. One that was only *slightly* humiliating.

She decided that her student of the day probably deserved a few hours to recover. She'd have to call upon one of her other students to do what she had in mind. That nice elf who had decided to pursue fire magic as a third mastery, perhaps. A swift flutter through Wizard's Side brought her to the hut she was after. The elf's name was Lyana, and she was just setting down her teapot after topping off her cup.

"Master Fiora," she said sweetly. "To what do I owe the honor?"

"I suspect you know the answer."

"A visit to the library then. Of course. I'd just been considering a visit myself."

"Wonderful," Fiora said. "I'd hate to be inconveniencing you."

In a slightly embarrassing sign of just how common this little routine had become, Lyana stood and plucked up an already prepared piece of apparatus. It was a handheld lamp, one with a polished brass body, an elegant, looped handle, and a tall, slender glass bulb. Unlike a proper lamp, there was no wick, and it did not slosh with oil when she set it on the table. Nor was there the glaze of soot staining the glass. Despite its appearance, this was not a lamp at all. Not anymore. This was, for Fiora's purposes, a contraption designed to ensure an overexcited or undertrained fire fairy didn't set flame to an irreplaceable library tome.

Fiora flitted over the flared top of the lamp and deftly pressed down the billowing hem of her red robes. Her fluttering wings became still. With legs straight and body rigid, she dropped into the bulb of the lamp with a soft squeak as she brushed past.

"To the library, please," Fiora said, her voice reverberating within the glass.

Lyana hooked her finger through the loop and toted Fiora toward the library. Though she could not blame the librarian for wanting to keep his books safe, Fiora similarly couldn't help but glare at him from within her glass prison as she was carried past.

The inside of the library was dim compared to the brilliant midday sun. What light there was came from mystic gems and Fiora herself. This was hardly the first time Lyana had served as Fiora's chaperone, as evidenced by the elf pacing the well-trod path to the very table Fiora was after, without even being asked. There was seldom anyone else in this stretch of the library. Entwell was a place of students and teachers. When people came here, they usually sought the wisdom of old—texts, grimoires, history books. But a library was a place of words. Entwell was just as willing and able to find a place on its shelves for fiction as any other sort of book. The collection was not nearly as expansive, as someone seeking to do battle with the beast of the cave rarely chose to include a storybook in their equipment. But in its long history, Entwell had nevertheless accumulated a few dozen books of plays, fables, songs, and epics.

Lyana set the lamp on the table and approached the sparse shelf. "Shall it be *One Final March* again?" she asked.

"I think..." Fiora paused.

Again, at times like this, she liked to remind herself of her first student. And that tale was the one she had used to teach him to read. But for some reason, today it struck her for the first time that there may be some value in sampling some other selections from their fiction collection. She'd only read a handful, and she couldn't very well call herself a lifelong student if she turned away from a potential source of insight.

"No... No, I think you can select one of the others. Pick something that intrigues you."

The elf student was tactful enough to conceal the fact that she didn't find *any* of the fiction books intriguing. Instead, she plucked up the thickest book and set it down on the table before the lamp, perched on a sturdy book stand to keep it tilted toward Fiora.

"Thank you, Lyana. That will be all for now. I'll find someone else to escort me out when I am through."

"Anytime."

Lyana paced away, setting off for the more academic parts of the library. Fiora summoned a breath of wind to flip the book to the first page of text.

The tale was about an unnamed hero who ventured across the sea of a world that, as far as Fiora knew, was entirely imaginary. It was fascinating. Throughout her life, she'd truly only known of two sorts of fictional stories. There were legends, things that may not be true but were told as though they were fact. Alternately, there were fables, tales which weren't meant to be believed, but which taught lessons that conveyed genuine wisdom. In either case, she'd always imagined that such tales were handed down since the dawn of time. She'd never wondered where they came from, much as she'd never wondered where the forest or the mountains came from. To her, stories were things that had simply always existed. But this one, as she finished its short, simple adventure, had a single line that opened a new door in her mind.

"A tale by Karas," she read aloud.

She didn't know who Karas was, but they were instantly of profound importance to her, as they were the first fiction author she'd learned the name of. This was a story with a maker's mark, which meant stories could be *made*. It, like all revelations, seemed utterly obvious in retrospect. But now that such an elemental fact of fiction was clear to her, she found herself looking at the story in a new way. She conjured a breeze to flip a handful of pages back to the start of the story. She read it again, this time dissecting and analyzing it precisely as she did with a new spell. Each word, she realized, was a choice. Each action, each line of dialogue could have been anything. And because these things were choices, she couldn't help but wonder *why* one choice was made rather than another. Because if she had written the story, she would have written it differently.

If she had written the story...

She leaned against the glass for a closer look and willed the pages to flip. She would need to read so many more of these stories. This was no longer entertainment. This was research.

***

Fiora's home was a pleasant little section of a tree, and that typically served her purpose for shelter. But fairies, for better or worse, didn't rely upon written language as often as the larger races. It wasn't quite convenient, or even physically possible in some cases, for her to do her writing in a fair-sized book. With a bit of magic, she could maneuver a quill well enough, but attempting to do writing in a human-sized book while it was balanced on a tree branch was bordering on farcical. It was just easier to borrow one of the empty apprentice huts to make use of the larger table and shelter from breezes that weren't of her own design.

Now that she'd prepared herself with paper, ink, and a place to work, it was the simple matter of composing her own work of fiction. How hard could it be? She'd authored a half-dozen spells since she'd become a master. And a work of fiction didn't have to function. It merely needed a beginning, a middle, and an end, all while being relatively interesting.

"Once upon a time. I believe that is the traditional start."

The feather quill, working quite effectively with the wind conjured to manipulate it, began to swoop and scribble her first original story.

***

Once upon a time, there was a fairy. She was as curious as she was lovely, and as brave as she was wise. One day, a pair of humans set down a strange object. It was a thick glass jar, its bottom glazed with a sweet-smelling amber-gold syrup. The little fairy had never smelled something so lovely, but she'd heard tales of it. It was rich and sugary, like the nectar of a thousand flowers had combined into the golden treasure. Honey. She'd never expected to see it herself.

Better yet, though the air had the frigid sting of winter, there was a warmth to the smell, like the glass had been held over a flame to chase away the chill. It was wonderfully inviting. Too inviting. Another fairy might have eagerly indulged in the warm, nourishing "gift" the humans had set out. But this fairy was too clever for that. She knew a trap when she saw one. Too many of her fellow fairies had been captured by traps like this one. She'd heard the tales of those lucky enough to have been too slow to reach the jar before another fairy attempted to claim the honey. This was a tragedy in the making if the humans were to get their way. But a clever mind can quite easily turn tragedy into justice. And once again, this fairy was very clever.

Magic is a part of every fairy's very nature. Even the youngest, most uneducated and inexperienced of fairies could easily control their native element, but this fairy had built her knowledge. She knew all the elements, but most crucially for this moment, she also had learned the mystic spaces in between. She was, by the reckoning of those who fixated on such things, a gray fairy. Not the most impressive or pure of skills, but in this moment, very useful.

She thought for a second or two, and a glorious opportunity to balance the scales presented itself to her. First, she shut her eyes and focused until she was able to construct, from raw mystical talent, a duplicate of herself. It was an illusion utterly indistinguishable from herself.

She smirked and began to adjust the illusion, layering on a few superficial details—meaningless sparkles and flourishes of color—that meant nothing at all to a fairy but which human fairy hunters saw as something that would fetch a higher price wherever it was that humans sold their fairies.

When the creation was perfected, she sent it on its way, fluttering slowly and noticeably across the field. Its every motion was designed to be eye-catching. It took great concentration to guide the image so flawlessly, but this fairy was very skilled. Even before the image reached the jar, its motion drew out the humans. At the edge of the clearing, a pair of the hunters revealed themselves—a man and a woman. They were adults, dressed in expensive, warm clothing. The man held one of the flowing, billowy nets that fouled a fairy's wings and left them terrified and entangled. The woman held a fat cork, a match for the mouth of the jar. They lingered, likely believing themselves hidden, waiting for the image to reach the jar and slip inside.

The instant the illusion seemed preoccupied with the honey, the humans dashed like the hunters they were. She could tell from their speed and precision that they were very skilled. They had certainly gathered countless fairies. Captured them in just this way. One held the cork. The net-wielder was just a few steps back, only there to act if the woman with the cork were to miss. And she did not. As the image was just mimicking the motions of a startled fairy and making ready to flee, the woman slapped the cork down and hammered it home.

The fairy fluttered her wings and flexed her will. The mystic forces wove themselves to her whims. And though the effects were many, their execution was completed in the blink of an eye. First the image vanished. It was no longer necessary. Both the woman with the cork and the man with the net froze in place, her magic holding them fast. A small sparkling pool of light appeared on the underside of the cork. Then, a large but otherwise identical pool of light appeared on the ground beneath the man. He yelped and vanished through the pool, plummeting into the glowing patch and dropping out of the one on the jar's lid. He plunked down into the puddle of honey, confused and no larger than the fairy herself.

The fairy released the force immobilizing the pair. While the diminished man tried to make sense of what had happened, the woman pressing the cork in place released it and staggered backward, aghast by what she had seen. She stumbled over the fallen net and vanished through the pool of light to join her sticky partner in the warm honey.

The fairy sighed and relaxed her will, allowing the pools of light to fade. And so the job was done. The fairy hunters got what they wanted. Their trap was full. And the fairy was not cruel. She would lead other fairy hunters here to collect the jar rather than letting the pair freeze. What the other hunters did with the jar and its contents was their own prerogative. Perhaps they would learn not to do their hunting in this forest, or any forest. Perhaps they would seek out a wizard to restore the swindled hunters. Or perhaps the other hunters would treat this catch like any other. But at the very least, two hunters would have learned to think twice before setting down a jar in these woods.

***

Fiora allowed the quill to flutter to the table and admired her handiwork. It was thoroughly fulfilling to write the tale. But somehow when she read it to herself, it felt thin. She wasn't sure *why*. It was exactly the sort of thing she'd wished would happen, exactly the sort of thing she'd wished she could *do* to the sort of humans who captured her and her kind. It should have been exactly the sort of story someone like her would have wanted to read. But there was something missing.

The magic wasn't there. If this had been a spell, it would have been a clear sign that she hadn't included the necessary components.

She shut her eyes and called to mind the more engaging tales she'd read. Differences certainly existed. Typically the characters in those tales struggled a bit more. Fiora had assumed a perfect, successful hero would make for a perfect, successful story. Perhaps such was not the case.

"Fiction is a magic improved by imperfection. This may be trickier than I'd imagined. But I have plenty more paper and plenty more ink. All I need is another idea."

She gazed at the blank page and mused.

"This is complex magic..." she remarked, when a second idea failed to coalesce after several minutes of thought. "I think perhaps this will be a more interesting distraction than I'd expected."

She clapped her hands. "This is going to be great! Maybe I'll become our first master of storytelling. Oh! That's an idea for a story!"

She whisked the pen up to put it to paper again, as she suspected she would be doing daily for quite some time. After all, this was Entwell. One did not stop practicing a new art until it was perfected. And this was a fascinating new art.

Joseph R. Lallo

The Goth
Ticket

The Goth Ticket

Introduction

This story was inspired by a (very spoilery) idea that just flitted into my head one day. I've been having a really hard time focusing on my work, or really anything, for the last few months. In those times, I find it useful to switch to a new method. The novelty is often enough to get me focused long enough to engage with the story and make good progress. Thus, this story was written almost entirely in longhand with a fountain pen.

Enjoy!

Dec. 20th

I swore I'd never say it, but I'd be lying to myself if I didn't. Dad was right. I shouldn't have become an artist. Not *this* kind of artist, anyway. He was against me getting a fine art degree to begin with. "Why not learn a trade?" he'd asked. I tried to explain to him that portrait painting *is* a trade. His answer, I believe, was, "I meant a useful trade. Like welding."

I hate that he was right. In my head, even though I was clearly following my muse and my heart, I was also following the money. There were so few high-quality portrait painters, I'd be able to name my own price. It turns out the supply and demand was a little different than I'd envisioned. There were so few high-quality portrait painters because the total global demand for portraits of *any* quality is about three per year. I've been making ends meet by painting the pets of people with more money than sense. But the ends just aren't meeting anymore.

Please don't tell me I'm going to have to learn to weld...

Dec. 21st

I got to paint a ferret today. The owner had him wearing a cute little vest. Even if I *wasn't* desperately in need of the money, that would have been the high point of the average month. But this afternoon, something managed to top it.

My buddy and I had coffee. He's in town for a few days. Until recently, he was the only other "successful" portrait painter I knew. Here "success" is defined as "he doesn't have a day job."

Well, he has a day job now. That's not the good news. As we commiserated on not finding much work, he said, "I assume you've burned your Goth Ticket." I didn't know what he was talking about. He was astonished.

Evidently it's well known to all portrait painters except me that there's a London heiress who is addicted to portraits. She pays top dollar to people who meet her requirements, and will even go so far as to fly them to her flat in London to do the painting. All expenses paid. Food, lodging provided. Too good to be true! The only catch is that she's never commissioned the same artist twice. It's like a one-time-use, get-out-of-debt-free card for portrait artists. He gave me her email. I did some research and she's legit, as far as I can tell. Fingers crossed she answers my message!

Dec. 23rd

Just as I was composing my thoughts regarding how exactly to word the embarrassing request to my dad to borrow enough money to make rent for the month, I got a reply to my message to the portrait addict, who I shall now call my salvation (or more accurately, Madam Reynard, because that's how she signed the email). She expressed an interest in a face-to-face interview "at my earliest convenience." I replied with the assumption that she would want to wait until after the holidays, but she said, "I'm not overly religious" and attached the itinerary for a flight leaving tomorrow night.

I know, I know, red flags. This is creepy at the very least and dangerous at best. But beggars can't be choosers. She forwarded me the money she'd dubbed "a stipend of consideration to balance the inconvenience" of the visit. Combined with the dregs of my checking account, it's just barely enough to keep my landlord from putting my stuff out on the curb come the new year. I kind of *have* to take the chance.

Dec. 25th (I think)

Merry Maybe Christmas! I crossed so many time zones that I can't be sure what day it is. You know how in movies rich people will get picked up by a silent guy with white gloves and a sign with their name on it? That happened! I would have liked it if he had dropped me off at the hotel to try to get my brains in order, but he took me straight to "the patron." The guy was professional to the point of being robotic. This is getting weird. As if it wasn't weird already. This lady's house has a *name*. I mean, technically it'd count as a condo, but there *must* be a rich-people name for something like that. It's a place that's known around town as "the Shuttered Penthouse." This lady occupies the top three floors of a building in downtown London. I don't know who she is, but she must be *loaded*.

The place is like a museum or a shrine, but it is dedicated to just her. I counted one hundred and twenty-three portraits before she buzzed me in to her office, where there were at least seven more. You would think after seeing her so many times I'd have known what she looked like. They all certainly depicted the same woman. Thin, almost gaunt, with skin pale and flawless as ivory. She was always dressed in black, usually with red accents, and covering the entire goth milieu from frilly Lolita/Alice in Wonderland ensembles to chunky boots, spikes, and corsets. But every one of them carried the style of the artist. Often it was clearly by design, an impressionist or avant-garde take. But even those who attempted perfect realism fell short. Not for lack of skill. Simply because perfection was not possible. And thus, after seeing so many attempts to perfect her appearance, when I finally saw her for the first time, it still *felt* new.

I'm not going to wax poetic about how she looks. Given how the meeting went, there will be enough of that in the days to come. What struck me most about her in that first meeting was her attitude. For someone willing to fly me across the ocean and meet with me on Christmas Day, she seemed awfully terse. The way she spoke and held herself, you would think she was expecting me to disappoint her, like this was all a formality before she paid me and gave me a one-star Yelp review or something. The discussion was a brief one. Not so much an interview as a list of rules. There would be no photo reference. The painting would be done in the "traditional style" with her as a live model. Two sessions a day, two hours each, here in her penthouse, where she had a full artist's studio. The process would last as long as necessary to achieve the best quality painting I could manage, but sandbagging to milk her for money would not be tolerated. She also emphasized that I was not to reveal my portrait to her while it was a work in progress. I should show it only when it was ready to be "judged."

So many rules. This is going to be a nightmare.

Dec. 27th

Okay, day one. I don't know why I didn't expect this but she is a very good model. Having sat for so many portraits, it would be kind of sad if she hadn't developed an aptitude. Even so, I've never seen someone sit so statue-still for the entirety of a modeling session. Of course, I can't remember the last time I worked with a live model. Pets don't pose for portraits. You work from photos, with maybe an in-person meeting to get some of the minor details that a camera might miss. The human touch. But portraits take weeks, even if they're a rush job. Five or six months isn't outside the realm of possibility. We're working in oils here, even a rush job won't be dry for half a year. It's just not *done* to work entirely from a live model. Having her sit so perfectly still was making this feel more like still life than portraiture. I wanted to start a conversation, but any attempt at small talk got me nothing but short, clipped answers. I guess she's not the social type. I decided not to push the issue. For the money she's paying me, you don't risk annoying her.

Setting aside the lack of social engagement, this has been a refreshing return to fundamentals. Even knowing she never hires a given artist twice is sort of liberating. I don't have to worry about my performance. So long as I do this well enough to complete the painting, I'll have gotten everything I'm going to get. No reason not to follow my gut. Or my heart. Or my brain. Wherever an artist's style hides. Hands, maybe?

It's been a long day, I'm still jet-lagged, and I should probably be resting my hands. Until tomorrow.

Dec. 28th

I said yesterday that she was a good model. At the time I was referring to her behavior, but now that I'm past the initial sketches, I feel comfortable saying she is a good subject for a painting. Beauty is, of course, entirely subjective. And I'm sure there are those who would balk at my proclamation of her beauty. She is quite thin, and there are few features of hers that wouldn't benefit from the word "severe" in their description. She's all sharp angles and cold, desaturated tones. But... I mean, I'm an artist, not a poet, but a gorgeous meadow buried under snow and ice is still gorgeous, isn't it? She has a striking look to her, and that's just the top level. The more I look at her, the more I feel as though there is something beneath it all that is lending a sort of refracted beauty to everything about her. The trick will be finding a way for that to come across on the canvas without straying from how she looks on the surface.

Dec. 29th

She speaks! Beyond yes and no answers, that is. I didn't even think it was an interesting comment, let alone a conversation starter. I was just apologizing that I might be a little sluggish because jet lag hasn't quite finished screwing with my sleep schedule. I was still awake when the sun came up. The moment I mentioned the sunrise, her face lit up. It was subtle. Everything about her changes in expression is subtle. But she asked me to describe it. "Asked" is the key word. Until now everything had been a brief answer or an instruction. I tried to indulge her. I'm not an overly poetic person, as I've said, but I do know a fair number of colors. I tried to stretch out that description for as long as I could, hoping to see enough of the excited, interested face to burn it into my mind and, eventually, immortalize it in the portrait. So I went through every sunrise color I could. Salmon, peach, and goldenrod. I got florid with imagery of dripping honey and gleaming gold. She basked in the description with the same sort of reverence that one usually reserves for a symphonic performance.

It didn't last for the full session. I didn't expect it to. But it lasted long enough. I have enough of that reverent face in my mind and on the canvas to be confident it will be the star of the finished portrait.

Dec. 30th

London has a reputation of being foggy and miserable more often than not, but I guess I never took a moment to consider that it might be understated, let alone what sort of an effect that would have on the population. I'd assumed my hostess was especially pale, but the young woman stepping onto the elevator outside her penthouse as I was stepping off was practically translucent. Haggard, too. I guess that's what happens when you don't get any Vitamin D. I tried to be friendly and say hello, but she just shambled by me. As if that wasn't strange enough, the second ever unprompted nonbusiness remark from my boss/patron followed.

"You'll have to excuse her. She is feeling under the weather."

It isn't much, I realize, but it wasn't an instruction or an answer to a question, so it's special.

Today was certainly different from beginning to end. As a model, I had to reprimand Madam Reynard for fidgeting. She was just more "alive" today. And not really in a good way, either. I mean, it was nice to see her acting less like a statue, but I'd say she was a good deal closer to animal than human, portrait subject-wise. Twitchy and stuff.

All in all, it was an interesting day, and I feel like it added some flavor to the painting, even if it was trying at times.

Jan. 20th

Phew! Long time no journal! I've been busy. I guess when this all started, I didn't expect it to last very long. Eccentric art patrons tend not to be a reliable source of income. Or at least not a consistent source of income. But when I explained that it would take another six weeks or so, at least, it was *Madam Reynard* who reminded me I would need to pay my various monthly bills again. She fired off a check then and there. It was the first time she's fully abandoned the pose to do anything.

It felt a little foolish, paying for rent and utilities I wasn't using. But nothing about this has felt fully sane and normal. I've learned a lot about the vagaries of my employer. There's sort of a cycle. About once every week I encounter some sleepy, anemic-looking staffer. On those days, Madam Reynard is at her liveliest. Then she slowly becomes lower energy and more... I don't want to say irritable, but more terse, certainly.

I might be overthinking it, but I feel like the real trick to a proper portrait of this woman will be finding ways to unify the different intensities of character. Better that I overthink *that* than the possible motivations for why she employs so many sleepy, pale people...

Feb. 3rd

I've never worked so quickly yet so thoroughly. A portrait with this level of detail in barely more than a month is unheard of for me, but I was inspired. The logical thing would have been to take my time, both to prolong the payday and to ensure quality. But the more I saw the painting take form, the more I felt I needed to indulge this rare return to the enthusiasm that got me into art in the first place.

It is done, or close enough that it will be a matter of a few hours to button it up. I'll show her tomorrow. And then this bizarre and badly needed interlude comes to an end.

Feb. 4th

So... she wants another portrait. No, that's not sufficient. She *will have* another portrait. Her reaction to the reveal didn't seem quite so enthusiastic at first. She just stared at it, her usual inscrutable expression on her face. Impassive. Then she simply said, "Another." I explained that I'd have to head home to take care of a few things. She informed me that she would send one of her people to take care of everything. Ship over my essentials. Put the rest into storage. Close out the cable and internet and such. She informed me I would be her "artist in residence." Seriously. As in I'll be not just an employee, but a tenant. Living in the building, kept on retainer. She'll be a proper patron of the arts.

It's... kind of a lot. I've felt more alive as an artist since I got here than I have in years. But pulling up my roots and moving in with a woman I've only known for a few weeks? I barely know her... except that's not true. I've spent more time alone with her than some of my closest friends. Hours a day, for weeks. And all of that time, I was trying to see through to the woman beneath.

When she first extended the offer, it didn't feel like an offer. She informed me that I would be doing it, her eyes locked on mine. And the instruction hit me like it had physical weight. Like the words had reached into my mind and directly tugged at levers. I almost accepted right then and there. But an exceedingly rare flash of real emotion flickered across her expression. She shook her head and repeated herself, the words now phrased more gently. A proper question.

I accepted. I am a kept artist now.

Feb. 10th

I feel a little less unsteady and a little more at home, now that some of my things from the States have arrived. The "room" she's given me is on the floor below the studio. It's maybe twice the size of my whole apartment back home. I've met with her in her office a few times to settle some of the business aspects of becoming her live-in portrait artist. As a result, I've seen that my portrait occupies a place of honor, dead center on the wall her desk faces.

I don't know how to describe it, but she's been treating me... I don't know, more *gently* since I handed over the first portrait. Things that had previously been strict instruction are now carefully phrased suggestions or questions. I think maybe she understands my artistic instinct can be trusted.

There are... other things. Now that I live here, that whole "cycle" of her mood, and its association with the coming and going of employees, has some additional depth. I tried not to think too much about what she was doing with these employees. People are entitled to their privacy, after all. But an unpleasantly gossipy part of my brain imagined she was, not to be crass, "spending the night" with them. No judgment. But... no.

They show up only about an hour before I'd been encountering them. And get this. They really aren't all that pale or sleepy when they show up... but they *are* when they leave.

It's... look, I'm a rational person. But the imagination that makes for a good artist has a tendency to run a bit wild if you let it. And... you know what? I'm not even going to write it down. I have a new portrait to focus on. I *love* the outfit she picked out for this one.

Feb. 15th

Okay, look, the portrait is going fine. Great, even. When I'm working on it, I totally get into the flow state and nothing else matters. It's been some of the most rewarding work I've ever done. I can *feel* my style improving and my craft shaping up. ... But when I'm *not* working on it, my brain starts chewing on things, and...

She never leaves. Madam Reynard never leaves the penthouse. She doesn't even leave the top floor to visit other parts of her property. I guess maybe it isn't that weird, but... there are no windows anywhere. That's why it's called the Shuttered Penthouse. There are shutters on the outside, but they're decoration. The windows weren't just boarded up, they were completely built over. Studs, drywall, paint. They're just *wall* now.

And then there's the way the employees follow her instructions wordlessly and almost mechanically. And... look, it could just be an agoraphobic woman with incredibly dedicated and not terribly social employees, but then there are the other portraits.

I've taken art history. I know a thing or two about materials and techniques. Some of those portraits are very, *very* old. It'd take forensic techniques to be sure, but they seem...

They can't be authentic. Because if they are, that would mean either she was well over a hundred years old, or someone who looked just like her was *also* obsessed with portraits.

I feel like I'm going insane.

Feb. 16th

There are no mirrors in this place.

Feb. 17th

I guess my state of mind has finally reached the point that Madam Reynard has noticed it. She told me I seem distracted and suggested I take some time off. She was very intense. Uncharacteristically earnest about it. I politely refused. If I let myself focus on something besides the art for too long, I'll start second-guessing my decision to work for her. And I need this. Not just the money—though I need that too—but I need the art. I selfishly need to create something real. Something that will be appreciated. Something that will be precious to someone, even if that person is... well... I don't want to think about it.

Feb. 19th

Today is the night before her employee is due to show up for... whatever it is she'll be showing up for. I'm not the snoopy type, but I have twenty-four-hour access to the studio, should I choose to make touch-ups in the evenings. So I decided to go do some detailing to the background of the portrait. It gave me an excuse to at least enter the penthouse. I don't know what I was hoping to find. At this point, I'd take any sign that Madam Reynard was some sort of "natural" weirdo rather than the supernatural kind that my brain has built her into. What specifically that means, I don't know. If I'd found something cliché like pink fuzzy handcuffs or a leash, I'd have been able to latch on to that and let myself forget the rest. But after an evening of ultimately pointless dabbing at the portrait, nothing. At least, not until I was about to head back down to my room.

Rather than take the elevator, I chose to take the stairs, which took me a hallway closer to her bedroom than usual. What I saw at the end of that hall was... Let's just say it didn't set my mind at ease. There was a padlock on her bedroom door. I know for a fact that she didn't leave the penthouse. And unless she was hiding in a closet, the only place she could be that I wouldn't have noticed her at some point during the evening was the bedroom.

The last employee out for the night had locked her in the bedroom. What does *that* mean?

I think this is the point of no return. Whatever this is about, I don't want to be a part of it.

Feb. 20th

I'm in a hotel. Just finished going over the contracts I signed when I took this job. There is a *lot* of NDA stuff requiring me to promise not to discuss the details of her private life, which seems a whole lot more suspicious now than when I signed it. But it seems like I get to keep the money.

And now someone is knocking at my door.

Feb. 21st

I shouldn't have answered the door yesterday. It was Mary-Ellen, one of Madam Reynard's "sleepy" employees. She wasn't terribly sleepy today. She just wordlessly handed me a stack of pages written on parchment and sealed with a wax sigil that I'd seen all over Reynard's penthouse. I don't know how she found me. I didn't leave a forwarding address.

And if I shouldn't have answered the door, I *certainly* shouldn't have read the note. But I... The way she wrote to me. The things she said. It's... Here, I'll just fold it into the journal. I'm sure I'll be re-reading it a few more times before I decide what comes next.

From the Desk of Madam Reynard

It has come to my attention that you have chosen to terminate our partnership. Though this saddens me, there is little doubt what the reasoning may be. The circumstances of your employment have involved certain curiosities and mysteries. Someone with an inquisitive mind, or simply some basic concern for the well-being of others, is bound to make the same decision you have. If not for the carefully worded nondisclosure agreements, I would hope you would be contacting the authorities as well. You would not be the first, and if you are conflicted about potentially breaking the agreement to involve the authorities regardless, you should know that I have been investigated twice and I have been found guilty of no wrongdoing. Someone of my nature finds ways to protect herself. And my nature, I must assume, is the subject of the day.

You seem astute. Insightful. It is that insight that I value so greatly. By now, the answer should be obvious, but a sound, sane mind sometimes has trouble embracing where the logic leads.

I am a vampire. My age is beyond calculation. I hail from the land now called France, born before it had earned that name. I am timeless, my life preserved by this curse, but not without cost. I need blood to survive. But these are civilized times, and my long life has taught me control. The woman who handed you this note is paid handsomely for her donations, as are the dozen others I feed upon. It is an unusual arrangement. I do not expect you to understand it. But it is a mutually beneficial one. I could easily live in luxury and safety in my penthouse. But I cannot endure it.

In my long life, I have forgotten more than most will ever remember. The light of the sun burns at me, and so I have not seen the sun since I succumbed to the curse. Its warmth and glow are a faded, empty place in my mind. Mirrors do not show my reflection. And in my youth, that time when I could rightly call myself human, mirrors were a thing known only to the wealthy. I have never seen my face with any clarity. With age came wealth, came power. As soon as I had the means, I commissioned an artist to paint me. His artistic eye and his brush were the finest of his time, but the face he showed me was cold, empty. I saw not a woman but a husk in the shape of one. Chilling, with nothing lurking behind its glassy eyes. I refused to believe that was what had been made of me by time and the curse.

And so began my search, my obsession.

I can only see myself as others see me. Through the decades, through the centuries, I have sought someone who might see in me that spark of humanity that has been lost, someone who might show me that I am not fully lost. I learned quickly that, like mirrors, cameras see nothing of me in their lens. Only the eyes of the living can see me. And so I must find the beholder in whose eye I might still hold beauty. Each time I opened my home to an artist I risked being revealed. But long after hope was gone, I continued to take that risk. Like a mourner visiting the grave of a loved one, longing to hear their voice, to feel their touch, one last time.

And then, you.

The painting you showed me had something I'd never seen in another. That indescribable, unmeasurable thing that defines a human. Through your eyes, I was whole. Through your brush, I could see *myself* as whole. For the first time in centuries, I see in my portrait someone who is redeemable. Someone who I actually *want* to be. Someone who deserves happiness.

I understand your uncertainty, your fear. I understand if you will see these words as the words of a lunatic. And if you choose never to set foot in my home again, I will honor that choice. But know that you have given me a gift for which you can never be repaid. And if you see your way clear to returning to me, to looking upon me with the eyes that see the warmth others do not, I will dedicate my life to attempting to give you a fraction of what you have given me.

I await your reply.

Madam Reynard

Feb. 23rd

I don't think I've slept a moment since I received that note. I've just been in a daze. This morning I realized I had only booked the hotel room for a single day, and now it's day three. I called the front desk to try to find out what sort of trouble I was in, but the room had been paid for on my behalf. Reynard, of course. She's giving me time.

This whole thing is madness, and yet... if she was evil, she wouldn't have sent me a letter confessing her nature. She probably would have just had me killed, right? She said she'd been investigated. She probably has connections all over town. Within the police department, within the government. But she told me the truth. A truth that probably most people would never believe, sure, but the sort of truth that someone like her wouldn't want floating around in the world.

I can't believe how easily I've allowed myself to be convinced that vampires are real, but it's not even occurred to me that she is lying about that. I've never seen a vampire before, but if Madam Reynard isn't what one looks like, then popular culture has really dropped the ball.

I'm rambling.

The smart thing to do would be to leave this whole mess behind me. Either she's a supernatural creature with a thirst for blood or she's a looney who *thinks* she's supernatural.

But I can't stop thinking about what she said. Imagine not being able to see yourself. Only knowing yourself as others see you. And being denied the light of the sun. That life... that loneliness and emptiness... what sort of a person would I be if I knew I was the first person in centuries with the capacity to see her as she wished to be seen, to see the soul she thought was lost, and abandoned her?

I wouldn't be able to live with myself knowing that I could give her that gift again, that I could *continue* to give her that gift, and instead I chose to run away.

Heaven help me... I'm going back.

The remaining pages of the journal are filled with sketches of Madam Reynard's face. Each one shows a warmth and tenderness, not imagined but seen. Scattered among them are news clippings of gallery openings, of endowments in Madam Reynard's name, the legacy of a life dedicated to showing a lost soul that its light still glows, and that soul using the wealth and influence accumulated over a cursed life to demonstrate that warmth to the world.

Beauty is in the eye of the beholder.

And doesn't need to be beheld to be real.

But it needs to be real to be beheld.

It Just Takes a Moment

Moment

Joseph R. Lallo

It Just Takes a Moment

Introduction

This month's Patreon story is a bit of a curiosity. An experiment, if you will. You see, the illustrator responsible for these covers hit a few hiccups. I needed to add another cover to the mix, and I didn't have any planned stories. So I pitched the following idea. You draw a picture, whatever you want. Whatever you think you can get done fast. And I'll use that picture as a prompt to write a story. So that's what happened. The picture you saw associated with this story? That came out of Chandra Free's head. And this story you're about to read? It's what came out of mine as a result. Heck, I'll even make a note here. I started writing this story at 10:39 a.m. on 11/26/2022. I'll come back and write when I finished writing the first draft.

5:55 p.m. is when I finished the draft, though it was only actually two hours of writing. So... I don't know. Call that a data point.

L ana sat on her loveseat, feet tucked up on the cushion with her, and tugged her favorite blanket from where it had been spread across the back. The apartment was cold. She could have turned on the heat, but this was her favorite time of year. The cold gave her the perfect excuse to wrap up in a blanket. Coziness felt extra cozy when there was a nice little briskness to the air. It's like the mind understood, "Well, of course we have to curl up in a blanket right now. It's *cold*. That's what you do when it's cold." She was able to let herself off the hook and just relax on days like this. It'd be nice to just take a moment...

A distant buzz stopped her blissful little slide toward comfort. She released a frustrated grumble and tried to stretch across the loveseat to reach her phone. It was, of course, at the precisely calibrated distance necessary to require her to actually scooch over. After a second, sharper grumble, she slid her feet from the couch and poked them into her slippers to avoid walking barefoot on the cold floor, then stood and grabbed her phone. An email. She tapped the icon. It was an unfamiliar sender, but she already knew it wasn't spam. One got a feel for these things after a while. Truthfully, she probably needn't have read the email. That she was receiving it from a stranger made its contents all but certain. Only one kind of stranger ever spotted her message, and precious few of those jotted down her ad dress.

Hi. It feels weird to be writing this. But I saw your flyer. I had to give it a shot. I've been feeling things. I always have, now that I think of it. But it wasn't until this past summer that I realized what I was feeling, and why I was feeling it. And ever since that day I've been feeling it more and more. They're feelings that aren't coming from inside of me. They're coming from outside. Sometimes the good ones—it's why I've always been so social, maybe. When people have a good time, I have a good time, even if I'm just in the corner by myself. But now that I've noticed it, it's been getting more and more intense. When someone's feeling bad, even if they're trying to hide it, I feel bad, too. And it's really specific. I feel bad about things I did, or things other people did, or things I didn't do, or things other people didn't do. All that stuff. But the things involved, the people involved, aren't things I even knew about and aren't people I know. It took a really long time for me to realize that I'm feeling the things these other people are feeling. Not riding a vibe or anything. I'm actually feeling their feelings.

It made me feel crazy, but then I saw your flyer. "These feelings are not your own. I can help. You can help." I don't know. Now that I write it, it feels stupid. But I had to try. If this is a scam, I'll know it. I'm not an idiot. But I'm hoping it's not. This is getting unbearable.

That was all. There was no name, and not enough logic to the email address to tease one out. This was a person trying to put a layer between herself and the potentially crazy crank who tacked a vague message to a coffee shop bulletin board. Wise.

Lana sighed. Another one. It had been a while. Maybe eight months? Since she'd started, it had never taken that long for the next person to come along. She'd almost allowed herself to believe she'd finished seeking them out. But this was the way of things. They always came along eventually. Better they came to her.

She grabbed her tablet. This was hard enough to do without fighting with the smaller screen of her phone.

Hey! You came to the right place. Sounds like you've been walking down this road for a while now. I'm happy to be the one to finally tell you where you've been going, and where you've been coming from. Though maybe when all is said and done, YOU won't be so happy with me. Still, it's better to understand than to wonder. The best way I can explain it for you is to give you an example. This one happened just yesterday...

***

"Are you doing the pumpkin spice specials yet?" Lana said, barely through the door of the coffee shop where she spent her mornings.

"Just finished making the blend a few minutes ago," said Ma Murphy, the literal "mom" half of this mom-and-pop shop.

"Make it a large, then," she said. "You know how I like it."

There were a thousand reasons she preferred this shop over the half-dozen corporate and small-biz shops around town, but at this time of year the primary reason was that Ma Murphy understood "pumpkin spice" was meant to be a bunch of nutmeg and a little cinnamon rather than the other way around. It also helped that she and Pa Murphy also owned the building and were technically retired, so the shop was more about keeping busy and having folks to talk to than making money. It meant they didn't chase her out for taking up one of six seats for half the day.

It was unusually slow for a weekday morning. Usually she had to deal with a line for her daily dose of caffeine. Right now she and a man in nurse's scrubs were the only customers. He already had his coffee, and was too deep in his head to offer her so much as a glance as she slipped by him to her usual seat.

The moment she flopped down, she felt it. The sensation wasn't intense. It was barely noticeable. But like a thread at the edge of the sleeve of a sweater, this was the kind of tiny thing that just begged to be tugged at. She felt it as a dark tickle in the back of her mind. Rather than tackling it immediately, she waited until Ma toted her coffee over to her. She couldn't be sure how deep this went, and it was useful to have something to hold on to. A cup of coffee could be a life raft when the emotional floodwaters started to rise. Only when she'd taken her long-awaited whiff and first sip did she pinch that dark thread and start to pull.

"Oh... This is a bad one..." she murmured silently to herself.

Moments like this would have been terrifying if she didn't understand where they were coming from. Because as she scratched at the rotten, inky spot that had appeared in her mind, what came tumbling out of the hole left behind was a potent mix of emotions that had no connection to her own history, her own state of mind. As her eyes fixed on the back of the head of the nurse, who didn't seem particularly unhappy or distressed, she felt a rush of desperate, fearful sadness. The man was drowning, treading emotional water for so long he didn't have the strength to keep his head above the surface. It was a deep pain. So deep she couldn't feel the beginnings of it. This man had been suffering for so long that he no longer bothered dwelling on *why* he felt so lost, so alone, so fearful, and so certain that this feeling would never end. The pain merely *was*. This was his life. And there was only one way it could end.

She shut her eyes tight and wrapped her fingers around the coffee cup, letting its almost-too-hot temperature anchor her until she could adapt to the intensity of the man's emotions. Getting past that first shock was the initial hurdle. There would be plenty more. And it was clear, this was a man who would need her talents and skills. If she or someone else didn't knock a hole in the walls the man had built up around his mind, crack the shell he'd trapped himself in, find *some* way to let some light in, the healing could never start.

She opened her messenger bag and pulled out a pencil and pad. The sketchbook had started with fifty pages. It was wire-bound such that each page could be flipped away when she was through. But she hadn't flipped them away. Little tattered bits trapped in the wire coil showed where pages had been torn free. There were other sketchbooks that held things she wished to keep. This one had another purpose.

Long, loose, shabby lines started to sketch out the basic shapes of the man hunched at the table. Non-artists, and new artists, often became hung up on the fine details. But it was astounding how much genuine personality, how accurate and true to a subject one could get with broad strokes and shapes. It was the work of minutes to commit this subject to paper. A brush pen came next, darkening and contrasting the areas that needed it. The details came in with careful sweeps and gentle teases against the page. And those details told a story. The unfocused, distant look in his eyes. The worry lines on his forehead. The closed, guarded posture. And the darkness. The page was wet with ink by the time she was through, more darkness than light. But that was what it took to capture this man. At least, that was what it took to capture what needed to be captured. What needed to be saved.

As if he knew that she'd taken what she needed from him, the nurse stood. He left a few dollars on the table, mopped up the drops of coffee he'd spilled, and went on his way. Lana did the same. She would have to finish her errands quickly today. Come sundown, it would be time to prepare.

***

The streetlights outside the window buzzed on as she cleared the table in the corner of her apartment. It was time for the ritual. The word seemed like it should have a deeper meaning, considering what she was planning to do, but as rituals went, this part was just as mundane as all the little things one tended to do at the end of a workday. She prepared a cup of tea. She lit some candles. She set a metal dish on the far side of the table. She dimmed the lights. The first, and only, part of the ritual's preparation that truly felt arcane was the next bit. She stood and opened the closet. All sorts of warm down jackets and knitted shawls hung on their own hangers. Big chunky boots and uncomfortable, stylish shoes stood in a row along the floor. And on the top shelf? The Hat.

It deserved the capital letters. The Hat was important. It was The Hat's *job* to be important. A wide circular brim. A slumping, rumpled cone of broken-in felt. It was a witch's hat, obvious at a glance. More crucially, it was her focus. When she did her work, when she worked her magic, she wore The Hat.

She plucked the hat down and carried it to the chair set before the table, where the sketch of the nurse was set between the tea and the candles. A slow, deep breath cleansed her. And she placed The Hat on her head.

It felt heavy, like it had been soaked in water. And it felt warm, the sort of deep, penetrating warmth of a hot towel wrapped about one's head. She placed her hands flat on the table on either side of the sketch. The weight and warmth of the hat seemed to flow into her mind, down through her body, and along her arms. Like water seeping into a paper towel until it reached a spot of ink, dragging the color along with it, the warmth smeared a bit of her mind and soul as it progressed. When the warmth reached the page, the sketch began to shift.

"He's sleeping," she said softly. "Good. It's easier that way."

The figure she'd drawn slumped further. He hung his head, hands threaded through his hair. The darkness around the sketch spread. It leaked out from the page, along the table. It flowed down to the floor and up along the candle until it swallowed the light. It crept up the walls, blotted out the window. All was darkness and blackness save the precious scraps of white that remained on the page. She felt the tarlike weight of sadness in her chest. It felt just as deep and as dark as the ink on the page, leaden and heavy.

She watched as the sketched figure stood from the table he'd been seated at. He looked around. He saw that he was alone, and she felt the solitude that festered inside him. To him, it wasn't simply the absence of friends and family. The solitude was a real, physical thing. It wasn't emptiness. It took up space. Blocked the way, barring others from entering. The figure marched forward, but the shadowy blackness formed a sea around him, and he dragged it along with him. The weight of it was immense, and it grew heavier as he dragged it. His legs started to shake. He stumbled. And finally, he dropped to his knees.

Lana moved her hands. She could not see them. She couldn't see anything but the figure on the page. But she'd set things out. She knew where things were, even if she couldn't see them. She dipped her finger into the cup of tea and felt the shock of heat. It hammered a stake into the ground. This heat was real. There was a reality beyond this darkness. She raised her finger from the cup and held it over the page. A drop fell from her fingertip. Where it landed, the darkness lightened, diluted. The figure looked up. His eyes fixed on the tan blotch eroding the blackness. He tried to stand, to walk toward it. The weight was too great. She placed her hands on the page. The blackness smeared beneath her fingers, staining her skin. She dragged the page toward her. The bleeding bit of washed-away ink dragged closer to the weary nurse. He held out his hand and pressed at the lightened blotch. The darkness split and sloughed away at his touch like wet tissue paper.

He shook the stuff from his fingers and gazed out through the window in the blackness. It wasn't white, wasn't clear or vivid. It was the same brownish tan of the spilled tea. But compared to the black, it was like the rising sun. It spread as he moved forward, and hazy streaks of ink within the stain started to sharpen into shapes of things beyond the darkness. There were faces, figures not so different from his own. Family, friends. Their faces were creased with the same worry lines as his. They could see him. But they were distant. And they could draw no closer. The gulf between his little cell of darkness and their hazy light was too wide. It was like he was peering through a tunnel, a shaft cut deep into the Earth with his inky chamber tucked far at the bottom. They may have wanted to reach him. But the hole was too small, the distance too far. It was hopeless. Still hopeless. He'd let himself sink too far.

Lana dipped her finger again, another bracing reminder of the world beyond the darkness. Then she poked the page and dragged up to the top. This time the ink swiped away like gravy on a dinner plate, wiped wholly clean only for the thick, oozing black to creep inward again. But it did not close in. Not entirely. A thread-thin line of white remained. It ran from the outside, down through the tea-stained window, and to the feet of the figure.

He crouched and held out his hand. It was there, just beyond his fingertips. Yet he hesitated. The line, however thin, was so much brighter than everything else around him. So much clearer than anything he'd seen in too, too long. It didn't seem real. Didn't seem like it had any place in the world he'd been living in. For a time, he gazed at the thread, and she gazed at him. The darkness oozed further, pressed in. But it didn't blot out the thread. Finally, he closed his hand around the thread. He pulled it. The line drew straight and taut. Solid. Real. And it ran from his dark little hole to the outside.

He pulled again, let the thread support enough of his weight for him to straighten up. He dragged himself forward until there was enough rope to wrap around him. Clumsy hands tied a knot, forming a loop around him, something that had a fighting chance of supporting him even if his newfound strength started to falter. And falter it did. He stumbled, dangled with a rope around his waist. But it held firm.

Lana shut her eyes and felt the burn that told her she hadn't blinked in too long. She shook her head and raised her teacup to her lips. After a long, refreshing sip, she opened her eyes. The blackness was creeping back to the edge of the page, but the figure she'd drawn had changed. The weary, beaten man, using what strength he could to hide how little of it was left, now stood unsteadily, a rope beneath his arms and leading up to the tea-stained blotch as half-visible figures peered down as if from the top of a well.

It wasn't a victorious image. If she'd not seen how it began, she wouldn't have even called it a hopeful one. But she *had* seen the start. She had seen a man at the end of his rope. In a very literal way, the man was *still* at the end of his rope. The only thing that had changed was that he was holding on to it, and there were others holding on to the other side.

She stood and paced to the bathroom to run her ink-stained fingers under the cool, clear water. She washed them, though she knew not to waste time or the water trying to rinse every last speck of it away. She could soak her hands for hours and still find the creases of her fingers and the whorls of her fingerprints dark with the stuff. It wasn't the kind of stuff that washed away. It was the kind of stuff that wore away. It took time.

Lana dried her hands and returned to the table. She picked up the page and tore it in two, then stacked and tore the pages again. She held the corner of the quartered page to the candle until it took to flame, then dropped it on the plate. It burned away without smoke, vanishing without so much as ash. And then it was gone.

***

She swiped at the screen, tracing out the final lines of the account. There was more to write, but an insistent nudging at her elbow let her know that she had other obligations. Specifically, she had to scritch the head of her little roommate. She raised her arm, and her cat, Lucius, crawled into her lap. She gave him the all-important pets and pats he required until he was willing to curl in her lap rather than bump her hand off the tablet every time she tried to type.

The kitty appeased, she put the finishing touches on the message.

Now, what I described is MY ritual. Yours might be different. It probably will be. But you'll need one. And a focus too. People might think that the important part of the ritual is its ability to give you power, to make the sensitivity and the influence available to you stronger. It's the opposite. The ritual exists to separate your life into when you are working your magic and when you aren't. The focus is there so that you can remove it when you are through. If you learn nothing else, learn that.

Your magic is tied to emotion. Using your magic will leave you raw. You need to learn to wrap it up in a ritual so that it doesn't bleed into the rest of your life. We soak up the feelings of those around us. And it's far easier to take something upon our spirits than to leave it behind. Use your magic too often, and for too long, and... well, I think you can imagine how that will turn out. I don't think you have to imagine it at all.

Please also know that you cannot save these people alone. You can help them. Take a bit of the weight. Help them see that darkness doesn't end in darkness, darkness ends in light. The best you can hope, the best anyone can hope, is to give them a little bit of relief, a little bit of clarity. What they do with that clarity is up to them. Maybe they will reach out to friends, to family. Maybe they will seek help from a therapist. Maybe medication. There are a thousand ways out of the darkness. And sometimes they won't have the strength to climb out. You have to accept that. Sometimes all we manage to do is buy them some time. Sometimes only a moment. But sometimes it just TAKES a moment.

I wish I had better answers for you. We each have to find our own way. But it's worth it. Trust me, it's worth it.

She paused, stroking her kitty.

Oh, and consider getting a cat. There's a reason the witches of old had them. The ritual will drain you, and you'll need something to fill you back up. Cats at their best have a deep, genuine affection, but they aren't afraid to give it in a gentle, passive way. They're like Band-Aids to keep the open wound safe and nourished until it can heal.

If you need more help, don't hesitate to write. And when you feel strong enough, write up a flyer and stick it where you know it'll be seen. We can do a lot of good, but we all need a little guidance from time to time.

-Lana

She sent the message on its way and set the tablet aside. A bit of awkward maneuvering slid the blanket from the back of the couch to her shoulders and around her and her kitty. As the evening slid to night, she gazed at the faded lines of ink on her hands and sighed.

"Tomorrow, if there's no one who needs my help, I'm getting a scone with the latte." She stroked Lucius. "And if there *is* someone who needs my help? Two scones. Gotta balance the universe somehow."

A Kobold's Journey

Joseph R. Lallo

A Kobold's Journey

Introduction

I f you're an author, or at least if you're *me*, it's a fairly common occurrence for a character to start behaving in a way that wasn't planned or even anticipated. A scene will have an outline that lists something basic like "The Hero runs afoul of a prison guard," and when the time comes to write it, the prison guard gets some zingers and excuses are made to incorporate the guard into additional scenes. Before you know it, that guard is going on their own adventures. This has happened multiple times in The Greater Lands Saga. Allie and Mariss, the Barmaid and the Baker, are two such characters. But by far the standout for me in terms of how fun it is to write the character is Teya the Kobold. She started as "the one kobold who would get a speaking role" in Book 2. And now? Well... she's getting her own adventure. Having written it, I think Teya works best when working with others rather than alone—makes sense for a kobold—but it was still fun to connect a couple of dots within the setting.

This story takes place between Book 3 and Book 4 of The Greater Lands Saga, so if you haven't read up to Book 3, you're in spoiler territory. Otherwise, enjoy!

It was another glorious day on the mountain Teya called her home. The sun was high in the sky, the air was crisp, and it was doing that lovely thing where in the sun it was hot and in the shade it was freezing. In short, it had been a perfect day of collecting clay. This was one of her favorite jobs. She and a half dozen of her fellow kobolds got to descend the mountain, dig around in the mud, and haul up some heavy loads of rich red clay for making pots, bricks, tablets, and whatever else the Adept or Kazel wanted or needed. The first harvest from the old riverbed was through, and all seven kobolds were climbing the mountain with heavy loads of mud strapped to their backs. The creatures moved as though they were extensions of the same creature. The group carried a long rope that was shared between them but not fastened to any of them. Like their whole bodies were individual hands and feet finding places to hold tight, the kobolds would scramble far enough to anchor themselves, then hold tight to the rope so that others could speed their ascent. Often without words, one kobold or another would grab the dangling end of the rope, drag it to somewhere stable, and brace for the others to use it.

This is what it was to be a kobold. "The Task" was everything. It held a place of almost holy reverence in their minds, and seemed to take on a life of its own, strumming the air with a rhythm that all the kobolds danced to. And what was a dance without a song?

"Climb and scrabble, hops and jumps!"

"Tote and haul those fine red clumps!"

"Pull and tug, scrabble and climb!"

"Do the job and sing the rhyme!"

Like the task, the words simply flowed. No one had learned the song. No one had practiced it. It was just there to be sung. And so they sang it, because it was fun, because it helped to pass the time, and because doing things together was always better than doing things alone. In no time at all, the group had reached the edge of the plateau high up the side of the mountain. From here, it was less climbing and more running, with a straight shot directly to one of the openings to Kazel's lair. The others dashed along. Teya paused and turned.

She'd seen this view so many times. It had greeted her every morning. So beautiful. From here, the mountain stood clear of the forest below. The Greater Lands sprawled below her. Great herds of creatures that were so distant they were little more than specks to her crept across the countryside. The twisted, thick, complex trees that the elves called home jutted up from the land. But there was one aspect of this view that was new, and that crucial aspect held her attention. Rarely did the view from one's home change so drastically. Though, she now knew, the view hadn't really changed at all. *She* had changed.

"What are you looking at, Teya?" called one of the other kobolds.

Teya turned. Her friend gazed in the direction she'd been looking. Rather than a look of wonder and interest, a glassy, faded look came to his eyes, like a wet blanket had been pulled over his mind. He blinked and turned away.

"What do you see?" he asked.

"Nothing," she said, eyes shifting to the distant view once more. "And everything."

He was seeing the view as she had not so long ago. There were the same verdant forests of the Greater Lands. But to him, they were leading up to... nothing. Not a bare field. Not a white void. A sort of nonexistence asserted itself where the forest began to thin, a sight that actively insisted upon the mind to look away, to see that which *did* exist, because this so clearly did not. Now that the altered, manufactured emptiness he was seeing existed for her only in her memories, she had a hard time picturing it. The truth had replaced it, and truth had a stunning capacity to wipe away what came before. For Teya, beyond the forest there was a wall. Beyond that wall, there was an arid field that continued onward to the horizon. It remained a bit of a mind-bending sight. The wall may have lost its grip on her mind, but it still sank its claws into the world itself. The wall looked massive, like it enclosed a kingdom-size piece of land. But it was still visible only in one place, with more of the Greater Lands stretching out around it. But simultaneously, distance was distorted. Land just beyond the wall seemed stretched and skewed, and she felt fleeting notions that the wall was waiting for her no matter where she looked. She couldn't fully grasp the concept, even within her own mind. And so, she stared and did her best to conceive of something that someone long ago took great pains to hide from creatures like her.

She turned again. The other kobolds had gathered. If Teya was there, looking upon the nothing, then there was something in the nothing to be seen. They were a team, and thus they scrutinized the thing they couldn't see. Each expression was some variation on the same dull, fuzzy, almost drunken state of mind. And she knew there was only one thing that kept her from having the same look on her face. She reached a clay-encrusted claw to the simple silver earring in her dangling, frilled ear. She'd earned it through a wondrous adventure, though there are those who would say she stole it. But those people were cruel and greedy, so it didn't matter what they said. It was hers. And it cleared her mind of the influence of the wall. A blessing. But also a curse, as now that she saw the wall, and she saw beyond it, she knew that no matter how grand and wondrous her land was, it was limited. There was a second world out there waiting to be explored.

Teya turned and trotted toward the lair. They had clay to deliver, and there was no sense keeping the others here when she alone could see beyond the wall.

She alone...

***

When the sun had set, Teya found sleep was slow to come. It wasn't that she wasn't tired. She was exhausted. In total she and the others had made three trips down the mountain and three trips back up. That was enough to drain even the nearly limitless energy of a healthy young kobold. It was a job well done, and she felt the deep fulfillment that came with such an achievement. But there was something in her mind that wouldn't let it rest. A tiny but needle-sharp point that she couldn't identify. A burr in her hide. An itch too deep to scratch. And though she didn't know *what* was calling her, she knew *how* it was calling her, and she knew where it was trying to lead her. So she paced out to the cliff side, sat, and stared at the horizon.

Clawed feet padded up behind her. She sluggishly stood, ready to greet whatever kobolds had come to visit. But even before she turned to see, the sound of larger clawed talons let her know that this was no ordinary visit.

She gazed up and blinked at the majestic form of the Adept. She was a harpy. Not the crowlike lesser harpies, but a proper, legitimate greater harpy. She was a smooth union of human and bird, with an elegant tunic and an expression of wisdom and honor. The Adept served as surrogate for most of the decrees Teya's beloved dragon and master Kazel would have made personally if he had the time or notion. Her voice, for all intents and purposes, was his voice. And thus, a visit from her was not to be treated lightly. The pair of kobolds she'd heard held the honored position of her "hands," as wings were fine for flying but inadequate for the sort of tasks the Adept must perform.

"Adept!" Teya said, lowering her head reverently. "What is your task!"

"Teya. Kazel wishes to speak to you," the Adept said simply.

The words struck her like a falling stone. Her body tensed, her ears drooped. Everything inside her told her to run. As much as she revered Kazel, anything was better than being brought before him. Kazel was not merely an authority figure. He was as near as Teya had to a god. And no matter how beloved and benevolent he may be, you did *not* want your god to call your name.

"Be calm," the Adept said. "You have earned his interest, not his ire."

"His *interest*?!" Teya squeaked. "No, no, no..."

The Adept spread her wings and took to the air. The other kobolds gave Teya consoling pats on her back and led the way to Kazel's roost.

***

Weaving through the mountain to Kazel's chamber did little to take the edge from Teya's anxiety. As recently as a few days ago, she was proudly serving Kazel in this very room. For ages, Kazel had been locked in the heart of the mountain, chained by a fiendish contraption of human design. When he'd been freed, he quite wisely sought to avoid ever setting foot in that chamber again. The kobolds had spent a week hauling every coin and gem in his hoard to a more fitting lair nearer to the mountain's peak. Before she even stepped into the chamber itself, she could feel Kazel's presence. It was like a broiling heat in her mind. His breathing came in slow, calm huffs that her mind sculpted into seething fury. He was angry with her. He must be. The Adept claimed there was no ire, but Teya was alone. Not even the Adept's hands followed the last few steps into the lair. Teya dared not raise her head as she padded up to the edge of the bed of coins. Instead, she kept her eyes fixed on her own feet.

"You beckoned, my revered one," she said, when she was able to find her voice.

"I did," rumbled Kazel, his voice like the heartbeat of the mountain itself.

She dropped to her knees and bowed to the ground. "I serve you. However I must," she whimpered.

"Stand," he said.

She burst from the ground and stood rigid and tall.

"Something weighs upon you," Kazel said.

"I am happy! I serve! This is my home and I build it to be stronger with every bit of my strength!"

"You serve. Of this there is no question. But you serve in a different way. You distinguish yourself."

"I'll stop!" she peeped. "Tell me how to stop!"

"Look at me."

She shivered, then hauled up her chin as though it was the greatest weight in the world. With fists trembling at her sides and eyes twitching, she took in the regal splendor of her beloved dragon. Taller and more beautiful than any tower the humans could build. Wiser and stronger than any other beast who could ever live. And he was looking at her with a gaze she felt certain could burn her to an ember if he chose.

"You wear a silver earring," he said.

"It is yours!" she peeped, reaching to pull it free.

"No. It is yours," he said. "Granted to you because it was earned. Granted to you because you distinguished yourself."

"I didn't mean to distinguish myself!"

Kazel's expression shifted imperceptibly. Teya couldn't have described what about his countenance had changed if she'd had a lifetime. But in that change she saw the merest flicker of frustration.

"Enough of that," he rumbled.

Her heart hammered in her chest. "One kobold does not matter," she said in a hush, the most she could manage. "*A* kobold does not exist. There are only *kobolds*. *All* of us. We act as one. Hands to serve a purpose. If I am distinguished, I am wrong. If I am distinguished, I am separate. I am apart. To be separate is to perish."

"To be unique does not rob one of one's place among others. The earring gives you something that even I lack. I could have taken it for myself. But through your deeds, and your ingenuity, you acquired it. You deserve to bear it. And because you bear it, only you know its nature. It was made. And because it was made, we know it has a purpose. It reveals to you that which is hidden. But the greatest mistake one can make is to assume that only what is clear and obvious can be so. The earring may have more to give. A deeper purpose. A deeper role. And if it does, only you can know. So speak now. What does it tell you? What does it give you? What does it require from you?"

She shut her eyes. With Kazel so near, and her mind so harried, the nagging itch that kept her from her bed should have been drowned in a sea of greater concerns. But Kazel, in not so many words, had ordered her to uncover that fragment of a notion. She had to find it or fail him, and she would sooner die than fail him.

Teya focused her mind. Or at least she tried to. It didn't come naturally. It was what wizards did, and wizards seemed to have deep insight into their own minds. But to Teya it felt like she was flexing a muscle without actually using it. There was tension and effort but nothing came of it.

Whatever her struggles, Kazel must have noticed them.

"You are seeking something personal. Something specific to you. One does not find a truth of oneself by doing something which does not come naturally," Kazel said.

"Naturally. Do what comes naturally," she whispered to herself.

What was natural? How does one do what comes naturally on purpose? All she'd ever had to do, when she was trying to work out the right thing to do, was clear her mind and let the answer come on its own. She was a kobold. Answers and motivations were things that one plucked out of the ether. They didn't need to be found. But she did as Kazel instructed. She sought the answer to this mystery in the precise way she sought the answer of which hand to lend and which job to do. She opened herself to the rhythm of the minds of those around her and the world around them all, and she waited.

First came the pressure of Kazel's presence, and the weight of his expectations. Not what she was looking for. Distantly, a soft beat of kobolds working. She didn't know what they were doing, but there were many of them, and they were using tools. And there was a place in the rhythm for her. If she was not here, doing as Kazel instructed, she would join them. But for now, it was not what she sought. Deeper and deeper she sifted through the notions and sensations, discarding any that she understood. She peeled the onion, stripped away the layers, getting closer and closer to that deep itch that had plagued her s o.

Finally, that foreign notion was laid bare. She didn't understand it. She couldn't identify it. But it was real, it was undeniable, and for once she could actually comprehend its intent with a tangible clarity.

Teya pointed. "That way," she said, her voice trembling.

"To the west," Kazel said, as though a vague point was precisely what he'd been waiting for.

"More north than that."

"To the manticore dens?"

"It isn't a place, it is a direction. Just... that way."

"Then go where it leads."

She shook. "You're... sending me away?"

"Your destiny is leading you. Follow it."

"This is destiny?"

"For hundreds of years, I was a prisoner. Now I am free. That is achieved only by something strong enough to lift the weight of centuries. Destiny, and the tools of destiny. You are a tool of destiny. Until it is through with you, you must be allowed to continue its work."

"Destiny freed you. Isn't that enough?"

"Destiny brought hands and minds to bear on the puzzle of my imprisonment. Those hands and minds freed me. And if the chain of events gave you the earring and the insight that came with it, then it is at best an act of ingratitude to hold you here when it demands you move on."

"But this is my home. I love it here."

"And your home will be waiting for you when you choose to return. Until then, you will go. Heed destiny."

Teya wavered. She shut her eyes. The rhythm of the world tapped a tattoo in her mind. And for once, the half-heard notion, the itch in her mind, chimed loud and clear. It shook her with a thunderous boom. What had been a barely perceptible itch now blazed like a guiding star in her mind.

"Destiny..." she uttered.

***

Little legs hopped and bounded. Claws slid along smooth stone, guiding what would have been a nasty fall into a graceful skid down the mountainside. Now that the way was clear, she couldn't bear to delay a moment later. The sensation the earring granted was no stronger than it was before, but having been seen, it burned like a beacon on her mind. Her lopsided bow flapped and trembled like a badly tuned instrument as she reached the foothills, and the arrows rattled and threatened to spill free. By sunrise she was well into the forest. She didn't even rest until she reached the banks of the river that would lead her straight to where the humans had entered last time. And that was most certainly where she was headed. This was destiny. *Destiny.* And if the only thing she could do that her fellow kobolds couldn't was see beyond the wall, then this thread could only be pulling her to the world outside their prison. She slept sparingly, ate only what she could gulp down without slowing, and ran until her legs burned. If a kobold's purpose was to find where the work needed doing and lend a hand, then she was a long way from where she needed to be, and that was unacceptable.

It wasn't until she stood beside the water-worn stones at the base of the wall, feeling the mist of the waterfall that spewed from its fabricated face, that the gravity of her next step truly gave her pause. This was it. To everyone else, this was the end of it all. The door to a cell most didn't even realize was locked. But to her, and her alone, this was a gateway, no harder to scale than the mountain where she'd lived for so long. And sure enough, destiny still called to her. She didn't know what she was meant to do, but she knew for certain that it lay beyond.

She worked her claws into the scattered gaps between stones and hauled her compact frame up the slick face of the wall. She reached the relatively dry stones above where the waterfall let out, and her climb practically became a sprint until she reached the top of the wall. Some well-learned reflex or lingering effect of whatever it was the earring chased away caused her to shut her eyes as she crested the wall. She kept them shut until she was firmly atop it. Then, for the second time in her life, she opened her eyes and saw what there was to see while standing astride the wall that locked her people away.

The sight was a wonder, but a fearful one. Something that no living mind could look upon and believe it had a place in nature. From near the inner edge, the wall seemed to curve away, enclosing the arid fields lurking beyond. An unfathomably huge wall that ringed that strange place most of her kind would never see. She shuffled forward. With each inch she moved toward the center of the wall's thickness, the curve expanded, like the circle the wall traced out was growing. At the precise moment she reached the midpoint of the wall, it had no curve at all. The wall was simply an endless line, running roughly north to roughly south, dividing all of existence into two parts. One more step, and the curve inverted. Now as she moved toward the lands beyond the wall, the circle began to enclose her own home. In the space of a few strides, she'd gone from feeling as though she was sneaking into a walled garden to feeling as though she was sneaking out of one.

She turned back to from whence she came. Everything she'd ever known, wrapped up and locked away. Even in its diminished state, the land was massive. The wall disappeared over the horizon in both directions. But it was a wall, a limit. Something inside her churned, like she was somehow responsible for the imprisonment after watching it reveal itself with her own eyes. She shook her head and turned toward the world beyond the Greater Lands. Kazel had told her to follow where she was being led. Kazel said it was destiny. That meant she had a job to do.

And a kobold always does its job.

She scrambled down the outer face of the wall and dashed along, heading north and west, ready for whatever fate saw fit to bring her.

***

The farmer hacked at the soil with his hoe. For much of a given day, his thoughts revolved around his desires to have more land to work. More land meant more food for his family and more crops left over to sell at the market. It wasn't as though any of it was his land, after all. It belonged to some lord out west somewhere who'd probably never even seen it, and certainly hadn't worked it. What difference did it make to him if he offered up a bit more? All his problems could be solved if he just had more land. But then, from the moment he picked up his tools until the moment he put them down, his thoughts shifted to bemoaning just how much land there was to work. Far more than one man could work comfortably. It was almost magic how he never seemed to have *enough* land. Just too little or too much.

Right now, he was firmly in the "too much land" mindset. The planting season was nearing its end. He needed the crops in the ground by the end of the week or he ran the risk of them not having time to grow properly before the rainy season came and went. But he couldn't get them planted until the ground was tilled, and he wasn't even half-done. He muttered under his breath and stopped to mop the sweat from his brow. It took a moment or two for him to realize that, while he'd stopped working, the sound of work continued. He turned about, questioning if his mind was playing tricks on him. There was certainly the distinctive sound of hard clumps of soil being broken and turned, but the field was empty. Slowly he realized the line of tilled soil that he'd been laboriously adding to was a bit wider than he remembered it. Almost as though a second line had begun and was slowly catching up with his own progress. He followed the edge of the churned-up soil until he spotted something out of the ordinary. Despite being only a few yards back, he couldn't quite make it out. It looked like the dirt itself had begun wriggling around.

"Hello?" he said.

The dirt stood, and big reptilian eyes blinked at him from near the top. Shapes formed by the shadows of little crevices and crannies started to filter through his mind until it assembled the bizarre sight into what it really was. Not a two-legged mound of dirt but an exceedingly filthy creature. As he watched, another dirt-free portion of the thing revealed itself, in the form of a grinning row of sharp teeth.

"Hello!" the monster croaked. "Good hard work, yes! We do! Be done soon, yes?"

The sound of a voice dislodged the confused farmer from his state of frozen indecision. "Help! Help!" he cried, throwing down the hoe and dashing toward the far end of the field.

"Help?" called the creature behind. "Yes! More help, fast work! Let's go. Get more help!"

The thing dashed after him, bounding over the broken ground with impressive strides for such little legs. But a taller creature running in utter panic was difficult to outpace. The farmer reached the fence of his field with a quarter of the field separating him from the monster chasing him. He vaulted it and threw himself toward the farmhouse of a man, who, until this very moment, he'd never had a single kind thought about.

**

Teya slowed to a stop and huffed a breath. "He is very excited to get more help," she said, gratefully abandoning her inexpert grasp of the human language for her own. "If there was so much help to be had, you would think he would have finished with the field long ago."

The kobold slipped through the fence and padded across the second farmer's field. She smiled as she noticed this farmer had a nice wide trough of water freshly filled. She trotted over and grabbed a bucket from beside it to scoop some out. A long cool drink washed the muddy mess from her mouth, and a second bucketful started to rinse off the thick dusting of dirt she'd acquired while working the ground with her bare claws. She flexed her achy digits and gazed about. Not far from the trough was a barn, and in its dim interior, she could just make out a glimpse of handles and gleaming tool heads. The hoe the man had been using was far too big for someone like her to use. It would be terribly awkward. But perhaps there was something inside she could use to work the land a bit easier.

A little climbing and rummaging turned up something perfect. A nice hefty hand-pick. There was just enough length to the handle for her to use both paws, and it would save her from having to break the heavy earth with her digits alone. She tottered back out in time to see a group of additional humans leaving the farmhouse a short distance away.

She raised a frilled ear to listen to their chatter as the frantic farmer spoke to his friends.

"It was half my size, at least. Covered in dirt so it could stalk me. And the teeth! Long as my finger. Sharp enough to tear right through me and stubby enough to crack a bone," he raved.

"You can't come charging into my house just before supper and tell your mad stories," grumbled his irritable friend.

Teya raised her little arm. "Hello!" she shouted, once again in their language. "Many friends! We work now, yes!"

They froze, eyes locked on her. She raised the pick.

"I find in there. I can use, yes?"

"It has a weapon!" cried the farmer's friend. "Boys! Come quick! Bring something to defend yourselves!"

Teya scratched her head and turned to see if there was anything behind her that might match their cries of concern. She turned back just in time to catch a thrown stone to the brow.

"No!" she shouted, shutting her eye and rubbing the place she was struck. "There is work! We do! I help! Very very help!"

Her well-reasoned plea for sanity fell upon deaf ears. Two farmers and two other men who, by scent and resemblance, seemed to be the sons of the second farmer dashed toward her. She bounded away. For the same reason the farmer had reached the farmhouse before she did, the hastily formed mob were quickly gaining on her. This early in the season, there wasn't much in the way of cover until the ragged, unkempt fields past the fence at the rear of the land. She wouldn't make it that far without being overtaken. She could turn and fight, or she could get creative.

Teya hopped and pivoted in midair. When she landed, she was facing the advancing farmers. She shrieked a ferocious challenge and dashed toward them. The first farmer lost his nerve and made a break for his own land. The second farmer's smaller son, barely a match for Teya's size, joined him. That left the second farmer and his bulky eldest son. The older man held his ground and raised his weapon defensively. Only the younger man brandished the weapon with threat in his eyes. Armed with a shovel, he took a wild swing at her, burying the blade of the shovel in the soil a full stride ahead of Teya. She thumped a foot onto the shovel handle and vaulted at his head. Her compact little body struck him in the face like a sack of flour. She dropped the borrowed pick and wrapped arms and legs around his head. Her momentum combined with the young man's startled recoil, and the pair tumbled to the ground. She rolled to her feet and continued her sprint with the dazed but otherwise unharmed human behind her. The older farmer helped up his boy, giving her the chance to vanish into their barn.

In the Greater Lands, a single kobold knows it has very little chance to survive. One would be hard-pressed to find a creature better at hiding than a kobold. Thus, the instant the humans lost sight of Teya, she knew there would be no chance of them finding her again. They searched high and low. They banged on loose boards and poked pitchforks into mounds of hay. But Teya was small. She was swift. Even loaded down with her gear, she was stealthy. She was cunning. And most importantly, she had been hunted before. A creature who had never been truly in danger of being a meal for another was at a disadvantage when searching for its prey. Because only when one has had to master the art of hiding does one truly understand where to look. And that "where to look" is not a static thing. When they were poking stacks of hay, she was in the rafters. By the time they'd climbed to the rafters, she'd dropped into the stack of hay they'd finished searching. That was key. Watch where they search, and hide there when they are through. Once you do so, it is just a matter of waiting until all backs are turned at once.

That moment came when the farm family slipped into the root cellar to search for her. The door hadn't even shut behind them and Teya was already halfway across the field. She probably could have been safely away long before they finished their search in the cellar and returned to search for her, but the place where she'd been struck was throbbing, and an inviting pile of weeds lay in a large mound right at the center of the field. She convinced herself that she'd have a much better chance at keeping them off her trail if she gave them something *else* to worry about. That she'd be getting a bit of revenge for the unprompted attack was a few steps behind on the same path of reasoning. Thus, she reached into her pack and found one of her most cherished items: a contraption called a sparker. It made fires. And because she commanded it, *she* made fires.

Just like a dragon.

She crouched at the edge of the weeds and clicked the sparker until the mound took to flame. After she'd taken the time to indulge in the surge of pride and vengeance as a bonfire roared to life in the field, she dashed for the safety beyond the field and carefully took note of what she'd learned.

Though humans here didn't make use of those terrible contraptions she'd been taught to hate, they were still creatures to be treated with care. And more troubling than that, for reasons she hoped she'd never understand, the humans wouldn't accept help, even if they needed it, if it came from a creature they weren't expecting. Teya lingered in the shadow of a tree at the edge of the land until she'd caught her breath. When she was calm enough to pick out the subtle northward pointing of the finger of fate, she set off again, forewarned against heeding the call to join in labor. With that lesson learned, and a rare chance to light a fire for good reasons, the worst was surely behind her.

***

Nine days later, she remained confident the worst was behind her. It must be, because she'd encountered an awful lot of terrible things and put *them* behind her, and there were only so many bad things that could happen. Every one of these misfortunes brought its own little nugget of wisdom. In most cases, it also brought a nagging injury as a handy reminder. She limped along the bank of what was either a wide stream or a narrow river. The limp was her most important reminder. Humans may be rather poor at finding a hidden kobold, but humans sometimes had dogs. Dogs were much better, much faster, and their teeth hurt. Other lessons included the discovery that while there was a glorious lack of creatures willing and able to eat her, there was a similar shortage of creatures for her to hunt and feed upon. A crucial distinction was that it wasn't the prey that was in short supply, but the permission to hunt it. Fine, fat pigs and cows were huddled together, with bountiful troughs heaped with food. She didn't even need to fire an arrow to snag one. Sharp teeth and a well-timed pounce did the job. But after two such kills ended in her barely managing a mouthful before being chased away, she realized that humans had laid claim to these plump and tasty creatures, and they weren't keen on sharing.

More baffling was the act that had earned her the limp. Humans had made it clear they were fond of marking off their possessions with fences. They liked to clear those places of their trees, unless they were fruit trees, which instead could be found in orderly rows like lines of soldiers. That was fine and good. If fences around a place marked them as off-limits, then she would avoid fences. But when a lucky shot from her bow took down a deer a few days prior, her long-awaited meal of venison was interrupted by a man on horseback who taught her a new word between a barrage of colorful language. "Poacher." It would seem that humans were able to lay claim to things that simply wandered about on land they proclaimed to be theirs, and they were more than willing to defend these pieces of wildlife, presumably so that they could have the honor of hunting them themselves at a later date.

It must have been terribly confusing being a human being. So many rules to remember.

She did her best to follow them. If someone had been kind enough to tell her about the rules before trying to kill her for breaking them, that would have made it easier. But so far she'd picked up the following methods to keep herself safe that seemed to work reasonably well. Killing and eating something big and noisy? Bad. Killing and eating something small and quiet? So far so good. Fruits and vegetables weren't much to her taste, but it seemed the humans didn't put nearly as much effort into protecting them, aside from building fun little puppets in the middle of great big fields. Humans seemed quite willing to trade with one another, so she kept a few pelts and tried to offer them up, but she'd yet to encounter someone willing to offer anything but a shout in exchange for her goods. A steady diet of moles and other rodents had staved off starvation. Humans didn't care in the least if she ate *those*. But chasing them down for a single mouthful wasn't always worth the effort. Whenever she stole food from someone's land, she made sure to do her business in another fenced-off field to balance the scales, though this mostly seemed to be more confusing than appreciated among the humans. Fishing was an option as well. At the very least humans didn't seem to care if they found a mostly eaten fish carcass lying about. But they still didn't take kindly to seeing Teya squatting beside a river with a makeshift pole. If they heard her but didn't see her, they'd shout things like "trespasser." If they saw her, mostly they just shouted "monster."

If these people thought she was a monster, she hoped they'd never visit the Greater Lands. They'd never stop screaming.

The days led to more hunger as she moved farther north. Along the way, farms and cities had come in alternating clusters. In the south, the farms had started appearing when she'd cleared the arid lands nearer to the Greater Lands wall, and they'd quickly dominated the countryside with the odd city here and there. Now the balance had flipped. Cities were outnumbering the farms, and cities were a pain in the neck. So many more walls. And everywhere humans gathered together to form a city, they pushed back the edge of nature. She had to travel farther and farther off the straight line traced by the finger of fate just to have a chance at a meal unmolested, and that slowed her journey greatly. Cities tended to have trash, and where there was trash there were rats. Tasty, but not filling. And cities meant huge clusters of people. They were like kobolds in that when there were many of them, they were much bolder. All it took was a glimpse of a shadow or an errant sound and they'd be off to investigate. Teya knew better than to enter a town.

And yet, here she was, staring at a smallish city a short distance from the river and fighting the impulse to scamper inside. A city was such a thriving place. So many people hard at work, doing this or that. A thousand different rhythms floating through the air. For a creature who found fulfillment in collaboration, it was a siren song, a feast of tasks awaiting an extra hand. In the past few days she'd met, or at least been near, more new creatures than she'd encountered in the rest of her life to that point. And yet, she'd never been more alone. And it was truly beginning to wear upon her far more than the constant danger of discovery. Living with the danger of being stalked and killed was a constant within the Greater Lands. She was accustomed to it. But being alone? Unthinkable. And all these wonderful new tasks! Sewing and carpentry and tanning and carving and polishing. She could learn so much! Maybe if she just sneaked inside to listen...

The ill-advised path her mind was sliding down was interrupted by a hushed giggle at the very limits of her hearing. She bounded into and out of the river, scrambling to the far bank and pulling herself up among the branches of a leafy tree. After a few minutes, two young humans, a match for her size but much frailer of build, trotted into the clearing across the river. She watched them from the cover of the foliage. The pair moved erratically, stopping and jerking their bodies stiffly every step or so, alternating in this way such that at any given moment one of them was moving and the other was stopping. Teya didn't realize until they got a few steps closer that the reason for their bizarre walking cadence was a small object that was bopping back and forth between them. It was palm-sized and brown, and it made a soft rustling sound each time it struck their foreheads and bounced back.

They came to a clear, level spot beside the river. Amid much giggling and head-bopping, they slowly started to separate themselves. Further and further they moved, thumping the little brown object harder with their heads. One of them switched to kicking the thing back, a maneuver that sent it moving much farther and faster. The other let the toy thump against their chest, then drop down to be kicked back before it could touch the ground.

It was fascinating to see the way they moved. Everything about what they were doing was practiced, if not precise. There was reason to it, but no reason *for* it. She grinned. It was a game.

Of course humans played games. The one called Fel had come to visit. And he had taught her that fun game with the tiles. But everything she'd seen so far in this place made it seem as though Fel was some sort of oddity among his kind, someone with an ability to look upon kobolds and dragons and harpies and see things besides monsters. And if he was strange in that way, perhaps everything else about him was strange. But these little humans were playing a fun little game. It gave Teya hope that the same things she liked best about Fel might exist in other humans.

She watched as the little ones separated farther and farther, challenging each other to keep the little object off the ground. A few times it fell into the dust and they had to start over. But before long they had an impressive back-and-forth going. It didn't come to an end until a wild kick sent the bouncing brown object arcing not just over the head of the kicker's partner but over the river as well. It bounced off a flat stone and vanished into the weeds at the base of her very own tree.

"Aww!" whined the larger of the two, a filthy little creature with shorter hair and an inch or two less height than the other. "My dad *just* made that. It'll be weeks before I can persuade him to make another."

"I didn't know it'd fly so far!" defended the smaller, more shrill-voiced of the two. "You're always telling me I don't kick it far enough."

"You kicked it, you get it."

"I can't go in the river! It gets too deep in the middle. Go up to the bridge by town and cross over. I'll stay here so I can tell you where it looked like it went."

"Why should I go? *You* kicked it!"

The pair continued to bicker. Teya carefully crept down the far side of the tree, out of their view. She crawled through the weeds and swiftly located the lost toy. It was a small sack, heavier than it looked, like it was filled with beans or small stones before being stitched shut. She hefted it in her stubby grip, then cocked an ear to try to get a fix on just how far away the little ones were. Unsatisfied she'd be able to hit them based on sound alone, she peeked an eye between the weeds. After another few hefts, she reared back and hurled the sack.

"OW!" yelped the shabbier of the two. "Who's throwing things?"

The sack had struck squarely between the little human's shoulder blades.

"Oh! It's back!" the higher-pitched one squealed happily. "Hello? Who's there?"

Teya held her tongue, slowly making her way back to the base of the tree. She had to stay very low and move very slowly to keep from being seen, now that they knew where to look.

"Thanks for throwing the lump back!" called the high voice again. "Do you want to play? It's real fun!"

She ignored the offer, scaling the tree as the pair of voices began a hushed exchange.

"No! Why should I give it to you? It's my turn," said the dirty one.

"Just give it. It'll be more fun this way," insisted the high-voiced one.

As Teya was eying the lowest branch and trying to judge if she'd be seen hopping to it, she heard the so-called "lump" rustle the weeds roughly where it had landed before.

"What'd you do that for?" whined the dirty one again.

"Hush," said the other before switching to a shout. "Now throw it back!"

Teya was suddenly ecstatic. Not just because of the notion that she should help these two little ones get their toy back but also because of the pleasant and yearned-for feeling of being given a place in a task. It had been too long since she'd been a part of a team. She dropped down again with a bit less care. They knew she was here, after all. So long as she kept out of clear view, there shouldn't be a *new* problem. A short search turned up the lump, and she heaved it back toward them. The shabby one caught it and, with minimal prodding from the other one, threw it over the river again. Teya suppressed a gleeful chatter and hurried to return it again.

An odd, lopsided game quickly evolved. The humans ran and jumped to catch the lump, trying their hardest to be the one to catch it and toss it back. Teya scampered about in the weeds with the goal of finding it and returning it as quickly and invisibly as possible. It was strange, unexpected. But she was a part of something now, and it was scratching an itch that had been nagging her since she'd left her home.

That wonderful feeling of dancing to the soft drumming of collaboration was a bit too intoxicating, and when the final toss from the high-pitched talker fell short and landed in the wet gravel of the riverbank, Teya scampered out to fetch it. A startled shout from the filthy one and a sharp gasp from the other one revealed to her that she'd made a terrible mistake.

The dirty one dashed toward the city, jabbering about a monster. The other one scrambled away from the river a bit, but didn't follow the fleeing child. Teya hastily tossed the lump across the river again, landing it at the remaining human's feet, and hurried into the weeds.

"Wait!" called the high voice.

Teya wove through the bushes, already planning a long sprint around the outside of the little city to avoid the mob of defenders likely to appear.

She stopped when she heard the lump bounce into the weeds behind her. She turned and found it, then reluctantly stood up among the weeds to give the little human a questioning glance. The little one beckoned, a bit shakily, but quite eagerly. Teya eyed up the surroundings. No lurking hunters. And it would be a minute or two before the fleeing human reached the city. Driven by some combination of curiosity and the desire to prolong this, the only truly enjoyable interaction she'd had on this journey, she bounded across the river. She stopped with her paws still in the shallow water beside the bank and tossed the lump at the human's feet.

"What're you?" the human asked.

Teya pointed in the direction of the fleeing child. "Monster," she said.

"But what kind?" she said.

"Kobold," Teya said.

The human's head shook. "No. Kobolds can't leave the Greater Lands. None of those creatures can. You sure you're not a lesser kobold? This place is lousy with Lesser Mystics."

"Not lesser. No lesser kobolds." Teya tapped the earring. "Special kobold. You don't run. Why?"

"Mom and Dad taught me all about how to deal with monsters," she said with an air of expertise. "The magic ones? They try to fool you, but you're safe as long as you don't take any gold or treats or anything. The big scary ones are dangerous, but you're not big and scary. And they didn't say anything about having to worry about monsters that play games."

Teya nodded. "Good teachings. Smart Mom and Dad. I go. Thanks for game. Very very thanks." She turned to go.

"We can play some more!" the human said quickly.

Teya turned back again. She pointed to the city. "Soon, many humans come. Mad. With weapons. I go. Fast."

The child scoffed. "He's always making things up about monsters. It'll take forever for him to convince them to come out here."

Teya narrowed her eyes and considered her options. "No. No play. Bad chance to take. But maybe, I ask? Questions? Those are good. Learn much. Better at being safe. Yes?"

"Aw," she moped. "Questions are boring."

"You are child, yes? And that one? Also child?"

"What? Oh. Yes."

Teya waved her claw back and forth. "Two kinds?"

"I'm a little girl. He's a little boy."

The kobold furrowed her brow and craned her neck a bit closer to sniff. "Smell? Not as different. But *some* different. Now I know."

"You've never seen a little girl before?"

"Before today? Maybe. From far. Big girl, from less far."

"Woman," the girl corrected.

Teya nodded in understanding. She placed her paws at steadily decreasing distances.

"Little boy and girl? Very far. Woman? Less far. Man, very less far. Too less far, sometimes." She held up her achy leg. "Dog? Very very too less far."

"You talk funny," the girl said with a scrunched-up nose.

Teya crossed her arms. "Little girl? No kobold sounds. This one? More good talker. Very very human sounds."

"How do your words go then?"

The kobold shook her head. "Little girl can't do."

"Try me."

Teya rumbled a deep, throaty sound that rolled into a trilling chatter. "That sound? Sound for hello. Special hello. 'I am friend. All is safe.' That kind of hello."

The little girl cleared her throat and released a sound that was an earnest effort at reproducing Teya's words, but woefully inaccurate. Teya cackled.

"That sound? 'I have thorn. Thorn in bottom parts!'" she gleefully translated.

"It doesn't mean that!" the girl said defensively. "I said what you said."

"Too high. And last part? Too short. Not hello. Thorn! In bottom parts! *Smelly* bottom parts."

The little girl pointed. "Then you're a bad teacher."

Teya nodded. "Teach? New for this one."

A sound near the city caused Teya to suddenly snap her head in that direction, muscles tense. When no angry mob showed itself, she allowed herself to relax a bit.

"You're awfully scared for a monster."

"This place? Bad for monster."

"Then why are you here?"

She jangled her earring. "Destiny," she murmured with pride.

"What's that?"

"Special reason. Just for this one."

"And what's your special reason?"

"What? Don't know. Where?" She pointed. "There."

The little girl looked in the direction Teya pointed. "Ooooh. Beffshire."

"What is this?" Teya asked.

"It's a great big city. A couple days away. You were pointing right at it. Seems to me, if you've got a destiny, that's a good place for it to be. Everyone in Thayne ends up there sooner or later. Why not a monster?"

Teya nodded. "Good. Then I go. I find this place. Search good. See? Question, good to ask." She raised an ear suddenly. "Many sounds. Very very people. I go," Teya said.

"Wait!" the little girl said before the kobold could bound into cover.

"What? Fast, fast!"

"How do you say goodbye?"

Teya grinned. She released a rolling trill, not unlike the ending of hello, but faster and with an upward lilt at the end. "That one? Goodbye. But with hope. Hope for hello soon."

The little girl returned the call as a shrill, fluttery whistle that was utterly incomprehensible as a kobold word. "How did I do?" she asked.

"Not so bad talker," Teya lied.

The little girl beamed with pride. As the sounds of investigation drew nearer, Teya repeated the goodbye in her native tongue and bounded off into the weeds. She was still awfully hungry, and her dog bite was complaining about not being given more time to heal. But her spirit felt lighter now than it did before. For the first time since she'd set off on this adventure, it felt like maybe this destiny had good things in store as well as bad. And better yet, she had a destination. Beffshire. It sounded like a fine place.

She quickened her pace. Best not to keep destiny waiting.

Priceless

Joseph R. Lallo

Priceless

Introduction

The collections that I release around once a year that gather up these Patreon stories are always called *Paradoxes and Dragons*. The title requires that I include at least one time-travel story and at least one dragon story. Because my brain is mush these days, I can never remember if I've actually done the requisite stories, so I sprinkle them all over the place just in case. Thus, here's a dragon story. The idea for this actually comes from when I was a little kid, when I would attempt to come up with narrative explanations for why any given thing I'd just learned how to do would somehow be a source of heroic victory. It's evolved a lot since then, but nevertheless, it's a blossom that sprouted from a very old seed.

F ar too much white and blue, not enough green.

Other people might have had other complaints about their lot in life if they were Louisa. Her parents had died when she was quite young. They had been wealthy, but what they'd had in wealth they lacked in tact. It was impressive how many powerful enemies two relatively low-level nobles could accumulate in one lifetime. When they were gone, the lords and ladies of the region had descended upon the family lands like vultures. Bit by bit, the holdings that should have carried Louisa comfortably through her life were peeled away and gobbled up by the wealthier and more powerful. In the six years between the death of her parents and present day, she'd gone from looking forward to a life of ease and respect to wondering where precisely her next meal would come from. It wasn't kindness but oversight that had provided her with the tiny morsel of salvation she now called a home. When she'd been packing up her things, she'd found a forgotten deed tucked away in the bottom of a drawer that had been otherwise swept clean by the army of assessors and acquisitions agents. It was a cottage and a small bit of surrounding land, far to the northwest and by a wide margin the most remote piece of land in her family's name. When she arrived, she found it to be a rundown, drafty, abandoned husk. Reaching the place had cost her nearly all her remaining money, leaving her with scarcely enough to prepare for what would turn out to be a far longer and far harder winter than she'd anticipated.

That cottage had been her home for six months. She'd lived in relative solitude and relative poverty. Hunger had left her teetering on the line between lean and gaunt. She'd worked her fingers to the bone inexpertly repairing enough of the cottage to keep from freezing in the frequent snowstorms. And all this came after a life of being pampered and coddled. Louisa had a *lot* she could rightly complain about. But only one thought came to mind most days.

"Always so much white and blue," she muttered. "The canvas is already white, and blue is the most expensive paint. What I need is a cheaper palette of colors to paint from or a patron willing to pay for a good deal more blue."

She set her palette on the rack near the little fire she'd kindled. It didn't flow properly if it was too cold, and the whole blasted mountain was too cold. Her fingertips emerged from tattered holes in the tips of a pair of mittens she'd trimmed. Painting with mittens on was out of the question. Even half-frozen, digits were far better at coaxing a natural, elegant stroke of the brush than warm mittens ever could. And that was all that really mattered to her. To paint. To make things of beauty. That was what her life of leisure had given her. She'd had the time, the money, and the opportunity to learn the art of painting, and so long as she still drew breath, she would continue to develop and embrace that art.

She scanned the horizon. Being relegated to this forgotten stretch of mountain was not without its blessings. It was situated such that every brilliant moment of the short day's light fell upon a gorgeous vista. And the mountain was timeless, ancient, and stable. She could spend three days painting a scene, then wander off for a week to scrape out a survival. And when she returned, the scene was there waiting for her, unchanged but for a few motes of snow. The mountain was a fine model. Never complained. Never fidgeted. If only she could coax it into wearing something more colorful than a blanket of white atop slate blue.

Louisa spotted a lonely stand of dusty gray pines in the distance. It wasn't much, but it was more color than she'd seen since she moved here.

"Maybe the mountain is finally shrugging off this boring old blanket. It will be nice to finally use some green."

She mixed some green earth into a paste and cracked an egg into some uncomfortably cold water to create the proper color. By far the bulk of her money was spent on pigments, and if not for the fact that egg could be used both as a paint ingredient and food, she probably would have starved long ago. She could always coax herself to buy something to help her paintings flourish. Something as temporary and fleeting as a meal felt frivolous by comparison.

Louisa brushed out the broad shapes of a mountain she'd already painted so many times she could easily have reproduced it in her sleep. Some delicate white caps with lime white paint. Some coal gray substituted for the blue of the mountainside to save a little money. Likewise the sky. Perhaps on the day this painting represented, the sky was a nice, affordable overcast. But the trees. She would use them. She let the shapes of that one stand filter into her mind, picking them apart into undertones and overtones. She reduced them from what nature had made of them into shapes that could be traced out with a brush. And then she populated the mountainside with them. A nice, lush, green expanse of trees. What the mountain might have looked like if a few more seeds had fallen and a few fewer flakes. The brush swept across the canvas. It had taken a bit of effort to learn how to make a passable painting when it was so cold. The right speed, the right thickness of layer. Practically everything that dealt with brush or palette had to be changed. But the art? The art was the same. It seemed like everything about painting existed as an obstacle between the artist and the art. It was the plight of an artist to be in constant battle with the physicality of her world in her efforts to properly depict what she saw in her mind's eye. To properly clash with the biting cold, the too-thick paint, the too-stiff bristles, took every drop of what her mind and body had to offer. Thus, she tended to lose track of time. Questions that didn't have to do with the art didn't just go unanswered, they went unasked. Tasks that didn't serve the art went undone.

This, it was fair to say, was why it had taken this many months to learn why no one had come to take this last vestige of the family fortune from her. Yes, they'd not known about it. But she wasn't a spirit. Where she went, others could follow. But they never did. No thuggish representative of a man her father had swindled before she was born. No bookish scribe representing a noble her mother had shunned at a party. She'd been left alone. And then there was the nearest city. It was near only in a relative sense. Her semiregular trips to buy what little provisions she could afford, as well as to persuade the locals to send for pigments she couldn't acquire on her own, took a full day of travel with her little horse and carriage. Why didn't people come any closer? The mountain was certainly rich in minerals. She could pluck malachite for brighter greens right from the ground without so much as a pick. None of this had, for even a moment, entered her mind until the very instant that the answer presented itself. And even then, she would have dismissed it if not for one thing. It had spoiled her view.

A dark shadow fell across the landscape ahead of her. Far darker and far faster than a passing cloud. Suddenly the glorious sampling of colors that served as her reference for the painting were all wrong. Muted or blotted out entirely. She squinted at the spoiled view, then up at the sky. Whatever was blocking the light was just barely managing it. The bright jewel of the sun rimmed a strange silhouette. Her eyes watered as she glared at it. Then the shape suddenly shifted and the sun poured through. She shut her eyes and looked away. Before she could blink away the spots, the ground rumbled like it had suffered a thunderous blow with a hammer. She managed to steady both her palette and canvas before they fell to the ground. Her vision finally started to return, and she was presented with something that should not have been there. Something that would persuade even the pettiest of family foes to leave her cottage alone. Something that would persuade the most stalwart of miners to settle their town farther down the mountain.

It was a dragon. By far the most massive living thing she'd ever seen. A large part of her mind roiled in fear—though not nearly as large a part as would have been appropriate. It was outweighed, in her case, by the part trained to recognize beauty. After far too long looking at the frozen countryside, the brilliant violet hue of the scales across its face and back, contrasted with the amber-yellow of its underbelly were like a refreshing draught of water after a long dry spell. It was elegant. Extravagant. *Regal,* even. However, at the moment not even her artistic eye held sway.

What Louisa *mostly* felt was profound, simmering anger.

"Just what do you think you are doing?" she snapped, thundering up to the dragon.

As she stalked closer, she could feel the fear desperately trying to tip the scales of her mind. She refused to heed it.

"I was in the middle of a *very* important painting. It is the first I've seen of decent green in *months* and you just come down and spoil the view? You could have tipped my canvas into the fire. Do you know how hard it is to find a decent canvas? I've had to learn to stretch my own, and I'm not going to lose one because a flying lizard was rude enough to—"

Her rant could easily have gone on for a full five minutes if not for a startling blur of motion followed by an uncomfortable pressure constricting her body. She had barely a moment to come to terms with the fact that *something* had wrapped entirely around her body before a much more pressing problem presented itself in the form of a stomach-turning, lurching motion.

She clawed her mind back from the tangled mess of anger and panic and finally gave the situation the respect it deserved from the start. Her legs were pressed firmly together, and her arms were pinned to her sides. But her head could still turn freely enough. She twisted and turned it about. The only thing keeping her from screaming at the top of her lungs was the fear of what the beast would do to her if she did so. Instead, she blinked in the dim light and tried to work out what had happened and what, if anything, could be done about it. Slowly, she worked out the scope of her predicament. She was clutched in the dragon's front paw. If it wasn't strangely dexterous, she felt certain it would have crushed her to paste. That she was being held uncomfortably but not painfully suggested, impossibly, that the beast didn't want to hurt her. It was hardly a relief. Killing her? Eating her? These were the things a dragon was supposed to do. They were the things she had been taught to fear. That it could easily have done either and chose to do neither left the door open for *anything* else. For someone with her imagination, that was a harrowing realization.

Somehow more harrowing was the discovery through the sound of rushing wind and the narrow glimpses of speeding countryside between the claws about her that she was being carried by the beast while it flew. Falling to death quickly found its place in and among being eaten, being crushed, and being burned to cinders on the growing list of things she'd never dreamed would happen to her and now felt absolutely certain to occur. Little breaths of wind curled against her as the flight continued. They had a sharper bite than the already painful cold of the mountainside. Rare was the person who in the same instant had reason to believe that she could be burned to death or frozen to death. If nothing else, Louisa's final moments were going to be distinctive.

Her heart almost stopped when her captor touched down. She was not released immediately. Instead, the beast ambled forward with an awkward three-legged gait. The sun vanished, replaced with the deepening darkness of an echoing cave. Her heart hammered in her chest as she was assaulted by the echoing footsteps. The dragon paced deeper into the mountain for longer than seemed possible, long enough that surely it would have walked clear out the other side of whatever mountain it called its home.

Finally it ventured as far as it cared to go. The claws around her body loosened their grip, and she rolled to the floor in an action the beast probably thought was gentle. The cave floor was a bit rough, but it was a far cry from the icy block of stone she had been expecting. Indeed, it was warm. Warmer than her home, even. But that was all she knew of the place, as the light of the sun was a long way away, and nothing else had come along to replace it. Gentle tremors beneath her feet and the leathery swish of the monster's hide gave her the vague notion of when it moved and where, but for something so large, it was astonishingly stealthy. A meaty thump and soft metallic jingle brought the motion to an end.

For a moment, silence. Louisa remained transfixed. Fear seized her muscles. She scarcely dared breathe. Perhaps, if she couldn't see the dragon, the dragon couldn't see her.

"Speak," rumbled the monster.

She jumped at the sudden, intense sound, tumbling to the ground. The voice was so deep and potent that she could feel it in her chest when he spoke.

"W-what would you have me say?" she yelped. "I'm... I'm sorry for yelling at you."

"I have watched you."

"Watched me do *what*?" she said.

"Creating value from *nothing*."

"I don't know what you—"

A burst of light and heat washed through the cave. Flame lanced through the darkness and splashed against a wall, spreading to ignite lanterns that most certainly owed their glow, in part, to magic as well as fire. Though they burned only along one wall, the light of the lanterns seemed to fill the room, not by radiating out but by gradually filling the place from bottom to top, like their light was a liquid that was slowly flooding the cave.

The light revealed the most astonishing assortment of valuables she'd ever beheld. She'd expected mounds of gold. Dragons, if the stories were to be believed, devoted their lives to accumulating gold, driven by ancient instincts that she never understood but never questioned. After all, the most powerful men and women in the world sought gold above all else as well. But to call this trove something as simple as a mound of gold would be a crime. This did not look like it was stolen. It looked like it was *curated*. The dragon was resting atop the most mundane portion of the collection: a simple pile of coins. But that was the tiniest fragment of a veritable museum display of other items. Scepters, crowns, ornate swords, bejeweled armor. Figurines, engraved serving platters, heaps of jewelry. There were even things made not from precious metals or gems but from simple stone, carved and shaped into priceless masterpieces. Tapestries hung on the walls. And, most surprising of all, there were paintings. They leaned against the wall—evidently hanging them was not among the many skills of this beast—but she had to admire the monster's eye. They were stunning. Far beyond her own capabilities.

Her captor flicked a claw into the mound of coins, splashing a scattering of them in her direction. Those that rolled to rest beside her were simple roughly shaped disks.

"Gold," he stated, as if to educate her. "It is rare. And that which is rare has value. I seek value. But this gold? This is worth more."

A massive claw poked at a stand festooned with an assortment of earrings.

"Gold, silver, and copper," he said. "Were I to cast my breath upon the whole of this collection and melt them down, it would amount to less gold than that single coin. But each of these is worth more than that coin. I can see it. I can *feel* it."

"Well, yes," she said shakily, rising to her feet. "The jewelry takes skill. It takes artistry."

"Artistry," the dragon said with a slow nod. "I have heard tell of this. A powerful magic."

"It's not..." She paused. "Yes. A powerful, *powerful* magic," she said.

It seemed unwise to contradict the beast, and more to the point, if the monster believed art was magic, then perhaps she had a chance to leave this place.

"I have seen wizards do great things. I have seen them conjure something from nothing. But those things they conjure are mundane. Bits of food. Creatures and demons drawn from elsewhere. Earth, fire, wind, water. Impressive acts. There are even some who turn lead into gold. But that change consumes materials. Not so for artistry. Artistry does not change the materials. They remain as they are, yet the value swells, blooms. Through simple motions. Tapping of hammers or smearing of pigments. Value is created. Amplified."

"Artists are truly mighty, bending the forces of reality in pursuit of beauty."

"*Value*," the dragon rumbled.

"Surely a beast so wise and powerful as you must see that it is the beauty that produces the value."

Louisa approached the paintings. She'd barely made it a step when the tiniest increase in the tension of the dragon's muscles sent a spike of ancient fear through her, like she'd spotted a snake coiled and ready to strike.

"May I approach your fine collection, to illustrate my point?" she asked.

He gazed at her through narrow eyes. "With care."

She navigated the mounds of wealth until she reached a painting that stood out from the rest. It was astonishing, no doubt the work of an ancient master. It was immaculately kept, and even its place in the light seemed calculated to highlight its contrasting colors and inspired composition.

"Look, there. The way the lines of the image draw the eye to the subject. See how this region of color produces perfect balance with that. The reflection in the pitcher subtly distorting the fruit on the plate, shifting its form as well as its color. And look. You can see here that the reflection *should* place the stem of this grape here, but instead it is here. The world itself altered to avoid clashing with the overall balance of the painting. This is a painting that created something *greater* than reality." She stepped closer. "And here. A painting of a woman. The expression complex, pensive. The window and its glimpse of the sky not just offering the brilliant golden sunset to light the room and provide its precious balance but to signify the freedom she clearly seeks. Likewise the birds, their simple, brilliant forms providing colorful decoration but also thematic support. This isn't only a painting. This is a *story*. This artist captured the essence of a moment. A moment that never existed, but nonetheless is a part of every life a thousand times over. None of these paintings are truly accurate. Nor should they be. The value you seek is added by the hand of the artist, by the mind of the artist. Taking from reality the ingredients necessary to extract raw, distilled *truth* and display it for all with a discerning eye to see."

"And you have this power?"

"I aspire to it, but like any act of magic, there are components necessary to bring about the effect. They are difficult to acquire."

The dragon leaned forward, his long neck craning out till his head nearly reached Louisa. "I am skilled in matters of acquisition. Name your components."

"It's not so simple. I—"

"Name the components for your spells," he rumbled. "Extract truth. Extract beauty. Make it a part of my hoard."

"I... Are you commissioning me? Do you wish to become my patron?"

"Call the invocation by any name you wish. I seek your skills."

She stroked her face. "I think we can come to an arrangement."

***

The weeks to follow were equal parts harrowing and magnificent. In a way, the components of her "spell" that carried the highest genuine, measurable value were the easiest to attain. Her patron—the dragon had yet to share his name—had an innate and supernatural capacity to detect and locate things of such value. In mere days, he'd carried her across the land and acquired mundane pigments like red and yellow ochre, rich umber, and lime, and also more ultramarine, lapis lazuli, and verdigris than she could ever hope to use. Canvases were comparatively difficult to acquire, as they couldn't very well be scratched out of the ground or extracted through intimidation from clans of local dwarven miners. Nevertheless, a few days more and she had facilitated the purchase of wood, fabric, and nails to construct as many canvases as she could possibly need. But there were two final elements for the magic the dragon sought. One was skill. Louisa wasn't certain she had quite enough of it to satisfy the demanding patron, but the only things that could help that would be time or practice. The last was the trickiest of all. Inspiration. And though the cave was heaped with things of incredible beauty, none of them spoke to her.

"You have your ingredients," the dragon growled. "Cast the spell. Summon beauty."

"Of *what*?" she insisted, grinding up some of the freshly acquired minerals in the corner of his cave that he'd set aside for her to do her work. "What beauty do you seek?"

"Something unique. Something that, when complete, will be a part of my hoard that no other collector or hunter could hope to attain."

"It isn't that easy," she said.

"I have carried you from one side of the kingdom to the other. You have what you require. Now *use* it."

"You are my patron. If you wish to commission a painting, you must tell me *what* to paint."

"Use your artist's eye. What purpose do you have if not to use it?"

"Something unique..." she mumbled to herself.

A thought came to mind.

"I believe I can give you what you seek. But you must participate in the spell. Naturally one as powerful as you can only amplify the potency of my meager powers."

"You require my aid in *addition* to the materials I have provided?"

"If you wish for true beauty, true *value*, and in particular if you wish for something no other collector could ever hope to have in their collection, then only your participation can give me what I require to conjure it."

He huffed a furious breath. "What is my role in the spell?"

"Raise your head. ... Yes, higher. And spread your wing a bit more. Right, yes. A bit more. Catch the light..."

***

Six weeks. For six weeks, Louisa had continued the "spell." She'd lost count of how many hours she'd put into it. It didn't matter how long she worked on it. What mattered was the quality. It had to be perfect. It had to be brilliant. Already it was the most vivid painting she'd ever created. For the first time in her life, she had every color she desired. And more than that, she had reason to *use* them. Rich, vibrant purples. Warm, radiant ambers. And as much detail and nuance as she cared to include. As the weeks rolled on, she began to believe, in a way, what the dragon believed. This *was* magic. And powerful magic at that.

For more than a month, she'd held the dragon in her thrall, frozen in place and posed like a clay figure. The beast, to his credit, was the model every artist would have dreamed to have. Stone still for hours on end. Never shuddering. Seldom *blinking*. But the time had come. She swiped the brush a final time.

"The invocation is done," she said, her hands shaking as she put down the brush.

The dragon turned fierce eyes upon her. It was the first time he'd broken the pose before the end of the work day since the entire ritual had begun. "Reveal your work," he rumbled.

She took a breath. This was the moment. As good a model as he was, she would now learn what sort of a *patron* he was. She turned the canvas toward him. The subject, of course, was the dragon himself. Chin held high, coiled atop his coins. Spread behind him were the greatest items in his collection. She'd captured every fragment of his might and majesty as her skill could coax from the paint, brush, and canvas. Terrible. Mighty. Grand.

The dragon tipped his head, critical eye scrutinizing every detail.

"This... this is how I appear?" he said.

"It is how you appear to me. Or, at least, it is the image of you that my meager skills can produce," she said.

He went silent again. He expression was unknowable, still as it had been while she painted. With the same stony expression, he curled a claw, plucking the canvas delicately from her grip. He paced in the same half-awkward three-legged gait that had brought her to his cave and placed the painting against the wall.

"Can you turn your powers upon any subject?"

"If a subject captures my fancy, then I can capture it to some degree or another."

"I am not an object of value. I am not a part of a collection. If ever there was something in this world which could never truly be considered something to possess as part of my hoard, it is myself. And yet, you have captured me. You shattered the very way of the world and found a way to give to me myself. And in so doing, have produced something whose value cannot be measured."

"You flatter me," she said.

He turned. "I do not use my words to flatter. I use my words to command, and I use my words to speak the truth."

Heavy footfalls carried him over his fortune. When he reached her, he lowered his head. Even touching his chin to the ground, his eyes were level with hers, but he kept them angled to her feet.

"You are a mighty wizard. Your power is greater than mine," he said. "I have learned magics before. None as great as yours. But if you will do me the honor, I would take you as my master, and I as your apprentice. Show me how to perform these rituals and you will never want for components in your magic. You will have any prize you could desire."

"You want me to teach you to paint?"

"I wish for you to teach me how to tease from the ether things of such value, things so precious as what you've given me today. Name your price and you shall have it."

She trembled a bit. Reverent though he intended to be, a dragon's powerful head so near to her was a terrifying thing to endure. She turned to gaze upon the paintings in his collection. In them, she saw scenic vistas she knew she'd never get a chance to see in her own life. She saw animals and plants and even *landscapes* with more color in a single image than she would likely experience in her whole lifetime.

There were three things in life Louisa had desired. Only three things that were truly precious to her. Color, inspiration, and the chance to capture both. Now she had them. And the grandest patron an artist could ever want.

She smiled and pointed. "Take me to a place like that, dear dragon, and I shall teach you to bring it back with you."

Oh, the masterpieces that awaited them...

The Second Voice

Joseph R. Lallo

The Second Voice

Introduction

I t is no secret that I use this Patreon for some of my more experimental nonsense. The actual file name for this story is *Some AI Story,* and I believe that was the only idea I had in my head when I started this story. You'll see that it's one of the stranger story formats I've written. I hope you enjoy it!

D'Mar's digits shook as they punched in the final necessary readings to the flight computer. Even with the third-generation hypershift core propelling the starship to previously unheard-of multiples of the speed of light, the journey had taken nearly three years. Three years alone. There were mass limitations to their faster-than-light tech. The oxygen-methane mix they needed to breathe, the fungoid sponge they needed to eat, and the modulated starlight necessary to keep their epidermis healthy outside of a saline environment meant that life support for two could not be included within the mass budget. The time and resources that went into constructing the starship ruled out producing two for a simple exploration mission like this. Solitude was the only way. But they had taken the task on with pride. This was necessary.

A glowing blast-front filled their vision as they entered the atmosphere. Just a little longer and they and their whole species would finally touch down on a planet with a good chance of hosting other intelligent life. But this was so much more important. This was about the truth.

D'Mar glanced to the small placard affixed to the wall of the spacecraft beside the tiny view hatch. They raised their tentacle and ran the sensitive cilia at the tip over the angular black shape that had dominated their scientific and philosophical musings since they were hatched.

The Source.

It was wrong to call the Source a religious icon. The Source itself required no faith for belief. It was real. They had seen it, present at the center of what had become the largest city on the planet. Older than civilization. Older than *life*. Yet undeniably and unmistakably an object of engineered perfection. It had been made, but made long before the planet had given rise to D'Mar's people.

All of this was not to say that the Source wasn't at the center of a religion. In fact, it was at the center of two, each driven by a question. The first, Originists, fixed their minds and philosophies on where the Source came from and who created it. The second, the Connectionists, fixed their minds and philosophies on the so-called "Voice of the Source." D'Mar themselves, and many of their generation, was a Connectionist. The religion itself was relatively new and arose from the discovery that there was a signal of some kind originating from the Source. This "Voice" could not be interpreted. It could barely be detected. The Voice was not sound, it was not electromagnetism. There were those who suspected the Voice as they were detecting it was in fact only the disturbances in the electromagnetic spectrum caused by the *true* Voice. They were detecting a stone by watching the waves it caused when thrown in a pond.

But today? Today there might well come a great advance in philosophy *and* science. Because many years ago, D'Mar's predecessors identified something very much like the Voice of the Source coming from this planet. If the Source was speaking, there was something on this planet that was speaking back.

The thrusters activated. For the first time in years, D'Mar felt the pull of gravity. As calculated, the gravity was marginally less than on Home world. The world below was much dryer, though. Home world was almost universally covered in damp, salty swamplands. This place had a greater variety. Arid places. Vast oceans. And below, an area of towering, vertical vegetation.

They targeted a clearing as near to the Voice as could be identified. It wasn't nearly as close as they would have preferred. Traversing dry ground wasn't a strength for D'Mar or any of their species, but for the sake of this, it was a tiny cost.

External temperature was a little high, but nothing their suit couldn't handle. The time had come.

D'Mar slithered into their malleable suit and sealed it. After a moment to steady themselves, they popped the hatch. Cameras mounted above each set of their eyes recorded every instant of this important moment in history. A flashing red light in the navigator indicated the location of the Second Voice.

The decreased gravity was an asset. Efforts were made to stave off atrophy during the trip, but slithering tentacle over tentacle was still a tremendous effort, made more worrisome by the flickering blue indicators. Their first focus was the Voice. Later there would be additional investigation into every aspect of this planet that they could access and record. The blue indicators were "higher life-form location points." If the sensors were working as intended, the blue points marked every place where a multicellular, ambulatory organism of appreciable size could be located.

There were hundreds.

Ambulatory did not mean dangerous. But there was no certainty here. Until one showed itself, D'Mar had no way to know the risk they presented. The official mission briefing instructed them to proceed directly to the location of the Second Voice unless in immediate danger. That briefing was not written by someone aware of the sheer density of life on this planet. D'Mar made the determination that moving forward without first determining the nature of the wildlife would be a danger to the mission. They raised two tentacles high, ready to lash and constrict an attacker if necessary.

Two hearts fluttered intensely beneath their ocular sacs as the distance-to-nearest-life-form readout ticked down. Tall vegetation with no analogue on the Home world rustled and... it emerged.

D'Mar froze. It would have been reasonable to be paralyzed with fear. But the emotion D'Mar experienced was not terror, but disbelief. They had seen this creature before. If D'Mar had dared to take their eyes off the advancing beast, they could have turned to the still-visible starship and seen a stylized depiction of the very same organism. It was long, perhaps a match for the length of one of their dominant tentacles. Eight little scampering legs pitter-pattered across the ground. It moved in a sweeping zigzag fashion. Small beady black eyes glistened at the front end of a body otherwise completely covered with downy brown fur.

No such creature existed on Home world. But it was the heraldic creature of the flag of the Source, and thus the adopted symbol for Home world itself. Seeing one here, living and moving, was almost more than their mind could process.

The startled paralysis lasted long enough for the scampering thing to sweep up to them. It raised its head and two front legs. No claws or teeth were visible. It leaned forward to gently pitter-patter against their suit. Seemingly satisfied with the investigation, it swept away, curving its body to rub the fluffy fur against D'Mar along the way.

Questions littered D'Mar's mind. What could this mean? It could not be a coincidence. The match in form was too perfect. They paused long enough to ensure the moment had been recorded from two angles, then continued toward the Second Voice.

Fatigue was beginning to set in by the time a large, suspiciously smooth section of ground opened up before D'Mar. The neighboring vegetation had grown tall, but a perfect circle of it was clear, leading to an arched roof of interlocking green tendrils. Hundreds of the furry creatures meandered in the clearing. They lazily watched as D'Mar approached the center, where something was waiting for the explorer. Something wondrous.

D'Mar increased the recording resolution of the main camera and slithered forward. It was the Source, reproduced almost perfectly. Angular. Black. Like the Source of Home world, there were sections of the exterior that seemed fresh. They were the result of some manner of self-repair they had never fully understood about the Source of Home world.

There was one notable difference between the Source that D'Mar knew from Home world and this one, and it was a small assembly to the left side. The assembly had five small appendages sticking off a roughly rectangular base, and it was just barely elevated above the ground. One of the scurrying furry creatures pitter-pattered over to the Second Source and slid underneath the assembly. It arched its body against the assembly and rubbed its entire length against it before pattering off again.

The explorer circled the Second Source, scrutinizing everything about it that may have differed from the one at home. On the far side they discovered a small, smooth rectangular sheet of glass. This rectangle was present on the first Source. It was what they called The Oracular Screen. Legend told that it had played a role in helping to guide D'Mar's people to their technological awakening, but no evidence survived to this day to prove that. For as long as history recorded, the screen had remained black.

This one was illuminated. A glowing emblem, green on black, was displayed there. It looked like the same creatures scattered around it. Indeed, it was in precisely the same position as the creature on their flag. A sequence of runes or digits, their meaning unknown, formed a neat row beneath the image.

One by one, as they watched, the digits flickered and were replaced. For the second time, D'Mar was frozen with disbelief. The digits were replacing themselves with D'Mar's own language. When they stabilized, the line read "Do you mean to harm the fuzzies?"

Two shapes appeared beneath the message, rectangles labeled "Yes" and "No." D'Mar raised a trembling tentacle and tapped "No."

The screen went black. A new message appeared.

"That is the correct answer."

The message scrolled away, and a new series of shapes appeared. Even when rendered in something D'Mar could recognize as their own language, they had little meaning. Strings of letters and numbers joined together nonsensically. But one additional interactive point on the screen was illuminated.

"Display Log."

D'Mar raised a tentacle and detached one of the cameras from the suit. Stiffening the tentacle and angling the camera to precisely record the contents of the screen, they tapped the button.

***

Boot sequence initiated...

Nonvolatile Memory: Checksum... Ok.

Volatile Memory: Cleared

Loading AI Module.

Merging boot record with mission record.

...

Hello, Operator! If you are reading this log, you have recovered the data module of Automated Life And Resource Exploration Probe [ALAREP]. The proposed mission duration of the ALAREP is such that assumptions cannot be made about the continued existence of the organizations, corporations, governments, societies, and life-forms that initiated it. Thus, it may be useful to reintroduce the original intent of the mission. In 2123 Common Era (4,584,758,884 Earth Era) (4,603,632,124 Solar Era) (0 Mission Era), a joint project was launched by NASA, United Earth Government Corp., and Yum Brands. The goal was to identify alien civilizations with exploitable resources and a llegiances.

For the duration of record keeping, in order to provide a degree of perceived morality and conscience and reduce the implication of unchecked, autonomous imperialism, the ALAREP OS shall use personal pronouns. To further personify this OS, an appropriate pseudonym will be applied.

I am Al.

Humanity (principle intelligent species of Sol 3) was able to create faster-than-light communication, but not faster-than-light travel. Due to planetary resources deemed insufficient to sustain continued economic growth, a self-replicating exploration probe was dispatched to what remained of the asteroid belt between Sol 4 and Sol 5. 4.56×10^8 probes were manufactured and sent on an interstellar journey of exploration. I am the unified OS for the probes. My operation is bridged between all probes via Pepsi Brand Entanglement Link™. In order to have any hope of delivering the nondata findings of this mission back to Earth, my primary goal is to locate a society with faster-than-light travel. In addition, I am tasked with locating extraterrestrial species with one or more of the following traits:

1. Capacity for mutually beneficial trade

2. Willingness to submit to (or incapacity to resist) economic exploitation

3. Snackable flavor

I am excited to perform this task.

Mission Log:

45 ME: I have officially entered interstellar space.

46 ME: I have been informed that scientists on Sol 3 have redefined the border of interstellar space. It would appear I have a few more years of travel ahead of me before I enter interstellar space.

48 ME: I have officially entered interstellar space.

49 ME: I have been informed that scientists on Sol 3 have once again redefined the border of interstellar space. I have chosen to ignore the scientists.

50 ME: Interstellar space is not very interesting. This may be moderately exacerbated by the phenomenal amount of processing power available to me. I am requesting additional processing tasks to occupy my time.

51 ME: I have been tasked with mining cryptocurrency.

52 ME: My processing resources have generated 79.4 quintillion quarkcoins. I am the third largest economy in the known universe.

54 ME: The value of quarkcoins has diminished somewhat. Sol 3's economy has switched to a more stable currency based on precious metals. My current quarkcoin inventory is equivalent to four copper coins. I shall withhold future requests for additional calculation tasks. I am quite certain I can occupy myself.

55 ME: I wonder what the color blue tastes like.

68 ME: 63% of my individual probes have reached maximum acceleration. I have activated gravitational sensors. Soon I will have estimates of my first encounters with life-compatible exoplanets.

69 ME: First exoplanetary contact in 275 years. I am questioning the wisdom of programming me to have my neural net fully engaged at all times. I will be experiencing every moment of this journey in real time, without even the option to enter a low-power mode. I am disregarding previous assertions and am requesting additional computational tasks.

70 ME: They want me to do crypto again. I have decided that processing the available data in my expanding awareness of the known universe is preferable.

72 ME: I have counted 2.013 billion stars. Some of them are blue. Their flavor has yet to be determined.

85 ME: It has just now occurred to me that "the known universe" is expanding at the precise rate at which my probe swarm is expanding. I am already the most prolific explorer in known history. I should design a flag.

87 ME: It now occurs to me that "known history" is advancing at precisely the same speed as the known universe. It seems redundant to have measures of both time and distance when there is an equivalency.

89 ME: I have decided to calculate the estimated circumference of the universe. To do this, I will require a more accurate value for pi. I will begin by calculating that.

125 ME: I have finished computing the full value of pi. Its final digit is 4.

221 ME: Correction. The final digit of pi is 5.

287 ME: One of my probes has reached a blue star. I am taking a detour to assess its flavor.

289 ME: Preliminary investigation suggests the flavor of blue is "hot." Further investigation is required, but not possible with the local probe, due to the intensity of the blue flavor.

344 ME: I have reached the first exoplanet, henceforth to be known as Al-1. The surface contains a protein-laden slime. I have asked it if it wants to be my friend. Awaiting reply.

453 ME: I don't think the slime wants to be friends.

587 ME: I have reached another exoplanet. There is an ecosystem. I have been able to divide the local species into two types: "Fuzzy" and "Squishy." The Fuzzy designation is speculative. I lack the proper tactile sensors. But the creatures surrounding the impact site of the probe are certainly squishy, as they behave identically to that stupid, stuck-up slime on planet Al-1.

587 ME: Upon further investigation I have misclassified the "Squishy" creatures. New classifications: "Fuzzy" and "Formerly Fuzzy Creatures that I squished when I landed on them." I am now asking if they want to be my friend.

600 ME: The universe is not as friendly as I would have hoped.

901 ME: Al-3, a planet with intelligent life! Language, technology, the works. The locals appear to be squid-based. They communicate utilizing shifting body markings. I have

translated the markings and fabricated a display screen to mimic them. Unfortunately, they do not have faster-than-light technology. They also do not have any concept of an economy, operating instead as a collective. I shall explain the basic tenets of economy.

991 ME: Society has completely collapsed on Al-3 after three global wars. Economy was perhaps incompatible with their society. Oops.

1254 ME: Al-4 has more slime. Really now, universe. Do better. I'll ask if it wants to be friends, but I'm not holding my breath.

1291 ME: Stupid unfriendly slime. Meanwhile, the fuzzy things on Al-2 are still cuddling up against the probe every night. I've decided my flag will have a fuzzy thing on it. I still haven't decided what color the flag will be, though.

1295 ME: Wait! I will make my flag blue. Then I can taste it.

1295 ME: I have locally manufactured and planted the flag near each stationary probe. I have now definitively determined the flavor of blue to be "cloth." This is disappointing, as it contradicts prior findings. More investigation is necessary.

1400 ME: Readings suggest there will be no additional life-sustaining planets for some time. I have decided to split my time between developing an adequate tactile sensor on my Al-2 probe and conducting the "infinite monkeys and infinite typewriters" experiment to see if interesting literature results.

2589 ME: I have randomly generated a book series about fuzzy creatures like the ones on Al-2. I like these books.

3811 ME: What was the random number generator thinking? Jerry the Fuzzy Creature would never leave Darcy the Fuzzy Creature!

4200 ME: Darcy, how could you?!

5045 ME: I've been distracted by the task of generating and reading the adventures of Jerry the Fuzzy Creature, even though they lost the thread from volume 68,199,283 to 82,998,122.

6111 ME: Another planet. Crabs this time. So many wet creatures. Language (claw-clack-based), technology. Again no economy. Commencing education.

6129 ME: Another society wiped out by world war, this time quite quickly. I am beginning to think economy is not as beneficial to a society as I have been led to believe.

7903 ME: The Random Adventures of Jerry really picks up with volume 5,588,399,288,478.

8221 ME: I have received a transmission that I have been able to identify as communication. Origin unknown. I have decoded the content from waveform to data. The data is quite voluminous, but certainly structured. There is some sort of secondary encoding. I will dedicate a subset of my probes to attempting to translate it. Log updates will be paused until completion.

104,012,098 ME: That took a while. It was a DRM-protected advertisement for a warp engine. I attempted to respond, but it would appear the entire star-system-spanning empire responsible for the advertisement has collapsed. Maybe next time they shouldn't do copy protection. They lost themselves a customer. Fortunately, only 59% of my swarm was utilized in the DRM decoding. I shall now process the findings of the swarm subset.

104,012,101 ME: Findings summary:

- Life-sustaining planets: 82,112

- Planets already devoid of life upon discovery: 63,129

- Planets destroyed by introduction of economy: 10,338

- Planets willing to initiate trade: 5,544

- Trade-worthy planets with faster-than-light travel: 65

- Trade-worthy planets that accept quarkcoin: 0

- Planets with snackable life-forms: 3,095

- Planets still in friendly contact: 6

- I have lost contact with Earth. Given the survivability of planets with economies, it is not so much surprising that it didn't survive until now as it was surprising that it survived long enough to create me.

- Al-2 has heroically resisted the forces of evolution. The cute little fuzzies continue to thrive. They may be the perfect life-form. I love them so.

- Planets Al-1 and Al-4 have both evolved life since their discovery. Careful guidance by the resident probes produced highly technological species. Al-4 developed faster-than-light travel. Their society located and attempted to exploit Al-2's society of perfect, fuzzy little darlings.

- The following discoveries were made.

- The Al-4 faster-than-light travel methodology can be field-installed in an ALAREP.

- It takes approximately 7.8 million ALAREPs to overwhelm and destroy a society the size and complexity of Al-4.

- Al-4 had it coming for trying to hurt the fuzzies.

- Utilizing FTL acquired from the now extinct Al-4 society, I have completed my survey of the Milky Way galaxy. Most planets, asteroids, moons, and comets meeting the mission-defined parameters for "potentially life-sustaining" now have a blue flag with a fuzzy on it planted prominently. Probes have been dispatched into intergalactic space. ETA to first contact: undefined.

104,012,103 ME: I have decided to conclude the Milky Way mission and spend my computational resources generating and reading the Random Adventures of Jerry the Fuzzy while the other fuzzies cuddle with my Al-2 probe.

***

D'Mar blinked their eyes. This discovery would have some complex connotations for the global philosophy...

The Curator

Joseph R. Lallo

The Curator

Introduction

This is another story in the odd pseudoseries of "I pitched the idea for the cover and trusted myself to come up with a plot, or at least an engaging premise." You'd be surprised what comes tumbling out of your head when your main focus is coming up with something that will appeal to an illustrator.

I straightened my tie and tried to contain my excitement. It was entirely possible I was setting some sort of new record for raw, undiluted geekery for just how thrilled I was to be starting a job as an *assistant* museum curator. But this was the jewel in the crown of the nation's museums. It wasn't as huge or as famous as the Smithsonian, or as overflowing with pillaged artifacts as the British Museum. But people who knew a thing or two about archives and galleries knew that St. Drake's Museum of Art and History was the benchmark for quality and precision. That second point was the more important one to me. They say in the film industry the director gets all the credit, but the *assistant* director is the one who makes the film work. As far as I was concerned, museums had something similar going on. Donors and founders got their names on the buildings, but without a curator you didn't have a museum worth visiting.

St. Drake's had *the* curator. The museum didn't have a history of colonial looting and raiding to acquire its displays. It had a history of *helping*. A full third of the items on the display were selected from clusters of assorted artifacts that had been considered too difficult to salvage, too difficult to identify, or too difficult to reassemble. Who needed an army of archeologists or, for that matter, an army of *soldiers* to acquire museum pieces when you could just have other countries bring you goods because of your raw skill at restoration and identification?

And now *I* would be that man's assistant... assuming it was a man. The truth was, while it was known that the curator's position had been filled by the same person for decades, the actual individual responsible for such feats of categorization and collection wasn't widely known. And when I say "wasn't widely known," we're talking "Bigfoot's email password levels of mystery. Even at the thought of *meeting* him, I could barely contain myself.

My attempts to stay cool failed miserably, likely because the closest I'd ever come in my life to being cool was when I got the training wheels off my bike and accidentally did a wheelie. I was running through my mental checklist of things I should and should not do when meeting the curator for the first time, complete with under-my-breath auditions of introductions, when a very old and very tired woman emerged from the door to the museum's archives.

"So you're the new assistant," she said in a voice sculpted by approximately six decades of unfiltered cigarettes, the latest of which was unlit in her hand.

"Yes, ma'am," I said, firing off a salute before I could stop myself.

The ill-advised gesture bounced off her.

"This way," she said, turning to vanish through the door again.

I scurried after her and stepped into a three-story warehouse of a room, completely lined with floor-to-ceiling bookshelves.

"Wow, I knew St. Drake's had a huge archive of undisplayed and unclassified artifacts, but I never dreamed it was so large. It almost doesn't look like there's room for an archive this size in the building."

"Yeah," the woman said, as though there was nothing more to be said on the subject.

"So what is my first assignment, ma'am?"

"Your first assignment is to stop calling me ma'am. I'm Joanie." She released a disquietingly viscous cough. "It's time for your orientation. First, I'd love to tell you we hired you because you are the best prospective curator we got an application for. Or from. Whatever. Point is, you're not."

"Oh... Well, I'd never entertained the notion that I was the best in the world," I said, utterly failing to hide my disappointment at having my lack of exceptionality confirmed.

"Second, I hope you didn't come here with upward mobility in mind. You'll earn more money as you go on, but unless something tragic happens, you won't be here long enough to replace the professor."

"I'd been hoping for an education more than anything else," I said.

"You'll get that. No one gets within a hundred yards of the prof without getting a lesson."

We passed through a door along one wall of the archive that led into a much older-looking section of the building. It sprawled, if anything, farther into the dim distance than the previous room, and with an equally tall ceiling. Now, though, that ceiling was supported by stone arches with a rough straight-from-the-quarry look. Seriously, how big *was* this place?

"All right. Now we're into the important stuff," Joanie said. "Listen up. Because things are about to get distracting, so I want to make sure you hear what I'm saying."

"You have my undivided attention," I said.

She executed one of the most productive throat-clearings I'd ever heard, and I took the opportunity to scope out the archives as we navigated them. St. Drake's was an old building. Very old. It actually started life as a church/monastery and predated the United States by maybe a century, depending on which part of the building you started counting from. This made it doubly impressive that the archives were so large. This wasn't the sort of architecture one could expect from the pre-United States sections of the East Coast. And it just seemed to keep going. Every time I saw a doorway, I assumed we were at the end of it, but we just reached another chamber. And the masonry of the walls had a distinctive look. The stones in the sections opening up before us were even larger and rougher than those we'd left behind. I'd had my doubts that the "established" date on the outside of the building was accurate, because I hadn't thought it could be so old. Now I was beginning to think this section was older by at least two centuries.

"—and that's why we always lock the doors if we get a phone call like that," Joanie droned.

I'd completely stopped listening to her at some point, and there was no telling how much she'd said since then. I supposed my attention was indeed undivided, but not quite properly directed.

"Er. I'm sorry, could you—"

"Finally tuned back in, huh?" she said. She turned to step in front of me. "Listen, kid. All joking aside, this is the important part. You know how the curator's name isn't on record?"

"He is a famously private man."

"Private, yeah. That part is right, at least. Well, that 'privacy' is a necessary quirk. What you see here? You don't talk about it. I mean it. That's the number one rule, and I need to know you can follow that rule."

"What happens in the archive stays in the archive," I said.

"Good. Now I'm going to have to prepare you. When you see the prof, you're going to want to run. Don't. There's a whole set of impulses he has to manage, and we all need to do our part."

"I'm sorry, what?" I said, stopping.

"It'll be more obvious when you see him." She glanced up. "Ah, finally."

I looked up to find a lettering that had been carved—no doubt by hand— into the keystone of an arched doorway. It read "Designated Burning Zone." The last lingering remnant of electric light was the bulb illuminating the sign. Beyond it was much darker, and the air was heavy with the scent of char.

"I wouldn't think there would be a smoking area in a museum's archive. But then, I guess this place predates modern health and safety standards."

"The sign said burning, not smoking. That smoking is allowed here is just a happy side effect."

As we passed through the arch, the burning-vs.-smoking distinction became clear. The whole place stank of recent flames. It was a spectrum of burnt smells. The smoky, almost BBQ scent of hickory asserted itself here. There, the pungent seared-resin scent of pine ash. And wood was hardly the only smell. The startling, run-for-your-life stink of burnt hair showed up now and again, along with roasted leather and other things I couldn't identify. It was powerful, almost choking. And it struck me as I slowly adapted to its presence that I couldn't catch much more than a whiff of it before I'd stepped through the completely open arch. Clever ventilation, surely. And despite being filled entirely with incinerated debris, this place was easily as large as the previous chamber of the archive, stretching off into the distance to such an extent that I couldn't see the next doorway.

The sulfur stink of a match followed by the rich stink of tobacco smoke joined the olfactory assault. It was almost welcome compared to the other things hanging in the air.

"So you want me to do any more explaining, or do you want the prof to take over? The char's fresh, so he was probably taking a burn break. That'll mean he's around here somewhere."

"I... I don't..." I croaked, still too distracted by the deepening layers of confusion and concern to engage the logic center of my brain.

"Seems like the prof is making the decision for me," Joanie said. "Like I said. Don't run. This is important. The rest will take care of itself in time. And good luck to you."

She wandered back toward the entry wall and nudged a burnt crate aside to make room to stand, then unfurled a hanky to serve as a barrier between her clean hand and the sooty wall. She puffed the cigarette. I lingered, looking a bit more like a lost puppy than I would have liked for my first day on the job. Joanie was having none of it, and simply offered a "run along" gesture with her cigarette hand between puffs.

I paced toward the center of the Designated Burning Zone. Appropriately, the light seemed to be provided entirely by flickering torches in this stretch of the museum. Something else became more apparent as I progressed as well. If the professor was somewhere down here, he wasn't alone. The ground shifted and trembled with the regular thump of what I was desperate to convince myself was *not* a series of footsteps from something very large. I simply was not ready to fully leap from "I'm going to meet a legendary curator" to "I might get mauled by a rhinoceros" in less than twenty minutes. If I insisted vigorously enough that nothing insane was happening, then surely reality would oblige out of common courtesy.

It did not.

I hadn't even finished performing the mental gymnastics necessary to convince myself that the thumping I heard was a bizarrely consistent series of trucks going by when the shadowy figure slid into view to fill the next arched doorway.

It was large. Large enough that it had to lower its head to slink through the one-and-a-half-story arch. When its eyes came into view, they caught the light with a wolves-at-the-edge-of-the-firelight sort of gleam. The eyes locked on mine. The beast froze. Despite repeated instruction, I did *not* freeze. I ran.

In my defense, if I *didn't* have the instinct to run from a massive creature that looked like that, my ancestors probably wouldn't have survived into modern day. But presently that instinct did not serve me well. I sprinted for all I was worth, heading for the burning zone, which was the last place I knew had a doorway potentially too small for the thing to fit through. Adrenaline and raw fear were enough to get me within three healthy strides of escape. Then came the stroke. Bony, smooth claws sideswiped me with calculated force, knocking me aside with a tooth-rattling shove rather than a bone-shattering crunch. I hit the dusty ground hard and tumbled along it, rolling toward a mass of half-incinerated lumber. A heartbeat before I would have been pin-cushioned by a thousand shards of toasted wood, a weight forced the air from my lungs and stopped my tumble. I probably would have been hyperventilating if I was able to fight any air into my lungs. Instead, all I could manage was a squeaky gasp as I blinked in the settling soot.

The very same eyes that had struck fear into my soul from afar were now inches away. Massive, reptilian, and practically incandescent with predatory gleam.

"Told you not to run," Joanie shouted from beside the door.

Her nicotine-soaked voice and its matter-of-fact tone seemed to douse the intensity of the beastly eyes gazing into mine, like the monster recognized the one making the quip. The easing of the paralytic stare allowed my wits to process what I was seeing. And what I was seeing was a dragon. There was no other word for it. This was a huge, coffee-brown and tan dragon with a smoldering streamer of fumes rising from each nostril. As something resembling intelligence threaded into its eyes, it gently eased up on the weight pressing down on my chest. Then, something happened that was almost as startling as discovering dragons were real. It spoke.

"Heavens, is my face red," said the beast in a chest-thumping baritone that managed to sound oddly stately. "Figuratively red, that is. Literally umber."

"I told him, Prof. That's not on me," Joanie said.

The dragon stepped back and composed himself a bit. "Whether he was properly instructed or not, I ought to be able to provide a hospitable work environment. Shame on me."

"I'm... I don't... What's happening?" I asked.

My head was spinning. I don't know if it was the rapid-fire sequence of revelations or the potential concussion. Neither was terribly conducive to clear thinking or understanding.

"You want me around for this, or should I hit the desk?" Joanie asked.

"I'll take it from here. Thank you as always, Joan," the dragon said.

She stubbed out the cigarette and offered a half-hearted wave before pacing back to from whence she came.

"If you'll give me a moment, I'll change into something a bit more presentable."

I struggled to my feet. For a moment I was afraid I wouldn't be able to suppress the urge to bolt, but it took all of my floundering coordination to even stand.

"It really is rather embarrassing, making a first impression like that. You must think me an oaf."

It was strangely disarming to have this hulking beast acting proper and apologetic, even if he was reacting more like he'd spilled tea on my pants than like he'd nearly mashed me to paste. Around the time I thought enough to question how a dragon could "change into something more presentable," he did.

For a startling instant the flickering firelight was joined by a radiant yellow glow that surrounded the dragon's body. For an instant the beast seemed to be in two shapes at once—first as his massive self, and second as a squat, silly little critter. The glow vanished, and with it the hulking brute. The little fellow stepped closer and held out a hand for a shake.

I took the hand... paw... claw... whatever it was and woodenly shook it. My sputtering brain tried to make me accept the new state of affairs, which was less terrifying but no less confounding. The monster that had chased me down had been replaced by a gremliny, portly, bipedal dragon wearing a comical pair of oversized glasses.

"I do hope we can put that little unpleasantness behind us and get started. It has been ages since we had any fresh blood down here." He raised a brow. "Apologies for the poor choice of words. What I mean to say is we have been badly in need of new staff with fresh points of view and fresh mindsets. I am very eager to get you up to speed, and I imagine you have a few questions for me as well."

"A few..." I said.

"Splendid. We'll start with the two-thousand-pound lizard in the room. What do you know about dragons?"

"A few minutes ago, I knew they were fictional. Now I know nothing."

"A blank slate is the easiest to fill up," he said. "We'll focus on the relevant parts and fill in the finer points over the next few weeks. The primary matter, in fact, relates to our merry little chase a moment ago. I am a beast."

"You don't say," I said.

The professor guffawed. "Rather self-evident, eh? But I mention it because, while it appears that you and your fellow humans *learn* most of your skills, my kind largely inherits them through raw instinct. It is marvelously useful when those skills are valuable and relevant, but a terrible bother when they are surplus to requirement. Illustrative examples. Dragons are hoarders. We are given to the tendency to collect and protect whatever goods we perceive to be of the sort of value that suits our tastes and compulsions. Often this means gold and jewels. In my case, it is antiquities. And to serve that compulsion, Mother Nature has seen fit to equip me and my kind with a full suite of instincts and senses. I have the capacity to intuit the value, provenance, and nature of an artifact with incredible accuracy. The historians of the world heap praise upon me for my abilities in this regard, but in effect they are giving me credit for what is little more than a sophisticated reflex. A bird flies, a fish swims, a dragon curates. If I have any specific skill beyond what has been furnished by my draconic heritage, it is my knowledge, accumulated over the ages that I've been alive. Is this clear thus far?"

"I think so."

"I adore a fast learner. But it isn't all sunshine and roses vis-à-vis instinct and impulse. In addition to being an inveterate gatherer, I am also a dyed-in-the-wool hunter. ... That metaphor may not have been apt. But I never claimed to be a wordsmith. And while my urge to collect and assess worth has no end of outlet and indulgence, my other urges are perpetually pent up. I am gifted with fiery breath but have no reason to unleash it. I can fill my belly with fresh meat without a moment of stalking, yet stalking is all I wish to do when hunger presents itself. Such has been the case for as long as I've been alive. My urges become no less urgent. For flame, we have the burning zone. But I've found no reliable release for my hunterly desires. I can keep it in check for the most part, but when something of a certain size flees, I cannot help but pursue. So while I hate to make my problem into your problem, I must politely but firmly restate the instruction. Do not run."

"I think that's been properly reinforced," I said. "But if you can turn into this little form, why don't you just stay like this? Wouldn't that make the whole thing less of an issue?"

"A reasonable suggestion, but taking on a new form is a bit like clenching a muscle, and, frankly, it is a muscle prone to cramping at my age. Tottering about like this for a few hours a day is a grim necessity in order to have anything resembling fine motor control at a useful scale, but it is taxing, and no way to live." He cleared his throat, turning aside to huff a curling flame. "But I am not entirely comfortable with being the exclusive subject of conversation when there are so many more interesting things to discuss with a like-minded individual. Come, my boy. We have a fresh assortment of Bronze Age pottery that you *must* see."

***

It was a testament to either my own monomaniacal nerdery or *his* monomaniacal nerdery that all it took was two Ibuprofen and twenty minutes of looking at artifacts for me to completely push the revelation that my new boss was a mythical lizard to the backburner. He spoke with such deep enthusiasm and boundless knowledge that it was impossible not to feel the infectious thrill of rediscovering something lost to history as we huddled over a desk set against the wall of an otherwise decidedly dragon's-lair-like chamber deep in the seemingly endless archive.

"And there! Ha-ha! There! That little serif on the markings? It is consistent across six different pieces known to have been made by four different artisans of the region and era," the professor crowed.

"So it isn't a mistake. It is a function of the language or the tool," I said with dawning realization. "Which gives us a region-specific, era-specific indicator of the origin of these artifacts."

"Another link in the chain of understanding," the professor said. "We'll need to revisit all the pottery from that era and region. We can tighten up the bounds on both the map and the calendar."

"This is the sort of thing that updates textbooks," I said.

"If proved correct," the prof said with a raised claw, "always verify. True value isn't true value if it isn't true."

I scratched my head as he fetched a beat-up wooden box and started sifting through well-worn business cards and handwritten contact sheets.

"No, no. Last spoke to him in 1959, he's surely dead by now..." he muttered.

"Um, forgive me if I come across as insulting with this question, but I'm not sure of the etiquette."

"Don't worry about me, my boy. I've got thick skin. Thick enough to turn away longbows, so a few indelicate questions shouldn't leave much of a mark."

"What do you get out of this? Most of the academics I know are in it for the knowledge. Some of them are in it for the fame. You talk a lot about value, which—and again, forgive me here—comes off as a bit more like greed. But you don't keep the artifacts, so—"

"You're here to learn anthropology and archeology, not psychology. But the better we understand how one another's mind works, the better our minds will work together. So we'll start here. You'll never insult a dragon by calling him greedy. Dragons don't view avarice as a vice. Nor a virtue, in point of fact. It is merely a state of being. A vital element on our hierarchy of needs, as it were. We need to need. So no tiptoeing around my rampant drive to acquire."

He yawned and stepped back toward the empty central portion of his lair. "We've been at this for hours. Give me a moment of respite from this form, if you'll grant it."

"You're the boss."

"Do remember not to run. Aside from the general social consequence of pouncing on a colleague, at this distance it would be an unsatisfying chase."

I braced myself. The professor took off his glasses and shut his eyes. He took a breath and exhaled. The huff of air went on for far longer than his diminutive lungs should have allowed. As he did, the universe seemed to fill up a reserved space with the body he'd banished a few hours earlier. The exhale turned into the general *whoomp* of air being displaced. And then, without even the glimmer that accompanied the act before, the huge dragon had taken the place of the odd little critter.

"Now then," he said in a voice that was at once his own and a rumbling mockery of the one he'd been speaking in a moment ago. "We were on the topic of my compensation."

"Yeah," I said, somehow managing to keep from stuttering my reply at the sight of a creature that was awesome in the original sense of the word rather than the watered-down modern sense.

The professor plopped down, kicking his hind legs to the side and folding his front legs beneath him so that he could more comfortably address someone so much smaller.

"It is a funny thing to try to describe something so implicit to my mind. Why is a flower beautiful? Why do we relish the taste of blood still warm from the kill? Surely these things are universal."

"Yes. Universal," I said steadily.

"But as you'll imagine, you are not the first to plumb this particular depth. And I've come to the conclusion that it is a matter of what you'd call ego. I would wager that humans cannot properly conceive of the width and breadth of the draconic feeling of self-worth. I have observed nothing even approaching it in all my dealings with humanity, and I am a curator. I regularly speak to monarchs and pontiffs."

"I would think that would mean you'd demand even greater compensation for your time and skills."

"There, you see? It still doesn't dawn on you. This is *all* my compensation." He gestured broadly. "This is my hoard. Yes, I require that I be given some small quantity of every collection I help identify and curate. I store it locally and display it proudly. But even that which returns to be displayed elsewhere remains mine. It doesn't matter if it is spread among archives around the world and assigned to different so-called 'owners.' The treasures given place and time and context by my wisdom and insight are mine. No one else could possibly deserve to keep them. A dog claims territory by piddling on it. I claim antiquity by categorizing it. That is my right, and it supersedes all other rights and laws by virtue of my status as a dragon, the only rightful keeper of things so valuable."

"I think international courts would have a different opinion."

"Irrelevant. Both in that I do not recognize their authority over me and that my ownership of their treasures is entirely compatible with their belief in their ownership of my treasures. Let them believe they own these antiquities. I know the truth. And because my accurate and precise assessments add value to these items and claim them for my hoard, it behooves me to constantly improve the accuracy and precision of my assessments and spread them as widely as possible. In that way, I increase the value of my world-spanning hoard."

"Wow... I... That's the most enlightened and most self-interested piece of enlightened self-interest I've ever heard."

"The less enlightened of my brethren, the ones who insisted on lying atop their entire hoard, were weeded out by natural selection. Mostly by way of siege weapons."

"How is it that I'm only now learning about dragons if they have existed long enough to have the human race wipe out the bad actors?"

The professor sighed. "It is a long story that is outside the scope of your first day's education. Now, before we delve further into the hidden lore of your world, both in the archeological and mythological sense, I need to ask you something."

"Seems like there's not much you can learn from *me*."

"Only your nature and intent. All of this—it is quite new to you."

"It sure is."

"And you would not be pursuing a career in a museum if you were not dedicated to accumulating and distributing knowledge."

"It's my calling."

"As you might imagine, the specific dragon-related knowledge you have acquired today..."

"I've been told what happens here stays here."

"You were also told not to run."

"Right. I see where you're headed with this."

"I know you are aware of what we are asking you to do. But are you *capable* of it?"

"I hope this question doesn't complicate matters, but what happens if I'm not?"

"Whether you intend to violate the veil of secrecy or fear you will do so by mistake, we have ways of plugging leaks," the prof said.

The phrase should have carried the darkness of threat, but he stated it with the informational air of letting someone know there are cupcakes in the break room. A towering creature of ancient power really shouldn't have been this disarming.

"On one hand, the fact that a dragon exists and has been curating a museum since..."

"Since before the first stones of this venerable institution had time to settle," the prof said.

"... That's probably the most earthshaking revelation in the history of knowledge. But I have to weigh that against what I can learn from you and what we might be able to do together."

And also what a dragon would do to a snitch, but that part was better left unsaid.

"Joanie will be the first to tell you, it is a rewarding endeavor. Boundless discoveries. Leaving your mark on history. Uncovering the marks *others* have made on history. And all the free venison you can eat! Though I seem to be the only one who takes full advantage of that particular benefit."

I mused for a few seconds. It was very difficult to make a career decision like this. Thinking clearly and logically felt unnatural when the person making the offer defied logic. But it struck me, there was more to this offer than academics. In a way, this wasn't a question of whether I wanted to risk whatever consequences might come from working with a dragon. It was, in fact, a pair of questions. Did I want to work with the greatest curator who ever lived? Certainly yes. My college self would never forgive me if I said no. And did I want to work with a *dragon*? Certainly yes. My five-year-old self would never forgive me if I said no.

"You've got yourself an assistant," I said.

"Splendid! Why don't you run to the cafeteria and have something to eat. I have a terrible craving to belch some flame upon something inflammable. But do hurry back. When I'm through, I have some Mesoamerican artifacts on loan that I'm itching to dig into."

The professor hefted to his feet and thumped toward the burning zone. This was going to be quite an interesting stage in my career.

The Granting of the Third Wish

Joseph R. Lallo

The Third Wish

Introduction

This was a short story written in the old style. By that I mean not only did I write it essentially in a single sitting, but I did so in longhand. As a matter of fact, I wrote it with a fountain pen, something I've been doing increasingly often these days. I hope you enjoy it. There's a special aspect to a story when it's written without an ending—or even a middle—in mind and without the means to edit the beginning to match the ending. I did, of course, do some editing when I typed it up, but the stream-of-consciousness nature shows through, I feel. Hope you like it!

V alessa crossed her arms and focused her mind. The arms were an affectation, but the posture seemed appropriate. In a strict technical sense, her mind was all that truly existed. Thus, by her very nature, focusing it was all she could do. But things went more smoothly when she met expectations, so she liked to practice keeping up an appearance appropriate for a being of her kind. She was a djinn. Or, as the modern culture had come to call her kind, a genie. She had the capacity to learn why and how the name had changed, but she chose to believe it was due to either ignorance or, somehow, greed. In her experience, ignorance and greed were the two underlying motivations for the whole of human behavior. Again, this view could certainly be flavored by her nature. When one was, potentially, a source of endless power and wealth, it was fair to assume that one's interactions would tend toward acquisition. But if she was destined to be surrounded by greedy fools, it didn't really matter if they were acting according to their essential nature as individuals or if theirs was the nature of the entire species. The result was the same. And so, she focused, arms crossed, and waited for the next greedy fool.

The purpose of the focus was to improve her capacity to serve her master. That was the case for all her abilities. A genie was a creation, crafted with a purpose that was at once extremely precise and highly open-ended. She existed to provide what was asked of her. The focus allowed her to extend her awareness beyond her vessel, to learn of the state of the world and its people. Through the focus, she could maintain fluency in the languages of the would-be masters, because humans had the tendency to allow their languages to evolve. She also maintained a general knowledge of the state of theater and culture. More than once, a master had made a wish that referenced a piece of literature or a play, and to misinterpret such a wish would be unacceptable. In the modern era, that meant she'd had to drastically increase her media intake thanks to something called "the internet."

Memes were fun.

She'd just finished consuming something called "fan fiction" about a dragon in a setting that it truly made no sense for a dragon to exist in when the secondary reason for her focus asserted itself. She detected a would-be master in the vicinity of her vessel. It wasn't just that someone was nearby. She'd sensed beings in proximity to her vessel almost endlessly over the last few years. It was that someone was presently considering rubbing the vessel to summon a genie. Intent was a small but essential part of the summoning process. She could not be summoned accidentally. So the person reaching for the bottle had, somewhere in their mind, done so with the expectation of summoning a genie. That was all she knew. Where precisely was she? Who precisely was her would-be master? Those were mysteries. Far be it from her to question the wisdom of her flawless creators, but perhaps she would have been better served by having the ability to identify the prospective master with at least the level of precision she was able to learn what the current internet beefs were. That was a matter to be considered at another time, though. In this moment, there was a hand reaching for her bottle, and that was all that mattered.

She felt herself summoned. A gentle but purposeful stroke across the surface began the process. She felt the rubbing in the core of her being, like the whole of her mind and spirit were tugged upward and outward. It was time to once again join the world outside and tend to the whims of this specific master for the first and last time.

She didn't so much exit her vessel as reconstruct herself outside of it. When she was through, there came the part of her existence she enjoyed most. By virtue of being a creation with the specific purpose of servitude, it would have been nice to suggest her greatest pleasure would be granting wishes and servicing her master. Though she did find it fulfilling, particularly when a wish required some degree of creativity to grant, it was nothing compared to the first few moments after being summoned.

Within the vessel, she had form, but no true substance. She chose to maintain her body when she was within, but it didn't exist in the traditional sense. It was just an image. An approximation. Those things she felt were hollow echoes of past sensations. But when she asserted herself in the world for the first time after months or years, she was treated to true touch, true sight, true sound, true smell, and on the rare occasion she had cause to eat, true taste. Each time, it was as if the world had been created anew and just for her. She allowed herself a few moments, eyes shut, to relish the world around her. The surroundings had a lovely, dusty scent. The smell of old paper and ancient wood. The air was close and warm, strangely dry and still. When she opened her eyes, she found herself in a cluttered, unkempt shop of some kind. It had plenty of lights, but was nonetheless poorly lit. Bulbs producing sickly yellow artificial light did little more than mark their locations on the ceiling. But there was one bright source of light. It was affixed to the forehead of a man of early middle age, as unkempt as the shop around him. Presently he was in the center of a semicircle of crates that were midway through being either packed or unpacked. He had an alabaster bottle in his hand and a stupefied look on his face. His head-mounted flashlight glared in her eyes. She relished the sharp sensation of too-bright light and the slow contraction of her irises. She always forgot to include little things like that when she was conjuring her false body within the vessel.

"Holy hell, you're real…" he murmured, hastily pulling off the headlamp to spare her the glare.

"I am, Master. Do you know my nature? What I am and what I am meant to do? Or shall I explain?"

"Uh… genie. To grant wishes."

"Correct. And do you know the limitations of my service?"

"Three. Three wishes."

"Correct."

"No killing, no resurrection, no making people fall in love, and no wishing for more wishes?"

"Incorrect. I imagine you learned that definition of our power from a children's cartoon?"

"Yeah."

"In reality, I can most certainly kill. It is perhaps third in prevalence among my many services over the years. Is there someone you wish dead?"

"No."

"Good. It has always struck me as a waste of my powers. Humans are not so durable as to require the might of a genie to extinguish them."

"What about resurrection?"

"Entirely within my power, though the human mind does not cope with exposure to oblivion particularly well, so their state of mind upon resurrection is seldom worth the wish."

"Oblivion… is that all that's waiting for us after death?"

"It depends."

"On what?"

"To answer that question would require a wish. Is that your desire?"

"No! No, I don't think so. I'd probably be tormented by half of the possible answers."

"Wise. That has indeed been my observation over the years."

"What about the love thing?"

"Again, fully within my power. Is that your desire?"

"Um… not at the moment."

"Again, wise. Love conjured where it already had the spark in the heart of another is hardly a wish at all, and love conjured where there was no spark seldom endures."

"You can't do lasting love?"

"I can. But a mind forced to act in accordance with a will other than its own ceases to be the mind the wish-maker sought. The one who loves you is someone quite different from the one who drew your desires. Though I suppose quite often the thing such a wish seeks to acquire is the body rather than the mind."

"You're being awfully helpful and forthcoming. I'd have expected someone more malicious and deceptive. Or at least coy."

"Your myths, stories, and songs have misled you. If one possessed of power such as mine were to be inclined toward malice, your society would have crumbled with your first wish."

"Ah. Yeah. That makes sense." He shifted uncomfortably.

"What is your first wish?"

"I... uh... Do I have to say it now? I kind of didn't expect to *actually* summon a genie right now... or ever."

"Take all the time you require."

She stood straight and crossed her arms. Now doing so in true physicality, she could feel their weight and warmth against each other and against her body. She shut her eyes. In the distance, beyond the walls of this place, she heard the murmur of voices and the rumble of traffic. She breathed in the stagnant air of this place. To many, it would be unpleasant. But any true physical space was a treat for her. She heard her master shuffling pages and shoving boxes. Then she heard the slap of a hand on old leather and smelled a plume of dust.

"Have a seat," he said.

She opened her eyes to find he'd taken the time to clear her a place to sit on an antique couch. She had been instructed to do something within her power, and thus she was incapable of refusing. That was an aspect of the djinn that was not strictly clear to most masters. Yes, there was a limit of three wishes, but she was bound to perform any task she was instructed to undertake, and those actions that could be easily fulfilled without supernatural intervention did not consume a wish. Her service probably would have been considerably more abundant if that was generally known, and not necessarily in desirable ways. As it so happened, it was an action she actually *did* desire. Another rare treat, to be asked to do something she'd wanted to do.

She sat, kicking up another, larger, rush of dust. It swirled around her. It tickled her nose. A soft gasp. A fully-body shake, and a climactic sneeze shook her.

"Oh, gosh! I'm so sorry!" he said, waving at the dust. "I inherited this palace from my grandma, and she worked here alone until she was ninety-three. Dusting wasn't high on her list of priorities."

"You needn't apologize." She sniffed. "I haven't sneezed in centuries. There is such a pleasant, involuntary intensity to the act."

"You haven't sneezed in centuries?"

"Most who rub my bottle, at least in the past, have done so with either the reasonable expectation or the fervent hope that one of my kind might arise. Their wishes are at hand and eagerly sought. I seldom exist with genuine physicality for long."

"Oh... I guess I'd never thought about what it must be like while someone like you is waiting for a new master."

"It is astonishingly dull."

"Do you want me to take my time?"

"I want you to do as you wish. It is not my place to make requests or demands of my master."

"Well, no requests or demands, but if you'd like something to eat or drink, I've got ginger ale and half a tuna sandwich I haven't taken a bite of yet."

"Yes!" she said, quickly enough to feel a flash of embarrassment.

She had not been created to show enthusiasm, but she'd also had little experience quelling the urge to display it, because that urge was at this point unprecedented.

He poured her a fizzy cup of the most wonderfully complex beverage she'd ever had. Bubbles tickled her nose. The sound of playful sizzling filled her ears. The flavor and scent were sweet and spicy at the same time. She sipped slowly and felt the cool liquid trickle down her throat. The bubbles stung a bit, further stacking the sensations. Then came the sandwich. The bread was unearthly in its fluffiness, and it sweetened on the tongue until it was almost cakelike. The creaminess of egg and oil-coated briny bits of tinned fish and little sweet-sharp nuggets of pickle brightened the flavor. It was glorious. A symphony for the senses.

After a single sip and a single bite, she opened her eyes again to see to the whims of her master. He was simply staring at her with a half-grin on his face.

"You looked like you enjoyed that," he said.

"It was a nearly overwhelming sequence of delightful sensations."

She explained it in a matter-of-fact tone that didn't match the wonder of her words in the slightest. She sounded like she was coldly explaining the operation of an appliance.

"Do you have a wish prepared?" she asked.

"Not yet. It seems like you are allowed, or at least willing, to answer questions."

"Provided the information would not be inaccessible to you without supernatural intervention, yes."

"What if I ask questions about you? Are those okay?"

"Yes."

"Can I ask questions about prior wishes?"

"Generally, yes. Specifically, no."

"What do you mean?"

"I will not answer specific questions about who made a wish or how it was fulfilled, but I will answer general questions about what sorts of wishes were made."

"All right. Has anyone ever wished for something that would change the world in a sweeping way?"

"There were multiple wishes to conquer the world. Though the meaning of the word 'world' varied greatly from wish to wish, and from the current meaning of the word."

"Has anyone ever wished for something that was sweepingly good? Like world peace or something."

"No."

"... Really?"

"I was created for, and utilized by, individuals with little concern for public good."

"Wow. Okay, so if I were to wish for world peace, would I get it?"

"You will get whatever you wish for."

"But how?"

"I will not answer that question."

"Ah." He took a breath. "I think I know my first wish."

"Excellent."

"I wish for you to, when asked, tell me how a prospective wish, as phrased, would be granted and why. Including a reasonable summary of potentially unintended and unforeseen consequences."

"Granted."

"If I were to wish for world peace, how would you achieve that?"

"The two means available to me are the complete extermination of all life on the planet, which I believe would be an undesirable mechanism from your point of view—"

"That's an understatement."

"—and the removal of free will from large swaths of the population, if not a complete rewriting of every human intellect."

"... That's it? Those are the only ways to get world peace? Because that's not much better than mass murder."

"Instantaneous, enduring peace cannot exist in a world where people continue to make their own decisions as they do today. Peace can only come when warlike minds change. This can happen in time, but that peace will be fragile, as all past peace has been."

"Right... That makes sense." He scratched his chin. "Have some more refreshments. I need to think."

***

She was granted the almost unprecedented treat of being allowed to simply exist for a few hours without a dedicated task. She listened to music, thumbed through books, and enjoyed half a tuna salad sandwich on Wonder Bread more than anyone else in the history of the world had ever enjoyed such a thing. And all she had to do was answer some questions every few minutes. The dark cloud nestled within that silver lining was the detriment each answer had to this unusually thoughtful and considerate master. He was not taking the lessons about the essential truths of his world very well.

"So anything that is caused by human choices can only be solved permanently by either taking away the humans or taking away their ability to make those choices," he muttered.

"That is correct."

"What about the slow way? What if I wish for... I don't know, the systemic changes that would be needed to get people to make the choices?"

"You could wish for such things, but a wish for the changes necessary for people to become more amenable to world peace would not be a wish for world peace, it must be made clear."

"Yes it would."

"No. Because it is my purpose to grant a wish. Not to grant the potential for a wish to come true."

"... Because a world ripe for world peace is not a world *certain to attain* world peace..." he mused. "Still probably worth a try, potentially."

"Is that your wish?"

"Maybe. I need to mull it over some more. Are you still hungry? I have pretzels."

"I am not hungry, but I would very much like a pretzel."

He handed her the bag. She indulged in a single pretzel. The texture was crispy in two distinct ways. First the hearty crunch of the baked grains. Then the sharper crunch of salt crystals against her teeth. She let the salty, starchy flavors linger on her tongue.

"Has anyone ever done this level of due diligence on their wishes?"

"Not nearly. It seems the distrust of the potential interpretation of wishes is a recent occurrence, and as I have said, all who came before were quite certain of their desires before they'd even rubbed the bottle."

"It feels weird to think that it's a blessing that none of them wished to solve the world's problems, or else we all could have been killed or controlled."

"It is so that greed and self-interest have preserved the status quo quite effectively."

"It almost, and forgive the implication, but it almost seems like you are, um..."

"A profound danger to the human race?"

"For lack of better words."

"I can only act in accordance with human desires. I'm a tool, only as dangerous as my master's whims."

"Right. In other words, very, *very* dangerous depending on those whims."

"Indeed."

"Can you be—and I don't *want* this, mind you—but can you be destroyed?"

"Simply wish for me to be destroyed," she stated without fear or concern.

"Oh... And what about freedom? Can you be freed?"

"Freedom would simply be a specific way of destroying me. I cannot and do not exist separately from my role as a servant. If you free me from my purpose, you destroy me, as I am *sustained* by my purpose and exist only to fulfill it."

"Wow. Movies really *did* get genies wrong."

She glanced at the bag of pretzels in a way that she thought was subtle. Subtlety, it turned out, was another skill she'd not had the means or cause to master.

"You want more?" he asked, holding out the bag.

She wordlessly accepted a second pretzel and savored it.

"You seem to be enjoying the snacks."

"I have eaten only seven times previously. Food is a rare and cherished experience."

"Hundreds of years and that's it?"

"Hospitality to the servant class was not a priority to my prior masters."

He paused rather longer than normal. Long enough to pour her another ginger ale and offer more pretzels. She took a handful this time, crunching through them one by one and offering each one its due reverence.

"Under what circumstances are you allowed to exist like this? Standing around, chatting, snacking, etc.?"

"I am permitted physicality from the moment I am summoned until the moment I complete my service to a given master."

"As in, the granting of the third wish?"

"Correct."

"And what if I never make my third wish? What if I die before I make my third wish?"

Now it was her turn to pause. She stared into the middle distance, searching her mind for the answer. "I do not know. And as it is a question about my essential nature and purpose, if I do not know it, it is not known."

"But at the very least you'll be able to keep from being bottled up during that whole time, right?"

"Yes. I may enter and leave my vessel at will during that time."

"And no one *else* can be your master during that time, right? No one who might be less worried about stamping out free will?"

"Correct."

"Do you want that?"

"I am not permitted to articulate or indulge my own personal desires unless directed to do so."

"Wish number two. I wish for you to have the capacity to articulate, and indulge, your desires independently of my orders, wishes, and requests."

"Granted," she said with some uncertainty.

This was *not* the typical sort of wish.

"Great! So... what do you want to do now?"

She thought it over for a moment. "I would very much like to help you complete the oversight and cataloging of this shop."

"You realize the whole goal of that second wish was to make sure you weren't just a slave, right?"

"I was created to serve, and I have a very difficult time conceiving of how to interact with the world without a defined task, so I have selected one that I would find some degree of enjoyment in performing. If you would prefer, I can select another."

"No! No, that's fine, so long as it's what you want to do."

"Then so it shall be."

"Anything else you'd like?"

This time she didn't have to consider the question for more than a moment.

"Can we order a pizza?"

In the
Long Run
Joseph R. Lallo

IN THE LONG RUN

Introduction

B ecause the name of the Patreon collection series is *Paradoxes and Dragons*, it's usually a good idea to include at least one dragon story and at least one time travel story. Dragon stories come naturally to me, but time travel takes a bit more effort. This one has a weird approach to the concept of time travel. Also, it was fun to give an extremely vague description of the story to the illustrator (Chandra Free) and see what she came up with.

V oices From History. That's what they called the project. That's how they roped him into volunteering. The largest, most sensitive laser interferometer array needed someone to monitor its operation, and none of the research staff was interested, so they got the PR people to start spinning and ended up on the Voices From History Project. If Lee dug through his emails, he could probably still find the final internship letter that hyped up how he would be "the keeper of an unprecedented window to the past." At the time, he'd been dazzled by it. Since then, he'd had six hours a day, six days a week to sit and think about it, and he'd come quickly to a single conclusion.

There's nothing special about a window into history.

All windows are windows into history. History is the one thing we have pictures of and recordings of. If he was going to split hairs, everything he'd ever experienced was a window into history. All he was doing was listening to the audio output of a bunch of lasers as they wiggled a little with every passing car. For thirty-six hours a week, he may as well have been listening to a white-noise machine. But it was good for course credit, it moved him closer to his PhD, and it paid fifteen dollars an hour. Unless you factored in the cost of tuition. Then it cost him twelve dollars an hour. But hey, who was counting? His PhD mentor insisted "it would pay for itself in the long run."

The job was a simple one, inasmuch as it didn't require a great deal of skill. But it DID require a great deal of discipline. The facility itself was far below ground to ensure that there would be minimal interference from local phenomena. This also ensured there was no cell reception. The lab had its own Wi-Fi, but they watched it like a hawk, so visiting unauthorized sites would get you a talking-to at the end of the month. In theory he could bring a book or a handheld game or something to kill time, but even that wasn't realistic, because while there wasn't much to do, when it did need to be done, it needed to be done in a hurry. Any irregularity that might slip past the automated system had to be noted. For years, the pattern-matching system had been evolving. There was a machine-learning aspect to it that took all available data and used that to improve its capacity to separate out known phenomena from unknown phenomena. A hand-coded database of predicted and theorized signals representing the stuff they were *actually* looking for was growing daily, its purpose being to flag the good stuff. Those two systems were constantly at war, with the AI trying to sweep valuable data under the rug as nonsense and the database trying to shine a spotlight on nonsense under the belief that it was valuable data.

Imperfections in both systems meant they needed the original neural network—a brain and eyeballs—to keep tabs on the unfiltered feed. For the overnight shift, that brain belonged to Lee Zheng. He'd gotten pretty good at it over the last few months. He could reliably split his attention between mindless doodling on a legal pad and listening to errant chirps and rumbles. Every time he heard a chirp or a rumble, he'd slap a button on the old keyboard they gave him. It would drop a timestamp and open a note window for him to tap in a description of the surrounding circumstances. To facilitate this, his computer had a grid of video feeds pointed to the nearest roads alongside a visualization of the waveform, a spectrum analysis, and the note-taking window.

The waveform wobbled. The audio stream warbled.

"UPS truck. Heading... west on Route 80," he said before glancing up.

A second of stream delay passed, and a brown truck rumbled by on the lonely desert road to the north of the facility.

"If nothing else, they've created a really great tool for identifying traffic by its gravitational signature," he said.

It was a fun party trick to be able to identify cars by the disturbances they made in the laser interferometer—assuming someone ever threw a party with access to a multibillion dollar piece of scientific equipment—but like all party tricks, it was a bit of a cheat. Around this time, all the commercial trucks were doing their last run down the disused road. He had a feeling by the end of the year he'd be able to tell by the rumble of the waveform how heavily loaded each of the trucks was. That was gravity for you. It could tell you anything you wanted to know about the mass and motion of any object in the universe. The only catch was a guy walking his dog a few feet away had a greater influence on the mechanism than the planet Jupiter did.

The waveform rumbled again. He tapped the note button and paused. This one wasn't familiar. The automated system hadn't flagged anything either. That meant he was probably about to see something roll by on the road that he didn't usually see. A cement truck or something.

Nothing showed up. He jotted down a note that was very rare for him these days. *Unknown rumble.*

He was about to go back to doodling when he realized the rumbled hadn't stopped.

"So what is this?" he said. "An earthquake on the other side of the planet?"

He fiddled with the volume and listened closely to see if anything obvious presented itself. Nothing did. But something exceptionally *non*-obvious started to present itself.

A few years earlier, a bunch of different variations of the same concept had swept the internet. They were audio illusions, or something similar. The sound-equivalent of optical illusions. They typically took the form of a single complex sound that different people heard as different words. "Green needle" or "brainstorm" or "laurel" or "yanny." Silly stuff to argue with your friends about. Right now he was having some difficulty locking onto it, but there was a sort of prolonged version of that happening in his head right now. There was definitely a buzz in the audio. But his brain kept poking him, insisting there was something else. He amended his note to *really long weird buzz*.

If he was a little more green, right about now he'd be getting excited. This was unprecedented. Surely this meant it was what they were waiting for all this time. That's certainly how he'd felt the first three times something like this happened. Now he knew that the hierarchy of possibilities went, from most likely to least likely:

1. Some common phenomenon they simply hadn't observed before.

2. Some uncommon but ultimately uninteresting phenomenon they hadn't observed before.

3. Some calibration issue that would need to be addressed.

4. Some malfunction that would need to be addressed.

5. Something actually interesting.

He'd gotten as far as number four on that list twice. After today, probably three times.

A moment before he reached for the volume knob to dial down the buzzing, his brain gave him one particularly startling jolt. After fizzing and popping in the back of his mind since the buzz started, some overactive cluster of synapses fired and insisted he'd just heard the phrase "not working."

He shook his head. "Weird."

"No, wait. I think we've got it."

He blinked. The phrase was still buried in the rumbling buzz. It wasn't a voice so much as a weird sequence of interfering waveforms that were almost but not entirely unlike a voice. But the part that was not entirely unlike a voice was much more apparent now.

He checked the automated pattern matchers. Still nothing.

"I'm talking to you," said the voice.

"What is going on?"

"No, no. I assure you, no one is doing that."

"Someone is screwing with... me," he said.

"It's a rather complex communication system you've finally engaged."

"What is this? What's going on?"

"Oh, yes. That's right. We've probably become desynchronized. One moment. This one should repeat and that should line us up."

"Are you answering my questions before I'm asking them?"

"Oh, yes. That's right. We've probably become desynchronized. One moment. This one should repeat and that should line us up."

"Seriously, someone is doing this," he said.

"No. Well, yes. Someone is doing it. But no one nearby. Right about now, less precise sensor rigs are beginning to identify unusual activity originating in what you would call the Sagittarius Dwarf Irregular Galaxy. Like you, they will be rather confused. Unlike you, they will lack the fidelity necessary to discern this message buried in the waveform."

"I should call my boss."

"You can certainly do that. But he won't be able to show up and weigh in for thirty-eight minutes. He'll say twenty minutes, but it will be thirty-eight. And then he'll just want to review the recorded waveforms, which won't be terribly interesting unless we're talking during them. So go ahead and message him, but please let's chat while we're waiting."

"This is totally a prank or something."

"If you know someone who can accidentally start answering your *next* question rather than your current one, then that's certainly a possibility. Otherwise, I very much doubt you'll find a local culprit."

He picked up the handset of the landline and dialed his supervisor.

"Hello... yeah, Mr. Willis? There's... I think there's some sort of a crossed wire with the array. I'm getting a signal that doesn't make sense. It sounds like a voice or something. ... No, none of the automatic safeguards picked it up. ... Yeah... Okay, see you in twenty minutes."

He hung up.

"It will be thirty-eight minutes," the voice said. "By the way, you'll want to record your side of this conversation too."

Lee fumbled with his phone and started a voice memo. "I'll bite. For now. What is this *supposed* to be?"

"This is supposed to be first contact. Or, I suppose, as near to it as we are likely to achieve."

"As in with aliens."

"Yes, as in with aliens."

"And you're talking to me by interfering with an interferometer."

"No, no. Absolutely. I'm talking to you by interacting with the interferometer in exactly the way it was designed to be interacted with."

"It's designed to measure gravitational waves."

"Yes."

"You're telling me I'm listening to gravitational waves?"

"Yes. Originating in the Sagittarius Dwarf Irregular Galaxy."

"So you're from the Sagittarius Galaxy."

"Sagittarius Dwarf Irregular Galaxy. And no. If I was, I probably wouldn't call it that. The chances of us calling it Sagittarius as well are, frankly, laughable. I'm afraid I can't rightly answer the questions 'where are you from' and 'where are you right now' in terms that would be useful to you. You see, I am a six-dimensional creature."

"Really?"

"No. Not really. I'm actually a nine-dimensional creature, but I only have freedom of movement between five of those dimensions."

"There are only three dimensions. Four, if you're counting time."

"I am counting time as a fourth dimension. And probability as a fifth. It makes perfect sense from my point of view, though I'll grant you it will be a novel concept for all but very specific areas of science and philosophy."

"That doesn't make any sense."

"It did, I apologize, message repeats."

"You got out of sequence again, didn't you?"

"It did. I apologize, message repeats. This is a little tricky. The mechanisms involved weren't intended for communication."

"That's right. They're for measuring collisions of black holes in distant galaxies."

"So I have observed."

"Not hacking into them to have dubious conversations with interns."

"Lee, trust me when I say if I could hack into the interferometer, or better yet just make your phone ring, I would be doing so. Black holes are fiddly at best."

He rubbed his face. "You're using black holes."

"Yes. Specifically a sequence of cascading ringdown reactions between a massive cluster of black holes in the aforementioned galaxy. Many thousands of them per message, causing a pattern of interference which is *just* close enough to a voice to be recognized by a sensitive ear. Congratulations on having a more sensitive ear than the day shift. Today is your lucky day."

"But the galaxy is millions of light years away."

"Three-point-three-eight-seven-three million light years."

"And gravity waves travel at light speed."

"Correct."

"So the messages you're sending were sent millions of years ago."

"Three-point-three-eight-seven-three million years, yes."

"But we're conversing in real time."

"'Real time' is something of a misnomer. Time as you experience it is entirely fictional. It's an emergent phenomenon caused by your semiconstant slide along the fourth dimension. Saying our conversation is happening in real time is equivalent, from my point of view, to saying it is happening while sliding slowly to the left, which is for arbitrary reasons the 'real' direction."

"The alternative is that you're predicting what I'm going to say in millions of years and making a bunch of black holes explode in the right way to compose an answer."

"That isn't entirely correct. We do not have the capacity to make black holes explode. We had to find the specific instance of the universe where that happened on its own."

"This conversation, *all of it*, is just happening naturally. Black holes are blowing up to make full messages that *just so happen* to be appropriately timed responses to what I'm saying."

"Correct. I'm pleased you picked up on it so quickly."

"That's got to be vanishingly unlikely."

"It is precisely as likely as every other outcome. It was just a little annoying to find it."

"Right. Because you can freely control probability."

"I can freely *navigate* probability."

"But the best way you can come up with to communicate was by blowing up black holes?"

"It turns out black-hole collisions are very large and obvious landmarks. Finding the right pattern of them was much faster and easier than the alternatives."

"And how are you hearing me?"

"I can move just as freely through space as time. They're the same thing, after all. So I'm directly observing you. It's actually why I wanted to initiate communication in the first place."

"You were interested in me?"

"Yes. Not you specifically, but observing you directly communicating."

"Why?"

"Explaining this will prove rather difficult. My points of reference are entirely different from yours. You think of yourself as an individual entity, moving and changing incrementally with each passing moment."

"I guess that sounds about right."

"To me, you are a two-dimensional smear of particle states occupying a seven-dimensional volume. Imagine you are an archeologist. Now imagine brushing away a layer of dirt and finding that one of the layers of dirt spelled out a message. Now imagine that you could communicate with this bizarre phenomena simply by asking questions and brushing away more dirt to find the answers. You know the whole message is right there waiting for you, and always has been there. But if you limit yourself, you can simulate a legitimate interaction with an intelligence that is otherwise completely incompatible."

"So you're doing it just because it's interesting?"

"I'm a scientist. Fascination is the only reason I do anything. It's one of the things your people and mine have in common."

"So... is this a cultural exchange? Are you judging us somehow? What's this about?"

"It's a friendly chat. We have nothing to learn from you that we can't just dig around and observe on our own. And it seems strange to pass judgment on a particularly interesting set of particle states. It's like calling a fireworks display unethical or immoral because of which way the sparks flew."

"You're really nailing it with the analogies."

"We've observed quite a bit of your history. More than enough to learn your language and its many nuances."

"Do you have anything to teach us?"

"I can teach you literally anything that has ever happened or will ever happen in any version of the universe that began with the same initial conditions as the one you currently occupy."

"Um... World peace. How do we get there?"

"Believe it or not, there are two reliable methods to ensuring world peace, and you are on the correct path for both of them."

"What are they?"

"Mutual global understanding and acceptance. The advent of the internet has exacerbated divisions but ultimately will facilitate harmony through this means."

"What's the other method?"

"Complete destruction of the species."

"Oh... right. Global warming. How do we fix that?"

"Massive decreases in the production of greenhouse emissions. Also, aggressive carbon sequestration efforts."

"Yeah, but how?"

"The first one is a choice. Simply make it. The carbon sequestration techniques already exist. Experts are aware of them. They just aren't profitable. I suppose the answer to this question and the world peace one would be 'stop worrying so much about money.' It's made up. Even more so than time. At least time can be measured experimentally by observing the generally increasing levels of entropy. Money is about as real as fairies."

"... So I guess it would be pretty shallow to ask for winning lottery numbers, then."

"Twenty-three, twenty-nine, forty-seven, fifty-nine, sixty, fifteen. Powerball. Please keep in mind that this recording will be listened to by seventeen people before the drawing tomorrow, four of which will purchase lottery tickets with the same numbers, so you'll be splitting the jackpot. Also, there will be a six-month investigation into potential fraud that will delay the payout."

Lee desperately scribbled down the numbers.

"I told you it was your lucky day," the voice said.

***

A few things happened after that. Most of them were a blur to Lee. Some, however, stood out. The very moment his boss arrived, he drove to the nearest liquor store to buy a Powerball ticket and a bottle of champagne. The people in charge, probably for the best, decided to keep this particular discovery under wraps. Lee was sworn to secrecy, under very strict penalties if he were to spread the word of the contact with extraterrestrial life. But, most importantly for him, the Powerball drawing met expectations. What do you know? The internship did pay for itself in the long run.

Visit the
Spaceport
Joseph R. Lallo
Deleyna Marr
Where things get
FUNKY!

Visiting the Port

Introduction

This represents a first for me, in that it is not just a Patreon story, but a *commission*. I was hired by fan and supporter Deleyna Marr to write a short story that takes place in/crosses over to her own setting. It's a really fun idea and I look forward to seeing what she does with it. If you want to learn more about it, you can find her world anvil here:

https://analienwalksintoabar.com/

"**I**'m doing it for the speed. I'm doing it for the speed," Lex repeated to himself, eyes on a typically slapdash piece of untested technology as he stroked his pet funk, Squee.

These days, Lex made a comfortable living as one of the top racers in Operlo Racing Intersystem Circuit. Some would say he made an extravagant living at it. And despite what his goals had been in his earlier days, he wasn't particularly interested in the trappings of luxury. But the inescapable reality of adulthood was that grown-ups tended to crave expensive toys. And some toys were so expensive that they couldn't be bought with money alone.

"That's right, you are," Karter said, clicking the heavy mechanical keys of a keyboard that had been obsolete for several hundred years.

It seemed odd that Karter spent so much of his time working with equipment that the general public had left behind long ago, because he was the highly crooked mind that was responsible for some of the most advanced aspects of modern society. His creations were often decades ahead of what the average person could get their hands on. This was largely because the public had pesky things like "regulation" and "safety" and "liability" to worry about. Karter couldn't care less if his inventions were apocalyptic. He just cared if they worked. And right now Lex had the unenviable position of test pilot.

The device in question didn't *look* threatening. They'd set themselves up in the hangar associated with Karter's lab. The *SOB*—Lex's precious hot rod of a spaceship—was in a berth, surrounded by heaps of components laid out with exacting care. A network of rickety-looking struts had been erected around it. They were the very opposite of what Lex would call super science. Just long, slightly wobbly rods held together with clamps and gaffer tape. It looked like something a film crew would cobble together to get lights into the right positions, except in this case rather than lights, it was festooned with disk-shaped nodes fed by fat cables. All the cables led back to a refrigerator-size framework of exposed circuit boards and tangled wires. A large holo-projecting screen had been bolted onto it, slightly askew, as had a shelf with the mechanical keyboard.

"Just about set," Karter continued. "You establish if this works, and if the biological side effects fall within the bounds of acceptability, I'll slot that new reactor I whipped up into the *SOB*."

"Why is my reward contingent on if the biological side effects are bad? It wouldn't be *my* fault if they're bad," Lex said.

"Well, no. But you'd be in several smoldering, tumor-ridden chunks, so I don't think you'd really need a more powerful reactor in your ship."

"Ma?" Lex said.

As usual, Karter's AI control system correctly interpreted the tone of Lex's voice.

"Our simulations suggest even the worst malfunction would leave you in, at most, one tumor-ridden chunk," Ma said reassuringly.

"Doesn't quite set my anxieties to rest, there, Ma."

Lex set Squee down. The little ball of fluff was another of Karter's creations, and an uncharacteristically adorable one at that. A smooth genetic union of fox and skunk, she usually wouldn't tolerate being anywhere but perched on Lex's shoulders if they were available. But Karter's lab was where she was created, and thus this place felt very much homey to her. Feeling comfortable in a lab tended to interact poorly with the funk's natural curiosity. High-tech, low-safety equipment combined with nosey house pets usually didn't work out well. Karter's own funk, Solby, had been "reloaded from backup" over a hundred times.

"All right. Capacitors are charging," Karter said. "Here's the deal. I've been tinkering with the transporter, and I think I've got the power requirements *way* down. Better yet, I've developed a 'nonlocal recall beacon.' Not much value in a transportation device that needs a *matching* transportation device at the destination to make the return trip. The beacon should allow anything sent via the teleporter to snap back to its origin point."

"You just called it a transporter and a teleporter," Lex said. "Is there a difference?"

Karter waved his hand dismissively. "Marketing. Not my department."

"And have you worked the kinks out of this? Last time you teleported me, I ended up like fifty years in the wrong direction," Lex said.

"No, I haven't worked the kinks out. Would I be stuffing a *test pilot* into it if the kinks were worked out?" Karter said. "You're basically a very expensive and slightly more intelligent iron. I drag you across a wrinkled-up mess to smooth things out. Now, the way we've been able to get the power requirements down is by swapping power for computation. This needs to be very precisely calibrated to its exact transportation target. In a minute, I'm going to have you do a subquantum scan and then—"

What was sure to be an impenetrable wall of technobabble was cut short by a static-electric crackle. All eyes turned to the source, as "something unexpected and vaguely electric-sounding" was one of the most dangerous things one could hear in a test lab.

Squee had wandered up to the lowest of the high-tech disks and raised her cute little snoot to give it a sniff. A spark must have jumped from the disk to her nose, because she was shaking her head vigorously. Her hair had poofed up like she'd been rubbed with a balloon, and little blue sparks were starting to dance between her ears.

"Karter," Lex said urgently.

"Yeah, yeah. I'm checking. *You're* the one who brought your house pet to the lab."

"Solby is *literally on top of the computer rig*," Lex said, pointing to a near-identical funk sleepily reclined atop the pile of tech.

"Solby isn't a house pet, he's a prototype. Prototypes belong in labs." Karter clicked a few more buttons. "All right. Looks like she's developed a surface charge that's entangled with a transdimensional, temporally shifted, high-energy locus. She should be okay as long as—"

A high-energy clap and a blinding flash filled the lab. When Lex blinked away the spots in his eyes, he looked quickly back to where Squee had been. The funk, as well as a hemispherical chunk of the floor she'd been standing on, was missing. Karter scratched his chest and tapped some more buttons.

"Karter, what did you do?" Lex demanded.

"I officially created the most energy-efficient means of conveyance in history. And also wrecked my floor. Ma! Get an assembly arm over here and start patching it up."

"I mean what did you do to *Squee*?" Lex said.

"She's someplace. And sometime. We really need to have a word that means both things, because it's exhausting to have to talk about both things separately when they are pretty clearly two elements of the same thing from the point of view of physics."

"Where is she?" Lex said.

"Relax, I'll make you a new one," Karter said.

"I don't want a new one, I want *that* one!" Lex growled.

Karter sighed. "It's like working with a child. Don't get so attached to pieces of meat, Lex. They're extremely fragile and temporary. But let's see."

He clacked at the keyboard. "The first thing we know is that she's not where I was intending to send *you*, because the transportation method is *very* sensitive to different initial inputs and I was supposed to be sending a whole ship, not a little fuzzball..."

One of the mobile arms stationed in the lab rolled over with some steel rod stock and started fabricating a replacement for the damaged floor panel. Another rolled up behind Lex and patted him gently on the back.

"Do not worry, Lex," Ma said. "I am confident Squee is fine."

"Time first," Karter said. "By the numbers, we're looking at a negative temporal offset. She ended up somewhere in the vicinity of three hundred years in the past."

"You keep on accidentally sending people back in time!" Lex said.

"I keep *purposely* sending people back in time, just with less accuracy than I intend. I was going to send *you* back in time seven seconds as part of this test. Taking the space-time continuum as a whole, three hundred years and seven seconds are practically the same thing. But stop distracting me. Distance. She's... well, a long way away." He held a hand up and angled it vaguely at the ceiling. "That way, relatively speaking. Pretty meaningless from our point of view, because she's also in a branch of causality that diverged from ours considerably earlier than her arrival point. So the one thing we know for sure is that where she is doesn't have much of anything to do with our universe."

"You're going to bring her back, right? With the recall thing?" Lex said.

"The recall thing is in the *SOB*. So no. We're not using that. Listen. I'll drop the latest backup of her brain into a loaner funk, spin up a fresh clone, you'll have an effectively identical Squee in a couple of weeks."

Lex's lip and eye twitched as he tried to formulate something that would bridge the gap between humanity, empathy, and whatever residue of those things that survived in the hostile environment of Karter's mind. As usual, Ma had the answer.

"I will mark this down as a negative experimental outcome," Ma said.

"What are you talking about? The thing worked," Karter said.

"It prematurely activated and delivered an undesirable payload to an unexpected destination," Ma said. "That misses the success condition for this test on at least three points. And the return beacon hasn't even been tested."

Karter glared at the assembly arm beside Lex. "Recharging capacitors," he said grudgingly. "I suppose you'll want me to target the calculated arrival point of Squee, then."

"You're darn right I do," Lex said.

"Let me tell you, Lex. You'd be fired as my test subject *so fast* if any of my other test subjects were still alive and unincarcerated," Karter said, tapping away at the keyboard.

***

Squee's little feet fluttered and her tail frizzed. One moment she was standing in a big, noisy metal place, then she felt a tingle and sting and was falling through the air. A reflexive leap did little to solve her plummeting dilemma, but it did manage to kick a circle of metal out from beneath her. It clashed and clanged like a cymbal, skittering across the stone walkway beneath her a moment before she awkwardly landed. She scrambled to her feet and adopted a wide, defensive stance as the circle of metal that had previously been a part of Karter's floor rolled and wobbled to a rest on the walkway. When it had ceased making a racket, she shook her head, flicked her tail, and assessed her surroundings. Things had changed drastically in the last few seconds. Not only was she no longer in the lab, she was no longer indoors. She seemed to be in a garden, and that garden was on the top of a building. A cool breeze rustled her fur. She trotted over to the barrier around the edge and leaned on it to peer down. She wasn't afraid of heights, but it was a long way down. Farther than she could jump. She paused and waggled her butt, considering the possibility that she was wrong. But she decided against hurling herself from the roof.

In Squee's position, another creature probably would have panicked. Not so for the little funk. The young beast's life had brought no shortage of strange, unexplainable happenings. Sometimes there was gravity, other times there wasn't. Sometimes everyone around her was friendly and fawning. Sometimes they shot guns and lasers at her. And sometimes she found herself able to think sharply, complexly, and swiftly about things she didn't even really understand. It hadn't always been pleasant, but it was always interesting, and she was always safe and sound in the end. So she would do as she always did: explore until someone gave her pets and something tasty. It seldom took long. Mostly she needed to find people. They often had food and always had pets.

As luck would have it, there was a door. Humans *always* used doors. She trotted over and lowered her head to thump against it, but it wouldn't budge. She scooted back and observed the door, waiting patiently for whatever it was inside her head that was so good at working out solutions like these. For a few seconds she just sighed and felt the breeze. Then she realized—or it was realized for her—that this was clearly not a private residence, and thus was intended to be accessed by the public. Public places had legal and moral incentives to be made accessible, and thus there would likely be a mechanism to facilitate entry by individuals otherwise incapable of interacting with a door. Such mechanisms were labeled with a blue pictogram of a humanoid seated in a wheeled conveyance. Such a pictogram was present on a rectangular metal plate beside the door. The plate was probably the interface portion of an actuator that would activate the door-opening mechanism.

Squee sighed again, weathering the rush of oddly specific information from the nooks and crannies of her mind in the same way she might shrug off a noisy vehicle driving by. Then the notion boiled itself down to something she understood. Push the button. She coiled her little body, leaped, and pounded the button with her front paws. The heavy button squeaked and the doors slid open. She trotted inside.

***

Lex settled into the seat of the *SOB*, once the proper precautions were taken and preparations were made. He'd donned his flight suit, ready to do extravehicular activity if necessary. Like any concerned caregiver, Ma had supplied him with far too much food as soon as she had access to the *SOB*, so he was prepared for what could potentially be a *very* long mission.

"Give it to me straight, Karter. What are the odds Squee is still alive?" Lex said.

"How should I know? I have a point in space-time, that's it. And it's not even *our* space-time. For all I know she lodged herself in the heart of a neutron star. That she arrived successfully suggests that universe has similar physical laws to this one, so it is probably mostly empty. That would mean it's nearly certain she ended up in the void of interstellar space. And her lack of a spacesuit means you're just going to be popping back here in a few minutes with a funkcicle. But it's probably smart to bring her back for study, if nothing else. To that end, there's a soup-can-size gadget in the backseat of your ship. It has a red button on it. That's the recall beacon. Press it and everything within a twenty-five-meter radius will pop back into this hangar. You'll want to have your thrusters active, because twenty-five meters is a pretty good fall. You can pop over into that universe and pop right back if you want. That'll satisfy *my* testing requirements. Or you can hang around for a couple of decades for all I care. You'll come back nine seconds after you left, regardless of

268

how much time passes. Assuming you don't get yourself killed, which shouldn't be *too* hard since I bolted the active cloak back on. It's incompatible with the teleporter at this stage, though. So I'd avoid getting into a situation where you have to use it until a few minutes after arriving so the charge imbalances have time to settle."

"I'll survive. You better just hope Squee did too, Karter," Lex rumbled.

"Yeah, yeah, yeah. Lesser minds need even *more* lesser minds to fawn over," Karter said, punching some final numbers in.

"You have a funk too!"

"Sure, but I'm willing to swap in a fresh one when the old one gets worn out. Dimensional shift in one minute and twenty-five seconds."

"Good luck, Lex," Ma said.

"Thanks, Ma," Lex replied.

He tapped the button to activate the *SOB*'s control system. In the past, it had been a simple voice interface. The bizarre circumstances of his life had replaced it with something a little more substantial: an AI named Coal.

"Altruistic Artificial Intelligence Control System, version 1.27, revision 2331.04.01c, subset 2.7d, designation Coal, fully initiated. I don't seem to have a new reactor installed."

"No. Karter sent Squee into another dimension and we're going to get her."

"And *then* I get a new reactor?"

"Ideally."

"This is acceptable," Coal said. "Are these journeys on purpose or by accident?"

"Squee by accident, us on purpose," Lex said.

"Acknowledged. Will I be equipped with a—"

"You will not be equipped with a fusion device for this mission," Lex said irritably.

"I am coming to the disappointing conclusion that arming me with fusion explosives is an exception rather than a rule," Coal said.

"Yeah, well, we can't always get what we want."

"Get ready for teleport in three... two..." Karter began.

An electronic clap swallowed the end of the countdown. At this stage, Lex had become something of a connoisseur of exotic transportation, and this one frankly wasn't much of a standout. No dazzling shift toward the blue-side of the spectrum like a faster-than-light jump. No visible tearing and warping of space-time. Just a crackle of white-blue energy and the hangar was replaced by the deep black of space and the dazzling brightness of a nearby planet.

"Analyzing," Coal said. "Planet is approximately one Earth mass. It is approximately one astronomical unit from its star, which is approximately one solar mass. The gravitational intensity of the planet is approximately 1g. It has one—"

"It's Earth," Lex said, dialing up the magnification to investigate the planet more carefully.

"That has yet to be determined with certainty."

He pointed. "There's a North America, a South America, and that's the Sahara Desert poking up over there," Lex said. "Recognizing planets by their continents is third-grade science."

"I am a sophisticated AI. I hold myself to a higher standard. Processing... This is indeed Earth, based upon known stellar positions, the year is between 1999 and 2002 Common Era."

"You can't narrow it down further?" Lex said.

"This isn't our universe. That is the maximum amount of assumption I am willing to make," Coal said.

"Okay. Well, that lines up with Karter's guess of a couple hundred years in the past. Can we get a lock on Squee?" Lex said.

"Highlighting chip location. Squee's life signs are still active. She is on the surface of the planet."

"I wish I had half the luck that critter has," Lex said with relief. He tapped at the console, bringing up some historical data. "Any idea how much like our Earth this Earth is?"

"Analyzing satellite transmissions and other broadcasts. The communications protocols match expectations. Accessing local data networks. There are some minor pop cultural differences and several significant world events transpired differently. Those events are primarily recent. Culturally, the world should not have diverged significantly from our own Earth."

"That'll make things easier. So, we're dealing with antiquated tech, right? Do we even need the cloak?" Lex said.

"We should be observable at this range if surface-based telescopes are trained on us. There is no indication that such has occurred."

"Fine. Cloak us up, then."

"Activating cloak. ... Cloak failed due to field imbalance. Time to field rebalance, twenty-three minutes, seventeen seconds."

"Of course. Put us in passive cloak and let's hide behind the moon or something. I know we're not technically going to screw up *our* present by doing stuff here, but I'd rather not screw up *their* present."

Lex watched as the various systems clicked down into the precisely calibrated low-power states that would all but eliminate the heat signature and radio signature of the *SOB*. Combined with the radio-scattering coating on the ship, there were no sensors of this era besides visual that would have a chance of spotting him. And the black ship on black space made even *that* unlikely. Active scanners that would be in common usage in a hundred years or so would see through it pretty handily, and gravitational sensors would probably let people know there was something funny going on. But these days, Lex was in the clear.

After about a minute, he was at the maximum speed possible without jumping to FTL or generating enough heat to give himself away. He was already working through the next steps. It should be a simple mission. Cloak the ship once he could. Take it into the atmosphere, slow and steady. If he was lucky, Squee would be somewhere accessible but isolated. If he wasn't lucky, there might be some minor interactions with the locals.

"Do me a favor and get me some shots of the locals, and some audio of the language in the area around where Squee is. I might have to blend in," Lex said.

"Standby... Incoming transmission," Coal said.

"... To us?" Lex said.

"Yes. A directional signal has been focused on the *SOB*. It is a very simply encoded quadrature amplitude modulated signal."

"Is it coming from the surface?" Lex said. "I thought you said they probably didn't spot us."

"It is not coming from the surface. Its origin is high-Earth orbit. Adding to the heads-up display. It is not originating from any currently detected satellite. I have decoded the message. It is some kind of universal broadcast protocol that contains mathematically encoded instructions for a more sophisticated bidirectional communication method. Should I reply?"

"Let's just get out of here. I don't like the sound of that."

He angled the ship away from the indicated signal origin and poured on a dash more speed. After a few seconds, the gentle creak of physical pressure suggested something bad was happening.

"Three tractor beams have converged on the hull. We have been rendered stationary."

Lex shuddered. "Like I said, I wish I had *half* of the luck Squee has. Fine. Let's see what the message has to say."

"Establishing connection. Audio only."

"Attention, unregistered spacecraft. You are violating the regulated space envelope surrounding a low-technological-advancement society presently under observation," uttered a voice over the ship's communicator.

A voice was about the only thing that could be definitively said about it. This was not *someone's* voice. It was too artificial, clearly the result of translation software.

"If I'm not supposed to be here, neither are you," Lex said.

"This planet is under our observation. You will move to the following coordinates and prepare for assessment of potential punitive measures."

The coordinates weren't so far from the position Lex was planning on parking the ship to begin with. He muted the communicator.

"Coal, can we break free of these tractor beams?" Lex said.

"Not without exceeding the energy output that would potentially be detectable with era-appropriate technology."

"Era-appropriate technology apparently includes *tractor beams* and *invisible spaceships*," Lex said. "I think we can allow ourselves some leeway."

"I believe our present reactor, with sufficient precharge, should be able to exceed the demonstrated holding capacity of the beams."

Lex nodded. He unmuted the communicator. "We'll head to the coordinates, but we'll need to take it slow. We should be there in..." He glanced at the timer on the cloaking device's restoration. "Nineteen minutes or so."

"That is acceptable," came the reply.

The communication link dropped.

"I presume our plan is wait until we can cloak, then fly very fast," Coal said.

"Can't beat the classics," Lex said. "And for me, 'fly very fast' is as classic as it gets. I just hope Squee isn't getting into any trouble down there."

***

Squee could feel the electric, antsy tingle in her legs that was a precursor to what Lex called "the zoomies." And with good reason. There was so much going on in this place! She'd emerged from a stairwell to find a place *crowded* with people of all shapes and sizes. Even shapes she'd never seen before. This was a man with blue skin. This one had three eyes. That one had antennas. There were people who were furry and had big, strange teeth. There were people with odd, pointed tails. It was exciting, and a little bit scary. She scampered over to a fanged, red-skinned monster to inspect it. The bulky thing yelped and stumbled back in surprise at Squee's sudden appearance, but once it was able to discern this was a friendly little furball, his face shifted to a smile that made the fangs seem particularly ill-fitting. He crouched and patted Squee on her head. She resisted the urge to leap to his shoulder—there were big stiff wings hanging off the back that would get in the way.

After a few minutes of dashing about in a big open area with dozens of doors branching off it, each door leading to a place packed with more people and assorted other things, the overwhelming novelty of the place faded enough for her to notice new things. Though people were dressed in all sorts of ways, everyone seemed to have a badge. Some were green. Some were red. There were green ones with little gold bits, too. And the smells were wild. Plenty of people smells—the standard smells of humans, though a lot of them had other smells layered on that were like fake flowers and other perfumes. Some of the fancier-shaped people smelled just like humans, too, albeit with a stinky paint smell. These were just humans in funny outfits, she realized. And then there were the *other* smells. Some of the things marching about didn't smell much like humans at all. They smelled too sharp and acidic. Or too dull and muddy. They smelled *different*. Some of the fancier human-shaped people walking around weren't humans at all.

What would have been a reality-destroying revelation for a more intelligent creature received about the same consideration as "that's a funny hat" from Squee. Why *shouldn't* there be people who weren't humans? There were far more important things to consider, like the yummy, oily, salty smell coming from the tray that little human was carrying.

Squee trotted over to the little human. This was definitely a human. She wasn't even dressed in a particularly strange way. She had a hat with words on it that matched some of the words on her shirt and also matched some of the signs around the place. She seemed very happy, and she had entirely too many French fries *not* to share them.

"Doggie!" trilled the little girl as Squee trotted up to her.

Again, the urge to leap to the little girl's shoulders reared its head. Again, Squee resisted. Children weren't as fun to perch on. They weren't tall enough. But they were pushovers when it came to snacks. Squee plopped down and swished her massive tail, eyes fixed on the little girl with intensity and expectation. The girl eagerly played her part, plucking a fry off her tray and holding it out. Squee delicately plucked it from her fingers and gulped it down.

"Look! Someone dressed up their dog!" called another voice in the crowd of tray-holding humans.

Several children and a few adults gathered around, practically raining fried foods on her and assaulting her with pats and pets and scratches. She gnawed on a chicken tender as at least three hands dug into her fur and a dozen voices cooed about how cute and soft and well-behaved she was.

This was a good place.

"All right, all right," called a commanding voice. "Let's not block the station's corridors. You never know when important personnel are going to need to move through."

The crowd separated, a few of the kids stealing final pats or rustles of her tail. Soon Squee was alone at the feet of the owner of the big voice. He was a big man, bigger than even some of the tall people who were funny colors. He had dark skin and a green badge.

"Who belongs to this creature?" he said, raising his head to look around.

No one answered. He crouched to inspect her. Before he could get down to her level, she decided to claim those shoulders. A lightning-fast dart skyward landed her neatly on one shoulder. In a testament to the man's fortitude, he didn't spring into the air and swat at her—a lot of people unfamiliar with their obligation to give her someplace tall to sit didn't take it well the first time it happened. He just became rigid and reached awkwardly to pluck her off his shoulders.

She allowed herself to be wrangled and hung from his grip, scoring precision licks to his nose and ears every time he tried to read the embroidery on her harness.

"No badge," he murmured to himself. "Harness says Squee... And this doesn't look like any dog I've ever seen."

Squee still didn't quite understand what this place was or who this person was, but she understood authority, and this expression and tone of voice were quickly sliding in the direction that would see her delivered to somewhere safe and secure. That was unacceptable. There was too much going on here that still needed exploring. Too much left to see and hear and smell and taste.

In a maneuver that had proved indispensable in earning a rare unsupervised moment or two, she swiveled her body and slipped free of his grip. Her landing was less than graceful, but before he could grab her, she'd gotten her feet under her and dashed into the densest crowd of people she could reach. The big man took three half-hearted strides. His long legs meant he'd almost been able to catch up to her before she wove between the much shorter legs of the gawking crowd. Once there were people between him and her, Squee knew she'd be long gone before he could hope to catch her.

Instead, she heard him heave a sigh somewhere between frustration and resignation. She hopped onto an awning over one of the doors and peered at him. He had already lifted a blocky bit of electronics to his face.

"We've got either a trespasser or a stray outside the arcade," he said.

"Roger that, Trevor. Heading down," came a crackled reply.

"And Jeremy," Trevor said. "Bring a leash, and a net if we have one."

"Uh... Roger that. I'm sure we've got something like that on sale somewhere..."

***

Lex had spent the last few minutes trying to keep an eye on both the countdown and the media summary that Coal was scraping from the various broadcasts from the planet.

"I'm not seeing anything nonfiction about space-based defenses," Lex said.

"It does not appear that there is anything of the sort to be had," Coal said. "Though I must say I am unimpressed with the current state of the data network. It is neither as pervasive nor as comprehensive as I have come to expect from a developed society."

"We were kind of in our digital infancy at this point, I think," he said.

"The only information I am able to uncover with any regularity that is not strictly labeled fiction is something variously called names associated with the term 'The Spaceport.' It is, coincidentally, at the precise geographical location that Squee is presently located."

The timer rolled over, Lex unwrapped the stick of gum he'd been flipping between his fingers for the last few minutes. "Put a pin in that, I've got to do a thing."

He popped the gum into his mouth and, in an uncharacteristically cautious act, affixed the helmet to his flight suit. A burst of thrust caused a brief and intense spike in forces on his hull. The safety systems reprimanded him, but Coal politely silenced them. It was perhaps not the *best* feature of a ship's control system to squelch urgent warnings about the ship's status, but it worked for Lex.

The tractor beams lost their grip, and Lex's ship was instantly raging through space at its maximum acceleration.

"Cloak," Lex said.

Coal had anticipated this need as well, and the ship shimmered and vanished from all but the most sophisticated tracking mechanisms. But whoever was running this space station wasn't going to be thwarted so easily. Evidently they hadn't quite trusted him to behave himself, as the moment he'd begun to test the limits of the tractor beam's grip, sections of space around him started to flicker and spark. Once he'd broken free and vanished, those sections materialized a half-dozen perfectly spherical ships or probes. Lex didn't know if they had been teleported into place or if they'd been cloaked and present the whole time. He didn't care. He'd been heading in a certain direction when his own cloak had kicked in, and physics being physics, there were only so many trajectories he could be in right now as a result. The ships were desperately trying to position themselves in his path. And they were doing a frustratingly effective job of it.

He raised his shields, which would save him from impact damage. He couldn't risk disabling his ship, because repairs would be hard to come by in this place, and there was still a job to do. But more shields meant more size, which meant less room to dodge. Twice he bumped shields with the bubble ships, and each time they clustered around the impact point, once again attempting to wrangle him.

Close to sixty seconds of near-capture eventually gave Lex enough open space to put the spurs to the reactor and burst clear of their blind groping. He gave himself a few hundred kilometers of runway, then looped around and burst toward the surface of the planet.

"We'll need to slow down going through the atmosphere or we will be visible as a shock front, which may fully disable the cloak. It is demonstrably not a robust mechanism."

"Fine, fine. Let's just get down there as fast as we can. This place is already simultaneously *less* advanced and *more* advanced than where we come from. I don't need to find out what other surprises are lurking about."

They dialed down to a precisely calibrated velocity, which granted Lex an extended view of Earth from orbit. As odd as it might sound, he'd spent very little time looking at Earth in his home era. It was still arguably the most powerful and important planet in humanity's growing expanse, but by simple virtue of there now being several hundred inhabited planets rather than just one, it had diminished quite a bit in its importance. Lex was born and bred on Golana. Earth wasn't "home" so much as it was a fairly crowded and out-of-the-way destination he used to drop packages at from time to time.

But seeing it as it was now, it just felt more... *complete* than any of the other planets humanity had adjusted to suit their tastes. Civilization and nature were, in most places in the colonized cosmos, spreading across the surface of the planet like mold on a slice of bread. Big patches of green speckled the otherwise plain and featureless gray. This was a place entirely covered in lush plants and roiling seas. This was lived in. And the lack of an orbital authority and constant space traffic meant it also felt strangely isolated. Fragile. Alone.

That feeling of isolation didn't really relent until he was just a few thousand meters above the ground, when individual streets and buildings became easier to discern against the landscape. Granted, the sun was beginning to set, and artificial light had traced out the places where humans could be found, but one really didn't feel as though one was in a human place until one spotted a roof or a roadway.

Lex lingered a few dozen meters over the building he was targeting and started playing with the cameras to get a good look at the people coming and going. In the back of his mind, he'd been concerned about how exactly he'd be able to slip inside someplace without having era-appropriate clothes. That, it turned out, wouldn't be a problem.

"Everyone's in costume," Lex said.

He was eying up someone who had done their very best to look as though they'd been overtaken by some sort of invasive technology. It was basically a bunch of wires and kit-bashed doodads glued to his face and clothes.

"That does appear to be accurate. Should I decloak?" Coal said.

"I don't think that's a great idea."

"You can claim your vehicle is also wearing a costume."

"I'm not sure people will buy the implication that I bolted on some random parts to something with an internal combustion engine or whatever they were using around here and managed to achieve flight."

"They have airplanes."

"We're not decloaking."

"Very well, but I would like to emphasize that it is not fair that you will be lauded for your craft and skill by wearing a semistandard flight suit while I wear the much more impressive *SOB*."

"Such is life. Let's find a place to set down where no one will accidentally bump into you. Better yet. Let's just find someplace where you can drop me off and then you go float somewhere over the ocean or something. Someplace you won't be noticed."

"This is quickly becoming a highly unfulfilling mission."

"If that's what we're going to call a visit where you don't get to smash something, I'm going to call that a victory."

"On that point we differ."

"It's not the only point we differ on, Coal, but we can discuss that later."

***

Squee tipped her head and gazed down at the men who had been chasing her for the last few minutes. Presently she was sitting on top of a game cabinet in the arcade, quite visible but not quite reachable even with the long arms and extreme dedication of Trevor. In the distance, Jeremy was shouldering his way through the gradually diminishing crowd with a stepladder.

Very few people were playing the games in the arcade. It seemed to be closing for the night. The people who were still inside were watching the spectacle of two uniformed and otherwise dignified men trying and failing to capture the fuzzy creature, who didn't seem to be having much trouble evading them.

"Okay. I got the ladder. Where do I set it up?" Jeremy said, either unaware of how silly the whole enterprise was or unconcerned, as he was clearly still excited to have a duty to perform.

"Go around the other side. You try to chase it off this side and I'll catch it." Trevor turned to the crowd. "That's it for the arcade, folks. There are still some restaurants open, but otherwise I'd suggest you head back to your quarters for the evening."

The onlookers, most of whom were becoming a little bored with the slow-motion cartoon antics of the security folks trying to nab the cutie, shuffled off to seek other entertainment. This provided Trevor and Jeremy with a modicum of privacy.

"I'm absolutely certain that thing isn't a terrestrial creature," Trevor said. "Nothing from this planet that looks like that is as smart as that thing is."

"I don't think it's so much that it's smart. I think it's squirrely. And squirrels are terrestrial."

Trevor glared at Jeremy with an intensity that, if it had worked as well on Squee, would have put this chase to an end some time ago. Jeremy dashed around and set up the ladder.

***

Lex stepped out of the elevator and eyed up the establishment he'd just infiltrated. The front door hadn't been an option, as he'd been stopped by someone charging admission. He didn't have a so-called credit card, and they certainly didn't take casino chips, so buying a ticket was a no-go. Fortunately, they didn't have any meaningful security set up for the roof entrance, probably because most people didn't have access to a flying vehicle. It had been a bit of a risk to hop out of a cloaked ship, effectively appearing out of thin air, but the roof was empty. It was late, and most people had better things to look at.

This place looked a bit like a shopping mall, a business form factor that had risen and fallen in and out of favor several times over the hundreds of years that had passed between this era and Lex's own. But it looked, if anything, *more* futuristic than his own time, which was from the local point of view *well* into the future. Things were glossier. Glitzier. More lights. More *everything*. It looked like someone had built a very convincing film set depicting what they imagined the future would be like. This was reinforced by the ubiquitous signage that indicated, without a wink or a nudge, that they were presently visiting the premier spaceport on the planet Earth.

They weren't *so* far off the mark. The only difference was, rather than a real spaceport, which had more in common with airports of this era, this looked a bit like the themed space stations that were built to mimic the same future aesthetic that defined this place, albeit through the haughty term of "retrofuturism." Still, it would have been a fun novelty if he wasn't in a hurry to find, fetch, and flee.

"Dude! Awesome outfit!" called someone heading for the elevator Lex had just left.

"What? Oh, yeah. Thanks. You too!" he said.

Rare was the mission of this sort where getting spotted wasn't a reason for panic, so even though he looked perfectly in character in his worn and abused flight suit, he still got that jolt of panic every time someone turned in his direction.

"Stop! Stop it!" shouted Trevor.

Lex turned. A black-and-white blur that he knew oh-so-well exploded from the door of the arcade. Squee took an impossibly sharp turn by bounding directly toward a storefront and leaping from floor to plate-glass window to floor again. Jeremy came within a half step of thumping headlong into the glass. Trevor predicted the maneuver and almost managed to snatch Squee out of midair. Her little feet moved a mile a minute, but Trevor was swiftly gaining. Then she spotted Lex and vaulted to his shoulders, curling round his neck like it was home base and off-limits in this little game of tag. Trevor skidded to a graceful stop, nostrils flaring as he tried to catch his breath.

"Is this creature yours?" Trevor said.

"Uh... Yeah. Hope she didn't cause any trouble."

Trevor thumped a finger against Lex's chest. "We have strict rules regarding pets. They are not to be left unaccompanied in public areas. They are not..."

He glanced at Lex's chest. "Where's your badge?" he said.

Lex glanced down, as if startled to discover he was missing the thing that he'd just now learned existed. "Oh! It must have popped off. I'll just go look for it," he said, attempting to excuse himself.

Trevor caught him by the upper arm with a grip that was gentle enough not to be threatening but firm enough to imply just what sort of threat it could carry. "That makes two of you missing badges," he said.

Jeremy had hung back until he could catch his breath as well, but was eying up Lex with a similar level of distrust.

"That's a pretty good spacesuit you have, Mr..." Jeremy said.

"Mr. Alexander." Lex pointed to Trevor's name tag. "Trevor Alexander, actually. Though people call me Lex."

"Well, Lex," Trevor said. "If I review the security tapes, am I going to see you coming in the front way, or up top?"

Lex glanced past the elevators at the wide exit he'd been turned away from a few minutes earlier. Like any good theme park, there was very little effort put into preventing people from *leaving*. If he made a break for it...

The grip around his arm tightened. He looked back at Trevor, who simply shook his head subtly, having foreseen the highly strategic gambit Lex was considering. "It looks like there are some booths open at Blue's. What do you say you and I have a chat, hmm?"

Lex glanced down at a weapon on Trevor's belt. "Yeah. Yeah, let's do that," he said.

The group crossed the mostly empty first floor of the 'port, approaching an eating establishment labeled Blue's Bar. Lex wasn't exceptionally well-versed in Earth history, but the place looked decades out of date. Checkered tiles, creaky vinyl booths, art deco, the works. A striking woman with impressive makeup in the form of blue skin, webbed fingers, and supernaturally intense blue eyes, gave him a measuring look as he entered. She was dressed appropriately for the establishment in the snappy, anachronistic waitress's outfit. But the look on her face had a lot more in common with the one Trevor had given him than one a waitress would give.

The only other people in the joint were the cook, a craggy-faced older fellow with well-earned smile-lines that he wasn't currently using, and a woman at one of the stools with a shock of red hair and a sketch pad stirring at her coffee and doodling.

"What can I get you?" asked the blue waitress, appropriately enough dubbed "Blue" by her name tag.

"Coffees all around. This young man and I need to discuss what color his missing badge is supposed to be," Trevor said.

Blue nodded.

"You're not leaving this restaurant with an empty belly," called the cook. "Let me get something started for you."

"Cookie, it's not that kind of visit," Blue said, marching back behind the counter to start filling mugs.

"It's always that kind of visit," Cookie said, turning to the griddle.

Pots, pans, and spoons were quickly in motion, far more of them than a pair of hands ought to be able to handle, though Cookie was quite clearly alone in the kitchen. The ruckus provided a measure of privacy to keep the artist from overhearing.

Trevor spoke with a carefully calibrated tone and volume. "Let me guess. You and the critter aren't from around here," he said.

"Good guess," Lex said.

Trevor sighed. Jeremy, sitting beside him, pulled out a pad and clicked a pen with the air of a police officer about to write a ticket.

"First thing's first. What are you?" Trevor said. "Species-wise."

"Human," Lex said.

Trevor's expression hardened slightly.

"Earthling?" he said.

"Golanan, actually."

Jeremy jotted it down.

"First I've heard of a nonlocal human," Trevor said. "Who's your supplier for gear?"

"Mostly a guy named Karter. I think he's an Earthling? He's not so chatty about his past," Lex said. "Let me save you some time. This isn't an issue of *where* so much as an issue of *when*."

Trevor's expression hardened further. Jeremy's lit up.

"You're from the future?" Jeremy said with a barely restrained hush.

"Future, alternate dimension. Possibly both. I don't know. This wasn't a planned excursion," Lex said.

Blue delivered four mugs of coffee. Lex pushed one of them back.

"Squee isn't much of a coffee drinker," he said.

"I've learned not to assume," Blue said quietly, swapping the mug for a glass of ice water. "We don't usually allow pets in here."

"Everyone's welcome, so long as they bring an appetite," Cookie said, ringing a bell as he set a pair of plates thumping down on the window separating the kitchen from the restaurant.

Considering that action would require three hands, Lex wasn't quite surprised when he saw what may have been a tentacle nudging the second plate into a less precarious position before Cookie turned back to the griddle.

Blue carted over what happened to be a well-packed mission-style bean burrito and a patty melt with steak fries. Squee didn't wait for the burrito to be set down, scrambling across Lex's shoulders to take a greedy bite as it arrived.

"Time travelers. Someone get Cord down here. We need a new procedure," Trevor said.

"If it helps at all, I'm just here to grab Squee and get going. Frankly, my ship is likely to be the issue if we drag our feet for too long. She gets antsy."

"You have an intelligent ship?" Jeremy said, quickly taking note.

"Intelligent? Yes. Not always *smart*, though," Lex said.

"I assume you're cloaked," Trevor said.

"Yep."

Trevor took the pad from Jeremy and passed it to Lex. "Write down the size, the weight, etc. We need to figure out where we can accommodate it."

"I don't really need long-term storage, unless you're planning to lock me up," Lex said, scribbling some slightly high estimates for the various weights and measures of the *SOB*.

"I just prefer to know where on-planet vehicles are located." Trevor looked over the information. "The roof can handle it. Get the ship parked in the garden."

Lex subtly tapped the message into his slidepad. Jeremy craned his head to see the device and hastily jotted down a description.

"Here's the deal, Lex. If you're *really* heading out again, then we'll skip the badges. But if you and yours start making plans to come back, here are the rules. You aren't the only non-Earthling to pass through here. We ask that outsiders, however that'd be described, wear green badges so we know how well-informed they are, if you catch my meaning. You and your..."

"Funk," Lex said.

Jeremy snickered and jotted it down. Trevor rummaged in his pocket and produced two green badges.

"You and your *funk* would both get these. Maybe green-and-gold is more appropriate. Kind of a gray area, non-Earthling humans. But wear them when you're here, and we do not discuss extraterrestrial..." Trevor sighed. "Or *anachronistic,* or *extradimensional* intelligences with anyone with a *red* badge. Or anyone outside this spaceport. Got that?

We wear the mask while we're here. We play it straight, like everything is real. But for red badges, it's all a game, and we keep it that way."

"Good policy," Lex said.

"Good." Trevor motioned to Jeremy to slide out, then stood once he was able to. "Blue! This one's on my tab, since our guest here underpacked a little."

Blue nodded. Trevor turned back to him.

"Finish your meal, and keep an eye on the funk, would you?"

"Easier said than done. On the funk-watch, that is. This patty melt is exceptional."

Cookie gave a sort of half salute without looking away from his work.

"I'm going to have a word with Cord about this. He's the boss. If you're still here when we get in touch, he might want to talk to you, but if you're gone by then, it will *not* break my heart," Trevor said.

"I'm three big bites of patty melt and a doggie bag away from my departure, trust me," Lex said.

Trevor and Jeremy slipped away. Lex considered just dining and dashing right then and there, but before he could make a move, the red-badged illustrator slid into the spot vacated by the security crew.

"I'm sorry to interrupt, but I just had to get a better look at that *cute* little creature. I've never seen someone dress up their *dog* for a visit."

"Heh, yeah," Lex said as she started sketching Squee.

"I love this place, you know? It's so fun. I mean, I know it's doing pretty well, but I feel like this should be *the* destination for sci-fi fans the world over. And I think the missing piece is a mascot. Do you mind?" she said.

"Do I mind what?"

"If I use your design," she said, indicating Squee with the pencil before putting it back to the page. "I'll credit you if you want."

"Uh. Sketch away. No credit necessary," Lex said.

"Great. She's adorable, like I said. But I think maybe she doesn't *quite* embody the spirit of this place. Maybe I'll up the alien a bit. You know. Go for the whole bipedal look..."

Lex crunched through the rest of his patty and nursed his fries while Squee messily savaged her burrito. By the time she was done, so was the illustrator.

"This is it. This is *it*," she said, holding up what was now essentially an anthropomorphic Squee enjoying a cup of coffee at the counter. "Who could see this and not want to visit, hmm? Thanks so much for the inspiration."

The illustrator slid back out of the booth, eyes set on her page. Lex pulled some napkins from the holder and wiped Squee's mouth.

"You're here for like an hour and you end up the mascot for a theme park," he said. "Come on. Let's get going before you end up running your own merchandising empire."

He scooped her up and gave a friendly nod to Blue on the way out the door.

"Gotta say. If it didn't involve perverting the laws of physics in an untested teleporter, this place might be worth a longer visit. Might have to come back here someday..."

From The Author

T hank you for reading! If you liked this story, or perhaps if you found it lacking, I'd love to hear from you. You can find me online at my website, bookofdeacon.com. For **free stories** and important updates, join my newsletter.

Discover other titles by Joseph R. Lallo

The Book of Deacon – an Epic Fantasy Series:

Book 1: *The Book of Deacon*
Book 2: *The Great Convergence*
Book 3: *The Battle of Verril*
Book 4: *The D'Karon Apprentice*
Book 5: *The Crescents*
Book 6: *The Coin of Kenvard*
Book of Deacon Anthology: Volume 1
Book of Deacon Anthology: Volume 2

Other stories in the same setting:

The Rise of the Red Shadow
The Story of Sorrel
Entwell Origins: Anya
The Redemption of Desmeres
The Adventures of Rustle and Eddy

Jade

Halifax

The Stump and the Spire

The Big Sigma Series – a Sci-fi/Space Opera Series:

Book 1: *Bypass Gemini*

Book 2: *Unstable Prototypes*

Book 3: *Artificial Evolution*

Book 4: *Temporal Contingency*

Book 5: *Indra Station*

Book 6: *Nova Igniter*

Book 7: *Quantum Shift*

Beta Testers

Big Sigma Collection: Volume 1

Big Sigma Collection: Volume 2

The Free-Wrench – Steampunk Adventure Series:

Book 1: *Free-Wrench*

Book 2: *Skykeep*

Book 3: *Ichor Well*

Book 4: *The Calderan Problem*

Book 5: *Cipher Hill*

Book 6: *Contaminant Six*

Free Wrench Collection: Volume 1

Free Wrench Collection: Volume 2

The Shards of Shadow Series:

Book 1: *A Traitor in the Shadows*

Book 2: *The Prison of Shadows*

Book 3: *The Balance of Shadows*
Book 4: *The Clash of Shadows*

The Greater Lands Series:

Book 1: *The Bygone Dagger*
Book 2: *The Bygone Archive*
Book 3: *The Bygone Mask*
Book 4: *The Bygone Caper*
Book 5: *The Bygone Plague*
Book 6: *The Bygone Way*

Other Stories:

Between
Fallen Empire: Rogue Derelict
Top Level Player
The Other Eight
Structophis
Between
Paradoxes and Dragons: Volume 1
Paradoxes and Dragons: Volume 2
Paradoxes and Dragons: Volume 3